The Scorching Sun of Egypt

Sunrise

Copyright © Jonathan A. Kruisselbrink, 2013

FOREWORD

While writing this book about the beginning of the Amarna period (the reign of Akhenaten and its aftermath) I have tried to portray Ancient Egyptian life as accurately as possible. However, there are many things about Ancient Egypt that we still don't know or which are disputed, especially when it concerns the chaotic Amarna period. As a consequence I have many times taken the liberty of using my own imagination and sometimes I have also knowingly changed historical facts for the purpose of the story.
Some of the characters in this book are based on real historical people; however, because about many of these people we don't know much more than names, titles and positions I have given them a fictive life history.
For some of the Ancient Egyptian temples and cities I have used the names under which they are known to us today or their Greek names.
In short: even though the Amarna period really happened this book is a work of fiction and should therefore be read purely for enjoyment, by those who already are knowledgeable about Ancient Egypt and by those who are new to it.

YEAR 37 OF THE REIGN OF AMENHOTEP THE THIRD

The first rays started to appear over the horizon; soon the Egyptian sun would unleash its scorching fury on the people of the Two Lands.

CHAPTER 1
A ROYAL FUNERAL AND A NEW LIFE

Ipi loved to slip away from his family's small farm and wander into the Theban Mountains. He was only twelve years old and the youngest child of a family with six children but he was not fit for the hard life of a farmer. He was a frail boy who physically was not strong enough and he also could not imagine himself spending his whole life working on the fields. He knew he was destined for something else but he did not know for what.

Although his parents loved Ipi, they often wondered why the Gods blessed their family with such a strange boy who did not automatically follow in their footsteps like all the other farmers children did.

That morning his father had left for Thebes early and his mother was on the field so Ipi could disappear easily.

He climbed to his favorite spot in the Theban Mountains from where he could oversee the Nile Valley. He could sit there for hours enjoying the view of the green fields and the Nile River with its busy traffic. He could see the fishing- and cargo boats coming to Thebes, the Egyptian capital on the east bank of the Nile, to unload their goods to be sold at one of the city's many markets or shops.

Thebes had always intrigued Ipi, not only because it was a big and bustling city but also because of its temples where mysterious rituals were carried out daily to keep the Gods satisfied so that They would give the Two Lands, Upper and Lower Egypt, and its people prosperity.

He had visited Thebes a couple of times on festivals or with his father or mother when they had to visit one of the markets in the city but since they were just a poor peasant family living on the west bank of the Nile he had had few opportunities to visit Thebes.

On that day the view on the Egyptian capital and the Nile was different than on other days because Crown Prince Thutmose, first-born son of Pharaoh Amenhotep the Third and High Priest of Ptah in Memphis, had died unexpectedly seventy days previously.

From his viewpoint Ipi could see a funerary bark, which held the coffin with the mummy of the prince in its deckhouse, being towed across the river by another boat.

On the stern of the bark were two big rudder oars, operated by a helmsman, which acted as steering gear and gave stability. The funerary bark was followed by another bark with the Royal Family and behind that other boats followed with state officials, professional mourners and boats filled with objects that prince Thutmose would take with him in his tomb for use in the afterlife.

The procession was flanked by other boats with common people who wanted to take the opportunity to say farewell to the deceased Crown Prince.

On both banks of the river people were watching the fleet, some had torn their clothes and threw dust over their heads as a sign of mourning.

Ipi followed the procession over the river until they docked at the west bank, the land of the dead. He could see the coffin containing the mummy being placed on a sledge pulled by two bulls and flanked by shaven headed priests wearing white robes.

When the Royal Family and the other mourners had disembarked from their boats the sledge with the coffin started moving and the long procession continued on foot towards the tomb that had been hastily prepared for the prince.

Even from where he was sitting Ipi could hear the mourners wailing and see the Royal family, including Pharaoh Amenhotep the Third, his Great Royal Wife Teye and the new Crown Prince whose name was also Amenhotep. Ipi could also see the Sem Priest who was wearing a leopard skin over his white robe. After arrival at the tomb the Sem Priest would perform the very important Opening of the Mouth ceremony on the mummy which would reanimate the deceased prince, enabling him to live in the afterlife and receive the offerings which would be given to him daily after his funeral to sustain his ka or soul.

The funerary procession moved past the new mortuary temple that Pharaoh Amenhotep the Third had constructed for himself as a preparation for his own death. It was the biggest mortuary temple in Egypt with two colossal seated statues of the Pharaoh at the entrance. It was a fitting reflection of

Amenhotep's prosperous and stable reign over the Two Lands.

Ipi watched the funerary party until they disappeared from view towards a, no doubt, beautifully decorated tomb. This was the first Royal funerary procession he had seen and witnessing so much wealth and ceremony made him feel a little resentful. The mortality rate amongst the farmers and their families was relatively high so, even though he was only twelve, Ipi had seen more than enough funerals of farmers. A dead farmer would simply be wrapped in a reed mat and buried in a pit on the edge of the desert with some clay pots and pieces of bread as gifts for the afterlife. There would be no Opening of the Mouth ceremony, only a few prayers from the family and friends. Ipi knew he would be buried like that as well, there would not be a beautiful tomb waiting for him.

He was, however, still excited to have seen the Royal Family. He did not know much about them but he did know the Royal Family played a very important role in keeping the Two Lands stable and prosperous. The Pharaoh was the incarnation of Horus on earth and it was his responsibility to maintain Ma'at which represented order, justice and balance. If the Pharaoh failed his responsibility the Gods would abandon Egypt and the country would descend into chaos.

It was still morning but the summer heat started early so the river-breeze was a welcome change for Aset. She had started early with the preparations for the funeral and after that she escorted the Royal Family to the Karnak Temple from where the funerary procession would depart by boat to the Theban necropolis on the west bank of the Nile.

On the Royal Bark, while crossing the Nile, Aset could not enjoy the cool weather for too long because as a servant of the Royal Family she had to tend to all their needs and always be available to them.

Aset's parents had died already but both had been servants at the Royal Palace causing her to grow up there and starting to work in the palace when she was still a young girl. Now she was a young woman and she had already been the servant of prince Amenhotep, the second son of the Pharaoh, for several years. She had always been comfortable around the Royal Family, it was hard work especially because the Royal Family was very demanding, but since she had grown up in their surroundings she had become used to their behaviour.

Lately prince Amenhotep had got married and just like his father he married a girl who was not of Royal blood, something which was unusual for Egyptian Royalty. His wife was named Nefertiti and was already pregnant with their first child which, if it would be a boy, might become a Pharaoh in the future. Nefertiti was a young woman with a strong character and she had a big influence over prince Amenhotep. Even though she was a commoner Nefertiti was a difficult and demanding person, even more than most of the Royal Family. The reason for her behaviour, Aset suspected, was that Nefertiti, as a commoner, was trying to prove herself worthy of being a member of the Royal Family.

Prince Amenhotep had always been different from the rest of his family, he was reserved but friendly, even though he could be short-tempered sometimes.

The biggest difference, however, was of a religious nature; the Royal Family had always been supporters of the State God Amun, the King of the Gods but Amenhotep seemed not very interested in Him and sometimes Aset wondered if he maybe even had an aversion towards Him.

Prince Amenhotep only visited the Temple of Amun on special occasions, when there was no excuse for him to stay away. The only temple which he visited frequently out of free will was the small Temple of the Aten, a relatively minor and unknown Sun God. Aset once overheard the prince say that the Aten did not get the devotion of the people it deserved and that he wanted to devote his life to Aten. Of course that was before the unfortunate death of Crown Prince Thutmose. Now Amenhotep was the new Crown Prince and his life had changed completely. When, in the future, he would become Pharaoh he would be expected to serve Amun just like his forefathers did.

Contrary to his late elder brother, Amenhotep had never been very close to his father, the Pharaoh, while he loved his mother, Queen Teye, the Great Royal wife. Lately, however, he was spending a lot of time with his father and other high state officials as a preparation for his future responsibilities of ruling the Two Lands and the relationship between father and son seemed to improve.

Aset wondered how long it would take before the young Crown Prince would become the new Pharaoh. Pharaoh Amenhotep was getting older and his health was deteriorating, the shock of his eldest son's unexpected death had hit him hard. Prince

Thutmose had always been a healthy young man until some unknown sickness took him while he was visiting his parents in Thebes. The Royal physicians stood powerless and within a week the prince had joined Osiris in the Netherworld.

Next to Aset on the boat stood Kiya, who had been the servant of Thutmose and had come with the prince and his family from his residence in Memphis to Thebes where he died in his father's palace.

After the death of Thutmose, the new Crown Prince Amenhotep offered Kiya a position as his servant. Kiya was reluctant at first because that meant she would be living and working in Thebes, far from her family in Memphis but Amenhotep did not give up and kept trying to persuade her. In the end Kiya gave in and agreed and now she was working as one of the new Crown Prince's personal servants.

Amenhotep seemed to be very fond of Kiya and gave her a lot of attention while he hardly gave any attention to his other servants. Some servants in the palace were jealous about Kiya's special position but Aset did not care, she and Kiya had become good friends. Aset was only worried what the prince's intentions with Kiya were.

The Funerary bark reached the west bank of the Nile, the Land of the Dead, and the coffin with the mummy of prince Thutmose was carried off the bark by priests and placed on the sledge that had been waiting there for the funerary procession to arrive.

The bark with the Royal Family and other boats full with mourners also arrived and Aset and Kiya immediately disembarked to be available for when they were needed. Aset carried a jug of wine and cups and Kiya a plate of fruit as refreshments for the Royal Family on the way to the prince's tomb.

Under the direction of Ranefer, the Head of the Royal Servants, other servants were also busy carrying refreshments and fans to keep the mourners cool.

Pharaoh Amenhotep and his Great Royal Wife, Teye, disembarked and climbed into a litter that was waiting behind the sledge on which their son's coffin had already been placed.

"The death of Thutmose has hit the Pharaoh very hard, I have never seen him like this," Aset spoke to Kiya and went on: "And did you see Queen Teye? Even she has tears in her eyes!"

Teye was a very cold and emotionless woman and she had never shown much emotion about the death of her first-born son, at least not in public. But all that changed at the funeral when she could not suppress her tears anymore.

"She is not only a queen but also a mother," Kiya answered. "I feel very sorry for her and the Pharaoh."

At that moment Teye beckoned Aset and she came over and offered the Queen a cup of wine. The Great Royal Wife emptied the cup and without saying a word returned it to Aset, gesturing with her hand that she could go. Aset looked at the Pharaoh but he shook his head, he did not want anything to drink.

Aset walked back to Kiya and spoke: "The Pharaoh eats and drinks too little. I have heard Ptahhotep, the Royal Physician, complain to him about that. He said his health starts to deteriorate."

"Is it that serious?" Kiya asked and continued with a worried tone in her voice: "Do you think the Pharaoh might die soon?"

"I don't know and I don't want to think about the Pharaoh's death!" Aset answered sharply and explained: "It might cause bad luck for him."

At that moment the Sem Priest gave a sign and the procession started to move preceded by a priest bearing a standard of the jackal-headed God Wepwawet whose name meant the Opener of the Ways.

Eight bearers picked up the litter containing the Pharaoh and the Queen and followed the sledge with Thutmose's coffin. The two bulls pulled the sledge over a path past the new mortuary temple which Amenhotep the Third had built for himself. Two big statues of the Pharaoh sitting on a mighty throne in front of the temple looked down upon them when they passed.

Aset whispered a short prayer to Amun to protect Amenhotep so he would not need the service of this temple for many years to come.

The funerary procession left the fields on the riverbank behind and proceeded into the desert valley where the ancestors of the Pharaoh had their tombs made.

The Theban necropolis was a large area and was being patrolled by soldiers to keep tomb robbers away. Unfortunately this was a necessary measure because even in these stable times there were people in the Two Lands who tried to rob the tombs of the deceased, an act that was possibly the greatest sacrilege a person could commit in the Egyptian society.

Aset was getting tired, the sun rose higher and there was no shade in the desert. She hoped they would reach the tomb soon so that she would be able to get a short rest. She looked at the Pharaoh, his litter had a roof to keep him and Teye in the shade and the fan bearers were walking next to them to keep them cool.

After a long walk, to her great relief, Aset saw tents erected in the valley close to the entrance of a new tomb. They had finally arrived.

The bulls pulling the sledge stopped and the coffin containing prince Thutmose's mummy was carried to a cleared area in front of the tomb's entrance and put upright. It was a beautiful human-shaped coffin with spells, prayers and the prince's names and titles written on it.

Aset, Kiya and the other servants did not have as much time to rest as they had hoped. Everybody was tired and thirsty from the long trip through the hot desert and before the funeral ceremony started they wanted to drink.

Amenhotep and his family went to one of the tents and the other guests went to the other ones. Despite having travelled in a comfortable litter even Pharaoh Amenhotep was thirsty and Aset was relieved to see that he was drinking several cups of wine and also eating fruit.

Next to Amenhotep sat a young woman with a little boy. Aset could see she had been crying a lot and she knew why; this woman was Meresankh and the little boy was Amenhotep, named after his grandfather the Pharaoh. They were the wife and son of prince Thutmose.

Meresankh was not only mourning the loss of her husband but also the certain loss of her son's chance to become Pharaoh in the future. If her husband's younger brother, the new Crown Prince, would become Pharaoh and have a son then that son would become the next in line to sit on the throne of the Two Lands.

Little Amenhotep, however, seemed not to care or understand yet what he had lost. He was enjoying this day out and the different kinds of fruit that were served. He was chatting constantly which brought a smile back on his grandfather's face and even on his mother's.

Opposite them, next to Queen Teye, sat Crown Prince Amenhotep with his new wife Nefertiti.

Amenhotep was talking to his mother but when Kiya came to bring some more fruit for them he started talking to her. Aset could not understand what was being said but she could see Kiya enjoyed talking with the new Crown Prince. Nefertiti, however, did not seem to appreciate her husband having a conversation with his servant. Aset feared Amenhotep's attention to Kiya could cause her friend problems.

As soon as the procession arrived at the tomb the Sem Priest went into meditation to become one with the Gods, which was required to perform the Opening of the Mouth ceremony. At the same time other priests washed the coffin with four jars of holy water and walked around it holding incense burners while constantly reciting prayers.

When everything was ready the Royal Family and the guests were warned and the Sem Priest was awakened from his meditation. The priest positioned himself in front of the coffin which still stood upright in front of the tomb's entrance and started reciting hymns and spells for prince

Thutmose to awake and for the Gods to protect his mummy.

Next came the most important part of the ceremony; the Sem Priest took a ceremonial adze and with this he touched the mouth of the human-shaped coffin four times while repeating the same spell four times, every time the spell was recited for a different God. This ritual helped the mummy to come back to life again, to be reborn. After this part of the ritual the mummy of the deceased prince could sustain his ka and all the prince's senses would be restored enabling him to receive offerings, hear prayers and even to help and protect his still living family members. While this ceremony was being carried out the other priests continuously chanted prayers to Osiris.

When the ritual had been completed the Sem Priest walked four times around the coffin containing the mummy while burning incense and addressing the ka of Thutmose, telling him his mummy was ready to receive him.

Having reanimated prince Thutmose the Sem Priest continued praying, asking Osiris to accept him in His kingdom.

The ceremony was nearing its end when a bull was slaughtered and offered to Thutmose together with fruit, bread and wine. After all the offerings had been made, Meresankh, as a last touching gesture, put a garland of flowers around the shoulders of her husband's human shaped coffin.

Then the Sem Priest declared that the prince was finally ready to enter his tomb.

Aset had followed the ceremony outside but she was not allowed to enter the tomb. Only the Royal Family and priests were allowed to escort the prince into his eternal home where his coffin would be placed in a stone sarcophagus and where the last rituals would take place.

The tomb had only just been finished; the last two months the workmen had been working extremely hard to have the tomb ready in time for the funeral. Nobody had expected Thutmose to need his tomb so soon because of his health and young age.

Aset was watching the priests, the Pharaoh and his family following the coffin into the tomb when Ranefer, the Head of the Royal Servants, called her and ordered her to help prepare lunch for the Pharaoh and his family.

While preparing the tent for the Royal Family's lunch Aset met Kiya again.

"You have to be careful with prince Amenhotep, Kiya!" Aset warned her friend.

"It is no problem, he is just being friendly to me," Kiya answered and added: "And don't forget he is the son of the Pharaoh, I cannot forbid him to talk to me."

"I understand that," Aset replied. "But please don't encourage him. I think Nefertiti does not like it and who knows what will happen when Amenhotep gets bored of you."

"Don't worry Aset, he is only being nice to me, nothing more!" Kiya spoke, starting to get irritated.

"Yes, and not much more will happen, we are servants and we will never be more than servants. No matter how much a prince will like us he will never marry one of us because we are too low for them," Aset spoke angrily and then added in a warning tone: "So be careful Kiya, whatever you do there is no chance for you to ever get any higher up from here."

"Who says I want to get higher up?" Kiya exclaimed, sounding almost angry by that time and after a short silence went on in a calmer voice: "Besides, Aset, you forget that both Nefertiti and Queen Teye were not of Royal blood when they married."

"You are right about that," Aset replied. "But they were not servants like us, Kiya, both came from noble families and we don't!"

"Stop arguing and continue your work!" Ranefer, who had entered the tent unnoticed by the two servants, intervened in the argument and continued in an angry tone: "Most of the nobility and the government of the Two Lands are here and you two were arguing almost loud enough for them to listen to your problems! And from what I have heard you were speaking about a sensitive subject and I advise you not to speak about that anymore!"

Ranefer was strict but good with his staff, Aset knew him well and was happy to work for him. He was an older man and just like her he had been working at the Royal Palace since he was young.

"We are sorry, it won't happen again," both Aset and Kiya replied meekly and continued their work in silence.

The Pharaoh, his family and the priests returned from the tomb of Thutmose. The doors had been closed and sealed with the special seal of the necropolis guard. It would be impossible to open the tomb's doors without breaking the seal; this made it easy for officials of the necropolis to see whether the prince's tomb had been opened or not. As an extra safety measure the entrance to the tomb would later also be hidden from view with sand and rocks to make it harder for tomb robbers to locate and reach it.

Pharaoh Amenhotep went to the tent for his lunch together with his family and the funerary priests. He had also invited the viziers of Upper and Lower Egypt: Ramose, an aging man who had been serving the Pharaoh from the moment he ascended the throne and in addition to being vizier also served as mayor of Thebes, and Aperel a younger person who had only recently become vizier.

Aperel who had his residence in Memphis had made the long journey to Thebes especially for the funeral.

Amenhotep did not eat much and did not speak, he seemed elsewhere with his thoughts. Aset thought he was probably thinking of his eldest son, the late Thutmose, but he continuously stared at his second son, Amenhotep, the new Crown Prince, who was sitting opposite him.

Suddenly the Pharaoh turned to Aperel.
"I know you have business to attend to in Memphis but I have to ask you to stay here in Thebes a bit longer," Pharaoh Amenhotep spoke to the Vizier of Lower Egypt and then explained: "Soon I will make an announcement and it is important that you will be here at that time."

Ipi was on his way back to his family's farm. It was already late in the afternoon but he was not in a hurry to arrive home. His parents did not like him to stay out all day so coming home too late usually resulted in a beating from his father and the longer he could postpone feeling his father's anger the better.

He made his way through the fields which had just been harvested. For many years the harvests had been bountiful but this year it had been disappointing causing his parents to worry about feeding their family during the coming flood season.

They had only a small plot of land which they leased from the Temple of Amun in Thebes and in return for using the land they had to give a small part of the harvest to the temple. Normally donating a part of the harvest to the Amun Temple was no problem but with this year's small harvest it was a different situation and to make matters even worse the Pharaoh's tax collectors were also visiting the farms to collect his share of the harvest.

In years with a good harvest the tax collectors often had an easy task but when the harvest was bad the farmers did not want to separate from the fruits of their hard labour. For that reason tax collectors always had an escort of soldiers with them; to guarantee their safety and to help them to collect the Pharaoh's share of the harvest from resisting farmers.

A part of this share of the harvest would be used for trade with foreign countries and to feed workers employed by the Pharaoh, another part would be stored and kept for times of famine so that even when the crops would fail the Egyptians would still be able to feed themselves.

Every year the Pharaoh also paid tributes to the temples, especially to the Karnak Temple of Amun, the King of the Gods; a considerable part of the tax-income was used to make these tributes possible.

It was almost dark when Ipi arrived home. His house was a small single room building made of reed and palm leaves which his family shared with a cow, their most precious possession. As he had feared his father had already returned from Thebes. He had hoped that with the chaos in the city because of the funeral it would have taken him longer to return home.

To Ipi's big surprise, however, his father, a dark man named Hor who looked much older than his real age because of a life of hard work on the fields in the blistering sun, was not angry; he was actually very friendly.

"Hello Ipi, there you are finally. We have been waiting for you," he spoke in an unusually friendly voice. "Come in quickly, your mother has just finished preparing a delicious dinner."

Ipi went inside the house which did not have any furniture because it was unaffordable for his family. The only things they had were a couple of pots, cups and bowls for preparing food and eating and they ate sitting on the floor. Inside, Ipi was surprised to see his father had not exaggerated, there was a delicious meal of bread, pork, fish and fruit prepared.

"What are we celebrating?" Ipi asked.
"First wash yourself and eat your meal and then we will talk," his father answered.

He did not need to say that twice, Ipi was starving. He quickly washed himself with water from the Nile River which they kept in a bucket and joined his family for dinner.

His father was telling about his day in Thebes: "It was so busy because of all the high dignitaries who came from all over the country to the funeral of prince Thutmose and all of these officials brought their servants and guards along with them. All the inns are full and I had to wait a long time before I could get a ferry to cross the river to return to the west bank."

"What were you doing in the city, father?" Aha, Ipi's eldest brother, asked. Aha had been married already and had gone to live with his wife in Thebes but after his wife and baby had died while she was giving birth he had come back to live with his parents and helped on their farm. After this tragic experience he refused to get married again.

Ipi had two more elder sisters who had married already and lived with their husbands on other farms in the area and two other elder brothers, one, Huni, lived with his wife, Tahat, and their baby son Djehuty, on his parents farm and the other, Ankhaf, was not married yet and also still lived with their parents.

Ipi's father looked uncomfortable after Aha's question.

"Don't worry, Hor," Nefer, Ipi's mother, spoke while she put her hand on his arm. "I will explain it to Ipi."

Ipi was wondering what was happening, what were his parents talking about?

"Ipi," his mother started speaking. "We know you are not happy growing up as a farmer and your father and I agree that a farming life is not suitable for you. We have been looking for alternatives for you and today your father went to the Karnak Temple to talk with the priests of Amun about you. They have agreed to take you into their temple."

Ipi's mother stopped speaking a moment while tears started to roll down her face but then she continued: "Tomorrow we will go to Thebes to bring you to Karnak. There the priests of Amun will take care of you."

Ipi felt like he had been hit in the face.

"What? Are you giving me away?" he shouted, almost crying.

"I know it sounds hard," his mother answered, still having tears in her eyes. "But it is the best for everybody. You will never be happy as a farmer and who knows what future there might be for you in the Temple of Amun."

"You just want to get rid of me because I am not a good worker like Aha!" Ipi replied, now crying with indignation.

"That's not it, Ipi," Hor, Ipi's father, now joined in, trying to speak calmly and putting an arm around Ipi's shoulders which he shook off angrily.

"There is another problem." Hor went on speaking. "You know our harvest has been disappointing this year. I don't even know if we have enough to eat for everybody until the next harvest!"

"So because there is a bad harvest I have to leave?" Ipi cried and then shouted desperately: "I want to stay here with you! I don't want to live in a temple!"

"We are sorry," his mother spoke softly. "But there is no other way. We already made an arrangement with the Amun temple and I am still sure this is the best solution for everybody."

After his mother's words Ipi did not say anything anymore. He threw his bowl with food on the floor and ran out of the house. His parents remained inside the house sitting on the floor both of them with tears in their eyes. Aha and his brothers and sister-in-law just sat there, too shocked to say anything. The only sound came from little Djehuty who had started crying during the argument. Nobody was hungry anymore and the meal that had been meant as a farewell dinner for Ipi and the cooking of which had kept Nefer busy all day, was left untouched.

Ipi sat crying on the bank of the Nile River. How could his parents do this to him? He could not understand it. But the more he was thinking about it the more he also started to see that maybe his parents were right after all. This could be the chance for him to escape the hard and monotonous life in the fields while in the temple he might even get the opportunity to learn how to read and write, a skill Ipi had always wanted to possess but which he never dared to hope he would actually ever get the chance to learn. And now that his parents were putting him on the path that might help him to realize his dreams, he was angry at them.

Life in Egypt always started early so the people could do as much work as possible before it got too hot. So just like most people Ipi and his family got up early but this morning his father and mother would not go to their field as they would on any other day.
After running away the previous evening Ipi returned home and said he would go to the Amun Temple, even though he was not happy about leaving his family.
Ipi and his parents left their house and walked through the fields to the riverside. Normally Ipi would enjoy this trip; he always liked to see the first sunrays of the day appearing over the mountains east of Thebes and to see them touch the tips of the obelisks of the city's temples. The sky went from dark to red and the Theban Mountains from black to purple and then orange while the Nile flowed like a silver stream through this display of colours.

But today Ipi could not enjoy all this; he was too depressed about leaving his family and nervous about how life in the temple would be.

They came at the riverside where it was already busy with people who were waiting for a ferry to cross the river to go to their work or to one of the markets in Thebes.

They did not have to wait too long before they got a place on a ferry, it was a small boat which was, just like all the ferries on the busy hours of the day, overloaded with people, animals and all kinds of goods.

The boat made it safely to the other side of the Nile and docked at the harbour of Thebes. At the harbour it was a chaos of boats coming and going while all kinds of products were waiting to be bought, transported to one of the many warehouses or to be loaded on a boat destined for another city. Fishing boats returned from their nightly fishing trip to unload their catch and sell it to traders who would later sell it at the markets. The harbour was noisy with the sounds of animals, of people advertising their products and of buyers and sellers negotiating a price. And everywhere were the smells of fresh fish and livestock, of all kinds of spices, fruits and vegetables.

Ipi was overwhelmed by the sights and sounds and for a moment forgot where he was going to. Here he saw rich people with their expensive linen garments and poor people with sometimes nothing more than a simple loincloth; all sorts of people came here to do their business. There were also many foreigners who came to Thebes to sell wares from their strange and faraway lands and to buy new products which they would sell again at home.

Ipi noticed a tall but poor looking man on the street with something that looked like necklaces which he was loudly promoting. His father went over to the man and Ipi followed him. He heard his father negotiating about one of the man's products;

"One copper deben," the street seller spoke. A deben was a weight unit and used as a way to express the value of products, Ipi knew.

"One copper deben?" his father exclaimed in dismay.

"But this is a very special amulet!" the seller spoke again, holding up a small linen bag hanging on a cord.

"Inside this small bag is a piece of wood inscribed with a powerful prayer which will protect the wearer of this amulet against evil, disease and bad luck," the man explained and then continued: "And do you know what makes this amulet even more powerful?"

The street seller did not even wait for a reply to his question before giving the answer himself.

"The piece of wood inside this small bag," he spoke while holding up the linen bag again in front of Ipi's father, "comes from the same tree under which the Goddess Isis and the little baby Horus hid in the marshes when the evil Seth was searching for them. The tree from which this amulet comes has protected Isis and Horus and he who wears this amulet will be protected too. Paying only one deben for such a powerful amulet is actually too cheap but I see you are not a rich man and I always try to help poor people, they need protection and help from the Gods more than rich people. So for you I have this special offer!"

Ipi's father had been listening to the seller's words and became impressed but spoke: "It is just too much, I cannot afford it. I can only offer half a deben."

The street seller was quiet for a moment but then sighed theatrically and finally spoke: "I accept your offer! I am losing on the deal but since I see you have a wife and son to take care of I will help you. I agree to the price of half a deben even though I am sure I will regret it later."

Ipi's father paid and the street seller gave him the amulet.

"This is for you," his father spoke to Ipi while he put the amulet around his neck. "It will help to protect you when you are in the temple."

The street seller watched and smiled.

"You are a very lucky boy," he remarked, "having such a special amulet and such a caring father."

A moment later Ipi and his parents walked up a road away from the harbour until they came on a big street. This was the main street in Thebes which ran between Karnak and the Southern Temple, the two temple complexes of Amun in Thebes.

Ipi and his parents turned to the right towards the Karnak Temple. Ipi could already see the enormous pylon which was the entrance of the temple from faraway; it was one of the biggest constructions he had ever seen. In front of the pylon stood large statues of the Pharaoh and flagpoles with flags in different colours.

Ipi had never been inside the Karnak Temple or any other temple yet, so the closer he got to it he got both more nervous and more excited; more nervous because soon he would have to say farewell to his parents and more excited because he would soon enter what was possibly the holiest place in the country; the earthly home of the God Amun.

They arrived at the entrance of the temple and his father walked up to a young priest standing in front of it and spoke: "Could you please tell the lord Wenamun, the Third Prophet of Amun, that Hor and his son Ipi are here to see him? He is expecting us."

The priest looked surprised as if he wondered what such a high ranking priest as Wenamun would have to do with poor peasants like these three people.

"Follow me," he finally replied and walked into the temple without any further words.

They walked across the forecourt and Ipi and his parents were struck by their surroundings: enormous pillars had been erected on every side of them and between them statues of Egypt's Pharaohs had been positioned. Ipi felt himself very small in such a big and impressive complex.

"Amun must be a very powerful God," he whispered more to himself than to his parents.

"He is the most powerful God, he is the King of the Gods," his mother, who overheard him, answered.

"Wait here," the priest curtly told Ipi and his parents. "Only priests are allowed further into the temple. I will see if the Third Prophet Wenamun has time to receive you."

As soon as he had finished speaking the priest disappeared through another big gate further into the temple without waiting for a reply. Ipi and his parents were left behind waiting, feeling both impressed and uncomfortable in these sacred surroundings.

Paneb was feeling good, his day had started well. He had been abandoned by his parents when he was still a young boy and grew up alone, surviving by stealing and deceiving. Usually he worked alone but when there was an opportunity he worked together with others robbing travelers and sometimes fencing items stolen from the tombs of one of Egypt's many necropolises.

He had just arrived in Thebes which was a good place to make a profit. He had been here already before but, to avoid the authorities, he never wanted to stay in one place too long.

Contrary to most other Egyptians, Paneb was not religious or superstitious but he was happy with the beliefs of the Egyptian population and he made good use of it. That day he was selling fake amulets and already he had sold one to a poor superstitious peasant who bought it for his son. He had made the amulets himself the previous night using whatever materials he could find. The amulet the peasant bought had been made from a simple piece of wood which he had inscribed with a text copied from another text he had seen on a temple wall. He had no idea what the text he copied meant since he could not read but neither could that peasant and all the other poor, superstitious people who usually were his targets.

The sun was rising higher in the sky and the streets in Thebes were getting quiet. Unless they really had no other choice people stayed inside to rest until the worst heat of the day was over.

Paneb did not have a house in Thebes. When he could afford it he would sometimes rent a room at an inn but usually he slept outside. He had grown up sleeping on the streets or under trees so he was comfortable with that.

Like most Thebans, Paneb also decided to take a rest during the hot hours of the day and he went to a tree on the riverside outside the city that provided a cool shade and had a river breeze. It was also surrounded by reed so it even offered some privacy.

Paneb came there frequently to rest and get away from the busy city and started to regard it as his home. There, without being spotted, he could make his amulets which he would later sell in the city.

He was almost asleep under his tree when he heard a movement close to him. He looked up and saw a man standing next to him, the man was poorly dressed and looked like he had been doing hard labour most of his life.

"I knew I would find you here," the man spoke. "When you are not busy deceiving the poor and naïve with your trash or drinking beer at one of your usual taverns you are always here."

"What do you want, Merenre?" Paneb asked, feeling annoyed. He did not know his behaviour was so predictable. In fact, he always wanted to be unpredictable so that he could not be found easily in case of trouble.

"I need to talk to you," Merenre spoke.
Paneb noticed the man looked a bit nervous.

"Should you not be busy digging a tomb somewhere?" he asked Merenre, who was a workman in the Theban necropolis on the west bank of the Nile.

Paneb knew Merenre relatively well, he knew the workman often spent his wage on gambling and drinking; that was how they had got to know each other.

"I left the work in the tombs, I found an easier way to make a living, it will actually make me rich," Merenre answered Paneb's question with a forced optimism in his voice.

"That's good for you Merenre but did you come all the way here to tell me that?" Paneb asked, pretending not to be interested.

"Well, actually, I need your help, Paneb. This is a big opportunity for you too," Merenre replied hesitatingly.

"Maybe then you should tell me about this great idea of yours," Paneb replied, still pretending like he did not care so much.

Merenre, feeling relieved that he was not turned down by Paneb immediately, started telling: "You must have heard about the death of Crown Prince Thutmose and his funeral yesterday."

"Of course," Paneb replied. "Nobody in Thebes could have missed that."

"I agree, everybody spoke about it," Merenre said and then went on explaining his idea: "I have been working on the prince's tomb so I know exactly where it is. I also know how we can get into the tomb easily and fast, we only need to dig a tunnel for a couple of nights. If we can find some reliable people who are willing to help digging for a share of the profit we can be rich beyond our imagination within a couple of days. Just imagine the treasures inside the tomb of the son of the Pharaoh!"

The more Merenre was speaking the more excited he got.

"And what do you need my help for?" Paneb asked, not yet convinced about the idea of robbing a Royal tomb.

"You are living outside of the law; with your contacts it should not be hard to find people who are willing to help us with breaking into a tomb. We only need about five people to help us to dig the tunnel," Merenre explained.

"What do you mean by 'us', Merenre?" Paneb asked and continued: "I haven't answered you yet. Besides, I don't like the plan. It is too dangerous. The necropolis is heavily guarded and you know what happens to tomb robbers when they are caught. I don't like to end up impaled on a pole in the desert."

To Paneb's surprise Merenre suddenly became desperate and begged: "Please Paneb, you have to help me. If you don't help me I will be in big trouble!"

"What do you mean? What kind of trouble are you in?" Paneb asked, wondering what Merenre had gotten himself into.

"I have gambling debts with people you don't want to be indebted to," Merenre explained. "And if I don't settle these debts soon they threaten to feed me to the Nile crocodiles. So please, help me to break into Thutmose's tomb so I can settle my debts and after that there will be enough left for us to live in comfort for the rest of our lives."

Paneb thought for a while and then spoke: "I am sorry but it is too dangerous, it is just not worth the risk."

"What do you mean too dangerous?" Merenre now cried in desperation. "I know you are sometimes selling stolen grave goods, isn't that dangerous? Please, I need your help! I am begging you!"

"First of all, stop crying, behave like a man and don't talk so loud. If there is somebody else around here he will hear everything you say," Paneb spoke angrily and went on: "Second, there is a big difference between fencing a few stolen goods and actually breaking into a Royal tomb. I am sorry but your problem is not my problem and I suggest you leave Thebes as soon as possible to save your life."

Paneb was genuinely scared about robbing a tomb because getting caught meant certain death. He was, however, also a greedy man who could not resist the temptations of a Royal tomb and here was a man who knew the location of such a tomb, knew how to get in it and was willing to share these secrets with him when he was willing to help.

After thinking it over quickly Paneb decided to help Merenre. But before he would tell Merenre he agreed to help him he waited until Merenre was very desperate, this would give Paneb a strong position to negotiate a large share of the treasures for himself.

He watched Merenre sitting there crying and begging and finally spoke: "If I would help you, how much will I get?"

Merenre looked both surprised and relieved and simply answered: "How much do you want?"

"I want half," Paneb replied immediately. Merenre now looked shocked, thought for a moment and spoke: "That is too much, we have to pay the diggers too and what about my own share?"

"Do you know how much treasure goes into a tomb?" Paneb asked. "If we do this carefully and camouflage the entrance of our tunnel we can enter the tomb every night over a long period and take everything we can carry with us."

Paneb stopped speaking a moment, looked at the desperate man in front of him and continued: "You don't have to worry about the diggers, I know people who will help us for just a small share of the treasure. Some people are even more desperate than you, Merenre. After you have paid your debts there will be enough left for you to live a comfortable life. So, it is half for me or you can try your luck with somebody else."

As Paneb expected Merenre did not know any other people who would be able to help him so he sighed and agreed: "Fine, you can get half of the share. When will you start looking for diggers?"

"Don't worry about that. Come back here in three days," Paneb replied and then suddenly snapped: "And now get out of here, I want to get some sleep!"

Merenre left quickly without any further questions and Paneb lay down again under his tree and tried to sleep. But sleep did not come, he did not want to show it to Merenre but he was very worried about their plan.

Ipi and his parents had been waiting for a long time in the forecourt of the Karnak Temple which went quiet around noon time. His parents were sitting against a wall in the shade while Ipi was walking around looking at the statues and the inscriptions on the walls. He saw pictures of strange animal-headed Gods, of the Pharaoh and he saw a lot of strange signs which he did not understand. He was looking at them, trying to make sense of them when he heard a voice behind him: "Are you interested in hieroglyphs? Maybe someday you will be able to read them."

Ipi turned around and saw an older man standing behind him. The man had a shaven head and was wearing a white linen garment and made the impression on Ipi of a person who occupied a high office and was powerful. Yet, in spite of this impression, he spoke very friendly to the speechless

Ipi when he continued: "When you learn reading our sacred hieroglyphs a whole new world will open for you. These walls here around you are telling something but only those who know how to read can understand what they are saying and once you have learned to read you will also be able to read the many wisdoms that priests and Pharaohs from times long ago have left for us in their inscriptions on many papyrus rolls that we keep here in our temple. Do you think that is interesting? Would you like to learn how to read and write?"

"Uh...yes..eh..my lord.." Ipi answered stammering, not knowing what to say.

"My name is Wenamun," the man introduced himself. "I am the Third Prophet of Amun and you must be Ipi, the son of Hor and Nefer?"

"Yes, I am Ipi and my parents are over there," a recovered Ipi replied, pointing to his parents.

"Let's go and meet them," Wenamun spoke in his friendly voice.

They crossed the temple court to the place where Ipi's parents were sitting. When they saw Ipi and Wenamun coming they quickly got up and greeted Wenamun with a bow but after that Ipi's mother started crying, put her arms around Ipi and pressed him against her as if she never wanted to let him go.

"I understand this is a difficult moment for you," Wenamun spoke. "But don't worry about Ipi, we will take good care of him and I will also personally keep an eye on him. You made a good decision when you came here, Hor, and I am sure the Lord Amun will reward you for bringing your son to his temple."

Ipi's father thanked the priest and put his arm around Nefer's shoulders and pulled her to him.

"I think we should go now," he spoke with tears in his eyes. They thanked Wenamun again for his help but he refused: "Don't thank me, thank the Lord Amun, He is the one who takes Ipi into His temple."

Finally they turned to Ipi and his father spoke: "Take good care of yourself, Ipi, listen to what the priests tell you and try to learn from them."

Ipi tried to hold back his tears but failed to do so and started to cry. He could not answer his father's words and simply hugged both his parents.

Then Hor and Nefer turned and started to cross the forecourt back to the exit of the temple. Ipi stayed behind with Wenamun, standing on the enormous court watching his parents until they were gone.

Wenamun put his arm around Ipi's shoulders and spoke reassuringly: "Don't worry, Ipi, everything will be fine. Come with me now and I will show you your new room."

Ipi followed Wenamun further into the temple, further than most people were allowed to go and in spite of his sorrow about saying farewell to his parents he felt a sense of pride that he was allowed to go where others could not. Meanwhile Wenamun was telling him about the temple and its history, trying to make Ipi feel more comfortable: "This temple has been started by our ancestors more than a thousand years ago when Amun was still unknown outside the Theban area and was yet to become the King of the Gods."

Wenamun stopped speaking a moment giving Ipi the opportunity to ask some questions but when he remained silent the priest went on: "Karnak started as a small insignificant temple but when after a period of unrest the Two Lands were reunited under a Theban Pharaoh the Lord Amun became more powerful and popular in all of Egypt. From then on all the Pharaohs paid tribute to Amun and his priests and expanded the temple by adding new buildings, obelisks, courtyards and pylons to it. What you see here is the result of centuries of construction and even today the temple still keeps growing. Pharaoh Amenhotep built a lot in Karnak and I am sure his son will continue the tradition and add his own construction in honour of Amun."

Wenamun kept talking but Ipi heard only half of what was being said; he was too overwhelmed by what he saw, everything in Karnak seemed to be on an enormous scale. Everywhere he looked he saw statues and depictions of Pharaohs and Gods staring at him. He was amazed to see that inside the temple complex there even was a large rectangular lake. The lake had stairways on each side leading into it and there was a boat moored at the side.

"This lake is used by the priests four times a day to purify themselves and the boat is used in religious ceremonies," Wenamun explained when they passed the lake.

"Do I have to purify myself there too?" Ipi asked.
"No, not yet, this lake is used only by the priests. At first you will be working as an apprentice but because you will be working in the temple you will have to purify yourself too, only at another place," Wenamun replied.

"When will I become a priest?" Ipi wondered.
"If you work hard and show you are willing to serve the Lord Amun you can soon become a priest, just do your best," Wenamun explained with a friendly smile. They came at a court from where a corridor went deeper into the temple.

"This leads to the Holy of Holies," Wenamun told Ipi while he pointed at the corridor. "Only a select group of priests and the Pharaoh are allowed to enter this most sacred part of the temple."

"Are you allowed in there?" Ipi asked curiously.

"Yes, I am the Third Prophet of Amun, I enter the Holy of Holies everyday three times to greet and worship the God," Wenamun replied.

Ipi was impressed and asked: "Is the Holy of Holies where the statue of Amun is being kept?"

"Yes," Wenamun replied again, this time in a reverent tone. "And the ka of the God resides inside that statue; that makes this temple the most sacred place of the Two Lands."

They did not enter the Holy of Holies but turned to the right instead and after a long walk they came at the big temple wall that surrounded the huge structure of Karnak and followed it to the back of the temple. Ipi wondered how large this temple actually was; it looked as if it would never end.

Eventually they came at a row of small rooms built against the temple wall. Wenamun stopped at one of the rooms and spoke: "This will be your room, Ipi."

Wenamun opened the door and inside Ipi saw a young boy, maybe just a little older than himself.

"Nebamun, say hello to your new friend and roommate, Ipi," Wenamun spoke to the boy.

Nebamun had been sitting on the floor bent over a papyrus roll but as soon as he saw Wenamun he got up to greet him with a bow.

"This is Nebamun," Wenamun introduced the boy to Ipi. "He has been living here for almost a year now and is studying in the House of Life to become a temple scribe."

"Will I become a temple scribe too?" Ipi inquired. "No," Wenamun answered. "But you will do something that is just as important, or maybe even more important. Tomorrow you will become an apprentice of Penthu, he is one of the best physicians in the Two Lands. He will instruct you and you will learn from him and if you learn well from Penthu and serve the Lord Amun you can become both a physician and a priest here in the Karnak temple."

After he had stopped speaking Wenamun turned away from Ipi and spoke to Nebamun: "Take care of Ipi and help him to adjust to life in the temple."

Next he turned again to Ipi and said: "Everybody here at Karnak will help you but if you have any problems you can always come to me. I will be following your progress so do your best. May the Lord Amun help you with your new life Ipi."

Having said that Wenamun left Ipi alone in the company of his new roommate.

Ipi remained standing hesitatingly in the doorway until Nebamun told him to come inside. The room was sparsely furnished with only two sleeping mats and a table on which lay Nebamun's writing materials, some papyrus and pieces of pottery which Nebamun used to practice his writing skills on.

"Where are you from, Ipi?" Nebamun asked.
"I'm from Thebes," Ipi answered shyly. "My parents have a small farm on the west bank of the Nile; they sent me to the temple because they are poor and think I will have a better future here."

"I will have to share a room with a poor peasant boy?" Nebamun mumbled annoyed to himself but then continued to Ipi with a proud tone in his voice: "I am from a noble family from Mendes in the Nile delta. My father is one of the biggest landowners in

Lower Egypt and has many farmers living and working on his lands. At home we have many servants and I had a private teacher. As a son of a poor farmer you will probably not understand anything about life here in the temple, it is too complicated for uneducated people like you."

Nebamun looked at Ipi to see how he reacted to his words and finally added: "I think they should not accept people like you for temple service. Only people of the nobility are worthy to serve the Gods."

Ipi did not know how to answer, his first impression of the Karnak Temple had been good and Wenamun seemed to be a very friendly man but the thought of having to share a room with Nebamun made Ipi doubt again about whether it was a good idea to come the temple. Without saying another word he sat down in a corner of the room, took the amulet his father had bought for him that morning in his hands and prayed it would help and protect him.

CHAPTER 2
A ROYAL ANNOUNCEMENT
AND
THE FIRST SIGNS OF UNEASE

Malkata Palace had been full of rumours since the funeral two days earlier. Everybody knew that there would be some important announcement from the Pharaoh but nobody could say for sure what it was going to be. It had to be important because Aperel was still waiting in Thebes until the announcement was made even though his office was far away in Memphis.

The Pharaoh and Crown Prince Amenhotep had been having many meetings which sometimes also included Queen Teye and Nefertiti. Nobody else attended these meetings except the Royal Scribe Merykare but he was sworn to secrecy and did not tell anything about what was being said.

Almost everybody thought it had something to do with the succession to the throne and some people said that Pharaoh Amenhotep was going to abdicate, something that was denied by others because a Pharaoh always reigned until his death.

Whatever it was, it kept prince Amenhotep busy, he seemed very preoccupied and ignored everybody, even Kiya. Kiya didn't seem to mind being ignored by Amenhotep, in her free moments she was often seen chatting with one of the palace guards.

"It did not take a long time for you to forget your prince," Aset remarked to Kiya when they were waiting outside the room where the Pharaoh, the prince and their wives had a last meeting before they were going to the audience hall where they would make the announcement everybody had been waiting for.

For this last meeting Amenhotep had also summoned Meryptah, the High Priest of Amun. This was not unusual because the Amun Priesthood was closely involved with the Royal Family and the business of governing the Two Lands.

The Pharaoh had ordered the viziers of Upper and Lower Egypt and other high state officials and priests to come to the palace where they were already waiting in the audience hall.

"As you told me before, I am only a servant girl so nothing can ever happen between the prince and me. Besides that, I think he is over me as well, since the funeral he has ignored me completely. The only things he says to me are: do this, bring me that. Now he also sees me as just another servant," Kiya answered to Aset but she did not seem to be bitter.

"I am happy you came back to your senses again," Aset spoke smilingly. "If you would have married Amenhotep maybe I would have ended up as your servant. Thanks to the Gods that did not happen. Working for you would probably drive me crazy and I would end up running away from you in desperation to some far away oasis."

"And I would send soldiers to fetch you and bring you back to me," Kiya replied laughing.

Aset looked serious again and continued speaking: "I noticed you are very close with the soldiers now, especially with one."

Kiya blushed and replied: "Yes, his name is Montu. I have known him already for some time and I think I love him."

Aset wanted to reply but at that moment the door opened and Merykare, the Royal Scribe, came out of the room and told Aset and Kiya, other servants and the Royal Guards to prepare, the Pharaoh could come any moment to go to the audience hall.

The audience hall was a big pillared hall in the palace with bright paintings of scenes of the Pharaoh's accomplishments in battle and religious duties. On one side of the hall there was a raised platform with two richly decorated golden thrones, one throne for the Pharaoh and one for his Great Royal Wife. In this hall Amenhotep received visitors from inside and outside the country and, like today, personally made announcements to his officials.

Pharaoh Amenhotep the Third sat on his throne wearing the pschent, the double crown of Upper and Lower Egypt, and holding the crook and flail, the symbols of the office of the Pharaoh. Next to him, on his right, sat Queen Teye, his Great Royal Wife, and on the other side two extra thrones had been placed for prince Amenhotep and Nefertiti; it was unusual for the Pharaoh to give an audience together with his son and his son's wife.

His selected listeners were holding their breath, some of them already guessing what the announcement was going to be. Meryptah, the High Priest of Amun, came to the audience hall together with the Royal Family but joined the other officials in the hall to listen to the Pharaoh. Aset noticed that he looked worried.

Pharaoh Amenhotep started to speak:

"As all of you already know my health has been failing me the past years. I pray the Lord Amun will bless me with many more years as your Pharaoh but we have to bow to His will and have to be prepared

if he decides it is time for me to join Osiris in the Netherworld. To my great regret my firstborn son Crown Prince Thutmose went before me to Osiris. This was not only a personal tragedy for me and my family but could potentially throw the Two Lands into chaos if there is not a well prepared successor to the throne. To guarantee a succession without any problems after I travel to the Netherworld and to prepare the new Crown Prince, prince Amenhotep, as well as possible for the responsibilities of the office of Pharaoh I have decided to name prince Amenhotep my co-regent. Next week there will be an inauguration ceremony in the Karnak Temple and from then on my reign will continue as a co-regency. Every command from prince Amenhotep should be regarded as if it came from me personally and he will be only responsible to me.
Some of you might say that my son is too inexperienced and not yet ready to reign over the Two Lands but this is my will. I Pharaoh Amenhotep, the Living Horus on Earth, know that my son will be a good ruler and command you to accept him as your Pharaoh."

Aset was standing with Kiya, Ranefer and other servants at the side of the hall and listened to the Pharaoh. The moment he said that he would continue his reign as a co-regency with his son she heard some talking amongst the listeners; even though she could not understand what was being said she sensed that not everybody agreed with Amenhotep's decision. It also explained the worried look on the High Priest of Amun's face because it was no secret that the future co-regent did not care much about Amun. Aset also wondered why the

Pharaoh was defending his idea already before anybody had voiced a protest. Was even Amenhotep not sure whether he made the right decision and was this a way of reassuring himself?

After he had finished speaking the Pharaoh and his wife left the audience hall but prince Amenhotep stayed together with Nefertiti to receive the congratulations from the officials who were present in the hall.

Aset heard people wish him good luck or say they hoped the Gods would protect him and give him wisdom and a long, prosperous reign. Most people probably meant it but Aset could see that some of them were just saying what they were expected to say. Meryptah, the High Priest of Amun, had already been informed during the private meeting with the Pharaoh and his family but he also came to congratulate the prince and said he hoped that under his reign he would continue the good relationship between the Temple of Amun and the Royal Family because, as the High Priest said: "It is this relationship which made the Two Lands as strong and prosperous as they are now."

Aset heard the prince reply with only a polite: "Thank you, I will remember your advice."

Then she saw him turn his back to Meryptah to start a conversation with Ramose, the Vizier of Upper Egypt and mayor of Thebes.

For a moment Meryptah looked surprised by such behavior towards him; as one of the most powerful people in the country he was not used to people turning their back to him, even the Pharaoh treated him with respect, but then he started to look worried and angry and he turned and walked quickly out of the hall.

Aset saw all this happen and wondered what the future would bring when prince Amenhotep would reign alone after his father's death.

Paneb lay sleeping again under his tree on the riverside when Merenre came back. He shook Paneb's shoulder to wake him and slowly Paneb got up. He had a headache because the evening before he had got drunk both to celebrate his future wealth and to calm his nerves over the risky business which he had planned.
"Did you find the diggers?" Merenre asked.
"Of course I did," Paned replied. "I told you I would take care of that. I found five reliable and experienced workers who are willing to help us dig a tunnel to the tomb. They only ask a small part of the treasure inside."
"That is very good news," Merenre spoke relieved. "We should start digging into Thutmose's tomb as soon as possible."
"No, not yet!" Paneb answered while throwing water from the river in his face, hoping it would relieve his hangover.
"But we should do it as soon as possible," Merenre complained. "If we wait too long some of the diggers could talk and the security guards of the necropolis might hear of our plan. You know what will happen if we get caught!"
"Yes, I know what will happen if we get caught! We will be impaled and then fed to the animals in the desert or to the Nile crocodiles!" Paneb replied angrily. "But if we are going to do this we will do it my way!"
Paneb paused a moment but then he went on more calmly: "Listen, if we are going to dig into a Royal tomb we have to plan it carefully and wait for the

right moment. The prince has only recently been buried so his tomb is probably still being kept under close watch. We just have to be patient. We will continue our normal daily business and when the right time comes I will get in touch with you."

Paneb stopped speaking again to see whether Merenre understood him and just when Merenre started again about the diggers Paneb cut him off and spoke: "Don't worry about our diggers, I told them I would cut out their tongue if they would talk to anybody about our plan. And even if they would talk; they don't know which tomb we are going to enter. As long as you and I keep quiet there won't be anything to worry about."

Merenre nodded and just replied: "Fine, we will do it your way."

He was disappointed because he had expected to be rich and out of his problems within a couple of days. Now he had to wait longer but he understood that Paneb was probably right.

"How long do you think we should wait?" Merenre asked, hoping to get some kind of estimate about when he would have his riches.

"How do I know?", was Paneb's annoyed reply, his headache still bothering him. "A day, a week, maybe a month or even longer. When the opportunity comes you will hear about it. But now you should go back home and don't contact me unless it is something very urgent. I will let you know when the right time has come for us to start."

Merenre didn't say anything anymore and got up. When he was about to leave Paneb put a hand on his shoulder and spoke in a, for him, unusually reassuring tone: "Don't worry, everything is going to work out fine."

His words were not only meant to comfort Merenre but also to reassure himself.

Life in Karnak Temple had been hectic the past days because of the coming inauguration ceremony of the co-regency. The forecourt of the temple was full of people coming and going, many were there on some kind of business but others came there just out of curiosity, wanting to see something of the preparations for the ceremony.

Ipi started to adapt to life in the temple, it was actually better than he dared to hope except for the fact that he and Nebamun, his roommate, did not get along very well.

Karnak was even bigger than Ipi initially thought and he kept discovering new parts. There was even an industrial area with amongst other things a bakery, a goldsmith, a pottery maker and of course Penthu's practice. Karnak Temple was a city within a city.

Every morning Ipi went to the House of Life to learn reading and writing hieroglyphs and in the afternoon he worked as an apprentice for Penthu, the chief physician of Karnak Temple.

Just like all the other priests in the temple Penthu had a shaven head and was usually wearing a white robe. He was a tall, middle-aged, difficult and short-tempered man but he seemed to like Ipi and Ipi liked to work for him and did his best to learn as much as possible.

Just like Ipi, Penthu had been brought to Karnak Temple as a young boy, he had grown up at Karnak and studied there to become a physician. Over many years Penthu had earned the reputation of being one of the best physicians in the country and people from all over the Two Lands and even from outside the country came to him for help. Being a physician Penthu did not only worship Amun but was also a devout follower of Imhotep, the famous physician and vizier of Pharaoh Djoser who had been deified after his death.

Ipi learned from Penthu how to prepare potions and treat simple wounds and diseases. Penthu had many physicians and apprentices working for him but he always personally took care of Ipi which made some of his other apprentices feel resentful.

Penthu's practice was in the back of Karnak Temple and was connected to the outside world by a back entrance so that patients from outside the temple could enter easily without having to pass through the sacred parts of Karnak which were only accessible for priests. The practice consisted of several rooms where he, his assistants and apprentices worked. Here they treated patients and prepared medicines. Penthu's practice even included a room where seriously sick or injured people could stay and receive treatment over a longer period.

Penthu was looking how Ipi treated the wound on the hand of a carpenter of the temple who had had an accident during his work.

"What happened to your hand?" Ipi asked the carpenter.

"I cut it when I was constructing a scaffold in the temple of the Goddess Mut," the worker replied.

Ipi knew that Pharaoh Amenhotep was expanding the precinct of Mut, the wife of the God Amun, which was located next to His temple and was part of the complex of Karnak which further included a temple dedicated to their son Khonsu and the precinct of Montu, the Theban God of war.

Accidents happened frequently at these construction sites and normally there were physicians on the site to help the wounded but sometimes they were taken to the practice of the temple physician, especially when they were seriously wounded. Penthu saw, however, that this carpenter was not seriously hurt and told Ipi to treat him.

"The wound is not very deep," Ipi reassured the carpenter. "You don't have to worry about it; it will heal in a short time. I will disinfect the wound with honey and bandage it."

Ipi looked at Penthu who nodded that he was doing well.

"Be careful with your hand and make sure the wound does not get dirty," Ipi warned the carpenter when he was ready. The carpenter was very grateful and thanked Ipi before he left.

"You did very well, Ipi," Penthu spoke after the carpenter had gone. "You will be a great physician in the future!"

Ipi felt very proud of himself, he had helped a person and Penthu had complimented him.

A moment later a young priest came into the room, he looked familiar to Ipi but he could not remember where he had met him before.

"Can I have a moment of your time, my lord?" the young priest asked politely.

"What do you want, Amenemope?" Penthu replied, apparently not very happy with the priest's visit.

"The Third Prophet of Amun, Wenamun, wants Ipi to help with the preparations for the inauguration of the co-regency. He wants him to come now," Amenemope explained.

Penthu sighed, feeling annoyed and spoke: "Well, if Wenamun wants him to come now, I guess I will have to send him with you. But I would like to have him back as soon as possible, he is my personal assistant."

"I am sure he will be back soon," Amenemope reassured the temple physician.

Ipi followed Amenemope through the temple, he regretted not being able to work with Penthu for some time but he liked to meet Wenamun again and felt honoured to be involved in the preparations of the inauguration of the co-regency. He wished he could tell his parents about this, they would be so proud of their son.

"Penthu seems to like you," Amenemope spoke when they walked through one of the many passages of Karnak.

"I think so," was all that Ipi answered, there was something in the manner in which Amenemope spoke to him that made him feel uncomfortable.

"Wenamun likes you too," Amenemope went on and then added in a vicious tone: "You are a lucky little farmer's boy, you have important friends here."

After these words Ipi remembered this man was the priest he and his parents had met in front of the temple the day he arrived at Karnak.

Ipi did not reply to Amenemope's words and they continued in silence.

Everywhere in the temple people were busy, cleaning, painting or decorating in preparation for the big day.

Finally they arrived at the open forecourt which was hot in the burning sun. But even here many people were busy, Ipi even saw people on their knees scrubbing the floor.

Amenemope turned to him and spoke in a commanding voice: "Take a piece of cloth and a bucket of water and help them scrub the floor!"

"But you said I had to help Wenamun prepare for the inauguration!" Ipi protested.

"I said, Wenamun wants you to help with the preparations and that is exactly what these people are doing. Now go and help them!" Amenemope replied with a triumphant tone while he pointed to the people who were scrubbing the temple floor.

Ipi took a piece of cloth and a bucket with water, got down on his knees next to the other people and followed their example. He felt disappointed; he did not mind doing this kind of work but had hoped to see Wenamun again and to be able to help him prepare some important part of the coming ceremony.

"Even Penthu could not save you from this humiliation, Ipi?" Ipi heard a voice speaking next to him. He looked up and looked straight into Nebamun's face.

In his disappointment he had not noticed his roommate next to him doing the same work as he did. Ipi had never seen Nebamun like this. He did not look like the proud son of a noble family who liked to taunt Ipi. Nebamun looked miserable; sitting on the floor, getting his clothes dirty and covered in sweat from working in the burning rays of the sun for a long time.

"I expected that Penthu's favourite apprentice would not have to do this kind of work," Nebamun continued. "But of course, with you being only a poor farmer's son, this kind of work is still a step up from what you did at home. For me, however, this work is humiliating! I am nobility and my parents are among the biggest landowners in Lower Egypt, I should not be doing this kind of work! If my parents were here they would surely get me out of this work!"

Ipi felt both anger and satisfaction rising within him; anger because of Nebamun's derisive comments about his humble roots and satisfaction because of Nebamun's present situation. He wanted to say a lot of things to him, to defend his origin and to taunt him a bit with his, in Nebamun's own view, humiliating work. But then Ipi remembered his sacred surroundings and simply replied: "Well, your parents are not here to get you out of this work."

This made Nebamun quiet for a short time but then he continued: "Wenamun is always taking care of you. Why does he not get you out of this?"

"According to Amenemope Wenamun is the person who ordered me to do this," Ipi replied and went on: "Amenemope doesn't seem to like me very much."

He didn't know why he said this and expected some kind of insulting reply from Nebamun. But to his surprise his answer was not unsympathetic: "Don't worry, Ipi, Amenemope doesn't like me either. Actually, I wonder whether he likes anybody at all. His family has held high positions in Karnak for generations and this makes him feel as if he is above everybody else."

Ipi wanted to comment and say to Nebamun that he was not so different from Amenemope but decided not to and asked instead: "Does Amenemope still have family working in Karnak?"

"No," Nebamun replied and explained: "He is the last of his family serving in Karnak. But I think his family's history in the temple makes him very ambitious, he is only a temple scribe and that puts a lot of pressure on him. I think he is afraid of being the family's underachiever, he is doing everything to be promoted."

Nebamun stopped talking for a moment and looked annoyed at a person who walked right over the place he was cleaning without appearing to notice him. He muttered some words that Ipi did not understand but then continued speaking: "Somebody like you, Ipi, probably scares Amenemope."

"Why would he be scared of me? I didn't do anything wrong and I hardly know Amenemope!" Ipi replied surprised.

"I think he is scared because you didn't do anything wrong," Nebamun explained. "You only just came here in the temple but Wenamun likes you and Penthu says you are very promising and intelligent. He is afraid you might be a threat to him in the future; you might get a better position than him in the temple hierarchy. And the fact that you are coming from a poor background only makes it worse."

At that moment Wenamun entered the forecourt together with a lady wearing the clothes of a priestess, they looked around and talked to some of the people working there.

"Look, there is Wenamun with his wife Tahat," Nebamun remarked to Ipi. Hearing the name Tahat Ipi remembered his elder brother's wife Tahat and this made him miss his family again but he quickly shook those thoughts off and asked: "Is his wife a priestess in the Temple?"

"Yes," Nebamun replied and added: "She is a Chantress of Amun and comes from a noble Theban family."

At that moment Wenamun and Tahat came to Ipi and Nebamun.

"Are you enjoying the break from your daily routine?" Wenamun asked.

"I prefer working with Penthu and learning to become a physician in the temple, my lord," Ipi answered.

"I also would rather study hieroglyphics than do this kind of work, my lord," Nebamun added.

"It pleases me to hear that both of you are so diligent about your study in the temple," Wenamun spoke with a tone that betrayed his satisfaction but then continued: "But don't forget that in order to become a priest in the Temple of Amun you must be able to perform humble tasks as well."

"A priest of Amun must be humble?" Nebamun asked surprised.

"Yes, Nebamun, don't forget that whatever our position in the temple is, we are all servants of the God," Wenamun replied.

"This is a very important lesson," Tahat added to her husband's words and after a short silence went on in a lower voice: "A lesson which too many priests serving in this temple unfortunately have forgotten. I hope the two of you will never forget it."

It was the night before the inauguration of the co-regency. Paneb, Merenre and the five diggers had already been busy digging a tunnel to the tomb of prince Thutmose for some nights.

A couple of days after he had told Merenre to go home and wait for him, Paneb had contacted him; the opportunity he had been waiting for had come sooner than expected.

With all the high dignitaries coming to Thebes to attend the inauguration ceremony most of the guards protecting the necropolis would be in the city on the east bank of the Nile leaving the tombs on the west bank almost unprotected.

The diggers and Merenre were experienced tomb builders and Merenre knew the exact location of the tomb so work went fast.

Paneb was not used to this kind of work so he spent most of the time outside of the tunnel on the lookout for the few soldiers who were still patrolling the necropolis.

Every now and then he saw a patrol but only once they had come close to where they were working. Paneb had told the diggers to stop their work and to be quiet. The patrol had passed without noticing anything and they continued their work.

Except for that one frightening moment they were not disturbed and Paneb was surprised about the ease with which they could dig to the tomb of the prince.

They only dug during the nights, during the day they camouflaged the entrance to the tunnel, left the necropolis and waited for the following night to return and continue their work.

Paneb was sitting on guard outside of the entrance of the tunnel wrapped in a blanket against the cool desert night. It was a clear night and the bright stars and the moon illuminated the desert around him, he could easily make out the shapes of the mountains and cliffs surrounding the valley.

Merenre had told him he expected to reach the tomb that night so Paneb had brought a wine-skin with him to celebrate his success.

He felt like he had been waiting for hours and he almost gave up hope of reaching the tomb that night when he suddenly heard loud cheers coming from inside the tunnel. Paneb just wanted to tell them to be quiet when a very excited Merenre shouted to him that they had reached the tomb. In his own excitement Paneb also forgot all safety precautions and shouted that he would come down the tunnel to join them.

The tunnel was narrow, just big enough for a person to crawl through, but Paneb was in such a hurry that even in the dark it took him just a short time to reach the tomb.

When he entered the tomb of the Crown Prince, Paneb was surprised to see everybody just standing there without doing anything. Looking around in the tomb he immediately understood why; in the light of the oil lamps they had brought with them he saw the glitter of gold, silver and precious stones everywhere. Paneb was struck with amazement by the treasures he saw.

When he took an oil lamp and walked a bit further he saw this was only one of several rooms. He could not believe the wealth this young prince had taken with him to the afterlife.

On the tomb walls Paneb saw mysterious texts in hieroglyphs and paintings of Gods he had never seen before. For a moment he felt uneasy by these depictions that seemed to move in the flickering light of the oil lamps; what if one of these Gods would come to life and punish him for committing terrible sacrilege?

It took some minutes for Paneb to pull himself together again and to start thinking clearly.

He saw the others looking at a big golden statue and spoke: "Leave that for now! It is almost dawn and we will have to be gone by then. Just take some small things which will be easy to carry and won't attract attention. Tomorrow night we will come back for more."

They started to gather small statues, pieces of jewellery and other small treasures and put them in bags they had taken with them.

"That is enough for now," Paneb spoke after a few moments and added: "I will go outside and see if it is safe, then I will call you and we will go."

Paneb took a bag he had quickly filled with small treasures with him and started to crawl up the tunnel. It took him much longer to get out of the tomb than to get in.

When he got outside it was still dark but the stars already started to fade, it would soon be morning.

Paneb took his wine-skin, which he had left outside. He wanted to have a quick drink by himself to celebrate his new found wealth before he would call the others.

He was just about to take a sip of the wine when he heard something. He dropped the wine-skin and looked in the direction where the sound came from.

What he saw sent chills down his spine. Out of the dark came a patrol of necropolis guards and they came straight towards him and the entrance of the tunnel.

It was too late to camouflage the entrance and the soldiers would surely hear him if he warned the others inside the tomb, so Paneb decided to quietly go further into the valley, hide there and hope the soldiers would not discover the tunnel.

Paneb counted fifteen soldiers, if they would discover the tunnel he, Merenre and the diggers would not stand a chance against them.

To his relief Paneb saw the soldiers pass the tunnel. He just started to breathe easily again when he saw the last soldier in the patrol stop and pick something up from the ground.

To his horror Paneb saw it was his wine-skin which he had left at the tunnel entrance. The soldier called something to his comrades and showed what he had found. They started to look around and it took them only a short time to discover the tunnel.

When he saw a couple of the guards entering the tunnel Paneb knew it was time for him to leave. There was nothing he could do for Merenre and the diggers, their fate was sealed. They would undergo violent interrogations before the inevitable painful execution.

He had to try to get as much distance as possible between him and the soldiers because he knew the others would most likely betray him.

Paneb ran away as fast as he could when behind him he heard people shouting in terror. He knew what that meant; Merenre and the rest were taken out of the tomb and might soon inform the necropolis guards about him.

Paneb knew he would have to leave Thebes but he was sure he would come back. What he had seen in that tomb was enough for him to risk a return to Thebes after the commotion that would undoubtedly follow this attempt to rob prince Thutmose's tomb had died down. Paneb was already planning his return; he would learn from his mistakes of that night. In the future he would not leave anything to chance; he would never again be surprised by any patrols.

That night Paneb had only seen the tomb of a prince; while running away from the tomb he started to imagine what treasures the tomb of a Pharaoh would contain.

After he had been running a for a long time Paneb became exhausted, he thought there was enough distance between him and the guards so he decided to take a rest.

The sun started to rise, turning the sky red and orange, when Paneb looked at the bag he was still holding in his hand. Fortunately he had not dropped it when the soldiers surprised him. He opened the bag and saw the glitter of gold in the first rays of the sun. Seeing the treasure, Paneb smiled and knew he would be living a good life until he would return to Thebes.

Pharaoh Amenhotep and his son, Crown Prince Amenhotep, had attended an early ceremony that morning in the temple of Malkata Palace. It was the first of several ceremonies to ask the blessing of the Gods for the co-regency of the Pharaoh and his son.

After the first ceremony the Pharaoh, his Great Royal Wife Teye, their son the new co-regent and his wife Nefertiti had breakfast. They were sitting on pillows around a low table on which the food was served. As usual, Aset, Kiya and other servants were present to help the Royal Family with everything they needed. The Pharaoh did not eat much, Aset knew he had badly worn teeth and had trouble eating solid food. She also noticed that Nefertiti looked very tired because of her pregnancy.

Aset saw Ranefer, the Head of the Royal servants, being called away, then return and talk quietly to the Pharaoh. Amenhotep nodded and Ranefer went to open a door and let in an officer of the army.

"The Pharaoh has granted you an audience," he spoke to the officer who looked both worried and tired but still kept his military posture. The officer walked into the room and bowed for the Royal Family. Aset wondered what had happened since this was an unusual moment for an audience, especially with an officer of the army.

"What is so important, Hesy, that it cannot wait?" Aset heard an annoyed prince Amenhotep speak before the officer could say a word. After hearing the officer's name Aset remembered him as the head of the necropolis guard.

Hesy ignored the Crown Prince and spoke directly to the Pharaoh: "Your Majesty, I apologize I have to inconvenience you on the morning of this holy day but I have to bring you terrible news."

"Get to the point and tell me what happened!" the Pharaoh replied, clearly worried as if he already knew what he was going to hear.

"Your Majesty, last night a group of criminals broke into prince Thutmose's tomb," Hesy spoke in an insecure voice.

After hearing these words the room turned silent, Aset saw Amenhotep turn pale and she worried the shock would be too much for the old, frail Pharaoh. But then his colour came back and he got up.

"How could this happen!" he shouted furiously. "The tomb should have been guarded!"

Aset hadn't seen the Pharaoh like this for years; his anger seemed to give him renewed energy.

Queen Teye now also joined in and asked: "Has anybody been caught? Is there much damage to the tomb?"

Teye spoke in a tone as if she was discussing some kind of business. But then, suddenly, the strict Queen turned into a worried mother and she asked emotionally: "How is my son's mummy? Has it been damaged or stolen?"

"No, Your Highness," the officer replied. "Prince Thutmose's mummy has not been disturbed, he will continue living his afterlife in the presence of Osiris."

Teye seemed very relieved after receiving the reassuring answer and the worried mother changed back into the businesslike Queen again.

"What is the damage to the tomb?" she asked and added: "and has much been stolen?"

"Have the robbers been arrested?" a calmed-down Pharaoh Amenhotep repeated Teye's first question with a voice that drowned his wife's words.

"Six robbers have been arrested inside the tomb, Your Majesty," Hesy spoke, answering the Pharaoh's question before Queen Teye's. "But during interrogation we discovered that there were seven in total. One of the robbers, according to his accomplices a homeless man named Paneb who also appears to be the leader of the group, has escaped. We also discovered that a small amount of items from prince Thutmose's tomb is missing. We believe that Paneb took this with him when he escaped."

Then, after a short pause to catch his breath, Hesy went on speaking, replying to Queen Teye's question: "The damage to the tomb is minimal. There is only damage to the wall where they entered the tomb but that will be easily repaired."

"What have you done with the captured robbers?" prince Amenhotep asked.

"One of them, a man named Merenre, has died under the first interrogation, the rest are being held at the barracks of the necropolis guard for further interrogation and trial," Hesy replied.

"Since they were captured inside the tomb the trial will be quick and there shall be no doubt about the sentence!" the Pharaoh spoke, the anger having returned into his voice, and continued: "Is there anymore information about the robbery, Hesy?"

"No, Your Majesty, this is all the information I have at the moment," Hesy replied.

"Then you can go now but keep me informed, I want to know every detail about this crime and your progress in catching Paneb," Pharaoh Amenhotep ordered the officer.

"Yes, Your Majesty," Hesy replied obediently, then bowed and left, leaving a silent room behind him.

That night's incident at the necropolis might have spoilt what was supposed to be a festive day for the Royal Family but for the people of the Two Lands, who were not aware of what had happened, that day was still cause for a big celebration.

All over the country there were celebrations and in every temple the priests were praying to the Gods to bless the Pharaoh and his co-regent and give them a long, successful and prosperous reign.

People travelled from far away to Thebes which was the center of the celebrations, they were singing and dancing and lining the streets which the Royal Family and their entourage would take on their way to Karnak Temple where the Pharaoh and his son would receive the blessing of the State God Amun.

The temple was thriving with activity, priests, priestesses and other people were running around taking care of last minute business. The entrance of Karnak was flanked by colourful banners and everywhere along the route which the Royal Family would take through the temple garlands of lilies and papyrus plants, symbolizing Upper and Lower Egypt, were hung together with palm branches, symbolizing years of reign; combined, this meant the priests of Amun were wishing the Pharaoh and prince Amenhotep many years on the throne.

The forecourt was full of waiting people who were hoping to see a glimpse of the Royal Family when they would cross the court; beyond the forecourt high officials were waiting while further down the temple only priests and the Royal Family were allowed. The Holy of Holies remained empty and would later only be entered by the highest priests of Karnak, the Pharaoh and the Crown Prince to conduct the most sacred part of the inauguration ceremony.

Ipi was standing close to Penthu in a large hall near the entrance of the Holy of Holies, the earthly dwelling place of Amun. Even Penthu was not allowed to enter this sacred part of the temple. The central aisle of Karnak was kept empty so the Pharaoh and his family would be able to walk up to the Holy of Holies unobstructed.

The Royal Family could come any moment, most of the activity had quieted down and everybody was waiting for the ceremony to get started. While waiting Ipi heard two priests in front of him whispering to each other.

"Did you hear what happened in the necropolis last night?" one priest asked.

"No, I haven't heard anything. What happened?" the other replied.

"I have heard that the tomb of Crown Prince Thutmose has been robbed by a band of thieves," the first priest spoke again.

"How could that happen?" was the reply. "And especially on the eve of such an important day. Do you think that could be a bad sign? Could that mean that the Lord Amun is unhappy?"

"That was exactly what I was thinking! Everybody knows prince Amenhotep does not worship Amun; he never visits Karnak unless he has to. Amun cannot be pleased with this man as a co-regent and future Pharaoh of the Two Lands," the first priest replied.

Ipi listened to the priests' conversation and got worried. What if Amun was unhappy with prince Amenhotep? What would happen to them? Would he bring bad luck over the country or maybe even something worse? Ipi was lost in his thoughts when suddenly he heard noise at the entrance of the hall; the Royal Family was coming! Ipi instantly forgot all about the priests' conversation and about his worries, he was too excited about seeing the Pharaoh and his family from such a close distance.

For a moment Ipi felt proud, not so long ago he was a poor farmer's boy but now he was in the sacred Temple of Amun, close to the Pharaoh and witnessing one of the most important events of his country.

It was only a small group which Ipi saw passing by from behind the people who were standing in front of him. Ipi had expected many servants to follow the Royal Family but instead he saw only five people, three men and two young girls. Ipi knew one of the men to be Ptahhotep the personal physician of the Pharaoh. The rest of the servants, guards and other followers stayed behind in the forecourt.

From the moment the Pharaoh and his family left the forecourt of Karnak Temple they were escorted by Chantresses of Amun and the High Priest of Amun, Meryptah. When the chantresses passed Ipi he noticed Tahat, the wife of Wenamun, amongst them.

Behind the Pharaoh and the prince followed the Great Royal Wife and the wife of the new co-regent. Ipi noticed a strong resemblance between prince Amenhotep and his mother Queen Teye. He remembered hearing once that the relationship between the prince and his mother had always been very close.

The Great Royal Wife, the wife of the prince and their servants stayed behind while the High Priest, the Pharaoh and his son the co-regent followed by a few high ranking priests, amongst whom Ipi recognized Wenamun the Third Prophet of Amun, entered the Holy of Holies. Ipi noticed prince Amenhotep looked uncomfortable and nervous. He had heard many rumours about the prince having a dislike for Amun and wondered if they could be true.

Ipi felt shocked and disappointed by the sight of the Pharaoh, he looked weak and old, not as strong and powerful as his statues in the temples made him appear. Contrary to the Pharaoh, his son, the new co-regent, appeared young and healthy, even though he also did not resemble the idealized portraits of the Pharaohs. The young Amenhotep was tall, slim with short black hair and an unusually long face.

It took a long time for the Pharaoh, the prince and the priests to return from the Holy of Holies. Ipi was intrigued about what was happening inside. It had to be a very sacred ceremony because it was carried out in front of the statue of Amun, the embodiment of the King of the Gods. The only thing Ipi knew that happened inside the Holy of Holies was that Meryptah, as a representative of the God Amun, would place the double-crown of Egypt, which symbolized Upper and Lower Egypt, on the head of the new co-ruler, an act which meant that Amun accepted him on the throne.

When they finally returned the Chantresses of Amun, who had been waiting at the entrance of the Holy of Holies, started singing again. The High Priest walked with a solemn look on his face in front of the Pharaoh and the new co-regent, who now wore the double crown of Egypt, they in turn were followed by the other priests. Prince Amenhotep now looked relieved and proud, almost as if he had won a big victory but the old Pharaoh looked even more tired and weak than before and had to hold on to his son to keep himself from falling. Whatever had happened in front of the statue of Amun it must have drained his energy.

When they were passing Ipi, the rest of the Royal Family and their entourage started to follow them on their way out. When they were about to leave the hall, suddenly, the unthinkable happened: the mighty Pharaoh Amenhotep, Lord of the Two Lands collapsed.

Everybody stood as if frozen, only Penthu acted and within moments was at the Pharaoh's side, checking his unconscious body. Then Queen Teye also regained her self-control and shouted at the shocked Ptahhotep to do something and to one of the two servant girls to fetch water.

Spurred on by the Great Royal Wife, Ptahhotep quickly ran to the Pharaoh and wanted to take over from Penthu.

"He should be taken back to the palace immediately," Ptahhotep spoke.

"Don't be a fool!" Penthu replied and explained: "You can't move the Pharaoh in this state, it will kill him. He will have to stay here in the Karnak Temple until his strength has returned."

Ipi watched in disbelief how two of the best physicians in the country started to argue. Soon however, Queen Teye intervened and decided Penthu was right and the Pharaoh should remain in Karnak. At that moment Ipi heard one of the two priests in front of him remark: "I am sure now, Amun does not approve of prince Amenhotep as the co-regent and future Pharaoh. The Two Lands have difficult times ahead!"

Penthu beckoned Ipi to come over and ordered him: "Prepare my private room for the Pharaoh, His Majesty will be staying there."

Ipi wanted to run but felt a hand on his shoulder stopping him.

"Wait a moment boy, I will be coming with you." It was prince Amenhotep.

"I have to make sure the room will be suitable to receive the Pharaoh," Amenhotep explained.

"Yes, of course, Your Majesty," Ipi replied feeling intimidated by the prince's presence.

The moment they were leaving Ipi saw the servant coming back with a small jug of water.

"Give the jug to me, Aset," Ptahhotep ordered the girl, but to his dismay Penthu already took it from her hands and carefully poured some water in the Pharaoh's mouth. To everybody's relief Pharaoh Amenhotep reacted to the water and slowly opened his eyes.

"He will still have to stay here. He is very weak and I would like to examine him," Penthu spoke to the Great Royal Wife.

"That's not...." Ptahhotep wanted to react but Queen Teye cut him off and spoke: "That is fine. Do everything you think is necessary to save our Pharaoh."

After seeing Amenhotep regaining consciousness prince Amenhotep seemed relieved and spoke to Ipi: "I will have a look at my father's room now. Show me the way."

When Ipi started to lead the way Amenhotep turned to the servant girl and ordered: "Aset you will come with us."

Walking through the pillared halls of Karnak the prince asked Ipi: "What is your name, boy?"

"My name is Ipi, Your Majesty," he replied politely.

"How did you end up in this temple at such a young age, Ipi?" prince Amenhotep continued asking.

"My parents brought me here, Your Majesty," Ipi answered again.

"Are you satisfied with your life in the Temple of Amun?" came the next question.

"Yes, Your Majesty," Ipi replied. "I am very happy here and grateful to the temple that they take care of me. They even train me to be a physician."

"That is great Ipi," Amenhotep spoke but went on in a warning tone: "But remember that the Amun Temple never gives anything without expecting something in return. Its main purpose is gathering wealth and power!"

Ipi's first impression of the new co-regent and future Pharaoh was good, he seemed very friendly.

But his last remark about the Temple of Amun made him feel uncomfortable. Could it really be true that this man did not like the Lord Amun and his priesthood? He looked back and saw the girl, whose name he heard was Aset, walking behind prince Amenhotep. She was a pretty girl with long black hair which fell over a simple but elegant white dress like most of the servant girls who worked in the palace wore. Aset did not show any sign of surprise or wonder about the words of the prince and looked straight forward with an emotionless expression on her face; maybe she was used to the prince making this kind of remarks.

The rest of the way to Penthu's room which was attached to his practice continued in silence. When they arrived in the well-kept, sunlit room with religious depictions of the Gods Amun and Imhotep next to medical texts painted on the walls the prince looked around and nodded, seemingly satisfied with what he saw.

"It looks fine but some adjustments will have to be made and, of course, the room has to be cleaned again," Amenhotep spoke and continued, while pointing at the bed: "The bed here might be suitable for a normal patient but not for a Pharaoh. I am sure there will be something more comfortable available in this temple."

Amenhotep looked around in the room, walked to the window that faced to the east and spoke: "The Pharaoh's bed should be placed here, close to the window so that every morning my father will be able to receive the life-giving rays of the Aten, the Sun Disc."

The prince continued pointing out other things in the room which had to be changed when Meryptah, the High Priest, together with Wenamun and a few temple servants entered the room.

"All the priests in the Temple of Amun will pray for a quick recovery of the Pharaoh and will spare no effort to give him everything he needs during his stay at our temple," Meryptah assured the prince.

"Just make sure the room will be in order as soon as possible," Amenhotep answered the High Priest without showing gratitude or the proper respect which even the Pharaoh showed the High Priest of Amun during their meetings.

Then Amenhotep continued: "I would like to return to my father now, tell one of your servants to escort me."

Wenamun beckoned one of the servants and told him to escort the prince back.

Before he left Amenhotep turned to Aset and ordered her: "You stay here and help to make sure the room is in order to receive the Pharaoh!"

After prince Amenhotep had left Ipi could feel a tension in the room. He could clearly feel the dislike from Amenhotep towards the Temple of Amun and this feeling was confirmed by the disrespectful way he talked about the temple and he behaved towards the High Priest. He also noticed the High Priest felt insulted even though he did his best not to show it.

Ipi decided to try to start a conversation with Aset when the opportunity came, maybe he would be able to find out something more about the new co-regent of the Two Lands.

The opportunity to talk with Aset came sooner than expected. Meryptah, Wenamun and the servants left the room, leaving Ipi and Aset alone together with a couple of servants who were busy cleaning and rearranging the room. Ipi was hesitant and tried to find a way to start a conversation.

Aset, however, seemed to have read his mind and asked: "You are worried about prince Amenhotep aren't you?"

For a moment Ipi did not know what to say; should he be honest and tell a servant of the Royal Family he doubted the son of the Pharaoh would be a good co-regent and future Pharaoh? Or should he tell a lie and say she was mistaken? Ipi decided to be honest.

"I worry prince Amenhotep will disrupt the divine order," he admitted and then went on explaining: "The Lord Amun and His temple have played an important role in our country for a long time and acted as a balance against the power of the Pharaoh. I worry that prince Amenhotep does not respect Amun and with his behaviour will upset this balance."

Aset thought about Ipi's words for a moment and replied: "You are very intelligent for such a young boy. But I think you are unnecessarily worried, I know the prince is different compared to all the Pharaohs that have ruled until now but I also know he is a good person who loves his country. He will be a good ruler and will do what is best for the Two Lands and its people."

While Aset was speaking she was feeling doubts in her heart. She had known Amenhotep a long time already and knew he wanted to do what he genuinely thought was best for Egypt but she doubted his ideas were suitable for her country. She also knew the prince to be a stubborn man who would not easily change his mind. Aset didn't want to admit it to anybody but she also worried about the future of Egypt.

The rest of the day all the ceremonies continued without the Pharaoh. The Egyptian people were not informed that the Pharaoh was ill and prince Amenhotep, the new co-regent, still attended all the necessary ceremonies.

The Pharaoh, who was slipping in and out of consciousness, had been taken to the room of Penthu who had taken charge of his care instead of Ptahhotep with the silent approval of the Royal Family.

Penthu's practice had been completely taken over by the Royal Family, court officials, Royal Servants and Royal Guards. The complete area was now closed to all temple staff with the exception of the highest priests of Karnak and Penthu and his assistants.

Ipi was one of the assistants who were allowed to stay but he could not come near the Pharaoh, only Penthu and Ptahhotep were allowed to treat him.

In the room of the Pharaoh there was a heavy scent of incense which was being burnt to please the Gods and next to the Pharaoh's bed there was always a priest of Amun praying for his recovery.

First this was done by the High Priest, Meryptah, himself but after a while he had been relieved by another priest, the Second Prophet of Amun, a man named Maya.

Aset did not stay with the Pharaoh, she had left with prince Amenhotep to escort him during his attendance at the remaining ceremonies. She and Ipi hadn't further discussed the prince but Ipi did feel less worried after Aset's reassuring words.

Later, however, something happened which brought back all his worries.

At the end of the day prince Amenhotep returned to see the Pharaoh. He was followed by Aset, another servant, two guards and another man who looked like a priest but not a priest of Amun.

"This is Meryra," Amenhotep introduced the unknown priest. "He is a priest of the Aten and he will pray here for my father. The priest of Amun is no longer necessary and can leave this room."

Surprised by the appearance of the Aten priest and not knowing what to do Maya looked at Meryptah for help.

The High Priest tried to protest but Amenhotep silenced him by saying: "Now my father is unable to rule I am the righteous ruler of the Two Lands and order your priest to go. I thank you for praying for the Pharaoh's recovery but that duty will now be taken over by Meryra!"

The High Priest of Amun backed down and, while Meryra knelt down next to the Pharaoh's bed and started praying to the Aten, told Maya he could go and then followed him out of the room. This time Ipi even saw a sign of surprise and shock on Aset's face; she must not have expected this.

When Meryptah and the Second Prophet of Amun walked out of the room Ipi heard the High Priest speak to the other priest: "I pray to Amun that I am wrong but I think that today, with the inauguration, we have taken the first step on a path which will lead the Two Lands into chaos!"

YEAR 1 OF THE REIGN OF AMENHOTEP THE FOURTH/ AKHENATEN

CHAPTER 3
A NEW PHARAOH
AND
A LOSS FOR KARNAK

One year after Pharaoh Amenhotep the Third collapsed in the Temple of Karnak he died in his palace in Thebes. His health had improved again after his collapse and he was able to return to the palace after spending a week in Penthu's room at the Temple of Amun. However, he never fully recovered and remained weak. His son, the co-regent, regularly had to rule the Two Lands without his guidance.

After the Pharaoh's death Egypt went into mourning. All over the country people tore their clothes and threw dust over their heads as a sign of their grief. Amenhotep the Third had ruled the country well for more than thirty years and had brought Egypt one of its most prosperous periods. Most Egyptians had been born and grown up under the reign of Amenhotep, he had been the only Pharaoh they had known and his death brought uncertainty for their future.

After an impressive funeral ceremony led by his son and successor, Pharaoh Amenhotep the Third was laid to rest in a tomb in the Valley of the Kings which befitted his long and successful reign. Amenhotep's tomb was filled with even more riches than the tomb of his eldest son, prince Thutmose, who preceded his father into the Kingdom of Osiris.

Pharaoh Amenhotep the Third was succeeded by his second-born son and co-regent Pharaoh Amenhotep the Fourth who inherited a rich and stable country from his father.

The co-regency of Amenhotep and his son was uneventful but the young Amenhotep did well. Even though the relations between him and the Temple of Amun never became cordial prince Amenhotep always faithfully performed the duties at the Karnak Temple which he was expected to do and the High Priest was always invited to attend meetings which were regularly held at the Royal Palace.

Everybody who had doubts about the new co-regent at the inauguration started to think they might have been wrong and that he would follow the example of his ancestors in keeping good relations between the Royal Family and the Temple of Amun.

Amenhotep's ascension to the throne included another inauguration ceremony in the Karnak Temple and was viewed by the Egyptian people as a national celebration. Every temple in the Two Lands organized a ceremony and made offerings to pray to the Gods to give the new Pharaoh a long and prosperous reign just like his father had.

After the new Pharaoh had been on the throne for some months without any significant changes in the

Two Lands life started to return to normal again and the people looked to their future with confidence.

Ipi had been working for over a year at Karnak and was a very promising apprentice.

After six months of work and study he had been accepted as a wab priest at the temple and just like all the other priests he now had to shave his head as a sign of purity.

He was still in training, both in the House of Life and as a physician, but he was at least certain his future would be in the Temple of Amun.

Penthu's assistants also had recognized his talent to become a good physician and gave him all the support he needed. Even his roommate Nebamun had become a good friend over the year. Ipi felt at home in the Temple of Amun, even though sometimes he missed his family whom he hadn't seen anymore since he entered the temple.

Ipi was treating a patient when a messenger of the Royal Palace came in with a message for Penthu. Penthu was surprised about this unexpected visitor and asked what he wanted.

"His Majesty orders you to come to the Palace immediately!" the messenger spoke.

"Why does His Majesty wants my presence in the palace? Is he ill? What about Ptahhotep? He is his personal physician," Penthu replied surprised.

"I don't know," the messenger simply answered. "I just know you have been summoned to the palace. His Majesty wants to see you immediately."

Aset was with Kiya in the audience hall; Kiya was in a good mood because she and Montu, the palace guard, had recently decided to get married. Her friend's plans worried Aset because she noticed that Pharaoh Amenhotep started to give more attention to Kiya again. She had talked to her about this but Kiya wasn't worried. Contrary to the more reserved Aset, Kiya enjoyed being the centre of attention, even when it came from the Pharaoh; she never saw any harm in it.

At that moment, however, the new Pharaoh had no attention for Kiya. He was anxiously waiting for Penthu to arrive.

"Where is Penthu?" Amenhotep complained impatiently and continued: "He should have been here already. A Pharaoh should not be waiting for a commoner!"

Aset noticed the Pharaoh often behaved very agitatedly lately, he seemed very nervous.

Next to Amenhotep sat his Great Royal Wife, the new Queen of Egypt, Nefertiti. During the co-regency of her husband and her father-in-law she had given birth to a daughter, princess Meritaten. The princess was a healthy girl and Amenhotep was a proud father but Nefertiti seemed disappointed she wasn't a son who would be the new Crown Prince and the future Pharaoh.

To her great relief Nefertiti was going to have another chance to produce an heir to the throne because she was pregnant again; maybe it would be a son this time.

The pressure on Nefertiti was growing, however, since soon after his father's death Amenhotep had also married Tadukhipa, the daughter of Tushratta, the King of Mitanni. She had been sent, along with many treasures, to marry Amenhotep the Third in order to cement the alliance between Egypt and Mitanni but due to his death Tadukhipa now married the new Pharaoh.

Fortunately for Nefertiti it was only a diplomatic marriage and her husband did not show much interest in his second wife.

Nefertiti was a strong Queen who took the example of her mother-in-law, the former Great Royal Wife, Queen Teye. Just like Teye, Nefertiti actively supported her husband ruling the country. But even after the death of her husband, Queen Teye continued to play an important role at the Royal Court, advising her son, the new Pharaoh, on state affairs and he always valued her opinion.

"Bring me a cup of wine! I am thirsty," the Pharaoh commanded, still impatiently waiting for Penthu.

Aset came to offer him the requested wine when another servant informed him of the arrival of Penthu. Amenhotep forgot about his thirst, gestured Aset to leave and ordered: "Let him enter immediately!"

When Penthu entered the audience hall Amenhotep's attitude changed abruptly.

"Penthu!" he exclaimed, welcoming the physician of the Karnak Temple in a friendly tone. "Thank you for coming. I hope I didn't inconvenience you when I asked for you."

Penthu bowed for the Pharaoh and replied: "You could never inconvenience me Your Majesty. I am your loyal servant and always at your disposal."

"I am very satisfied to hear that because I have an important task for you," Amenhotep answered.

"I will be honoured to serve Your Majesty," Penthu replied again and added: "I will perform any task Your Majesty asks from me."

"Good!" Pharaoh Amenhotep spoke bluntly. "I want you to become the new Royal Physician!"

For a moment Penthu looked at his Pharaoh as if not understanding what he meant. Aset and Kiya, who were overhearing the conversation, were also surprised. Did Amenhotep want a priest of Amun as his personal physician?

"But I am the chief physician of the Temple of Amun. I cannot leave the temple. I have promised to devote my life to the service of the Lord Amun," Penthu stammered.

Everybody in the audience hall was holding their breath. They expected the Pharaoh to become furious at this man who dared to refuse to accept an offer to work for him. To their surprise, however, the Pharaoh remained calm and friendly.

"I know you have devoted your life to Amun," Amenhotep spoke. "But what better way is there to serve Him than to take care of the health of His representative on earth?"

Penthu did not know what to answer and after a short but uncomfortable silence Amenhotep went on: "I was very impressed by the way you helped my father when he collapsed at Karnak and I know you have the reputation to be the best physician in Egypt. Don't you think the best physician of Egypt should work in the service of the Pharaoh, the Living God?"

Penthu wanted to reply but was cut off by Amenhotep who continued with a friendly voice which, however, contained a threatening undertone: "Could you refuse a request of your Living God?"

Penthu capitulated, he knew he had no choice but to do what his Pharaoh demanded. In a soft voice he replied: "I could never refuse a request from Your Majesty. If Your Majesty asks me to serve him I will obey. It will be my honour to serve you."

"I am glad you agree to work for me, Penthu," Amenhotep spoke with satisfaction and continued in a businesslike tone: "I expect you to be here in the palace tomorrow. You don't have to bring any assistants from the temple of Amun; we have excellent physicians here who can work with you when you require any assistance."

After Penthu acknowledged the Pharaoh's words Amenhotep told him: "That would be all for now Penthu, you have a lot to do to prepare for your new position so I won't hold you up much longer."

Penthu bowed and a short time later left Malkata Palace, feeling like a broken man.

Amenhotep's decision surprised everybody at the Royal Palace but also brought relief. If the Pharaoh would take a priest of Amun as his personal physician that would probably mean he respected the God and his priesthood.

One person who did not feel happy was Ptahhotep. He had expected to continue his service under the new Pharaoh.

While passing his practice in the palace Aset saw him sitting behind his desk staring blankly at the wall with tears in his eyes. He had at least some consolation that he could remain in the palace as a physician for the palace staff.

Later that day Aset and Ranefer, who kept his position as Head of the Royal Servants under the new Pharaoh, entered the Pharaoh's office to serve him fruit and wine.

The office was a large bright room with big windows that allowed as much sunlight as possible to enter the room. Unlike his father, the new

Pharaoh did not want to prevent the rays of the Aten to enter his office which resulted in the room being very hot compared to the rest of the palace but this did not seem to bother Amenhotep.

The walls of the room were decorated with images of the Sun Disc and Amenhotep and his family; between these images there were many inscriptions proclaiming the Pharaoh's titles and prayers to the Aten. It did not resemble the office of the Pharaoh's father which had been decorated with depictions of his accomplishments and images of the traditional Gods.

Amenhotep was alone in his office and stood in front of a window staring outside. He did not turn around or say anything when Aset and Ranefer entered the room and greeted him. Aset put the bowl of fruit she was carrying on a table next to the jug with wine which Ranefer had brought.

"Will you require anything more, Your Majesty?" Ranefer asked politely.

"No, that would be all. You can leave," Amenhotep replied, turning around to pour wine in his cup. Aset noticed the expression on the Pharaoh's face; it was sad, maybe even angry. She wondered what could have happened since the Pharaoh was in such a good mood just a short time ago.

Upon leaving the room Aset glanced outside through the window Amenhotep had been standing in front of and she immediately found out what had made him upset; outside, in the palace garden, she saw Kiya and Montu in a passionate embrace.

When Penthu arrived back at his practice at Karnak Ipi immediately noticed something was wrong. The normally self-confident priest looked worried and did not want to say anything about what had happened in the palace. The only thing he said before he rushed out of his office again was that he needed to speak with the High Priest as soon as possible. Later Ipi saw him coming back together with Meryptah, both now looking worried.

He tried to overhear what the two priests were talking about and heard Meryptah say: "But it doesn't have to be all bad. The fact that the Pharaoh wants a priest of Amun to be his personal physician is actually a very good sign."

Ipi was shocked when he heard the words of the High Priest. Was Penthu going to leave Karnak? He was needed in the temple, he could not leave. The Pharaoh had many good physicians already, why did he need Penthu?

Meryptah continued speaking: "Regrettable as it is, we will have to obey the Pharaoh and let you go. But we can make the best out of a bad situation. When you are in the palace try to gain the Pharaoh's trust. Until now his reign has not been bad for us but we don't know what might be coming. Having a priest of Amun working closely with him can maybe help to prevent possible future hardships for us. If, may our Lord Amun prevent it, it ever becomes necessary you might be able to help us to protect the interests of the Temple of Amun."

"I understand," Penthu replied and added: "I will always be loyal to the temple and to Amun. I will act as your representative at the Pharaoh's court."

"May the Lord Amun help us all," Meryptah spoke and after a short pause went on: "I have the feeling we will need His protection soon."

Having said that Meryptah turned and left, leaving Ipi and Penthu alone.

"You probably already understand what has happened, don't you Ipi?" Penthu spoke after an uncomfortable silence.

"You are called to Pharaoh's court?" Ipi replied.

"Yes, I am afraid so," Penthu spoke in a sad voice. "I have dedicated my life to Karnak, I expected to stay here and serve the Lord Amun until the moment Osiris will call me to the Netherworld but now I have to leave to the palace and serve the Pharaoh."

For a moment Ipi thought he saw tears in Penthu's eyes but the physician recovered immediately again and went on with a forced smile: "But there is nothing for you to worry about Ipi, Intef, my assistant, will replace me as the chief physician of Karnak and you know he is a very good physician. He will help you to improve your skills just as I helped you. Trust in the Lord Amun, Ipi, trust that everything will be fine in the end, that is all what you have to do and all what I have to do."

"What do you want me to do?" Kiya asked desperately. Aset found Kiya in their sparsely decorated room in the Royal Palace. Their only possessions in the small white walled room consisted of two sleeping mats, two boxes for their clothes, an oil lamp and a few cups and bowls. In the corner stood a small shrine dedicated to Aset's favourite Goddess Hathor in front of which Aset burnt incense every day. The only source of fresh air and sunlight was a small window high in the wall.

Aset informed Kiya about what she had seen at the Pharaoh's office and now Kiya also started to get worried.

"Maybe Montu and I should run away!" Kiya continued impulsively.

"No, of course not. You will only make things worse like that," Aset replied. "What do you think will happen when Amenhotep decides to look for you and finds you? I think the best solution is not to marry Montu and to see him less or even not to see him at all."

"No! I could never do that," was Kiya's stubborn reply and she continued in the same stubborn tone: "I would rather move with Montu to a small oasis somewhere faraway in the desert where I am sure we would never be found than live without him! The Pharaoh can not stop me from marrying whoever I want, that would be against Ma'at!"

"Yes, you are right, it would be against Ma'at!" Aset agreed but then continued: "But will the Pharaoh care about that? I know he is a living God but I have been working at the Royal Court long enough to know that Gods on earth can be just like people; they do not always obey Ma'at. I am sorry I have to say this but I'm just trying to help you and Montu."

Kiya looked angrily at Aset and spoke virulently: "Really? Are you trying to help me? Every time I have a relationship you complain and say I should be careful. You have never supported me! I think you are just jealous because you are one year older than I am and have never been in a relationship!"

Aset got flushed with anger and wanted to answer but Kiya told her to get out of the room. Aset hesitated a moment, waiting to see if Kiya would change her mind because in spite of her anger she still wanted to help her friend. When Kiya did not say anything anymore and ignored her Aset finally turned and left the room. Closing the door behind her she heard Kiya started to cry.

The next morning Penthu got up early. He had a lot of things to do and a lot of people to say farewell to. He was talking with Meryptah when he was told that a Royal Bark was waiting at the dock of the temple to bring him to Malkata Palace.

"May Amun be with you," Meryptah spoke when they parted. Then other priests and priestesses came, including Wenamun, the Third Prophet of Amun, his wife Tahat and Penthu's replacement, the new chief physician of Karnak, Intef. Ipi also came together with Nebamun to say goodbye to Penthu, who besides being his mentor over the past year also had become one of his best friends in the temple.

"Take good care of yourself, Ipi," Penthu spoke. "Do your best, learn from Intef and the other physicians and priests in Karnak and I am sure you will be a great priest and physician in the future."

Ipi felt tears welling up in his eyes and could not say anything more than: "Thank you, I will."

"Don't worry Ipi, I have the feeling we will see each other again in the future," Penthu spoke reassuringly before he turned to go to the temple dock.

Penthu arrived at the dock of Karnak Temple where he saw a beautiful boat lying in the water, waiting for him. The moment he boarded the boat Penthu was welcomed by a bald man wearing an expensive multicoloured robe and a lot of jewellery.

"Welcome on board His Majesty's bark, my lord Penthu. My name is Ranefer and I am the Head of the Royal Servants of His Majesty," the man introduced himself.

"His Majesty has sent me to escort you to the Royal Palace. All your belongings have already been brought on board. Are you ready to depart, my lord?" Ranefer went on speaking to Penthu who felt depressed about the prospect of leaving Karnak. Penthu just nodded and Ranefer gave a sign to the boat's crew who immediately pushed the bark away from the dock and started to return to Malkata Palace.

"The palace life will suit you," Ranefer spoke. "It is much more comfortable than life in the temple. And if you ever need anything don't hesitate to ask me. I will always be ready to serve His Majesty's physician."

Penthu wasn't listening to Ranefer's words. He stood on the stern of the bark and watched the distance between him and his temple getting bigger and bigger.

Aset was serving breakfast to the Royal Family; that morning, she was in command of the other servants because Ranefer was out on other business.

She noticed Kiya was missing and wondered where she could be. Kiya had still been angry at her earlier that morning but could she be so angry that she refused to work with her?

To her relief Aset saw Amenhotep's mood had improved again since the previous day. He was talking with his mother Teye, his pregnant wife Nefertiti and playing with his daughter Meritaten.

Suddenly he became serious and spoke: "I have arranged a meeting for this afternoon, today is going to be a very important day. Everything I have been thinking about for a long time is going to be realized soon. Aten will finally receive the honour he deserves."

Teye nodded approvingly but replied: "You know I will always support you but be cautious, my son. Be careful not to upset the Amun priesthood, do not underestimate their power."

"The Pharaoh always knows what is best," Nefertiti countered her mother-in-law's warning and added: "When necessary he will know how to deal with a couple of priests."

"Don't worry, mother," Amenhotep replied reassuringly to his mother's words. "You know I am always careful and I will always ask your advice before I take an important decision."

Aset overheard the conversation. She had got used to overhearing the Royal Family talking about state affairs and normally she didn't really care about what was being said since it often bored her. But today she felt that the conversation was about the beginning of something important. Had the Pharaoh finally decided to change his ideas into actions?

After she had taken care of the Royal Family's breakfast Aset had a short time to rest, so she decided to look if Kiya was in their room. When she arrived at the room she found Kiya very upset.

"He is gone!" Kiya cried.

"What do you mean?" Aset asked, wondering who she was talking about.

"He is gone!" Kiya cried again with tears running down her face and went on: "I went to look for Montu early this morning and I could not find him anywhere. Then Hekanakht, the Head of the Royal Guard, came to me and said that the Pharaoh has sent Montu to Kush."

"To Kush?" Aset exclaimed in surprise, referring to the Egyptian protectorate to the south of the country, and asked: "What does he have to do there?"

"The Pharaoh sent him to work as a guard in the palace of Thutmose, the Viceroy of Kush," Kiya replied, still crying.

"He did this just to get him out of his way. I could never forgive the Pharaoh for this!" Kiya shouted furiously.

"Don't talk like that!" Aset replied horrified. "You will make things only worse."

For a moment there was a silence in the room during which Kiya calmed down before she went on speaking: "I am sorry I was angry at you yesterday, you were right and I should have listened to you."

"Forget about it," Aset replied while putting an arm around Kiya's shoulders and then spoke: "I would probably have acted the same if I were in your situation. But even if you had listened to me it would not have made any difference, when we talked yesterday it was too late already."

Aset suddenly stopped speaking, looked Kiya straight in her face and cautioned her: "Now the most important thing for you is not to make the Pharaoh upset with you. Don't let him notice your anger about what he did!"

Kiya managed a smile and replied: "I know, I will come back to work, serve the Pharaoh and his family and act as if nothing has happened."

"Welcome to Malkata Palace!" Ranefer cheerfully spoke to Penthu when they arrived. "I will bring you to your quarters first, later His Majesty would like to meet you."

Penthu followed Ranefer into the palace to his living quarters. He had been to the palace a few times before but he never came past the audience hall. It surprised him how large the palace actually was.

They walked through a long corridor until Ranefer opened a door and spoke: "This is where you will live and work. All the equipment of your predecessor, Ptahhotep, is at your disposal but should you need anything more just let me know."

Penthu looked around in his apartment which consisted of several rooms and nodded with satisfaction.

"I think this will do," he replied.

"Then I will leave you now," Ranefer spoke but before he left he added: "When His Majesty wants to see you I will have you called."

Penthu stood alone in his room and looked around again, the walls were white and without any decorations except for an image of Imhotep, the deified physician of Pharaoh Djoser, which reminded him of his practice at Karnak where he had a similar depiction. After only a short time Penthu heard a knock on the door.

"Does Amenhotep want to see me this soon?" he wondered.

Penthu opened the door and saw Ptahhotep with a bundle of papyrus rolls under his arm standing in the doorway.

"I see you have not only received my position as the Pharaoh's physician but also my former living quarters," the previous Royal Physician spoke jokingly even though his eyes did not smile.

"Did you come here to inspect my lodgings?" Penthu replied sarcastically.

"No," Ptahhotep answered, this time speaking seriously. "I thought you would need these."

While Ptahhotep spoke he held up the papyrus rolls he had been carrying and added: "These are the documents containing His Majesty's medical history. They are strictly confidential so I wanted to give them to you personally."

"Thank you," Penthu replied, much friendlier now. "Can you please come in and tell me more about the Pharaoh's health?"

The friendly expression which Ptahhotep had maintained during their brief conversation suddenly disappeared and he replied curtly: "His Majesty chose you as his physician instead of me. In these documents you have all the information you need."

As soon as he had finished speaking Ptahhotep handed the papyrus rolls to Penthu and immediately left without any further words, leaving Penthu standing alone in his doorway holding the bundle of documents.

After Penthu's departure Ipi was feeling depressed. He had become so used to working with him that he could not imagine it being any different. Penthu had become one of his best friends in the temple; whenever Ipi needed anything or had problems Penthu had always been there for him just as he had been there during the difficult period when Ipi had just arrived at the Karnak Temple. Ipi still had other friends like Wenamun and Nebamun but that did not make him feel the loss of Penthu any less.

Ipi was working when Intef, his new mentor, came to him.

"I know you miss Penthu, Ipi," he spoke. "But you don't have to worry about your future as a temple physician. Penthu told me you are a promising apprentice and I will give you every opportunity you need to develop yourself and improve your skills."

"I know and I will not disappoint you," Ipi replied and continued confidently: "I will become a priest and physician worthy of the Lord Amun."

After his parents' sending him away and Penthu's being called away by the Pharaoh, Ipi had suddenly realized that the only stable factors in his life were the Karnak Temple and the God Amun. These were the only things he could not imagine disappearing out of his life and, for some reason he did not understand, it gave him strength and made him feel better.

"Amun will be proud to have such a dedicated apprentice in His temple," Intef complimented Ipi.

"Amun has given me a lot and I will show Him my gratitude by living my life in His service," Ipi answered.

More than ever before, he felt he belonged somewhere and that his life had a purpose.

Penthu entered the Pharaoh's office. He had been studying the papyrus rolls which Ptahhotep had given to him when he was summoned by the Pharaoh. Penthu had expected to go to the audience hall and was surprised when a servant took him to the Pharaoh's private office.

Upon entering the office he was even more surprised to see it full of people. Why would the Pharaoh invite his physician to a meeting?

"Penthu!" Amenhotep welcomed his new physician cheerfully, a tone which Penthu did not expect from a Pharaoh. Then, in the same tone, Amenhotep went on: "You have come at the right time, I am just going to announce a very important project of mine!"

Next, looking at the other people in the room, he introduced the physician: "All of you probably know Penthu, the physician who helped my late father so well last year when he collapsed in the Temple of Karnak during the inauguration of our co-regency? I have decided to offer him the position as my personal physician."

Penthu looked around in the room. It looked unusual; it didn't have the traditional religious scenes on the walls which he expected in a Pharaoh's office. Instead he saw many images of the Aten giving life to the Pharaoh and his family.

Many of the people attending the meeting Penthu knew already but there were also new faces. As usual the Great Royal Wife, Nefertiti, was sitting next to her husband while his mother, Queen Teye, was sitting on his other side.

What was unusual was the attendance of Meryra, the Aten priest, and the prominent position he was sitting at, together with the members of the Royal Family. All the other attendees, including Penthu had to remain standing. Even the old Ramose, the Vizier of Upper Egypt and mayor of Thebes, was amongst those who had to remain standing.

During the meeting Amenhotep was wearing the double-crown of Egypt, as if he wanted to emphasize his authority over the Two Lands and, maybe more importantly, over the people who were attending the meeting.

The Pharaoh got up from his gilded chair, picked up a papyrus roll, and started speaking:

"During the long history of the Two Lands we have always worshipped many Gods in as many temples. Every Pharaoh built new temples and expanded the existing ones. However, the most important God has only a few small temples which are being neglected by everybody. It is no wonder that the Egyptian people hardly know this God even though He gives them life everyday. So I have decided to do what my forefathers have failed to do. I will give the Aten, the Sun Disc and supreme life-force, what He deserves."

Amenhotep walked over to a table which had been placed in the middle of the room. He unrolled the papyrus roll he had been holding on the table and put weights on both ends of the roll to keep it from folding and to ensure that everybody would be able to see its contents.

Penthu saw the papyrus contained a drawing of a temple but it looked different from the traditional Egyptian temples.

The Pharaoh continued to speak, more excitedly this time:

"I am going to build a large temple complex for the Aten which shall be named Gem Pa Aten. As you see the Gem Pa Aten differs from all the other temples in Egypt. This temple will not have a roof, this temple will be open, it won't block the life-giving rays of the Aten. And since the Aten's rays are always able to enter the temple there is no need to build a shrine to hold a statue of the God. The Aten will at all times be everywhere in His temple!"

Amenhotep stopped speaking a moment to catch his breath but then went on in the same excited manner as before: "This temple will stand forever as a testament to the might of the Sun Disc which gives life to all of us every day. Soon everybody in the Two Lands will know Him and worship Him and Aten will finally get His rightful place as the supreme God."

The last words of the Pharaoh sent a chill through Penthu's spine. Was Aten going to be the supreme God? But what about Amun? He was the supreme God in Egypt, the King of the Gods, how could He be replaced? Amenhotep could not be serious about this?

The Pharaoh stopped speaking, creating a silence in the room and looked around at his listeners, seemingly trying to read their minds, trying to find out what they were thinking.

Then, one person carefully asked a question: "Your Majesty, where is this temple going to be built?"

It was Ramose, the old vizier and mayor who asked the question.

"Only the most prominent place in the Two Lands is good enough for the Aten," Amenhotep answered. "So what place is better than in the capital of the country? The Temple of the Aten will be built in the center of Thebes, next to the Karnak Temple."

When the Pharaoh spoke these last words Penthu noticed the Pharaoh's eyes were fixated on him. Amenhotep clearly wanted to see how he reacted on this second shock. Suddenly Penthu realized there was no representative from the Temple of Amun in the room. This was highly unusual since the priests of Amun were always invited at important meetings.

"What was the Pharaoh doing?" Penthu wondered. And, maybe more important, could he do something to prevent this from getting out of hand?

Penthu remembered what Meryptah had told him the previous day about gaining the Pharaoh's trust, so he decided to try that first. Maybe that way he would be able to have some influence on Amenhotep.

"Penthu!" Pharaoh Amenhotep suddenly called him and asked: "As a former priest in the Temple of Amun, what do you think of my project?"

Penthu was thinking fast about what answer he should give; but since Amenhotep had clearly already made up his mind and would not change it again he decided to give an answer he would like to hear: "I think Your Majesty has a very good idea, it is about time the Aten receives His own temple complex."

The Pharaoh seemed delighted with this answer and spoke: "Did you hear that, gentlemen? If even a priest of the Amun Temple sees the importance of a temple dedicated to the Aten then surely the rest of the Egyptian people will see it as well?"

For a moment Penthu worried he had actually encouraged the Pharaoh and asked himself whether he made a mistake and maybe should have been more critical of the Pharaoh's idea. Maybe Amenhotep would have listened? Penthu decided to try to carefully confront the Pharaoh without criticizing his temple: "Your Majesty, every Pharaoh has always contributed to the expansion of the Temple of Amun as one of their first acts as ruler of the Two Lands. Is Your Majesty going to continue this tradition before starting the new Aten Temple?"

For a moment Amenhotep was surprised about the directness of the question but then smiled and answered: "I will give the Amun Temple and its priests everything that is due to them when the time is right!"

After these words there was a silence in the room during which everybody was thinking about what the Pharaoh meant.

Then the Pharaoh went on speaking, while pointing at Meryra who stood up from his chair: "Most of you already know Meryra, a priest of the Aten as well as my personal advisor. I have appointed him as the High Priest of the Temple of the Aten; he will be responsible for the functioning of the temple."

"Your Majesty," Penthu heard a middle-aged baldheaded man wearing the robes of a court official remark, while looking at the papyrus roll containing the plans for the Gem Pa Aten. "As mighty as the Aten may be, it is still relatively unknown to the people. Where will we find enough personnel to make such a large temple function?"

"That is a good question, Aye," Amenhotep answered and then explained: "But Meryra has already taken care of that. He knows enough loyal servants of the Aten who are willing to dedicate their life to him. And when in the future the people will see the power and influence of the Sun Disc finding more priests will not be hard."

"So that is Aye," Penthu thought, looking at the person who had asked the question.

He had heard about him already. Aye was a rising star at the Pharaoh's court. He had a successful military career and, perhaps the most important, he was the father of Nefertiti, the Pharaoh's Great Royal Wife. After ascending to the throne Amenhotep invited his father-in-law to come and serve him at his court. Aye impressed the Pharaoh with his loyalty and ambition and the Pharaoh rewarded him with important titles such as God's Father and Fan Bearer on the Right Side of the King.

"Your Majesty, allow me to ask how such an ambitious project will be funded?" another court official asked.

"Sutau, you, as Overseer of the Double Treasury, should know that we have enough funding to build this temple. My late father left us a prosperous country and Aten will bless the Two Lands with even more prosperity when we will honour Him with a temple," Amenhotep reassured the official.

Penthu listened to the Pharaoh and the officials in the room. He still did not understand why he was invited to this meeting; did Amenhotep really want the opinion of his physician? Or maybe he was here in the role as a priest of the Temple of Amun? The Pharaoh did mention him as an Amun priest. But even if that were the case, did the Pharaoh value his opinion or was he only taunting him? It was clear he did not favour Amun and his priests.

Penthu was confused and did not know what to think of his situation. One thing he did know was that he had to inform Meryptah in Karnak.

It was late in the evening and after finishing his duties in the temple Ipi sat in his room practicing his writing skills by copying religious texts when Nebamun burst into the room.

"Have you heard the rumour, Ipi?" he asked excitedly.

"I haven't heard anything. What rumour are you talking about?" Ipi replied, looking up from his work wondering what could have happened.

"They say the Pharaoh is going to build an enormous new temple right next to Karnak!" Nebamun told Ipi, still speaking in the same excited tone.

"Well, his father also built a lot. He expanded Karnak and built new temples," Ipi answered, turning his attention back to his work and continued speaking: "But I am relieved to hear the Pharaoh is going to build a temple for Amun, this means he probably is going to follow the traditional Gods and our worries about him were unfounded."

"But this temple is not going to be dedicated to the Lord Amun but to the Aten!" Nebamun exclaimed and added: "It will be built right next to this temple!"

This time Ipi looked up at Nebamun, his face turning pale.

"Are you sure about this?" he asked.

"I am not sure about anything," Nebamun replied. "As I said already, it is a rumour but everybody in the temple is talking about it."

Ipi got up and spoke: "Let's go into the temple and see if we can find out something more about this rumour."

They were walking through the dark halls of the temple which were illuminated by torches and oil lamps that cast dancing shadows on the walls which made the depicted Gods and Pharaohs from Egypt's past seem to come alive. Normally the temple was quiet at such a late hour; the evening ceremony had finished a while ago and most priests and temple servants would have returned to their private rooms or left the temple. Only temple guards and priests on duty, taking care of the nightly rituals of the God, would be out at this time of the evening.

But this evening the halls in the temple were busy, everywhere priests and priestesses were talking excitedly.

"Let's try to find Wenamun," Ipi suggested. "I am sure he will know what is going on."

Ipi and Nebamun walked through the central aisle of the temple. The aisle had large pillars rising on both sides of them and disappearing in the darkness above. Halfway down the aisle they came across Amenemope, the temple scribe. He looked upset and seemed to be in a hurry.

"Do you know what is going on?" Nebamun asked the scribe.

"I don't know, but I am very busy so even if I knew I would not have the time to explain it to two mere apprentices," Amenemope replied curtly and rushed off again.

When they came closer to the Holy of Holies they met Tahat, the Chantress of Amun and wife of Wenamun who came towards them together with other chantresses. They probably had just finished a ritual in front of the Holy of Holies, Ipi thought to himself.

"My Lady," Ipi asked Tahat politely, "we are looking for Wenamun. Do you know where he is?"

"He is busy at the moment. He is in a meeting with Meryptah and other priests," Tahat replied.

"We have heard the Pharaoh is going to build a temple for the Aten right next to our temple. Do you know if that is true?" Nebamun asked Tahat.

"It is probably true. We heard it from a reliable source," Tahat answered again.

"Did you hear it from Penthu?" Ipi asked excitedly.

"Yes, we heard it from Penthu," a voice came unexpectedly from behind him.

Ipi and Nebamun turned and saw Wenamun who just came out of the meeting with Meryptah and other high ranking priests of the Amun temple.

"We received a message from Penthu in which he explained the Pharaoh's plans. We are waiting now for an official messenger from the Pharaoh to inform us about his intentions but until now we haven't heard anything from him yet," Wenamun continued speaking.

"Doesn't the Pharaoh want to contribute to the expansion of Karnak first?" Nebamun asked.

"Apparently not," Wenamun replied.

"That is not really surprising," Tahat told her husband. "The Pharaoh has never shown any interest in our temple or the God Amun."

Ipi remembered his meeting with Amenhotep in the temple, now already more than a year ago. He remembered the future Pharaoh's remarks about the temple and his attitude towards the High Priest. Thinking about his past experiences with the Pharaoh, Ipi remarked: "Maybe this Pharaoh will be hostile to Amun and His temple."

"I would not go that far," Wenamun replied and went on in a warning tone: "And, Ipi, be careful with what you are saying. Until now the Pharaoh has not done anything against us except for not showing us the respect that other Pharaohs have shown us. This is indeed alarming but it doesn't mean that he is hostile."

"I understand, my lord. I apologize," Ipi answered to Wenamun's reprimand, but he noticed that Wenamun did not sound very convinced about what he himself had been saying.

CHAPTER 4
NEW OPPORTUNITIES
AND
A BREAK FROM THE PAST

Hemienu was in a good mood; the future seemed bright for him and his family. For generations his family had been working on the construction sites of the Pharaohs. If a Pharaoh built a lot that meant good business but if a Pharaoh was not interested in building projects then his family could experience hard times.

Under Amenhotep the Third his family had prospered because of the enormous projects of this Pharaoh. But when his son ascended to the throne it was an anxious time, would this Pharaoh be a great builder like his father or not?

This anxious period ended a day ago when Hemienu was informed about a big project of the new Pharaoh. This project, however, was not what he had expected; Hemienu had expected the Pharaoh to contribute to the expansion of Karnak, as most Pharaohs traditionally did as one of their first projects. To his surprise Pharaoh Amenhotep was going to build a completely new temple complex which differed totally from the traditional temples he and his family normally had been working on. As an overseer and architect of the Pharaoh's construction sites Hemienu found this new and unusual project very challenging.

Hemienu had a busy day ahead of him; he had a quick breakfast with his wife Ahotep and two twin children of four years old, a son and a daughter named Hemaka and Achtai. After his breakfast which consisted of bread and fruit washed away by a cup of beer, Hemienu kissed his family goodbye and left his house to inspect the area where the new temple was going to rise and to meet other officials who would be in charge of the construction of the temple.

Coming from a family that had greatly prospered during the reigns of the previous Pharaohs, Hemienu had a villa on the southern outskirts of Thebes so he had a considerable walk ahead of him to reach the construction site. But Hemienu did not mind, he enjoyed walking through the fields and the beautiful city which he loved and to which his ancestors had contributed so much.

On his way he passed the Southern Temple, it used to be only a small shrine but the great builder Amenhotep the Third expanded it to a great temple dedicated to Amun. Hemienu remembered working there as an apprentice under the guidance of his father who had been an overseer at the building site. Passing the temple Hemienu continued north on the main avenue in Thebes which connected the Southern Temple to Karnak three kilometers further.

Every year, during akhet, the season in which the Nile River floods, the holy statues of Amun, His wife Mut and Their son Khonsu traveled in a festive procession from Karnak over this avenue to the Southern Temple. This occasion was called the Opet Festival, one of the most important and popular festivals during the year. Every year Hemienu and his wife took their children to see the procession of the holy triad which was accompanied by priests and priestesses, singers, musicians and acrobats.

Like every morning the avenue was busy with people going to their work or to one of the markets in the city. As always there were the street sellers trying to sell their wares to the many passers-by, even the priests and temple servants on their way to or from one of the many Theban temples were not spared from their attention.

Wearing an expensive robe Hemienu frequently attracted these street hawkers but he was a calm man and, on that day, in a particularly good mood so he did not mind and without stopping turned them down with a couple of friendly words.

When he arrived at Karnak Hemienu made his way to the eastside of the temple. He knew that was where Amenhotep planned his new temple to be built. Coming at the eastside he saw that he was not the first to arrive.

Most of the people Hemienu saw at the site he knew already, they were colleagues with whom he had already worked many times before. Some of them were architects, others were foremen, overseers and artists such as sculptors and engravers. All had come there to discuss how they would proceed with the construction of the new temple. Hemienu also saw priests with sticks and ropes walking over the field where the temple was going to rise. He knew what these priests were doing; they were measuring the exact position for the Aten Temple. Measuring the correct position of a temple was perhaps the most important part of the entire construction since a temple needed to have a favourable position compared to the stars or in the case of the Aten Temple, to the sun.

When Hemienu came closer to the group of people he recognized his good friend Thutmose, the Royal Sculptor. Thutmose was a tall, muscular man, used to hard and heavy labour. Just like Hemienu he came from a family that had prospered from the previous Pharaoh's projects. His father had been a famous sculptor and Thutmose followed in his footsteps. Their families had often worked together on various building sites, including the Southern Temple which was how Hemienu and Thutmose had met and became friends. Where Hemienu's father had been responsible for the construction of the Southern Temple Thutmose's father had been responsible for the carving of the statues of the Pharaoh and the Gods.

After exchanging greetings and inquiring about each other's family Thutmose came to business: "It seems like this Pharaoh will be very good to us. Maybe even as good as his father."

"He does start with a very ambitious project," Hemienu replied.

"Indeed, and the Pharaoh is even more ambitious than you think," another person intervened in their conversation. It was Nebtawi, the Pharaoh's new chief architect and chief of construction.

The previous chief of construction had been replaced by Amenhotep because he reminded him too much of his father's construction of temples dedicated to Amun.

Nebtawi was an experienced architect and construction worker but this was the first time he was in charge of such a large project.

The new chief architect wore expensive robes and jewellery, as he appeared to think befitted his elevated position. He had always been a proud and vain person but he never shunned hard labour and always showed care for his workers.

"As you all know," Nebtawi went on speaking in a loud voice so everybody could hear him, "the

Pharaoh wants to build a temple for the Aten. This temple will be named Gem Pa Aten. However, the Pharaoh demands the Gem Pa Aten to be finished within five years!"

After his last words Nebtawi paused for a short time and observed the reactions of his listeners.

"That is impossible!" Hemienu exclaimed and everybody else agreed with him.

"I expected you to say that," Nebtawi answered and continued: "I thought the same when I heard about this project for the first time. However, our wise Pharaoh has found a way of constructing a large temple within a short time period."

Nebtawi paused again and for a moment everybody was talking at the same time. Everybody seemed convinced it was impossible to construct a temple in such a short period as the Pharaoh demanded.

"The answer to the problem is the size of the stones we use for the construction," Nebtawi finally spoke again, while raising his voice so he would be heard above all the other voices that were still continuing their protests. "His Majesty has given me specific guidelines for the construction material for the Aten Temple. We will be using bricks measuring $27 \times 27 \times 54$cm. The small size of the bricks will make it possible for us to transport and handle them easier and faster. This will enable us to build the temple within the period the Pharaoh demands from us."

During Nebtawi's speech everybody went quiet but when he had finished speaking there was a lot of talking again amongst his listeners but this time there were also some positive voices amongst them.

One of the positive voices was Hemienu, who spoke: "It is a very tight schedule but this way it might be possible."

Thutmose was still skeptical however: "Yes, it might indeed be possible but we will need extra workers. I know I will need more workers if the Pharaoh wants his statues ready on time."

Nebtawi was not bothered by Thutmose's comment and replied: "The Pharaoh has promised us everything we need to finish his temple within the time he gave us. We will get extra workers and if you, Thutmose, need more workers you will receive them."

"Where will the building material come from?" another overseer asked.

"We will be using our usual quarries in the south for the granite but will quarry the limestone in the Theban quarries. For the temple enclosure we will use mud brick, this way we will be able to work faster," Nebtawi explained and went on: "The quarrying has already begun and we expect the first shipment of material to arrive soon."

"You are right!" Hemienu remarked to Thutmose, "The new Pharaoh is going to be good for us, he will give us many new opportunities but he appears to be very demanding as well."

"I agree but I think not everybody is satisfied with him," Thutmose answered and pointed to the Karnak Temple. Hemienu looked in the direction his friend pointed to and saw a large group of Amun priests looking at them from the temple's roof. He could see from their posture that they were not happy with the new situation.

Two weeks later it was, as usual, a hectic day at the Royal Court. The Pharaoh was excited about his new project and wanted to stay informed about even the smallest progress or setback.

Aset and Kiya were both at the court to be available to the Pharaoh for when he needed something. Kiya had still not forgiven Amenhotep for sending Montu away but working as a servant for most of her life had taught her to hide her emotions.

Pharaoh Amenhotep was sitting on his throne with his Great Royal Wife Nefertiti sitting next to him on his right side. On the floor, next to the Pharaoh's throne, sat Merykare, the Royal Scribe, with a clean sheet of papyrus making notes of everything that was being discussed at court.

Amenhotep was having an audience with Nebtawi about the construction of the Aten Temple when a court official told him a messenger had arrived.

"Tell him to wait, I am having an important meeting now," the Pharaoh replied.

"Your Majesty," the court official insisted, "this is a message from the King of Hatti."

Amenhotep was going to say something to silence the official when Nefertiti put her hand on his hand and whispered in his ear. He sighed but then replied: "Let the messenger deliver his message now."

The messenger entered the audience hall holding a sealed box. He kneeled before the Pharaoh and spoke, while holding out the box: "Your Majesty, His Majesty Suppiluliuma, King of Hatti, sends you his greetings and this message."

Aye, the Pharaoh's loyal servant and Nefertiti's father, took the box out of the messenger's hands and handed it to the Pharaoh.

"You can go now," Amenhotep told the messenger and added: "As soon as I will send a reply to your King I will send for you."

Aset watched the messenger deliver his message. She knew it was not uncommon for the Pharaoh to receive letters from the King of Hatti, the Pharaoh's father, Amenhotep the Third, had regularly corresponded with him and in this way tried to maintain good relations with this country that was quickly becoming more powerful and dominant in its region.

Amenhotep broke the seal on the box and opened it, it contained a clay tablet on which a text was written. He took out the tablet and started reading the message.

The Pharaoh kept staring at the tablet for a long time even though the message was not very long and he must have finished reading it quickly. Finally Amenhotep put down the clay tablet. Aset looked at him and saw his face had turned red. Whatever the message contained, it had upset the Pharaoh!

"Nebtawi," Amenhotep spoke, his voice almost being a whisper, "there are some important issues I want to discuss with you, your master sculptor and your relief artist. But that will have to wait until tomorrow. Come back here tomorrow morning with Thutmose and Rensi."

"Yes, Your Majesty," Nebtawi answered, bowed and left the court.

The Pharaoh waited until Nebtawi had left the hall while everybody watched him in expectation.

"Is everything all right, my husband?" Nefertiti asked worriedly. "I am fine," Amenhotep replied but then complained: "I just wish other kings would stop begging us for gold."

"What does Suppiluliuma say?" Nefertiti asked again.

"Listen to this," Amenhotep spoke in a voice that clearly betrayed his annoyance. He picked up the clay tablet and spoke: "Suppiluliuma says he wants to have a friendly relationship with me just like he had with my father. He says my father always gave him what he asked for and then criticizes me for refusing to send him what he demands. Then he again says he would like a good friendship to exist between us, just like the friendship he had with my father. But then again he continues saying I should not refuse to give him whatever he wants and goes on to demand the following: two golden statues one standing and one sitting, two silver statues of women, a piece of lapis lazuli and some additional gifts. He finishes saying that if I cannot deliver these gifts to him he is willing to send chariots to pick them up. Finally he also offers me gifts, whatever I want he will send to me."

Amenhotep put down the message and continued speaking: "Last month I received a similar message from Tushratta, the King of Mitanni, reminding me to send him two statues made of gold and lapis lazuli, one statue of himself and one of his daughter Tadukhipa plus extra gold and valuable goods. My father had promised Tushratta these treasures in return for the right to marry Tadukhipa. Due to his death, however, he never got the opportunity to send these gifts or to get married. For diplomatic reasons I married Tadukhipa but now Tushratta expects me to send him what my dear overly generous father had promised!"

The more Amenhotep spoke the more upset he became and in an angry voice he went on: "All these foreign kings seem to think our streets are paved with gold and my father always gave them everything they asked for. Maybe he could afford spending the wealth of the Two Lands on other kings and diplomatic contacts but I have better use for it. I won't send gold and other treasures abroad that could be better used for building temples dedicated to the Aten!"

"But my dear husband," Nefertiti intervened in a tired voice, her pregnancy being hard on her. "You know I support you completely with constructing temples for the Aten but we should not neglect our foreign contacts."

Aset was surprised, this was the first time she saw Nefertiti disagree with the Pharaoh.

"I won't do it!" Amenhotep shouted being more angry than annoyed now, even though he did not seem to mind his wife disagreeing with him.

"May I offer a solution, Your Majesty?" Aye broke into their conversation.

"What solution do you suggest?" the Pharaoh asked agitatedly as if he had already decided not to like Aye's suggestion.

"Your Majesty, I suggest we send them gold and silver plated wooden statues. This way we spend only a small part of our gold and silver but Tushratta and Suppiluliuma will still receive their statues," Aye spoke.

Amenhotep's face suddenly brightened and he exclaimed: "Aye, you are as cunning as the evil Seth! But I like your idea! We will send them gold and silver plated statues!"

Aset had been listening to the conversation and quietly spoke to Kiya: "I have a bad feeling about this idea. I have been working for many years at the Royal Court and often overheard foreign correspondence. A king can easily feel insulted and sending them gold and silver plated wooden statues can be a good reason for them to be insulted. The Pharaoh's father would have never done this."

"The Pharaoh's father also would have never sent Montu away!" Kiya mumbled angrily, more to herself than to Aset.

The Pharaoh, however, had no doubts about the plan and before Aset could hear Kiya's reply she heard him say in a good mood: "Write down what I am going to dictate Merykare. I am going to send Tushratta and Suppiluliuma a reply and tell them that they will receive what they asked for!"

That evening Penthu sat in his room by the light of an oil lamp trying to read Ptahhotep's documents about the Pharaoh's medical history but he could not concentrate. He felt alone and powerless. He wanted to do something in support of the Temple of Amun but he did not know what he could do.

After a while he gave up his attempts to read and pushed the papyrus rolls away. He got up from his desk and kneeled in front of his private shrine dedicated to Amun that he had set up in his room. Just when Penthu was whispering a prayer to Amun for help the door opened and Pharaoh Amenhotep entered his room. He was not wearing his Royal tunic but instead was wearing a simple white robe and he came without his usual escort of servants.

Penthu got up quickly to welcome the Pharaoh but before he could say anything Amenhotep already took a chair and sat down.

"Did I come at an inconvenient moment, Penthu?" Amenhotep, who saw that he disturbed Penthu in his prayer, asked.

"No, Your Majesty, of course not. I am honoured to receive you in my quarters," Penthu replied while trying to hide his uneasiness.

"Penthu," Amenhotep went on in a friendly tone, "what do you think about your life in the palace?"

"I have everything I need, Your Majesty. My life here is very good," Penthu replied.

"But are you happy?" Amenhotep asked again and before Penthu could answer already gave the answer himself: "I have been watching you and I know you are not happy here."

Penthu thought for a moment and then decided this might be a good moment to remind the Pharaoh of his duties towards the Karnak Temple.

"Your Majesty," he started speaking, "I am still a priest of Amun and I see you haven't got any plans yet for any contributions to the Karnak Temple."

He was worried his blunt remark would upset the Pharaoh but to his surprise Amenhotep stayed calm and replied: "Penthu, I am thinking about the Temple of Amun too. Don't worry, the Amun priests will receive what is due to them under my rule. But, Penthu, you have to remember that as Lord of the Two Lands I have to serve all the Gods of Egypt and Aten has been neglected for a very long time, I am just planning to give Him what He deserved already so long ago. Remember that the Aten hasn't got a single large temple complex yet, only a few small temples which don't do justice to this great God. Amun, on the contrary, has many large complexes all over the Two Lands. So do you think it is unreasonable of me to start with building a temple for the Aten before expanding the already enormous Karnak Temple?"

"But Your Majesty, I heard you say that Aten is going to be the new supreme God. What is that going to mean for Amun?" Penthu asked.

He wanted to say more but before he could Amenhotep got up from his chair, started pacing the room and spoke again: "I know the priests of Amun are worried about my reign, but, Penthu, you have to believe me that I am trying to do what is best for the Two Lands. When I build the Gem Pa Aten next to Karnak this should not be considered as an insult by the priests of Amun but as a tribute. The temples of the two most important Gods of the country will be standing next to each other! Do you understand what I mean? Aten will get its deserved position but the Amun priesthood should not feel threatened by this. I want Aten and Amun to exist side by side!"

"I understand what you intend to do, Your Majesty. You want to correct what you believe is an injustice towards Aten," Penthu replied.

"It is an injustice!" Amenhotep shouted angrily, which caught Penthu by surprise. But then just as sudden as he got angry Amenhotep calmed down again and repeated quietly: "It is an injustice, a great injustice towards a great God."

"Forgive me, Your Majesty," Penthu spoke, still shaken by the Pharaoh's outburst and added: "I understand what Your Majesty means."

"I am pleased to hear that, Penthu," the Pharaoh answered. He had stopped pacing the room and stood now in front of Penthu's shrine of Amun.

Looking at the shrine he remarked: "Tomorrow I will go to visit the building site of the Gem Pa Aten and you will come with me. You can visit the Karnak Temple and tell your friends there what I just told you. You can explain them that they have nothing to fear and have no reason to protest against the construction of the Aten Temple."

Speaking on behalf of the Pharaoh with the priests of the Karnak Temple could be difficult but Penthu looked forward to visiting the temple again so he replied: "Of course Your Majesty, I will speak on your behalf with the priests of Amun."

The light of the oil lamp was almost burned up and the room started to get darker when Amenhotep walked to Penthu, stopped in front of him, and went on speaking, this time in a tone as if he was telling a big secret: "Penthu, I have great plans for my reign, plans I haven't yet told anybody about. To realize these plans I want your help."

Penthu wanted to answer but the Pharaoh stepped closer to him, his face close to Penthu's, making him feel very uncomfortable. In the dying light of the room Penthu saw the Pharaoh's dark eyes staring directly into his. For a moment they stood there in silence when the Amenhotep put his hand on Penthu's shoulder and spoke: "I will need your support. Help me Penthu, please."

Having said that Amenhotep turned and walked out of the room, leaving Penthu behind in confusion.

Penthu sat down on the bed and thought about the strange conversation with the Pharaoh. He wondered why the Pharaoh wanted his help and especially why the Pharaoh used the word 'please'. In all his life he never heard about a Pharaoh using this word to a subject.

The oil lamp burned up and the room went dark but Penthu did not bother to refill it and light it again. He lay down and tried to sleep. But there were too many thoughts going through his mind, sleep would not come for him that night.

It was early in the morning and the sun had not yet risen when Aset and Kiya got up to prepare for the coming day. Contrary to Kiya, who preferred to sleep longer, Aset liked getting up early. Early morning was her favourite time of the day, the palace was still quiet, the always busy state officials did not start as early as she did, and outside she could see the bright stars fading during the sunrise which made the sky turn from black into purple to red, yellow and finally clear blue. She also enjoyed the river breeze which was still cool early in the morning but would turn hot later.

Every morning after washing and a quick breakfast in the palace kitchen Aset and Kiya walked up to the palace bakery where they would pick up freshly baked bread and cake and then to the store rooms from where they fetched freshly picked fruit for the breakfast of the Royal Family. Both Aset and Kiya enjoyed this short walk, especially the visit to the bakery which always smelled of baked bread and sweet pastries and was run by the friendly and cheerful Harkhuf, the chief baker, and his staff who usually gave them a piece of cake or still warm bread to eat and brightened up their morning with a couple of friendly words and jokes.

Aset and Kiya hurried back to the kitchen with baskets filled with food for the Royal Family's breakfast. They were late already as they had lingered too long at the bakery chatting with Harkhuf and his staff and worried about the scolding from Ranefer they would most likely receive. However, just before they reached the kitchen, they were shocked to be stopped by the Pharaoh.

Aset and Kiya bowed and Aset quickly spoke: "Apologies, Your Majesty, we did not know Your Majesty was up already. We will prepare the breakfast immediately."

Amenhotep ignored Aset and looked at Kiya.

"I have been very busy with affairs of state and I feel I have neglected you, Kiya," he spoke earnestly and went on: "To make that up to you I want you to accept this small gift from me."

While he was speaking Amenhotep produced a beautifully crafted golden bracelet and gave it to Kiya. Kiya was speechless and Aset looked on in amazement.

Finally Kiya managed to stammer: "Thank you, Your Majesty."

"I want you to wear this bracelet at all times so you will never forget about me," Amenhotep spoke and before he left Aset and Kiya alone he promised: "You will never be neglected again Kiya!"

Aset and Kiya did not have much time to think about what had happened. Immediately after Amenhotep had disappeared Ranefer came looking what kept the two servants and, not knowing of their meeting with the Pharaoh, started to reprimand them for being late. Aset and Kiya, however, were still too shocked to care about Ranefer's words and continued their work without taking notice of him.

That morning they served breakfast for the Royal Family like they had done many times before but this time Kiya felt unsure about how to behave in front of the Pharaoh. Amenhotep, however, treated her as if nothing had happened, being friendly but nothing more. That morning he spent most of his breakfast playing with Meritaten, his baby daughter of which he was very fond.

Kiya filled the Pharaoh's wine cup with his favourite wine from the Nile delta but he did not acknowledge her, all his attention going to his daughter. Kiya continued with Amenhotep's mother, Queen Teye, and then came to Nefertiti; she filled her cup and wanted to continue with Nefertiti's father, Aye, who often joined the Royal Family at breakfast, when Nefertiti suddenly grabbed Kiya's wrist.

"You have a very beautiful bracelet, Kiya," the Great Royal Wife remarked in a tone that sounded threatening.

"I wonder how a servant can afford such an expensive piece of jewellery," Nefertiti went on, glancing at her husband, already expecting it to come from him.

Everybody looked at Nefertiti and Kiya, the latter not knowing what to say and looking helplessly.

Then Amenhotep intervened and without looking away from Meritaten, who noticed nothing of the tension in the room and continued smiling at her father, spoke: "That bracelet is a gift from me to her as recognition of her service to our family."

Nefertiti let Kiya go but looked angrily at her when she continued her work, her hands trembling with shock because of the Great Royal Wife's unexpected action.

Aset was sure Nefertiti knew the bracelet was not just a gift of appreciation, the Pharaoh had an affection for Kiya and the Great Royal Wife was jealous.

Penthu was feeling tired, he hadn't slept during the night as many thoughts had been going through his mind. What did the Pharaoh want from him? What should he tell the priests at Karnak Temple that day? And, most important, was the rise of Aten really not going effect the position of Amun?

He decided that staying in his room would not bring him a solution, a walk along the Nile River would probably help to clear his mind. After his morning prayer to Amun and the burning of incense in front of the God's shrine he left his room intending to go for a walk outside. But just as he walked through the palace corridor he heard somebody behind him calling his name.

Penthu turned around to see a palace servant who spoke: "The Pharaoh requests your presence in the audience hall immediately, my lord."

Penthu followed the servant, wondering why he had to attend the Pharaoh's audience. The audience had not yet started when Penthu entered the hall but many officials were already there and the Pharaoh was already sitting on his golden throne ready to receive his visitors. Unusually, his Great Royal Wife who normally attended her husband's meetings was missing and she was replaced by the Pharaoh's mother Teye, who was possibly an even more formidable woman than Nefertiti.

Amenhotep noticed Penthu and beckoned him to come nearer. Penthu bowed and the Pharaoh spoke: "You look tired, lord Penthu, did you not sleep well?"

"The honour of your visit last evening has kept me awake, Your Majesty," Penthu replied.

Amenhotep smiled and spoke: "This morning I honour you by letting you attend the meeting about the construction of the Gem Pa Aten. This might be interesting for you and knowing more details about the new temple might be useful to you when you visit Karnak this afternoon."

At that moment a baldheaded priest entered the hall followed by a small group of other priests. Penthu recognized him as Meryra, the High Priest of the Aten. The priests walked straight to the Pharaoh's throne and bowed.

"I am here as you requested, Your Majesty," Meryra spoke reverently.

Amenhotep turned away from Penthu, towards the priest and spoke in a businesslike manner: "Today I will give the directions for the new art form, which will be used for the Gem Pa Aten, to the construction workers."

Meryra, who had advised Amenhotep on this matter, smiled to the Pharaoh and started speaking: "Aten deserves a temple that stands apart from all the other temples in the Two Lands. The people will see Aten is different from the traditional Gods. Your Majesty, for centuries, under the traditional Gods, our civilization remained static; we live the same way as we lived hundreds of years ago, today we build the same temples as we built hundreds of years ago but now Aten is giving us the opportunity to change and to move forward. This is the start of a new era, the era of the Aten. The Two Lands shall never be the same again."

Meryra had been addressing the Pharaoh when he spoke but he spoke loudly and Penthu had the impression he was actually addressing all the other people in the audience hall.

The Pharaoh gave a signal and a servant let three people into the hall; they were Nebtawi, the architect and chief of construction, Rensi, head of the relief artists, and Thutmose the head of the sculptors.

Just like Meryra and his priests and Penthu before them the workmen walked up to the Pharaoh and bowed.

"We are honoured to have been requested to come in your presence, Your Majesty," Nebtawi spoke on behalf of all three persons.

"How are the preparations for the temple proceeding?" Amenhotep asked, getting to business immediately.

"Everything is going according to schedule, Your Majesty," Nebtawi answered and explained: "At the moment we are clearing the land and preparing it for construction. We expect to lay the first stone next week."

"I am pleased to hear that. You are doing well, Nebtawi," the Pharaoh replied and then went on: "But that is not why I have ordered you to come here. As you already know the Gem Pa Aten has a completely different design than all the other temples in the Two Lands. This is to show the different status of the Aten compared to the other Gods. However, a different temple design is not enough! What I want is a complete break with tradition. As an emphasis on the special status of the Aten, the Gem Pa Aten and all His future temples will be decorated with a new art form."

Amenhotep stopped speaking for a moment to see the reaction of his workmen but they did not show any sign of protest or disagreement, so he continued: "The artwork in the temple should emphasize the life which Aten gives to all creatures on the world. It should show life as it is, it should be natural, realistic, not strict and formal or idealized as in the other temples. I want scenes out of real life on the walls of the temple, scenes of both the lives of the Royal Family and the common people. These depictions will be a tribute to the life that Aten has given to us all. These representations must be made in a lifelike, natural style. We must break with the rigid traditional style!"

The Pharaoh stopped speaking and then asked, looking at Nebtawi and Rensi: "Can you do that? Can you decorate the temple in such an art form?"

Nebtawi looked at Rensi who was the specialist in creating temple reliefs.

Rensi thought for a moment before he answered: "We can do that, Your Majesty. But we will need some time to perfect this new style and train the workers."

"We haven't even started building the temple so I expect you have time enough. Use the guidelines I gave you to make sketches and show them to me. After I have approved them you can start training your workers. When the construction of the temple has proceeded far enough I will give you specific details about the scenes and their locations in the temple," Amenhotep spoke.

"I will start making sketches according to your guidelines and submit them for Your Majesty's approval as soon as possible," Rensi replied to the Pharaoh while he made a bow.

Next the Pharaoh turned to Thutmose the sculptor. "I have some new directions for you too, Thutmose."

"Whatever Your Majesty wishes I will be honoured to do," the sculptor replied humbly.

"Just like the temple architecture and the relief work the statues should also represent a clear break with the past," Amenhotep explained. "They should show the real person, not an idealized portrait. I want you to show Aten's creations as they really are. As for statues of me..."

The Pharaoh had been speaking but suddenly stopped in the middle of his sentence, stood up from his throne and after a brief silence announced: "I am the earthly representative of the Aten!"

Every person in the hall was silenced by those last words. Even Merykare, the Royal Scribe, who, as usual, sat on the floor next to the Pharaoh to record what was being said stopped with his work and looked up in surprise.

The only person who showed no sign of surprise was Meryra, the High Priest of the Aten, who looked content.

A Pharaoh normally called himself Horus on Earth or even a Child of Amun but calling himself the earthly representative of the Aten was an even more radical break with tradition than everything the Pharaoh had planned for his new temple.

When the silence became uncomfortable Teye, the Pharaoh's mother, in an attempt to minimize any damage her son might have caused with his impulsive action broke the silence.

She stood up from her throne and spoke: "His Majesty means that as Pharaoh of the Two Lands he is the representative of every God, which includes the Aten!"

Her words did not have much effect; everybody knew that was not what Amenhotep had meant.

The Pharaoh looked around the hall, observing the reactions to his words on the faces of his listeners. Then he sat down again, looked at Thutmose and went on speaking as if nothing happened: "The Aten has both a male and female aspect, as the creator of everything that is alive Aten is both father and mother. So as his representative on earth my statues should have both male and female features."

Thutmose did not understand what the Pharaoh meant: "Your Majesty, how can a Royal statue be both male and female?"

"You will make a statue of the Pharaoh but with female features such as wide hips and breasts. You will also portray my eyes smaller as a sign that the Aten's rays constantly shine on my face and give me life," the Pharaoh explained.

Thutmose felt uncomfortable with this break from his usual style but he had no choice and replied: "I will do as you wish, Your Majesty."

"Design a statue for me according to my guidelines and show it to me for approval," Amenhotep ordered and gestured that the three men could leave.

Penthu had followed the meeting and was left with conflicting feelings racing through his mind. For a moment he had actually really believed the Pharaoh merely wanted to give the Aten the status he thought it should have but after what just had happened Penthu doubted that. However, in spite of the fact that he clearly felt no love for the God Amun and his priests, Penthu could not imagine the Pharaoh doing anything to harm them, not after his conversation with him the previous evening.

But how far would Amenhotep go? And if he would act against Amun and his priesthood what would he, Penthu, do? To his own surprise Penthu had to admit to himself that since he had met the Pharaoh personally he actually felt some sympathy and a kind of loyalty towards him. He would like to support the Pharaoh as he had asked Penthu to do during their meeting. How could this happen to him? He used to be a loyal priest of Amun! Did Amenhotep put a spell on him? How far would he be willing to go in his support of Amenhotep?

Ipi was walking along the Nile River, he did not have to work that day and there were no lessons in the House of Life to attend, so he took the opportunity to leave the temple. Just like during the time when he lived on the farm with his family Ipi still liked to wander away while he lived in the temple; even though that time he rarely got the chance to leave because he was always kept busy.

Ipi had wandered out of Thebes and stared across the river to the west bank of the Nile and saw the Theban Mountains rising behind the lush green of the fields and the palm trees. There, somewhere, was the farm of his family. He hadn't seen them for a long time and he wondered how they would be doing. He touched the amulet his father had bought for him on the day he went to Karnak. Ipi knew by then the amulet was a fake and that his father had been cheated by the street seller but he still valued it because it reminded him of his family. Ipi wished he could cross the river to visit them but he knew that for the time being he could only dream about that.

Walking back to Thebes Ipi saw an impressive temple built against the desert cliffs. He knew it to be the mortuary temple of one of the few female rulers of Egypt, Queen Hatshepsut. Ipi had visited it once when he still lived with his parents but he had not been allowed to enter the temple.

There were mortuary temples of many former rulers on the west bank of the Nile but Hatshepsut's temple, in Ipi's opinion, was the most spectacular one.

Priests at Karnak had told Ipi about this remarkable queen who had been chosen by Amun to rule as Pharaoh over the Two Lands. In return Hatshepsut did a lot for the Temple of Amun during her successful reign. She expanded the temple and erected two impressive obelisks whose golden spires caught the first rays of the sun every morning. Her peaceful reign had been a golden age for Egypt.

"Pharaoh Hatshepsut was loyal to Amun. Times are very different now," Ipi thought to himself. "Pharaoh Amenhotep does not seem to care much about Amun."

It was midday and the sun was rising high in the sky burning down on Egypt forcing everybody who had the opportunity to find shade and wait until the worst heat was over before continuing their occupations.

Having reached the harbour of Thebes Ipi noticed there was little activity and that most boats were deserted; it was a remarkable difference from the chaos he had witnessed there earlier in the morning with people from all corners of the country and even abroad arriving and departing, buying or selling any kind of product he could imagine.

Ipi passed through the quiet harbour; most boat crews and workers had just finished their lunch and, like most people, tried to get some sleep until the end of the afternoon when the temperature would be more comfortable. Ipi turned away from the river and walked through the empty streets of the city back to Karnak. He passed a few shops where somebody called him, trying to sell him something, and in some taverns Ipi heard people talking and laughing, amongst them he noticed some foreign languages which he did not understand; "probably crews of some of the deserted foreign boats in the harbour," Ipi thought.

Approaching the Temple of Amun Ipi saw that even at the hottest hour of the day the workmen were still busy at the site where the Aten Temple was going to be built.

"The Pharaoh must be in a hurry," Ipi concluded.
A few moments later Ipi entered the Karnak Temple through the gate in its enormous pylon and hurried across the forecourt to find cool shade inside.

Like Thebes the temple court was also quiet, except for four people having a conversation in a shaded corner but Ipi did not pay any attention to them. He left the forecourt and continued into a pillared hall intending to go to his room when behind him he heard a voice calling his name: "Where are you hurrying to, Ipi? Wait a moment! Come here!"

It was Nebamun, who was one of the four people on the forecourt.

Ipi came over and heard Nebamun say to the other three persons: "This is my room mate, Ipi, the apprentice physician."

Next he went on speaking to Ipi: "This is my family. They arrived today from Mendes."

Ipi looked at Nebamun's family, existing of his parents and a younger sister. All of them wore expensive clothes and jewellery; Nebamun had not been exaggerating when he said he came from a rich family.

Ipi gave a polite bow to the parents and the young girl and spoke: "It is an honour to finally meet you, my lord, my lady and my young lady. Nebamun has told me a lot about you."

"Did he?" Nebamun's father exclaimed in a mocked surprise and continued jokingly: "I thought he would have forgotten about us a long time ago. But we are also pleased to finally meet you Ipi. In his letters to us Nebamun has also told us about you. We are very happy that he has a good friend here in the temple."

Now it was Ipi's turn to be genuinely surprised. He did not know that Nebamun had been writing about him to his family.

Nebamun quickly changed the subject and spoke: "Let me introduce my family to you, Ipi."

He pointed to the man who had been speaking and said: "This is my father, Khuwyptah."

Next, pointing to the lady, he went on: "This is my mother, her name is Mut."

"Mut, like the Goddess and wife of the Lord Amun," Ipi could not help remarking.

"You will make an excellent priest some day, Ipi," Mut replied smilingly.

"And this is Sithathor, my younger sister," Nebamun finished, pointing at the young girl.

"Did you have a pleasant journey to Thebes?" Ipi asked.

"It was a beautiful trip and the boat was very comfortable," Khuwyptah replied.

"The Nile valley is very scenic. That keeps the journey interesting," Mut added and then asked Sithathor: "Don't you think so? Didn't you enjoy the boat trip?"

Sithathor, who seemed a couple of years younger than Ipi answered: "It took too long and was boring. But I liked seeing real crocodiles."

Everybody smiled and Ipi thought about how different the first impression of Nebamun's family was compared to his first impression of Nebamun.

"Nebamun did not tell me you were coming to visit," Ipi remarked.

"That is because I did not know they were coming," Nebamun replied before his parents could say anything.

Nebamun's father smiled and explained: "I have to be in Thebes for business so I thought I might as well take my family with me and pay Nebamun a surprise visit. We will be staying for a month in Thebes before we will return to Mendes."

Nebamun looked at his sister, who went to sit down against the temple wall, and asked: "Are you all right, Sithathor?"

"It is very hot here," she replied and then remarked: "I don't understand how you can live in this place!"

"You are right, my daughter," Mut spoke and suggested: "It is very hot and we had a long journey. Why don't we go out for a good lunch and some refreshing drinks. Ipi, you will of course come with us."

Ipi was feeling tired but thought it impolite to refuse so he agreed to join them.

"There is a good tavern close to the temple. We can lunch there," Nebamun spoke.

The tavern had tables and small stools both inside and outside and they decided to sit at a table outside in the shade of a large tree. Nebamun's father said it was a special occasion so he ordered the best food the tavern had to offer. The young girl who took the order was not used to have such a wealthy family as guests and seemed overwhelmed but only a short time later the family enjoyed a delicious lunch of beef, duck, vegetables and fruit.

The landlord of the tavern personally came outside to ask if everything was to their satisfaction.

"Do you have wine from the delta?" Khuwyptah inquired.

"Of course," the landlord replied but then added: "But it is our most expensive wine."

"Nothing is too expensive today. Bring us one jug of your delta wine!" Khuwyptah ordered and explained to his family: "The best wine in the country comes from the delta."

Next he told Ipi in a tone that betrayed a sense of pride: "Some of the vineyards in the delta actually belong to my family."

Ipi had heard most of the vineyards in the delta belonged to the Royal Family and only a few very rich families owned their own private vineyards. Ipi had no idea Nebamun's family was that wealthy.

After a good meal everybody was feeling tired but satisfied. The worst heat of the day was over and the streets were becoming busier again. Suddenly they heard commotion further down the road.

"What is happening there?" Sithathor asked wondering but nobody had any idea.

Sithathor got curious and walked to the street with Ipi and Nebamun following her. They saw a man wearing the robes of a palace servant who came walking down the road, shouting: "The Pharaoh is coming! Make way for the Pharaoh!"

The man was followed by palace guards who cleared the road of people who did not immediately obey him.

"Father, mother! The Pharaoh is coming!" Sithathor shouted excitedly to her parents.

She ran onto the street hoping to get a closer view of the Pharaoh but was roughly pushed aside by one of the guards who shouted: "Out of the way! Make way for the Pharaoh!"

Sithathor fell on the ground and Ipi quickly ran to her to help her up again. For a moment Sithathor was angry and cried but when the litter with the Pharaoh came down the street followed by a large escort of palace officials the excitement got hold of her again.

Nebamun's parents now also came to the roadside to see what had happened to their daughter and hoping to see a glimpse of the Pharaoh who was a Living God in the eyes of the Egyptians.

Ipi, still standing next to Sithathor, did not share the girl's excitement. He already knew where Amenhotep would go to; not to Karnak, where he would never set foot unless there was an event the Pharaoh had no choice but to attend. Amenhotep would go to his new project, the construction site of the Aten temple.

The curtains of the litter were closed so they did not get to see the Pharaoh. However, Sithathor was so impressed by having been so close to the Horus on Earth that she did not notice her knee was bleeding from her fall. Ipi did notice and went inside the tavern to ask for some honey which he used to disinfect the wound and then covered it with fresh herbs which would keep the wound clean and help it to heal faster. Finally he bound Sithathor's knee with a piece of cloth the landlord of the tavern had given to him.

"Does it hurt?" Ipi asked.
"No, but I cannot bend my leg. That soldier is a very bad man! I hope the Pharaoh will be very angry at him!" Sithathor complained, being upset again about the palace guard.

"Don't worry," Ipi comforted her. "Your knee will heal quickly. Come back to the temple tomorrow and I will clean the wound again and change the bandage."

"You are a very lucky girl to have a friend who happens to be a physician at the Temple of Amun, Sithathor," her father spoke.

"Uhm, my lord," Ipi answered, feeling a bit uncomfortable. "I am only an apprentice."

"Then you are a very promising apprentice. Thank you very much for helping my daughter, Ipi," Khuwyptah replied.

A short time later, Ipi returned to the temple. Nebamun went with his family to the house where they would live during their stay in Thebes and would return to Karnak later. Ipi was in a good mood, he liked Nebamun's family and hoped he would see them more often during the coming month.

It was busier in Karnak when he arrived back, visitors who came to worship and priests were coming and going. The visit of the Pharaoh to the construction site next to the temple also did not go unnoticed. Priests were following his visit from the roof platform which was normally used to track the movements of the stars at night. Some priests even left the temple to visit the site of the Aten temple, hoping to find out something about the intentions of the Pharaoh.

Ipi crossed the forecourt and the large pillared hall and a short time later he passed the sacred lake.

Next to the sacred lake Meryptah, the High Priest of Amun, Maya, the Second Prophet of Amun and Wenamun stood talking with a tall man wearing the robes of an official of the Royal Palace.

Ipi recognized him immediately.

"Penthu!" he called him happily, forgetting for a moment the company Penthu was in.

"Nice to see you again, Ipi," Penthu replied simply, in a tone as if he was disturbed by Ipi's intervention and then added: "I am sorry I can't talk with you now. I am having an important meeting. Maybe I will visit you later."

Penthu turned back to the priests, continued his conversation and ignored Ipi, who continued on his way to his room, wondering why Penthu seemed so distanced.

"I am telling you that I am sure the Pharaoh means no harm to the Temple of Amun," Penthu spoke full of conviction to the High Priest Meryptah. "He sent me here to convince you about that. He wants a good relation with you!"

"If he wants good relations with us then why doesn't he work harder on those relations?" Maya, the Second Prophet of Amun, replied.

"I agree," Meryptah spoke. "The Pharaoh has not given us any reasons to trust him."

Penthu sighed and countered: "I am not saying the Pharaoh loves Amun, I agree with you that he does not love Him. He gives preference to the Aten which I regret but has he actually done something to hurt the temple? Except for reducing the usual contributions to the temple I cannot think of anything."

Penthu spoke with a passion that surprised himself and after he had finished speaking everybody was silent for a moment.

Then Wenamun spoke: "It is not so much what the Pharaoh does but what he does not do! The

Pharaoh is neglecting the duties that come with his sacred office."

After Wenamun's words the old Meryptah spoke again in a voice that sounded very tired: "The Gods and their temples are the foundations of our country. Our country is built on the people believing in the Gods with Amun as the King of the Gods. The temples are not only houses of worship but also economic centers on which the people depend. Our rulers have always respected that principle. Now this Pharaoh is kicking against these foundations by giving priority to an obscure God and by not only neglecting the temple of Amun but by neglecting all the old Gods. I don't understand that and the people will not understand that. Explain this to the Pharaoh, Penthu."

Ipi was sitting in his room, hoping Penthu would visit him. It was getting dark but Penthu did not come. He lit an oil lamp, took some pieces of broken pottery and started to practice writing hieroglyphs by the small flickering light. Ipi had left the door open to let the cool evening breeze enter his room which was still warm after the hot day. He was concentrating on his work when he heard somebody enter his room.

Ipi looked up but it was not his former mentor Penthu.

"Good evening, Ipi," Wenamun greeted.

"Good evening, my lord," Ipi replied politely.

"You must be disappointed Penthu did not come to visit you today," Wenamun spoke.

Ipi did not say anything and just nodded.

"I can tell you we are all a bit disappointed in Penthu," Wenamun went on, that time more to himself than to Ipi but then spoke in an attempt to comfort Ipi: "But Penthu is a very busy man, Ipi. He has many responsibilities to the Pharaoh. I am sure he would have come to see you if he had had the time."

"Why are you disappointed in Penthu, my lord?" Ipi asked, having heard Wenamun's earlier remark.

"Penthu is in a very difficult position at the moment and seems to be torn between the Pharaoh and Amun. He appears to have forgotten that a priest of Amun serves the God before the Pharaoh," Wenamun explained with a sad expression on his face.

Ipi could not understand it; he had admired Penthu who always had seemed to be a loyal priest of Amun. How could he have changed so radically in such a short time?

"Don't worry, Ipi," Wenamun spoke reassuringly. "I am sure Penthu will find his way back to Amun."

After Wenamun had left Ipi felt very tired. It had been a hectic day, a day that had brought happiness and disappointments. He fell in a deep sleep and did not hear Nebamun returning to their room after spending the evening with his family. That night, however, Ipi had a terrible nightmare. A nightmare that was going to haunt him for years to come.

CHAPTER 5
TENSIONS IN THE TEMPLE OF AMUN
AND
AN UNEXPECTED PROPOSAL

Three months later, early in the morning, Nefertiti gave birth to her second baby. Birth was a dangerous moment for both mother and baby. Not only were there the normal dangers to their health but demons also posed a great risk. For this reason priests were always present at the birth of a prince or princess, they would perform rites to keep demons and evil influences away and pray for the health of the mother and baby.

Popular Gods for women during pregnancy and childbirth in Egypt were the dwarf God Bes and the hippopotamus Goddess Tawaret. Bes and Tawaret were especially popular with the common people and Bes was not only honoured as a protector of women in labour but also as protector of the people's homes.

Pharaoh Amenhotep, however, decided the traditional priests and Gods were not necessary for his Great Royal Wife; instead he called for Meryra to take care of the spiritual protection of Nefertiti.

Being the Royal Physician, however, Penthu was also present. Penthu, still a priest of Amun, quietly, without anybody noticing, prayed to Amun to protect Nefertiti and her child. Except for the Pharaoh, Meryra and Penthu, only women were allowed to be present when Nefertiti gave birth.

At the moment the baby came Nefertiti was helped onto a special birthing stool on which she would sit while giving birth. She cried from the labour pains while Penthu supported and encouraged her. It was an important moment, not only for the Royal Family but for the whole country. Would the future Pharaoh be born that day?

The birth went smoothly and as soon as it was over Nefertiti was quickly put to rest on a bed.

She seemed to recover almost immediately, looked up from her bed to her crying baby and asked anxiously: "Tell me Penthu, what is it? Is it a boy?"

"You have given birth to a beautiful and healthy princess, Your Highness," Penthu answered her.

Nefertiti's head fell back on her bed in disappointment; she still had not produced an heir to the throne.

Everybody else in the room seemed happy with the new addition to the Royal Family, including the Pharaoh who did not seem to care he did not yet have a son who could succeed him.

The baby was washed by servants and after that given to Amenhotep.

"Her name shall be Meketaten, which means Protected by the Aten," he spoke while smiling to his new daughter.

"The Great Royal Wife has given birth to a princess early this morning!" Meryptah announced that afternoon to a group of priests assembled in a hall built by the famous Pharaoh Thutmose the Third. "I have been informed her name is Meketaten. As is the custom we will organize a ceremony for tomorrow to pray to the Lord Amun for the health of mother and daughter."

A young priest stepped forward, out of the group of priests and asked: "My lord, please forgive me my question, I mean no disrespect, but did the temple receive an official message from the palace about the new princess or did we receive it through other, unofficial, channels?"

The High Priest appeared to think for a moment before deciding to give an honest answer: "We have received this message through unofficial channels. Until now we have not yet received any official word from the palace."

"Thank you for your reply, my lord," the young priest spoke again but he did not step back into the group, instead he continued with another question: "Once more, I don't mean any disrespect, my lord, but why do we need to organize a ceremony for the blessing of members of a family who don't care about the Lord Amun or His temple, who are actually, now at this very moment, building a temple dedicated to another God right next to Karnak? A temple for a God the Pharaoh has also named both his daughters after!"

After his question there was an agreeing murmur going through the group. Ipi, who was standing in the group, was surprised about the blunt questions and especially to find out they came from the scribe Amenemope. He did not expect him to be critical of his superiors.

Meryptah listened to the questions and sighed. Ipi saw he looked tired, he had aged considerably during the last months. He was a man who had devoted his life to the temple only to see its existence threatened in the end.

"We pray for the Great Royal Wife and the newborn princess because our tradition demands it and contrary to the Pharaoh we don't break our traditions easily. We also pray because it is the right thing to do. Princess Meketaten cannot be held accountable for the actions of her parents. Further, may I remind everybody that until now the Pharaoh has not done anything against our temple? Until now he has only ignored us but that is no reason for us to forsake our holy duties towards Amun and the Royal Family. I will ask for a blessing of both mother and child and leave it up to the Lord Amun to decide whether they deserve it or not," Meryptah had spoken with an unexpected energy and then he finished, speaking directly to Amenemope in a tone that sounded a little threatening: "Or do you think that you, a temple scribe, can take the decisions for the God Amun?"

"No, my lord. I cannot," Amenemope replied softly and returned to his place between the other priests.

This time there was a quiet laughter going through the assembled priests but Ipi knew that Amenemope had said what many priests were thinking and, he had to admit to himself, he was thinking the same.

"Why are you getting upset, Meryptah?" another voice suddenly sounded from the back of the group of priests. "Can't you take any criticism from your subordinates? Maybe you should listen to what this young priest said."

Everybody looked at the person who spoke, an old priest, who went on: "If we keep ignoring this crisis like you do, then in a few years there will not be much left of this temple that all these priests here have dedicated their lives to!"

Ipi knew who this old priest was: it was Wahankh, the priest who was in charge of the distribution of offerings. He had been living and working in the temple all his life and had risen to his position more because of seniority than achievements. Most priests disliked him and thought he was more interested in the power the Amun priesthood held than in the actual religion itself. For this reason he had, in spite of his age and long service, never reached the highest ranks of the priesthood, something which made him very bitter.

All the priests moved aside and Wahankh walked forward towards Meryptah with a menacing glare in his eyes.

Meryptah was caught by surprise by Wahankh's rude interruption but he recovered quickly and spoke, referring to Wahankh's usual absence at meetings: "So nice of you to join us this time Wahankh. Since you apparently know how to handle this crisis I hope you will join our meetings more often so you can share your ideas with us."

After he had finished speaking Meryptah seemed to hesitate a moment but then added with a smile: "Everybody who is genuinely concerned with the future of our religion and our temple instead of wealth and power is welcome to join the temple meetings but you, Wahankh, are also welcome."

Suddenly the renewed energy that had for a short moment taken hold of the High Priest disappeared, he looked drained of energy again and a young priest who stood behind him had to support him when he turned and walked away. Wahankh was left behind feeling taken aback but this time there was no laughter among the other priests.

The construction of the Gem Pa Aten was going ahead of schedule. The Pharaoh's new method of working had proved itself Hemienu noticed with satisfaction that afternoon.

He had been surprised when he heard of the Pharaoh's new directions for the relief artists and the sculptors which he thought were very unusual.

Shortly after having received these directions Rensi and Thutmose handed in their designs to the Pharaoh which he, after making a few alterations, approved. Now all the artists on the construction site were practicing working according to the new style so that by the time the construction of the temple would have proceeded far enough for them to start their work they would master the new style perfectly. Hemienu did not doubt Rensi and Thutmose would see to that.

Nebtawi was not on the construction site and he left Hemienu in charge during his absence. He was discussing with an overseer about how to construct the gate at the temple's entrance when he heard a lot of noise and screams coming from the back of the construction site.

Everybody dropped their tools and ran in the direction where it came from, including Hemienu.

When he saw the cause of the noise Hemienu was horrified. A large section of the back wall had collapsed on top of some of the workmen.

Since Nebtawi was not on the construction site Hemienu was responsible for handling the unexpected crisis.

"Start clearing the stones away and get the wounded from underneath them," he shouted at the workers who stood hesitatingly around the accident site.

The physicians who were on duty on the temple site immediately started their work of treating the wounded that had been rescued from under the rubble first. Hemienu himself also started to help clearing away the stones.

Shortly afterwards he found a badly wounded worker and yelled: "I found somebody, come here and help me!"

Together with two other workmen he got the unconscious worker out of the rubble and took him to the physicians who were already overloaded with wounded men.

Hemienu looked at the physicians for a while; they were very busy so he did not disturb them with questions. A bit farther away he saw five or six workers lying on the ground, they did not move and no physician paid attention to them. Shivers ran through Hemienu's spine when he looked at them.

"May I have a moment of your time?" Hemienu woke up out of his thoughts and saw it was one of the physicians who spoke to him.

"Yes, of course. What can I do for you?" he answered.

"At the moment we have eleven badly wounded workers and more are coming in every moment. There are also six deaths but that number will probably increase as well," the physician started speaking and went on: "We have only four professional physicians working on the site which is not enough and we are also short of medication and equipment. I would like your permission to ask the help of the physicians of the Karnak Temple."

Hemienu had always cared about his workers so he agreed immediately, feeling angry for not having thought about that himself.

"You are right! I will send someone to Karnak to ask for help," Hemienu replied and stopped the first worker he saw and told him: "Go to Karnak right now and tell them we have an emergency and need as many physicians and medical equipment as possible!"

The man ran immediately and Hemienu shouted after him: "Tell them to hurry, time costs lives!"

Ipi and Intef had just returned to their practice after the meeting with Meryptah and the other priests.

"Wahankh ought to be removed from the temple! And how dared that mere scribe talk to the High Priest in that tone!" Intef remarked angrily to himself.

Ipi overheard him and could not help replying: "My lord, I was, just like you, shocked about Wahankh's behaviour and agree a man like him doesn't belong in the temple. But, even when this was not the right place to mention it, don't you agree with Amenemope that maybe we should stop fulfilling our obligations towards the palace until the palace continues fulfilling their obligations towards us?"

Intef wanted to answer when a priest ran into the room.

Out of breath, gasping for air, he spoke: "There was a big accident at the construction site of the Aten Temple! The wall at the back of the complex has collapsed on top of many workers. There must be many wounded, if not deaths!"

"Are you sure it is that bad?" Intef asked, wondering if the priest could be exaggerating.

"I am sure, I saw it happen myself from the temple roof," the priest replied.

"Then we must help immediately!" Intef spoke decisively.

"But my lord, that is the Aten Temple!" Ipi remarked in surprise.

"The victims are workers who in the past probably worked on temples for Amun, Ipi. Now get your medical supplies and follow me to the Aten Temple!" Intef urged his apprentice and went to call other physicians and apprentices to come with him to the accident site.

On their way they ran into a dirty looking construction worker who, just like the Amun priest before, was completely out of breath and could hardly speak a word.

"My lord!" he gasped to Intef: "There has been an accident."

"We are already on our way to help," Intef cut him off before he could say anything more and asked: "Can you tell me anything about how many wounded there are?"

"I am sorry, my lord. I don't know but there are many," the worker informed Intef while still trying to catch his breath.

When they reached the unfinished and deserted gate of the Aten Temple Ipi could hear the screaming and yelling of the wounded and their helpers in the distance. It gave him an eerie feeling.

Working as an apprentice with Penthu and Intef Ipi had seen many terrible things but nothing could prepare him for what he witnessed when they reached the site of the accident.

There were many wounded, Ipi counted twenty-three, and still more were coming from under the collapsed wall. Some of them, Ipi expected, would not survive. In a corner, a short distance from the wounded, Ipi saw about ten dead workmen, a number which most likely would grow during the coming hours.

There were clearly not yet enough physicians on the site for the number of casualties so Ipi said a short prayer to Amun and went to the first wounded person he saw.

Intef had a short meeting with Hemienu and the head of the on site physicians who thanked him for coming and briefed him quickly about the situation before he installed his makeshift practice close to where Ipi was already working. Intef took out his medical equipment and supplies which his assistants had brought for him and laid it out in preparation of his work.

Intef himself had carried a small statue of Amun to the Aten Temple which he always brought with him when he worked outside of Karnak. Through this statue Amun would guide Intef's hands and help him save the lives of his patients. He set up the statue next to his working place, burnt incense and said a short prayer and then started his work.

Ipi had just finished setting the broken leg of a workman who was screaming in agony when Intef asked him to help him treating an unconscious man whose scull was severely fractured. Intef had helped the seriously wounded man as well as he could under the basic circumstances of the unfinished temple but then needed help with applying the bandage. He told Ipi to take care that none of the pieces of the broken scull moved while he bound the unconscious worker's head.

When they had finished their difficult task Intef spoke: "We will have to bring the severely wounded men to the temple. It is impossible to give them proper care here."

"But how can we transport them? We have to be very careful with moving them," Ipi replied.

Intef wanted to speak again when suddenly a voice shouted: "What has happened here?"

Everybody looked up at the man who had just arrived at the scene of the disaster. Ipi also looked up and saw a man in clean white robes wearing the insignia of a priest of the Aten.

"What happened here?" the man asked again, looking around in horror until his eyes finally remained resting on Intef.

"Obviously a construction accident," Intef replied, feeling annoyed about the priest interrupting his work and went on: "If you would like more details you can ask the overseer of the construction site. I don't know what exactly happened and even if I knew I would not have the time to explain it to you. As you see we are very busy here."

The high-ranking priest looked irritated, he was clearly not used to being spoken to in the manner that Intef just did. He did, however, take Intef's advice and ignored him further, passing him while looking for the person in charge of the construction when he suddenly stopped.

"What is that?" the Aten priest asked angrily while pointing at Intef's statue of Amun.

"That is a statue of Amun. As you see, we are physicians of Karnak and that is a representation of our Lord. He will help us to save the construction workers of your temple," Intef replied with an emphasis on his last words about saving the workmen.

"I appreciate your help," the Aten priest spoke but then added in a strict tone: "But I cannot allow idols of other Gods on the sacred land of the Aten. I have to ask you to remove it immediately!"

Intef could not believe what he heard and exclaimed: "But Amun helps us to save your workmen's lives!"

"This is the Gem Pa Aten and Amun is not needed here! If the Aten wants the workers to live He will help them!" the priest retorted unemotionally.

Intef almost begged in his reply to the priest: "Please let us work a short time longer. We are almost finished anyway. We will bring the seriously wounded people to Karnak to continue their treatment there."

"You can work here as long as you like but Aten does not tolerate other Gods on its land. So I tell you one last time: remove that statue or I will remove it! And I can assure you that when I remove it, it will not happen very respectfully!" the priest threatened.

Intef finally capitulated and spoke: "I will do as you wish."

He called one of his physicians and ordered him to take the statue of Amun back to the Karnak Temple.

"Treat it respectfully!" Intef told the physician while giving the Aten priest an angry look.

When the physician left with the sacred statue, Hemienu appeared.

"What is the problem, Hatiay?" he asked, apparently knowing the priest already and noticing the tension between him and Intef.

"Nothing!" the priest answered. "My problem has just been solved. These Amun priests had brought their idol onto the construction site which belongs exclusively to the Aten."

"I know that and I agreed to that," Hemienu replied.

"You have nothing to agree to, Hemienu! You are only an overseer! You are in charge of construction and have no authority over religious matters!" Hatiay spoke angrily.

While berating Hemienu, Hatiay took him by the elbow and when they were walking away from the priests of Amun, Ipi heard Hatiay saying: "And now I want you to explain to me what has actually happened here!"

It was almost evening, there were no more dead or wounded coming from underneath the rubble and the Amun priests had done everything they could at the accident site. Some of the wounded were well enough to return home that same day but many had to be brought to the Karnak Temple for further treatment. The workmen from the Aten Temple had taken some boards used in the temple construction and bound them together to make makeshift stretchers and helped transporting their colleagues to Karnak.

When Ipi finally left the Gem Pa Aten he saw Hatiay investigating the accident site, getting his robes dirty while climbing over the collapsed wall.

"The Great Royal Wife is very worried, she was actually crying," Sitre, a personal servant of Nefertiti, told Aset and Kiya that evening. "What would happen if she would never give the Pharaoh a son? Would he still retain her as his Great Royal Wife or would he marry another girl to replace her?"

"I am not worried about the Great Royal Wife!" Aset replied to Sitre and explained: "She is a very strong woman and the Pharaoh respects her too much to replace her. But, to prove to her husband that she deserves her position she will probably support him even more than she already did until now."

"Do you think she has to do that?" Sitre asked. "Doesn't she support the Pharaoh enough yet?"

"She supports him more than enough but the Pharaoh has many radical ideas, which are not popular with everybody. The Pharaoh wants to realize these ideas and he will need people on whom he will always be able to rely. The more Nefertiti will support him, the more he will appreciate her," Aset explained her view on the situation.

"Nefertiti is one of those persons who seem to be blessed by the Gods," Kiya added in a tone that hinted both respect and fear.

Since Amenhotep gave Kiya the bracelet Nefertiti treated her even colder than the other servants.

"No matter how difficult her situation is, in the end she always seems to come out stronger than before. You don't have to worry about Nefertiti, Sitre, she will be the Great Royal Wife for many more years to come," Kiya went on speaking to Nefertiti's servant.

Sitre was a young girl who was new in the Royal Palace. She was a quiet and shy person, in many ways the opposite of the more outgoing Kiya. Aset liked Sitre and tried to help her getting used to the life in the palace and working with the Royal Family.

They had been talking in the palace kitchen where they had a simple dinner. The kitchen was always hot from the cooking fires and busy with many cooks running around and often shouting at their junior staff when they did something wrong or were not working fast enough.

Aset never liked to spend too much time there and when she had finished her meal she went outside for a short time, hoping to catch a cool evening breeze before returning to work. Kiya and Sitre followed her a short time later and they continued their discussion in the more comfortable surroundings.

After a short while they returned back to work; Sitre to Nefertiti's chambers, Aset and Kiya to Amenhotep's office.

When Aset and Kiya arrived at the Pharaoh's office the Head of the Royal Guard, Hekanakht, a tall veteran soldier who started his career in the army of Amenhotep the Third before joining the Royal Guard and being promoted to its head under the new Pharaoh, was waiting for them and informed Kiya that the Pharaoh wanted to see her immediately.

"Why does he want to see me?" Kiya asked both surprised and worried.

"I don't know," the soldier simply answered, opened the door and told her to enter Amenhotep's private office.

Without thinking Aset wanted to follow her friend but Hekanakht pushed her back roughly and spoke: "Not you! His Majesty wants to see Kiya alone!"

Not understanding what was happening, Aset decided to remain waiting in front of the Pharaoh's office in case Amenhotep should need her but also out of concern for Kiya.

More than an hour had passed before Kiya came out of the office again, looking pale and in tears.

"What happened?" Aset inquired worriedly. "Did he do something to you?"

Kiya did not reply but just shook her head.

"Let's go to our room. We can talk there," Aset suggested to her friend.

Just when Aset and Kiya were leaving, a dirty and tired looking Aten priest arrived at the Pharaoh's office with an urgent message.

Arriving in their small room where they had some privacy Aset asked again what had happened.

Kiya had calmed down by that time but hesitated before answering: "The Pharaoh made me promise not to tell to anybody about what he told me this evening. He will make an announcement soon."

"An announcement?" Aset asked wondering, louder than she intended and went on in a lower voice: "Do you mean...? Does he...?"

Aset could not say the words so Kiya finally finished her sentence: "He wants to marry me, Aset! The Pharaoh wants to marry me!"

Hearing her friend's words Aset did not know what to say but then Kiya begged: "Aset, please don't tell anybody about this until the Pharaoh has made it public."

"You know you can trust me, Kiya, I won't tell anybody about this," Aset replied and having gotten over the initial shock she started to get curious and asked: "What position will you have at the court after the wedding?"

Before Kiya could reply Aset remembered their previous conversation with Sitre and remarked: "Maybe I was wrong and Amenhotep does want to replace Nefertiti. Maybe he will replace her with you, Kiya!"

Kiya had also calmed down, shook her head and spoke: "No, Nefertiti will remain the Great Royal

Wife. I will become his second wife but I don't know yet what my titles will be."

"Isn't Tadukhipa, the daughter of King Tushratta of Mitanni, the Pharaoh's second wife?" Aset asked.

"I also wondered about that but Amenhotep told me that it is only a diplomatic marriage. He sent her to a palace in the delta, she will never play an important role at the court," Kiya explained.

For a moment there was a silence, then Kiya took Aset's hands and asked: "Aset, when I am the Pharaoh's wife will you please be my personal servant? I want you to stay with me at that time."

"Isn't that a decision of the pharaoh? I am his servant now," Aset replied.

"I have already asked him about that, Aset, and he agreed," Kiya spoke again.

"In that case I think I have no choice haven't I?" Aset remarked, feeling annoyed, and pulled her hands out of Kiya's.

"Are you not happy I asked you to be my personal servant?" Kiya asked surprised.

"I want to be your friend, not your servant, Kiya!" Aset exclaimed angrily.

"I understand that but unfortunately the situation is going to change Aset," Kiya replied and went on speaking: "I did not ask for this and I am as unhappy about this as you are. I wanted to marry Montu and have a normal life with him!"

While she was speaking Kiya started to cry again and after a short silence she added: "I just want to have you with me when I will have to live at the court."

"I am sorry I got upset Kiya. Of course I will stay with you after you get married," Aset replied and then added smilingly: "But don't expect me to call you My Lady or Your Highness."

"What happened today at the Gem Pa Aten?" Amenhotep asked furiously. It was the middle of the night but the Pharaoh did not want to wait until the next day to hear a report about the accident.

As soon as he had received the information about the disaster at the Gem Pa Aten from Hatiay, the Aten priest, he had sent for Nebtawi and Hemienu.

When they arrived at Malkata Palace the Pharaoh was already waiting for them on his throne, which was placed on a raised platform, in an almost empty audience hall. Except for the guards, a few servants and the usual writer next to the throne there was nobody, creating an eerie atmosphere.

"Amenhotep was going to deal with this business alone," Hemienu thought to himself when he entered the hall; and he was not sure if that was a good thing or not.

"Nebtawi, you are the chief of construction, explain to me what happened!" Amenhotep spoke again with a face flushed with anger.

"Your Majesty, I was not at the construction site during the accident. Hemienu was the man in charge at that moment," Nebtawi replied in an attempt to direct the anger of the Pharaoh away from him and towards his overseer.

"But you have inspected the site after the accident, haven't you?" Amenhotep retorted and went on: "I repeat: You, Nebtawi, are the chief of construction and that makes you the first person responsible. Tell me, what happened at the Gem Pa Aten?"

The Pharaoh stopped speaking for a moment to see if Nebtawi would give a reply. When no reply came, Amenhotep continued speaking in a calmer tone: "A wall does not collapse without a reason. The cause of the accident lies most likely in the design or the construction method. Hemienu, can you give me an explanation for this disaster?"

Hemienu thought for a moment and answered nervously: "Your Majesty, the cause is probably the new building blocks we are using. At the Gem Pa Aten we use smaller blocks than normal. The traditional building blocks are bigger and heavier and create more stable structures than the blocks we are using now."

"So if your theory is correct, do you suggest we use bigger building blocks?" Amenhotep asked.

The Pharaoh spoke calmly but Hemienu could see from his face that he was still very upset.

"Your Majesty..." Nebtawi started and wanted to go on speaking but the Pharaoh cut him off: "I asked Hemienu a question and he will answer. You already had the opportunity to speak but you did not take it."

Amenhotep looked at Hemienu and spoke agitatedly: "I asked a question and I am waiting for an answer, Hemienu!"

"Your Majesty, using bigger blocks is a solution but if we look for ways to join the smaller blocks better together we can still build a stable construction. We are using a new material and are still in a learning process," Hemienu answered in a voice shivering with nervousness.

"How much time is this learning process costing me, Nebtawi?" Amenhotep asked his chief of construction and immediately continued with another question: "When will we be on schedule again?"

"Your Majesty, we haven't lost much time. We can build this wall up again within a month. In the meantime we can go on working on the rest of the temple," Nebtawi replied reassuringly.

"Do you agree with the chief of construction?" the Pharaoh asked, looking at Hemienu.

"I am afraid I don't agree, Your Majesty," Hemienu answered, his voice sounding scared when delivering the disappointing news to the Pharaoh.

Forgetting court protocol for a moment Nebtawi turned to Hemienu and exclaimed with a horrified look on his face: "Hemienu, what are you doing?"

Ignoring Nebtawi, Amenhotep asked: "And why don't you agree with your superior, Hemienu?"

"Your Majesty, first we have to find a good solution for our construction problem, which I am convinced we will find within a short time. Only after we have found this solution we can start rebuilding the collapsed wall," Hemienu replied and after nervously taking a deep breath he went on: "But, Your Majesty, as an overseer at the construction site it is my duty to bring the fact to your attention that everything we have built until now has been built in the same way as the collapsed wall was built."

When he had finished speaking Hemienu feared the Pharaoh would explode with rage after hearing the unpleasant news but instead he remained calm and just spoke: "So you mean you have to rebuild everything?"

"That is a possibility. We will have to examine everything that we have built until now on stability. After that we can decide whether we need to rebuild or not," Hemienu explained.

"Is there any more bad news or was that it?" the Pharaoh asked, still remaining surprisingly calm.

"There is one more, important thing, Your Majesty," Hemienu spoke, getting more confident again when seeing the Pharaoh had regained his calm and businesslike manner. "We have lost a lot of workmen today, thirteen dead and thirty-two wounded, they..."

"Don't bother me with these petty problems, Hemienu!" Amenhotep unexpectedly snapped and went on as angry again as before: "I don't care about a few workers more or less! They will be replaced! What I care about is my temple to be ready according to schedule!"

The Pharaoh stopped speaking, looking at Nebtawi and Hemienu with glaring eyes.

"Nebtawi," he continued speaking in an angry voice: "I have come to the conclusion that you are incompetent, therefore you are not working at the Gem Pa Aten anymore!"

Nebtawi cringed and paled but did not say anything.

Having fired Nebtawi, Amenhotep turned to Hemienu and spoke while still being agitated: "Hemienu, you are the new chief of construction. From this moment on you will be in charge of the construction and responsible for everything that happens at the Gem Pa Aten."

But Hemienu's promotion came with a warning: "And you had better not disappoint me, Hemienu! I will not tolerate another failure!"

CHAPTER 6
A SIGN THAT CANNOT BE IGNORED
AND
FOREIGN DIPLOMACY

During the night, hours before sunrise, Aset and Kiya were woken up by a fully uniformed and armed Hekanakht, the Head of the Royal Guard.

"My ladies," he explained to them politely. "I am ordered to escort you out of the palace immediately. His Majesty wants you to stay somewhere else for the time being."

Aset and Kiya did not understand what was happening.

"Why?" Kiya asked.

"We have to work this morning," Aset protested.

"I don't know why," Hekanakht replied curtly. "I am just doing as I am told. Now, pack only your most important belongings and hurry up, it is important that we leave the palace before everybody wakes up. His Majesty wants you to leave without anybody noticing!"

A short time later they were outside of Malkata Palace. Except for a few guards nobody saw them leaving. They went to the palace dock where the Royal Barks were moored with one of them already prepared for immediate departure. The crew had clearly been expecting them and politely welcomed them on board.

While Aset and Kiya boarded the boat they were still confused and did not understand why they had to leave the palace. Hekanakht also joined them on board and the crew immediately set sail.

The Royal Bark had a luxuriously furnished cabin, lit by oil lamps but Aset and Kiya decided to sit on comfortable seats on the boat's deck. Hekanakht did not join them but instead went to speak with the boat's captain.

It was a clear night and the moon and bright stars threw a silvery light over the river, the surrounding farm fields and the desert. The world was still sleeping, there were no other boats on the river and there was no sound except for the whispered conversations of the ship's crew, the splashing of the water against the boat's hull and the occasional call of a bird.

Aset looked back at the palace but all she could see were the torch lights which were kept burning all night, against the black background of the Theban mountains.

"Where do you think they are taking us to?" Kiya asked, breaking the silence and waking Aset out of her thoughts.

"I don't know. I have no idea what is happening," Aset answered.

"It looks like we are going in the direction of Thebes," Kiya spoke and went on with a tone that betrayed her fear: "Maybe Amenhotep has changed his mind. Maybe he does not want to marry me anymore and now wants to make us disappear before we tell anybody the Pharaoh considered marrying a servant."

After a short pause Kiya continued speaking to Aset while looking at the fully armed Hekanakht: "Why else would Hekanakht come with us? And why else would he bring his sword and daggers with him? The Pharaoh wants us to disappear!"

Kiya was getting on Aset's nerves and noticing they were indeed going to Thebes she replied: "You are not making any sense, Kiya. People disappear in the desert, not in Thebes. If your fiancé really wants us to disappear we would be taken west, into the desert, where nobody would see or find us ever again. They would not take us by a Royal Bark into the capital."

Aset was trying to calm Kiya down but she herself was also not feeling comfortable with their situation.

The boat was getting closer to Thebes. There was still some time to go before sunrise but the many torches and oil lamps illuminating the city proved that life in Thebes never completely stopped.

After a while Hekanakht came over and asked politely: "I hope this unexpected journey is not too inconvenient for you?"

Aset noticed Hekanakht was addressing Kiya and not her. Kiya did not seem to notice this and instead of answering his question she asked: "What is happening? Where are we going to? Can you please tell us something?"

"We are sailing to Thebes," Hekanakht informed them and then went on, speaking directly to Kiya again: "His Majesty wants you to stay at a different location until he calls you back to the palace."

"But why do we have to leave the palace?" Aset asked, joining in the conversation.

"I don't know," Hekanakht replied. "I am only following orders."

Hekanakht did not seem to be in the mood for any more conversation with Aset and Kiya; he turned around and walked back to the captain.

Aset noticed he never lost Kiya out of his sight and wondered if he had been informed by the Pharaoh of her new status as his future wife.

The boat arrived at Thebes but did not dock at the city's harbour. Passing the almost deserted harbour, Aset knew they were probably going to the dock near the Karnak Temple which was built specially for boats carrying members of the Royal Family.

When they arrived at the dock Aset saw the temple in the distance with the silhouettes of its pylons and tall obelisks clearly visible against the night sky. She could even hear chanting coming from the direction of the temple. The morning ceremony at Karnak always started early, she knew.

Aset, Kiya and Hekanakht disembarked and found two chariots waiting for them together with two charioteers and an armed guard.

One of the ship's crew brought the few belongings Aset and Kiya had taken with them to one of the waiting chariots. Hekanakht then ordered Aset to climb into that same chariot while he himself helped Kiya into the other and then joined her; standing protectively behind Kiya as if he was worried she would fall out or something else could happen to her.

The guard who had been waiting for them on the dock climbed behind Aset in the chariot and Hekanakht gave the charioteers the order to go.

Each chariot was pulled by two horses and they moved fast over the bumpy roads. Aset had to hold-on to the side of the chariot to keep herself from falling into the guard or the charioteer.

When they raced through the city's streets Aset saw the first people appearing, it would not be long before the sun would start to rise and a new day would begin.

Aset was nervous; she had never ridden in a chariot before and even though she did not doubt the skill of the charioteer, the speed he was driving with scared her.

The charioteer himself seemed to enjoy the ride; he was laughing and yelling at the horses, encouraging them to go even faster. Aset looked at the soldier behind her on whose face she could not see any sign of joy or fear, if there was any kind of emotion it was boredom.

When they had left the city and rode into the surrounding green countryside the charioteers pushed the horses to go even faster.

Every now and then they startled farmers on the way to their fields or people on their way to one of the many markets which would open soon. Aset wondered if Kiya, who was riding in front of her, was as scared as she was but it was impossible to see, the tall figure of Hekanakht was completely blocking her from view.

When the first rays of the sun turned the sky red they arrived at a walled compound set in an orchard of date palms.

The gates in the wall opened immediately upon their arrival and, in the early morning light, revealed a lush green garden with a pond in the middle. In the back of the garden was a beautiful two-storey villa.

"Welcome to my humble home!" a friendly looking middle-aged man welcomed them as soon as they arrived at the villa.

The man had clearly been waiting for them. Aset remembered seeing him at the palace sometimes and knew he was close with the Pharaoh but did not know his name or position.

As soon as the chariots stopped, the man walked over to Kiya, helped her out of the chariot, made a bow for her and spoke: "My lady, my name is

Panehsy, it is my honour to welcome you in my humble house. Please consider me your loyal servant during your stay here."

Ipi had been working almost all night. He had only slept a short time, lying on the floor in a corner of Intef's practice. He had been busy, together with his colleagues, taking care of the casualties of the accident at the Aten Temple, two of whom had died during the night. Immediately after their death the bodies of the workmen had been taken to the House of Death where the embalmers would embalm the bodies before decomposition would set in. Since they were only simple workers Ipi expected the embalming treatment they would receive would be of a low standard, not the same treatment the nobility or the Royal Family would receive.

While the temple physicians were working, a priest had constantly been burning incense and reciting prayers to Amun and to the deified Imhotep, who became a God of healing, asking Them for Their help in the recovery of all the wounded.

That morning there was a ceremony in Karnak in honour of the daughter of the Pharaoh, princess Meketaten, and Nefertiti. Ipi however was too busy to attend and so were all the other physicians. Even Intef, who supported the decision of Meryptah to hold the ceremony, could not attend to his great regret.

The chanting and praying was clearly audible for Ipi and the other apprentices and physicians during their work.

Hearing Meryptah reciting a prayer for the health of the newly born princess and the Great Royal Wife while looking at an unconscious worker who he doubted would survive his wounds, Ipi remarked to nobody in particular: "It should be clear now to the Pharaoh that he is going down the wrong path."

"What did you say, Ipi?" an older temple physician named Mereruka asked.

"I said that the Pharaoh must understand now that the Lord Amun is not satisfied. The accident at the Aten Temple must be a sign that Amun is unhappy about the Pharaoh refusing to worship Him," Ipi explained.

"I don't believe that," Mereruka replied. "I don't believe Amun would let walls collapse on top of a lot of workers. That would be the act of a cruel God."

Another apprentice now also joined in the conversation and spoke: "I do believe we should see this as a sign for the Pharaoh. Maybe the Pharaoh needed a sign he cannot ignore. And his temple, the Gem Pa Aten, collapsing over his workers is definitely a sign he cannot ignore."

"This is a sign I cannot ignore," Pharaoh Amenhotep spoke excitedly. "I have been thinking, Penthu, and come to the conclusion that this accident was a sign from the Aten to me."

Penthu did not understand it. How could the Pharaoh see the accident at the Gem Pa Aten as a sign from Aten?

Penthu had been working at his office at Malkata Palace that morning when the Pharaoh came to him, complaining about a headache.

After a quick examination Penthu concluded the Pharaoh was simply suffering from a lack of sleep. He advised the Pharaoh to rest but Amenhotep replied: "How can I sleep after receiving such a sign from the Aten?"

"Forgive me, Your Majesty," Penthu spoke and then carefully asked: "I don't understand this sign from the Aten. Why would Aten destroy His own temple?"

The Pharaoh got up from the chair he had been sitting on and walked to a window that looked out over the Nile in the direction of Thebes.

"Penthu!" he started, "you, as a priest of Amun, should know as no other that Thebes is a city that belongs to Amun. This is the center of His cult; the biggest temple complex of the country belongs to Him and is located here."

Amenhotep stopped speaking, returned to his chair and sat down again opposite Penthu before he continued speaking: "For a long time I have been having a vision about creating something extraordinary for Aten on virgin land, land that has never been dedicated to another God. With this accident the Aten tells me that He is not satisfied with only a temple in Thebes. He needs a temple on land which is untouched and far from the holy places of the traditional Gods!"

The Pharaoh stopped speaking for a moment but then added, sounding very excited again: "Don't you understand Penthu? Aten tells me that I have to realize my vision!"

"Does that mean you are going to build a temple outside of Thebes, Your Majesty?" Penthu asked, wondering about the Pharaoh's plans.

"I am going to do much more than that. Penthu! Much more!" Amenhotep replied, completely calmed down again.

For a moment nobody spoke, the Pharaoh sat opposite Penthu, his eyes staring over Penthu's shoulder at the wall as if he was seeing his vision coming into reality in his mind.

Penthu did not dare to wake him up out of his daydream but soon the Pharaoh's eyes turned to Penthu again and he went on speaking: "I am going to offer the Aten much more than just a temple."

Penthu now got curious about the Pharaoh's plans with the Gem Pa Aten; he was, after all, still a priest of Amun and knew about the opposition among the priests in Karnak against the Aten Temple being built next to their temple.

"Your Majesty, if the Aten is not satisfied with the Gem Pa Aten and you are going to realize your vision on new, untouched land; what does this mean for the Gem Pa Aten? Will you abandon the construction site of the Aten Temple?" Penthu asked, not being able suppress a hopeful tone in his voice.

If the Pharaoh noticed the hopeful tone he ignored it.

"No!" he simply answered and explained: "I have started building a temple for the Aten so now I will have to finish it. Leaving the Gem Pa Aten unfinished would be blasphemy. Besides, my architect told me the workers are now in a learning process so while finishing the Gem Pa Aten they will perfect their skills and be ready to realize my vision."

Aset and Kiya installed themselves in comfortable seats in the living room of Panehsy's villa. They were offered cool water from his private well and bread, freshly baked in his own bakery as Panehsy proudly remarked.

Hekanakht had returned immediately to the Palace but left the other guard behind at the villa where he joined two other guards who were already there.

"My lady," Panehsy spoke to Kiya, "I have prepared the best room in my house for you. It is not much but I hope it will be to your satisfaction."

Then, looking at Aset, he went on: "Your servant can of course sleep together with my servants."

Aset paled and wanted to protest before remembering that she was not in the position to do so or to even speak.

"My servant?" Kiya asked surprised and completely overwhelmed by being treated in such a respectful manner by a noble man who in normal circumstances would not even notice her.

"My lady, His Majesty informed me he would send you together with your servant," Panehsy explained, wondering what the problem was.

"Ah, yes," Kiya replied, suddenly understanding the situation better and then told Panehsy, trying to sound like a real Royal Lady from the palace: "But I don't want to separate from my personal servant. I want her to stay with me, in my quarters."

"Oh, if that is what my lady wishes than I shall make the necessary arrangements," Panehsy reacted surprised.

Aset gave Kiya a grateful look, feeling relieved they would not be separated while staying in this unfamiliar environment.

"Has His Majesty informed you why we are here?" Kiya asked, hoping to finally receive an answer about what was happening.

Panehsy thought for a moment before he replied in a proud voice: "His Majesty and I have known each other for a long time, even already before he became Lord of the Two Lands. I not only consider him as my lord but also as my friend. We have both been loyal worshippers of the Aten for many years and this has created a strong bond of trust between us."

Panehsy paused a moment while pointing at painted depictions of the Aten on the walls of his villa as if he wanted to prove the sincerity of his claim of worshipping the Aten.

Aset looked at the scenes of the Aten shining on the Pharaoh and Nefertiti. The rays of the Sun Disc ended in hands which gave the Royal couple the ankh, the symbol of life. Aset had seen these representations before in the palace but was surprised to see them in Panehsy's villa. On these scenes Aten also only gave life to the Royal Family, never to Panehsy himself or his family. There were also brightly coloured depictions on the walls of Panehsy and his family but for some reason these never included the Aten.

Aset woke up from her thoughts when Panehsy continued speaking: "Yesterday evening I received an urgent message from Amenhotep, saying he wanted to send the Lady Kiya and her servant to my villa early this morning. Naturally I was honoured and agreed. I had to promise to keep your stay here a secret. I even had to send my wife and two children and most of my servants to my house in the city. Amenhotep does not want anybody to know about your stay here."

"Did His Majesty give you a reason for our stay, or how long we will be staying here?" Kiya asked, still not having received an answer to her earlier question.

"His Majesty did not give me a reason but he did say it would just be for a few days," Panehsy answered.

That afternoon the Pharaoh was receiving an important messenger in the audience hall of the palace.

Since he was still not feeling well he requested Penthu to attend in case he would need him.

The Great Royal Wife, Nefertiti was still too weak after giving birth to Meketaten so Queen Teye, the Pharaoh's mother replaced her.

The messenger entered the hall, kneeled for the Pharaoh and delivered the message while saying: "Tushratta, the great King of Mitanni sends his brother, Lord of the Two Lands his greetings."

After the messenger had left Amenhotep broke the seal and opened the message.

Penthu, standing close to Amenhotep's throne, watched the Pharaoh while he was reading the message and saw him first turning pale and then red. Tushratta's message clearly angered the Pharaoh.

"What does King Tushratta have to tell you?" Penthu heard Queen Teye ask.

Teye had always kept her interest in diplomatic relations with foreign kings, even after she was replaced as Great Royal Wife by Nefertiti.

"King Tushratta complains that I sent him gold plated wooden statues instead of the solid golden statues father promised to him and also that I sent him fewer treasures than father had promised. According to Tushratta father showed messengers from Mitanni what he intended to send to him. Due to father's death it was never sent but now Tushratta still expects me to do it," Amenhotep told his mother, his voice sounding as if he was depressed.

"Your father was a wise man," Teye replied. "He spent a great part of his reign establishing and improving diplomatic relations with other countries. Your father understood the value of these contacts and because of his good relations with other powerful kingdoms he was able to make the Two Lands the stable and prosperous country you have inherited. I suggest you continue maintaining these diplomatic contacts, my son. Do not underestimate their importance."

Teye had spoken softly and in a calm tone but Penthu could hear she was very serious about what she had been saying.

"Thank you for your good advice mother," Amenhotep replied but then went on speaking: "But Tushratta seems to think that our country is made of gold. He actually says in his letter that gold in the Two Lands is as common as dust. The fact is, however, that I don't have any gold to spare now."

Amenhotep stopped speaking a moment, waiting for his mother to say something but when she remained silent he continued, that time addressing everybody in the audience hall: "The situation of our country has changed since my father was Pharaoh. We cannot afford anymore to send our wealth abroad. It will remain here in the Two Lands where I will use it to realize a vision that the Aten has given to me!"

Before anybody could say anything a man in military uniform advanced to the throne, bowed and spoke: "Your Majesty, may I bring another important detail about our relationship with Mitanni to your attention?"

The Pharaoh sighed and replied irritated: "What have you got to say, Sethnakht?"

Sethnakht, the Pharaoh's military advisor, started speaking in a loud commanding voice: "Your Majesty, since your grandfather, the great Pharaoh Thutmose the Fourth, made a peace treaty with the Mitanni they are our allies and as such they are important to our strategic position in their region. Lately the Kingdom of Hatti, which lies next to Mitanni, has been growing in power and this makes good relations with Mitanni vital to us. Hatti is unpredictable, Your Majesty, they threaten Mitanni and if they decide to go to war and come out victorious we will most likely be their following target."

The soldier finished speaking but then added in a warning tone: "Your Majesty, remember what King Tushratta wrote: 'Gold is like dust in the Two Lands.' The wealth of our country is the envy of every kingdom and that is why we have to keep our allies close to us to help us protecting it."

"What are you trying to say?" Amenhotep asked feeling annoyed about the opposition of his advisor. "Are you suggesting we should send military aid to Mitanni?"

Trying to reassure the Pharaoh, Sethnakht replied: "I don't think that will be necessary, Your Majesty. For the time being the Mitanni are strong enough to keep Hatti under control. However, we don't know what will happen in the future because Hatti is building up its military strength. For this reason we have to maintain close ties with Mitanni. If we lose Mitanni to Hatti, either by military force or through diplomacy, all the small city states and kingdoms in that region that are now under our control will likely follow and that means we will lose our control in that region, a region which is vital to our trade. And what could be even more threatening is that when we have lost Mitanni and our vassal states the road to the Two Lands will be open for Hatti's armies!"

"If I understand you correctly, Sethnakht," the Pharaoh replied, "you are suggesting that we buy the friendship of Mitanni by giving them everything they ask for?"

Sethnakht thought for a moment and then answered: "To put it simply, Your Majesty, yes, that is what I am suggesting and what your father, the wise Pharaoh Amenhotep the Third, did. By having Mitanni helping us maintaining security and stability in their region we will ultimately win more than it costs us."

"I understand what you mean, Sethnakht. I will keep your advice in mind when I compose a reply to Tushratta," Amenhotep curtly told his advisor and got up from his throne, which was a sign the audience was over. Amenhotep looked at Penthu and spoke: "I am still not feeling well. Help me back to my office."

Amenhotep sat in his comfortable, gilded chair in his office, his head was leaning back against the chair and his eyes were closed. In front of him, on his desk, stood an empty cup which had held an herb mixture given to him by Penthu, against the Pharaoh's headache and which would help him to sleep.

Opposite the Pharaoh sat his mother, Queen Teye, who said nothing and just looked at her son with a concerned expression on her face.

Penthu was standing together with a servant in a corner of the room, waiting for when he would be needed. He wondered if his mixture had been too strong and the Pharaoh had fallen asleep but then he started speaking, his voice sounding tired and his eyes still closed: "All these people telling me what to do! They know only part of the picture. I am the only person who knows the whole picture!"

"What are you trying to say, my son?" Teye asked worriedly.

"I am saying that I cannot give Tushratta what he wants," Amenhotep replied and then, lifting his head from the back of the chair and opening his eyes, went on: "Mother, the Aten wants me to perform an important task. He has given me a vision that I am going to realize. I will need all the resources of the Two Lands to do this and for this reason it is impossible for me to send so many treasures to Tushratta or any other king. When I have finished my work for the Aten I can see what I can do for our allies but for the moment they will have to wait!"

Penthu expected Queen Teye to get upset at her stubborn son who was neglecting his father's legacy but to his surprise she remained calm and replied: "You know I always support you with your work for the Aten and I will keep supporting you now. If this is your final decision I will accept that."

"This is my final decision, mother," Amenhotep simply answered.

Teye resigned herself to her son's decision, got up from her chair and, followed by her personal servant, walked out of the Pharaoh's office without any further words.

The Pharaoh rubbed his hands over his face in a gesture of tiredness and told his servant: "Tell Merykare, my scribe, to come into my office. I am going to dictate a reply to Tushratta."

It was Hemienu's first working day after his unexpected promotion. Normally he would have been proud of his new position but at that time he felt guilty about replacing Nebtawi who had disappeared without saying anything after they had left the palace the previous night.

He had always respected Nebtawi whom he had known for a long time already and whom he regarded as an able architect.

Hemienu's wife Ahotep had been elated when she heard about her husband's promotion.

"I knew it would happen sometime," she had exclaimed after hearing the news. "You deserved it more than anybody!"

She did not ask about what had happened to Nebtawi and Hemienu decide not to tell her.

As soon as he arrived at the Gem Pa Aten Hemienu called his overseers together and informed them of his new position and told them Nebtawi was not working at the construction site anymore.

Hemienu did not want to say the Pharaoh had fired him, he did not want to cause any further damage to the previous chief of construction's reputation.

After explaining the new situation he turned to business; he ordered everybody to stop their work on the temple immediately and told them to examine the whole structure on stability.

Hemienu himself personally participated in the examination of the temple, he walked through the whole complex looking everywhere for any signs of weaknesses in the construction.

The sun rose in the sky and it was getting almost unbearably hot. Walking through the temple with its unfinished walls and pillars Hemienu wondered again why the Pharaoh did not add a roof in his design. How could the priests of the Aten work and worship under such conditions?

It was already in the afternoon when Hemienu's inspection brought him to the scene of the accident.

He stood there for a while, reflecting on what had happened and then said to one of his overseers: "I am going to the Karnak Temple. I want to see how the wounded workers are doing."

During the short walk to Karnak Hemienu got angry at himself for not thinking about his wounded workers earlier.

He entered through the entrance which led him directly to the practice of the physicians of the Amun temple. Inside he encountered a chaotic situation with physicians running from one patient to another and some of his wounded workmen screaming in agony when their wounds were being treated. Everywhere Hemienu smelt the scent of incense which the priests were burning constantly, not only to please the Gods Amun and Imhotep but also against bad smells coming from putrefying wounds or seriously injured patients.

"Can I help you?" an exhausted looking young boy asked.

Hemienu recognized him immediately; he remembered seeing him amongst the physicians at the Gem Pa Aten the day before.

"Yes," he replied and spoke: "My name is Hemienu and your name is Ipi, if I remember correctly. You were at the Aten Temple yesterday?"

Ipi nodded and replied in a voice that betrayed his exhaustion: "Yes, my name is Ipi and I was at your temple yesterday. Is there something I can do for you?"

"I am the Pharaoh's new architect at the Gem Pa Aten and I want to inquire about the situation of my workers," Hemienu replied and went on asking: "Is their situation improving?"

"Most of your workers are improving but unfortunately two of them have joined Osiris in the Netherworld last night and one more will probably follow them soon," Ipi informed Hemienu, his weariness making him sounding detached, even though he always cared about his work and patients.

Hemienu was struck by the news that two more workers had died with one more about to die and for a moment did not know what to say.

At that moment Intef came over and immediately recognized Hemienu.

"I expect you come to inquire about your workers?" he asked.

"You are correct and your apprentice Ipi has already been very helpful," Hemienu replied, quickly recovering from the bad news Ipi had given him while greeting Intef with a polite bow.

Intef went on to take Hemienu to each of his remaining workers and informed him about their situation.

While Intef and Hemienu were talking, Ipi, feeling exhausted, went outside.

Since the evening of the previous day he had not left Intef's hectic practice and had been working almost constantly, getting hardly any sleep. He needed to rest, to be away from the screaming of the patients and, especially, he needed fresh air; the incense in the practice did not completely cover the smell of putrefying wounds and excrements.

Arriving outside Ipi felt relieved, the fresh air and the sunlight made him feel better almost immediately.

He decided not to go to his room and catch up on his lost sleep but instead took the stairs inside one of Karnak's great pylons and climbed to the rooftop of the building that connected to it. The worst heat of the day was over by then and there, on the rooftop, Ipi could enjoy the refreshing breeze and the view of Thebes and its surroundings.

Ipi was not the only person on the rooftop, many priests used to come there at the end of the afternoon to seek coolness after the afternoon heat.

The temple roof was also the place where during the night the temple's astronomers came to follow the movements of the stars. This was a very important task because by tracking the stars the priest maintained the Egyptian calendar and determined when it was the right time to celebrate religious events and ceremonies.

To his surprise Ipi saw Nebamun sitting alone near the edge of the roof, staring out over the Nile River which was now busy with all kinds of boat traffic coming from or on their way to the Theban harbour.

Ipi sat down next to his friend who, upon noticing him, asked: "Should you not be working? I heard you have many wounded to take care of."

"I know I should but I could not take it anymore. I needed to get out of there for a moment. I will return to work later again," Ipi replied.

"Did you hear the rumours that are going through the temple?" Nebamun asked again, without looking at Ipi, still staring over the Nile instead.

"No, what rumours are you talking about? Is the Pharaoh going to do something against the temple?" Ipi replied sounding both curious and worried.

Nebamun then turned to Ipi and said, speaking in a low voice as if he was telling a big secret: "No, this is not about the Pharaoh, Ipi. But many priests in the temple are not satisfied with the way Meryptah is dealing with the Pharaoh. They want him to take a harder line but he refuses to do so."

"That is probably just a couple of young priests agreeing with Amenemope yesterday," Ipi replied and added: "Actually, I have to agree with them that the temple should remind the Pharaoh of his responsibilities towards Amun. Don't you agree with that, Nebamun?"

Nebamun turned his face back to the river again before speaking, while sounding worried: "This appears to be going much further than just a couple of young priests, Ipi. There is dissent amongst some of the higher ranking priests as well."

Nebamun stopped speaking for a moment, thinking about Ipi's question before he replied: "I am not against a harder line of the temple against the Pharaoh but I think it is much more important that there is unity amongst the Amun priests. Divided we can never pose any opposition to the Pharaoh and then it will be easy for him to replace Amun with the Aten."

"Do you think that is what the Pharaoh wants to do? Do you think he wants to replace Amun as the

King of the Gods with the Aten?" Ipi asked in disbelief.

"Why not?" Nebamun spoke and explained: "Pharaoh Amenhotep thinks he can do what he wants. He loves the Aten and clearly does not love Amun. I think it is only a matter of time before he declares the Aten to be the most important God of Egypt. What that will mean to us? I don't know but we have to be prepared and not fight amongst ourselves."

Ipi was surprised, he always had the impression that the only reason Nebamun was in the temple was because his parents sent him there. He never gave the impression to care very much about it. But this time Nebamun had been talking with a conviction he had never heard before from him.

Without noticing Ipi's gaze had been drifting to the other side of the river, to the area where his family's small farm was located.

"Maybe you are right," Ipi admitted. "And maybe Meryptah is also right in not provoking the Pharaoh unnecessarily."

"I am sure Meryptah is right about that," Nebamun answered concurringly and, following Ipi's gaze, he suddenly changed the subject of the conversation and asked: "Is that where your family is living?"

Pointing in the direction of his family's farm, Ipi replied: "Yes, they live there but you can't see it from here. It is faraway, on the edge of the desert."

Nebamun's question surprised Ipi since he was rarely asked about his family.

"Why have you never returned home to visit them? You should go there sometime to see how they are doing," Nebamun went on speaking.

Ipi did not really know what stopped him from visiting his family. He knew he would get permission to leave the temple for a few days if he asked.

Ipi's hand went automatically to the amulet around his neck which his father had given to him and he replied: "I never have the time to go home, I have too much to do here."

Immediately after his reply Ipi knew his answer would not be accepted and Nebamun quickly proved him right.

"Ask Intef or Wenamun. I am sure they will give you some days to visit your family," Nebamun spoke and added smilingly: "You are going to be a good physician Ipi, but you are not that good yet that the temple cannot do without you for a few days."

CHAPTER 7
IN THE EGYPTIAN COUNTRYSIDE

Panehsy had shown Aset and Kiya to a beautiful room on the first floor of his villa. Even though it wasn't as luxurious as the apartments of the Royal Family they knew from the palace, this room was by far the most luxurious place they had ever stayed in. The room even had a real bed; it would be the first time they would sleep on a bed since until then they had always slept on a sleeping mat on the floor.

In the room a chest had been prepared with new clothes and jewellery for Kiya. "A gift from the Pharaoh," Panehsy explained.

The brightly painted room had windows on three sides which offered a view over the surrounding area and allowed a cooling breeze to enter the room.

From the room stairs led to the roof where a table and chairs had been set up and the occupants of the room could come in the evening to enjoy the cool weather. Aset suspected that they stayed in the room that under normal circumstances belonged to Panehsy and his wife.

At midday a servant entered the room bringing a tray laden with food.

"My master apologizes he cannot invite you to have lunch with him, my lady. He has been called away on an urgent business but hopes you will accept his invitation to join him this evening for dinner," the servant told Kiya while preparing the table for lunch.

The table was filled with roast meat, vegetables, fruit and cakes sweetened with honey and another servant came into the room bringing a jug of wine.

Aset noticed the table had been set up for one person even though there was enough food for three or four people.

Shortly after they had left one of the servants returned with a plate of bread and fruit and a cup of water.

"This is for your servant, my lady," the girl informed Kiya and then added: "I will be waiting right outside your room, in case you need anything more."

The servant left the room without waiting for a reply, leaving Aset feeling uneasy and not knowing what to do but Kiya looked at her and spoke with mocked impatience: "What are you waiting for, Aset! Come and help me to finish this food!"

After the meal Aset slumped in one of the comfortable chairs of their new home while Kiya lay down on the bed and stretched out.

"I could live like this forever!" she remarked with satisfaction, clearly enjoying her new living conditions.

"You probably will, Kiya," Aset replied wryly. Kiya was quiet for a moment, not sure whether she should be happy about this or not, but then she smiled again, got off the bed and spoke to Aset: "Don't be so sulky, Aset. Try to have some fun sometimes! Enjoy life while you can! Come here and try the bed, it is really comfortable."

"No thank you," Aset replied while looking at the newly painted depictions of the Aten on the wall. Here also the hands of the Aten only stretched out to the Royal Family, again offering only them the ankh, the symbol of life.

Except for the Aten and the Royal Family the walls contained scenes of nature and of Panehsy and his family. One of the depictions showed Panehsy offering tribute to the Pharaoh.

Aset noticed Kiya was looking at her.

"What is wrong with you, Aset?" Kiya asked annoyed.

"Haven't you noticed? Since we are here, I have been ignored or treated as if I am inferior!" Aset replied angrily and went on: "You asked me to lie on the bed but in case you haven't noticed there is only one bed and that one is meant for you. I am probably expected to sleep on the floor and nobody has even thought about bringing me a sleeping mat! In the palace at least I feel I am being respected but here..."

Aset could not speak anymore and started to cry. Kiya came over and, not knowing what to say just put an arm around her shoulders.

After a while Aset calmed down and spoke apologizing: "I am sorry Kiya. I know this is not your fault and that you did not ask for any of this. But I am scared, I have seen many things change in the palace recently and now I am worried I am going to lose you as a friend too."

"I am scared too," Kiya answered. "I don't know what is going to happen, how Amenhotep is going to treat me or what he will expect from me. If I had any choice I would prefer to stay a servant. But we have to accept what happens and make the best out of our situation."

After Kiya's words Aset got up from the chair, walked to the bed and lay down on it.

"You are right!" she spoke and added with a smile: "It is very comfortable. Just think about it that you will sleep like this for the rest of your life, Kiya."

Kiya also smiled but did not say anything.

"I think I know why we are here," Aset went on speaking, still lying on the bed and staring at the ceiling.

"Why do you think we are here?" Kiya asked curiously.

"I think the Pharaoh does not want his fiancée to work as a servant but, since he does not want anybody to know about his intention to marry you before he announces it officially, he cannot leave you in the palace. So he sends you to a villa in the countryside where nobody will notice you but where you can live in luxury until he calls you back to the palace to get married," Aset explained and then added: "And as we already found out, I am only here to serve you."

Kiya thought for a moment about what Aset had told her and answered: "You are probably right. But why would Amenhotep not inform us about this?"

Aset got up from the bed and looked at Kiya. "How long have you been working for the Royal Family, Kiya?" she asked and before Kiya could answer she continued speaking: "You should know by now that the Royal Family never explains their actions to anybody. They always do what they want and everybody just has to accept it."

Aset stopped speaking for a moment but then added: "Maybe you will be better informed after you are married."

"I hope so," Kiya replied and went on laughingly: "I don't want to be surprised by the whims of my husband all the time."

"We are all surprised by the whims of your husband, Kiya," Aset replied to her, but in contrast to her friend she sounded very serious.

Ipi had decided to listen to Nebamun's advice. He had waited until most of the wounded workers from the Gem Pa Aten had left the Karnak Temple and he did not have much work to do anymore and then asked Wenamun and Intef for permission to visit his family on the west bank of the Nile.

As Nebamun already predicted they immediately agreed. Now, ten days after Nebamun urged him to go, Ipi was sitting on a ferry crowded with farmers, traders and people on their way to visit tombs of relatives on the west bank. The ferry was moving slowly but Ipi enjoyed the trip.

After a while his thoughts went back to the Karnak Temple. After his conversation with Nebamun, Ipi had also noticed dissatisfaction amongst the priests in Karnak. This worried Ipi because he loved Amun and His Temple and did not wish to see it go down because of quarrels amongst the priests.

When the ferry reached the west bank of the Nile Ipi disembarked and immediately forgot all about the temple politics. His family did not know he was coming and he looked forward to surprising them.

Since his family was poor Ipi brought delicacies from Thebes with him so they could have a festive meal that evening. He had also bought sweet cakes for his little nephew Djehuty who, Ipi remembered, had a sweet tooth.

Ipi still had a long walk ahead of him, past the river, through the fields and forests of fruit trees.

The closer he came to his home the more people he recognized. These people, however, did not recognize him, looking older and wearing fine temple robes instead of the simple loincloth he used to wear before. Ipi smiled when people who used to ignore or sometimes even scold him, Ipi the lazy son of Hor, bowed politely for the young priest who was passing them.

It was late in the morning when Ipi walked down the narrow track that led to his family's small farm and finally past the border stone that marked the border between his family's field and that of their neighbours.

He saw two people working in the field, his father and mother. They were ploughing the field with a wooden plough, pulled by their cow. His mother was leading the cow and his father followed behind, making sure the plough stayed in its track. They were too busy and did not notice Ipi entering their farm.

Ipi stopped next to the field and waited for his parents to notice him. His mother saw him first. She looked up, not recognizing him at first, but surprised to see a priest on their property. Then she suddenly recognized him.

"Ipi!" she yelled. She immediately forgot about the cow she was leading and ran to her son. His father then also abandoned his work and followed his wife.

Ipi's mother hugged her son and started to cry. His father came and, without any words, took both his wife and son in his arms. Finally he simply spoke: "We have missed you so much, Ipi."

Ipi's mother now let go of her son, took a step back while looking at him and spoke: "You have grown up and you look very handsome in your temple attire."

"You are looking strong and healthy, Ipi. Life in the temple must do you good," his father commented.

Ipi looked at his parents and wished he could say the same of them. They had aged considerably since he last saw them and they looked very exhausted.

Before his arrival at home Ipi had felt as if he would have many things to tell to his family but now that he was finally there he started to feel a bit uncomfortable and did not know what to say. For a moment they just stood there, looking at each other until Hor, Ipi's father, said: "Nefer, take Ipi inside and give him some water, he must be thirsty. I will get the cow and join you soon."

Already before they reached their house a young woman came towards them, it was Tahat, his brother Huni's wife. She smiled, hugged Ipi and spoke: "Welcome home!"

Ipi noticed her smile was forced and wondered what could have happened. He remembered Tahat as a girl who even under difficult circumstances always remained cheerful.

At his family's house Ipi discovered they had added another room. Before he could ask the reason for this addition he already found it out.

A pregnant young woman came outside and spoke: "You must be Ipi, I have been looking forward to meeting you."

Ipi's mother noticed the expression of surprise on her son's face and quickly introduced the girl: "Ipi, this is Tuya, Ankhaf's wife. They got married about six months ago."

"Where are Aha, Huni and Ankhaf?" Ipi asked after greeting Tahat and Tuya. He wondered why his brothers were not home to help on the field.

"They are working on other farms in the area now because our field does not yield enough anymore for our family to live on. They will come home in the evening," his father explained and then went on:

"Come inside Ipi, you must be thirsty from walking in this heat."

A moment later everybody sat inside the house on the floor with a cup of water.

Hor, Ipi's father, pointed at the newly added room and explained: "That is Ankhaf and Tuya's part of the house. Our house was getting too small and soon we are going to get another addition to the family."

While saying the last words Hor looked smilingly at the pregnant Tuya.

Suddenly Ipi remembered he was missing somebody.

"Where is Djehuty? I haven't seen him yet," he remarked.

After these words all the smiles in the room suddenly disappeared, everybody went silent and Tahat started to cry.

The silence seemed to hang in the room for hours before Ipi's father started to talk with tears in his eyes: "Two months ago Djehuty woke up in the morning with a terrible fever. A local physician came and said he could do nothing about it. He said a demon was plaguing him and advised us to take him to Thebes where the temples have priests who are specialized in exorcizing demons."

"Why did you not take him to Thebes? Why did you not take him to Karnak?" Ipi shouted while he almost started crying himself.

"We were intending to do that, Ipi," Nefer, Ipi's mother, spoke and went on in a trembling voice: "We planned to go the next morning but Djehuty died during the night."

Ipi felt tears rolling over his cheeks and, understanding the importance of a proper funeral, asked: "Did you give Djehuty a decent funeral?

Does he have everything he needs to sustain himself in the afterlife?"

"We have given him everything we had!" Tahat cried out and buried her face in her hands.

"And you know that is not much," Ipi's father added. "We could not offer him anything more than a sleeping mat, a cup and a bowl and some grain, bread and a small jug of local wine."

"Did a priest conduct a ceremony at the funeral?" Ipi went on inquiring, his voice trembling with grief.

"No," Tahat replied, upset with the thought that she maybe had not been able to provide her son with everything he needed for the afterlife, and then explained: "We could not afford that but the physician held a short ceremony for him. I hope that will be enough for the Gods to accept him in the Netherworld."

Ipi thought for a moment and exclaimed with dismay: "Why did nobody inform me? I could have helped!"

Then, without waiting for an answer from his family, he continued speaking in a calmer tone: "I will go to the market this afternoon to buy everything necessary for a funeral ceremony and tomorrow I will conduct a ceremony for Djehuty myself."

It had been more than a week since Aset and Kiya had arrived at Panehsy's villa. Panehsy had told them they would only stay for a couple of days and they wondered why it took so long before they could return to the palace.

Even though Aset and Kiya enjoyed the luxury of Panehsy's villa they started to get bored, especially since they were not allowed to leave the confinement of the villa. Even Kiya who at first had reveled in her new found lifestyle eventually got tired of it.

To Aset's relief she was treated better after Kiya had insisted to Panehsy and his servants that Aset was not an ordinary servant and should be treated with more respect. However, Aset never felt comfortable with Panehsy, even when he appeared friendly she had the feeling it was not genuine and he still looked down on her.

During their stay they had gotten to know Panehsy better and found out his family had become rich by trading products coming from Nubia, the country to the south of Egypt. Panehsy had taken over the family business from his father after his death and, after prince Amenhotep had become Pharaoh, served as his advisor and confidant.

"Look at this orchard around the villa, Aset," Kiya spoke. "Don't you want to get out to explore it? Don't you want to walk to the edge of the desert over there?"

It was midday and they were standing on the roof of the villa, overlooking the surrounding area.

Panehsy had been called away to Malkata Palace and the servants were taking their afternoon rest and would not bother them unless they were called.

"It doesn't matter what I want," Aset replied and, pointing at the guards at the gate, went on: "The guards here are keeping an eye on us, or actually, they are keeping an eye on you. They will make sure we will stay within these walls."

Kiya smiled and spoke in a secretive tone: "I know but I found a way out."

"How do you want to get out of here? The villa is surrounded by a wall with only one gate and..." Aset suddenly knew what Kiya was thinking of.

"You want to use the small door in the wall at the back of the villa?" she asked.

"Yes, why not? I have tried it, it is easy to open from the inside and the guards never seem to watch this door. We can get out and return without anybody noticing," Kiya spoke, trying to convince Aset of her plan.

Aset had doubts about Kiya's idea but since she also wanted to get off the premises of the villa she let herself be persuaded.

They told the servants they were going to take a rest and did not want to be disturbed and then, when nobody was paying attention, sneaked out of the villa, through the garden to the wall. They looked around to assure themselves there was no guard, opened the door and quickly stepped outside.

Aset and Kiya ran through the orchard of date palms that surrounded Panehsy's property until there was enough distance between them and the villa.

When they were far enough they started to walk more slowly until they finally stopped at the edge of the desert where they sat down in the shadow of a tree. Aset suddenly started to laugh.

"What are you laughing about?" Kiya asked surprised.

"I just realized that I haven't been this free since I was a child," Aset replied.

Kiya unexpectedly turned serious and asked: "Aset, when I marry Amenhotep will that give me more freedom or will that only restrict my life even further?"

This question surprised Aset and she asked: "Why are you asking this?"

Kiya stared into the desert and replied: "The wives of the Pharaohs always have everything they want and sometimes even can make decisions for the Pharaoh but I never see them going out unless it is with the Pharaoh. I never see them having any fun. Their lives seem so empty."

"Not all the Pharaoh's wives live like that," Aset replied. "Look at Nefertiti and, when Amenhotep the Third still lived, Queen Teye. They are very powerful and enjoy a lot of freedom."

Kiya remained silent for a while before she answered: "I know that but they are exceptions and even they are caught in a web of servants, officials, guards and they have to behave in the manner that is expected from them."

Kiya stopped speaking for a moment, breathed heavily and then went on: "Aset, the more I think about becoming the Pharaoh's wife the more I hate it! As only a servant I at least have some moments when I can behave and do as I feel like, when I can be myself, but as the Pharaoh's wife I will be watched all day long and expected to behave as a member of the Royal Family all the time. That is no freedom! I will go crazy living like that!"

"It won't be that bad, Kiya," Aset reassured her friend and in an effort to cheer her up continued: "Most girls in Egypt would give everything to be in your place. Don't forget there are many advantages to being the Pharaoh's wife, you will live in luxury and you will have me to serve you."

Kiya smiled and spoke while she kept staring into the desert: "Wouldn't you like to live in the desert Aset? There is nobody there, nobody who tells you what to do, nobody who expects anything from you.

The desert is real freedom Aset. Wouldn't you like to just leave everything behind and go into the desert?"

"Maybe if there would be an abundance of food and water, Kiya, but there is not. The desert is chaos and Egypt is order. We cannot leave our country. What would happen if we would die in the desert? Who would bury us or provide for us after our death? Our souls would be lost forever!" Aset answered excitedly, trying to talk Kiya out of her idea.

Kiya recovered quickly from her depression, looked at Aset and spoke with a forced smile: "I know that, Aset. You are always too serious. Of course I would not walk away into the desert. But it is nice to think about walking away from everything."

As soon as she had finished speaking Kiya got up and before Aset could say anything more Kiya told her: "Let's go, we will explore the rest of this orchard before it gets dark."

It was almost evening when Aset and Kiya returned to Panehsy's villa. Coming nearer they heard people calling their names and saw the guard who had arrived together with them at the villa walking around, apparently searching for them.

As soon as the guard noticed them he looked very relieved and immediately escorted them back to the villa.

Arriving there all the servants and even Panehsy himself, who had returned earlier than expected from the palace, were searching for Aset and Kiya together with the other guards who were still somewhere outside trying to find them.

Upon seeing them, Panehsy, looking pale but relieved came over, gave a small bow, and spoke: "My lady, we are relieved to have you back at our home. Your unexpected outing had us all worried."

Aset and Kiya followed Panehsy inside where he offered both of them a cup of wine.

"This is the best wine I have," Panehsy told them and went on reverently: "We will be drinking to your health, my lady. His Majesty has announced his upcoming marriage to you today."

Aset and Kiya said nothing and sipped their wine while Panehsy emptied his cup in one gulp and continued speaking: "My lady, you will be happy to hear His Majesty asks you to return to the palace tomorrow."

"Did the Pharaoh announce our marriage to everybody?" Kiya asked.

"Yes, my lady. He made a public announcement. You can imagine my surprise when I found out I had the Pharaoh's fiancée in my house," Panehsy answered smilingly and then added: "You must be hungry and tired from your little trip today. You can wash yourself and take a rest while I will have a special dinner prepared. I hope my lady will give me the honour of joining me for one last dinner tonight before your return to the palace tomorrow."

That evening Panehsy went out of his way to be the perfect host during their last dinner together. He even treated Aset courteously and she enjoyed the evening.

After dinner Aset and Kiya returned to their room. They wanted to go to sleep early because they were going to be picked up early the next morning to be taken back to Malkata Palace.

They had only just entered their room when a servant knocked on the door.

Aset opened the door and the servant spoke: "My master asks if he can speak with you for a moment."

"Your master wants to speak with me?" Aset asked surprised.

"Yes, he wants to meet you now," the servant confirmed.

Aset followed her to the room that Panehsy used as his office. Inside the office she saw Panehsy sitting behind his desk on which an oil lamp was burning; it was the only source of light in the room.

Panehsy's face appeared red in the dimmed light of the lamp and Aset could see he was drunk from all the wine he had drunk during dinner and upon seeing the wine jug and cup on his desk Aset concluded Panehsy probably had continued drinking after dinner.

"You have sent for me, my lord?" Aset asked politely after the servant had left the room.

Suddenly the face of the man who had been so friendly during dinner became flushed with anger and he got up from his chair. Aset was shocked and automatically took a step backwards but it was too late; Panehsy's fist hit Aset in her face, making her tumble backwards on the floor.

Panehsy grabbed the crying Aset by the arm, pulled her on her feet and pushed her against the wall.

With his face close to hers he yelled: "How could you be so irresponsible!"

Aset was confused and scared, she had no idea what was happening or what the reason for her host's behaviour was.

"I don't know what you are talking about!" she cried while blood started dripping from her nose.

Panehsy slapped her again and shouted: "How could you let Kiya leave my villa! You should have stopped her!"

He finally let Aset go and went to sit behind his desk again. Aset fell on her knees and spoke, still crying: "We only went for a walk and did not go very far."

Panehsy got up again after Aset's words, making her cringe but he remained standing behind his desk, not making any move towards her. He kept silent for a moment before speaking again, more composed this time but still with a lot of anger in his voice: "Do you know what the Pharaoh would do to me if anything would have happened to Kiya?"

Aset wanted to say something but was cut off by Panehsy: "His Majesty trusts me with his future wife. How would I explain it to him when she would have been assaulted by somebody or if she had been attacked by a snake or some other dangerous animal?"

Aset wanted to speak, trying to say something in her defense but Panehsy went on: "You have been extremely irresponsible and there is no excuse for your behaviour! Get out of my sight!"

Aset gladly followed the last order and left Panehsy's office as quickly as she could.

When she entered their room there was a look of horror on Kiya's face when she saw Aset.

"What did he do to you?" Kiya asked.

Aset looked down on her white dress and saw it was stained red with blood which still continued streaming from her nose.

Kiya told Aset to lie down on the bed so she could look at her face.

Aset wanted to explain what had happened but Kiya told her not to bother.

"I could hear everything here in the room," she spoke while cleaning Aset's face and trying to stop the bleeding.

After a moment Kiya went on softly: "I am so sorry. This was all my fault. If I had not talked you into following me then this would not have happened."

While Kiya took care of Aset, they could hear Panehsy yell at his servants or the guards downstairs, scolding them for not paying more attention that day.

The following morning Ipi and his family got up early to get on their way to Djehuty's grave. Ipi was tired, he had not slept well that night and had been woken up by the same nightmare that had plagued him regularly. After that he had not been able to get back to sleep anymore.

Ipi's brothers had taken a day off from their work on the farms to attend Djehuty's ceremony and Ipi's sisters who were living with their husbands on other farms in the area also joined their family.

Looking at the small group of people wearing cheap clothes and bringing only a few gifts Ipi could not help thinking of the difference with the lavish funeral procession of Crown Prince Thutmose.

The previous afternoon Ipi had been busy buying and preparing everything he needed for the ceremony for Djehuty's ka. He had even written a short letter to his nephew on a piece of pottery that he would read at his grave and then bury there.

Djehuty's grave was not very impressive, the only monument his family had managed to give him consisted of a large undecorated rock. Underneath this rock the un-mummified body of Djehuty had been put to rest, wrapped only in a sleeping mat.

His family hoped this simple burial would be enough for Djehuty to continue his life in the Netherworld.

After arrival at the burial site Ipi and his family kneeled down in front of Djehuty's grave and Ipi started the ceremony by burning incense. Then he prayed to Amun to protect Djehuty in the afterlife and to Osiris to receive him in His Kingdom.

After the prayers everybody helped digging a small hole next to the grave in which every member of the family placed products such as fruit, bread and meat and a jug of cheap wine. With these simple offerings they hoped Djehuty would be able to sustain himself in the afterlife. As an extra gift Ipi also gave his nephew the sweet cakes he had brought especially for him from Thebes.

Ipi was glad he had been able to obtain a shabti statue for Djehuty. He blessed the small statue and ordered it to come to life in the Netherworld to perform every task that Djehuty would give to it. After blessing the statue Ipi put it in the hole with the other offerings. Having a shabti would guarantee that Djehuty would not have to work in the afterlife.

Ipi knew the Pharaohs would normally take hundreds of shabtis with them after their death while most farmers could not even afford a single statue. Ipi hoped that only one shabti would be sufficient for a young peasant boy like Djehuty.

When the ceremony was almost finished Ipi read the short message he had written for Djehuty's ka:

"To the ka of my nephew Djehuty,

I deeply regret not having been at your side during a large part of your short life.
I deeply regret not having been able to support you during your illness.

To make up for my failure to be there for you during your life I promise to take care of you during your afterlife.

Your uncle Ipi"

After Ipi had finished reading his message he added the piece of pottery containing the text to all the other offerings to Djehuty, after that his family helped him with the task of filling the hole containing the offerings with sand.

As the final act of the ceremony Ipi burnt incense one more time and walked around Djehuty's small grave while holding the incense burner and praying to the jackal-headed God Anubis to protect his nephew's resting place.

When the ceremony was over Ipi's family had breakfast next to the grave.

During the ceremony for Djehuty, everybody had been very solemn and some had even cried but while they were having breakfast together everybody started to cheer up. This meal next to the grave was a festive occasion for the family because Djehuty's ka was now able to join them. It resembled the Beautiful Feast of the Valley, a celebration where the Egyptians went to the tombs of their deceased loved ones to hold a feast in which the ka's of the deceased were expected to participate.

Ipi knew his family could not afford a feast every year but they would visit Djehuty's grave regularly and Ipi would make offerings for him in the temple and visit his nephew as often as he could. As he had made a promise he was now obliged to take care of Djehuty and a promise to a deceased person should never be broken.

It was early in the morning when an escort was already waiting to return Aset and Kiya to Malkata Palace.

Upon seeing the escort they were overwhelmed. Aset and Kiya were not returning by chariot, as they had expected, but instead there was a litter flanked by soldiers and servants waiting for them.

The escort was led by Ranefer and Hekanakht, the Head of the Royal Guard who had also escorted them on their way to Panehsy's villa.

Ignoring Aset, Ranefer greeted Kiya with a bow and spoke: "My lady, it is my honour to escort you back to Malkata Palace."

Kiya did not know what to say, she had not expected to meet her former superior under such circumstances.

Feeling confused she simply answered: "Thank you."

Adding to Kiya's confusion Ranefer replied: "Don't thank me my lady. Please consider me as your loyal servant."

Then, while holding out a beautifully decorated box to Kiya, he went on speaking: "This box contains a dress and jewellery. His Majesty asks my lady to wear these upon her return to the palace."

Aset and Kiya went back to their room in the villa followed by an older woman who had taken over the box containing the dress and jewellery from Ranefer.

In their room the woman asked Kiya to undress and then washed her at the washbasin which had been refilled by Panehsy's servants. Aset wanted to help but the woman, whose name she knew to be Titi and who worked as one of the Royal Family's beauticians, told her not to interfere.

After Kiya had been washed, fragrant oil was rubbed into her skin and her hair was oiled and combed. Then Titi started to apply cosmetics on Kiya's face and on her finger- and toenails.

When finished with the cosmetics she took a high quality white linen dress out of the box Ranefer had given to her and helped Kiya to put it on. When Kiya was wearing the dress Titi continued with jewellery including bracelets, rings, earrings and the wesekh collar, a broad collar made of many rows of beads strung together.

After she had finished Titi took two steps back to look at Kiya who was standing in middle of the room and clearly felt uneasy.

"Perfect!" she exclaimed, satisfied with the result of her work and told Kiya: "As soon as you learn how to assume the self-confident bearing of a member of the Royal Family you will be a real queen!"

In the space of only an hour Aset had seen her friend change from a young outgoing girl into a member of the Royal Family. She was very impressed with Kiya's new appearance.

"You look like a real queen," was the only thing Aset managed to say to Kiya in a whispered tone.

The beautician looked at Kiya one more time to convince herself once more that her work was perfect and then bowed for Kiya and spoke: "My lady, you are ready to meet your husband. Allow me to escort you to your litter."

When they returned outside everybody was still waiting, as if they had been away for only two minutes.

Like nothing had happened the night before Panehsy was standing in the doorway of his villa to say farewell and to wish Kiya good luck in her new life at the Royal Court. Kiya, however, ignored him, walking past Panehsy without looking at him. Aset followed Kiya and, while passing Panehsy, demonstratively rubbed her face which was still hurting.

Outside Ranefer invited Kiya to enter the litter. Unfortunately for Aset, Ranefer did not accept a servant in the litter, not even when Kiya pleaded with him.

"The Pharaoh would not allow it," the Head of the Royal Servants explained.

After Kiya had taken her place in the litter Ranefer gave a signal to Hekanakht who shouted a command to the soldiers who immediately jumped to attention.

Four bearers picked up Kiya's litter and the procession started to move.

They were followed by four more bearers who would take over the task of carrying the litter during the second half of the journey to Thebes where the Royal Bark would be waiting to bring Kiya to the palace.

With her litter flanked on both sides by fan bearers who kept her cool Kiya traveled to Thebes while Aset followed her friend on foot.

CHAPTER 8
RETURN TO THE PALACE
AND
ANOTHER DELAY FOR HEMIENU

"The Great Royal Wife welcomes her sister at Malkata Palace!" Nefertiti spoke to Kiya when she disembarked at the palace dock.

"Thank you, my lady, I am honoured to be personally welcomed by the Great Royal Wife," Kiya replied politely.

"Nothing is too much for my sister," Nefertiti spoke again with a friendly smile and went on: "And don't call me 'my lady' or Great Royal Wife, we are sisters now."

Nefertiti put her arm around Kiya's shoulder and escorted her past the assembled guards and servants to Amenhotep and the rest of the Royal Family who were waiting to welcome the Pharaoh's fiancée.

Aset followed behind them, she was exhausted from the long walk from Panehsy's villa to Thebes but luckily had had some time to recover on the Royal Bark during the crossing of the Nile to the west bank.

She was pleasantly surprised by the warm welcome Kiya received from Nefertiti. Aset had not expected such a friendly welcome from the Great Royal Wife after her previous behavior towards Kiya which had been especially cold and distant since the moment Amenhotep had given Kiya the bracelet.

Hopefully, Aset thought, Kiya and Nefertiti would be able to maintain a good relationship, this would make Kiya's life at the court much easier.

When Nefertiti and Kiya met the Pharaoh, Nefertiti announced solemnly: "Your Majesty, my sister Kiya has arrived to join your court."

"I have missed you, Kiya. Welcome home!" Amenhotep spoke and then asked: "I expect you had a comfortable journey?"

"Yes, Your Majesty, it was very comfortable," Kiya replied.

"Did lord Panehsy take good care of you during your stay at his villa?" Amenhotep continued asking.

"Yes, Your Majesty, I was very well taken care of by lord Panehsy," Kiya answered again.

Aset heard Kiya emphasizing the word 'I' in her reply but nobody noticed it or cared about what she meant by that.

The Pharaoh's mother, Queen Teye, was the only person who did not seem happy.

When Kiya greeted her, Teye replied in her typical strict voice: "As a mere servant you will have a lot to learn, Kiya. It takes more than a pretty face to be part of the Royal Family."

After all the smiles and the warm welcome she had received Kiya did not know what to answer but the Pharaoh saved her, putting his arm protectively around Kiya's shoulders he spoke: "Please mother, let us all enjoy this moment. We can talk about the more serious business later."

"You are right, my husband," Nefertiti added and looking at Kiya she continued: "Kiya must be tired from her long journey. She should be taken to her chambers where she can rest."

Nefertiti personally escorted Kiya to her private apartment in the palace.

Being Kiya's personal servant Aset followed her together with Nefertiti's servants.

Queen Teye's unfriendly reaction to Kiya's arrival had surprised Aset almost as much as Nefertiti's friendly welcome. Remembering that Teye also was not of Royal origin, even though she was nobility and not a member of the common people like Kiya, Aset had hoped Teye would show more understanding for Kiya's difficult position.

"Hello Aset," Aset heard somebody whisper to her from behind while they walked through one of the palace's brightly coloured passages. She looked behind her and stared in Sitre's face.

"Nice to see you again, Aset," Sitre spoke smilingly.

"I am also happy to see you again," Aset replied. Sitre's smile disappeared almost immediately and the young girl turned serious. She took Aset by her arm and slowed her pace down until there was enough distance between them and Nefertiti and Kiya with the rest of their escort.

"Aset," Sitre whispered. "You have to warn Kiya to be careful of Nefertiti!"

"Why?" Aset asked and went on in a voice that betrayed her wonder: "Nefertiti seems to be very friendly to Kiya."

"I know," Sitre replied and explained: "She is friendly because the Pharaoh wants her to be friendly. Or maybe she wants to gain Kiya's trust and later use that against her. But I know how she really thinks about Kiya. Nefertiti is very jealous of her and regards her as a threat to her position!"

"Are you sure about this?" Aset asked.

Sitre looked around to see if nobody could hear them and then spoke: "Just imagine that Kiya would give birth to a son, the heir to the throne, instead of Nefertiti!"

As soon as Sitre had finished speaking she let go of Aset and quickly joined her mistress again, leaving Aset behind with her thoughts about the warning she had just received until she also hurried to rejoin her own mistress.

Two days after he had conducted the ceremony for Djehuty Ipi returned to Karnak Temple.

In spite of the tragic news of Djehuty's death he had still enjoyed the time with his family and he hoped he would get the opportunity to visit them more often.

On his way back Ipi hoped that the tensions he had felt in the temple before he left would have been eased but not long after his return he found out they weren't.

As soon as he arrived at Karnak Ipi went to see Intef at his practice to notify him of his return.

When he arrived there he did not find Intef but instead he found Mereruka who told him Intef went to a meeting of all the high ranking priests of Karnak in the Precinct of Mut.

Seeing there were not many patients at that moment Ipi decided to go to the Precinct of Mut.

Wenamun would most likely be there too and he wanted to ask him whether what he had done for the ka of Djehuty was enough or if more was needed for Djehuty to survive in the Kingdom of Osiris.

Ipi walked down an avenue lined with trees that connected the Precinct of Amun to the precinct of his wife, the Goddess Mut.

Arriving at her temple Ipi saw a group of priests and priestesses standing next to a crescent shaped lake, which Ipi knew to be the sacred lake of Mut's Temple.

As he expected Wenamun was there too together with his wife Tahat who by now had risen to the rank of First Chantress of Amun.

Ipi remained standing at a discreet distance but was close enough to be able to overhear that they were talking about the donations from the Royal Palace to the temple.

Maya, the Second Prophet of Amun, was addressing Meryptah, the High Priest: "It is a fact that the donations to the temple coming from the Royal Palace are only half of what we received during the reign of the previous Pharaoh."

After his remark Maya looked to another priest and asked: "Isn't that correct, Hai?"

Hai, the treasurer of the Temple of Amun, answered: "Yes, my lord. Our current Pharaoh is not as generous as his father. However, I would like to add that I have heard from sources in the palace treasury that the Pharaoh gives less donations and gifts to all the temples and diplomatic relations. So the Pharaoh giving us smaller donations does not necessarily have anything to do with his obvious dislike to the God Amun. I have heard the Pharaoh is saving his resources for some big project."

"Probably to build more temples for the Aten," Maya remarked wryly and went on speaking: "So maybe his small donations are not meant as an insult to the temple. But the way he ignores us is an insult! The Royal Palace and Karnak Temple have always maintained a good relationship until this Pharaoh came on the throne."

Maya looked at Meryptah again and urged him: "My lord, we have been waiting for too long now, we have to do something. The Pharaoh ignores us but right next to our temple he is constructing a new temple for a God that might replace Amun in the future. It is time for us to act!"

The old and visibly exhausted Meryptah had patiently listened to the Second Prophet of Amun and asked: "What is it that you suggest to do Maya?"

"We have to remind the Pharaoh of his sacred duty towards the Karnak Temple," Maya replied with a strong conviction.

Intef, who favoured Meryptah's cautious policy towards the Pharaoh, broke into the conversation and spoke: "If we would remind the Pharaoh of his duties towards us he would most likely regard that as an insult. It will not make our situation any better."

"I know that," Maya spoke again. "But it will force him to talk to us, or give some kind of reaction. Maybe then we will know how much the Temple of Amun is still worth to him."

"The idea is good," Meryptah replied but then continued: "But, as Intef mentioned, the Pharaoh will regard it as an insult and, Maya, I also would like to start a dialogue with the Pharaoh but on positive terms."

The younger Maya respected his older superior, who also had been his mentor, very much but sometimes he thought Meryptah was too cautious to lead the temple during this crisis period.

"The Pharaoh is not going to invite us for a friendly dialogue, my lord. We have been waiting long enough for that," Maya replied with his annoyance clearly audible for everybody.

"Maybe I have an idea," a new voice interrupted the discussion. It was Tahat, Wenamun's wife.

"We all know the Pharaoh is getting married in two weeks," Tahat spoke. "Traditionally every Royal Wedding includes a blessing ceremony in the temple. Why don't we send a delegation to the palace to personally invite the Pharaoh and his new wife to Karnak for a ceremony. The Pharaoh cannot be upset by us inviting him and his reply to our invitation will most likely tell us something about how much we still mean to him."

"That is a good idea!" Meryptah exclaimed. "Do you agree with that, Maya?"

"Yes, my lord, I agree. We can await the Pharaoh's reaction to our invitation and after that we can decide our policy towards the Pharaoh," the Second Prophet of Amun replied.

Ipi had been overhearing the discussion. He was shocked by the appearance of Meryptah who looked older than when he last saw him, the responsibilities of his high position during this difficult period were taking their toll. He wondered how much longer Meryptah would be able to survive and what would happen after that.

When Meryptah would die, the more aggressive Second Prophet of Amun, Maya, would succeed him as the next High Priest and Ipi was not sure anymore whether he favoured a High Priest who searched the confrontation with Pharaoh Amenhotep.

"Hello Ipi, what are you doing here?" Wenamun's voice woke him up out of his thoughts.

Startled, Ipi for a moment forgot why he came there but then he remembered Djehuty and spoke: "I came to ask your advice about offerings to the ka of a dead relative."

It was the evening of the day they arrived back at Malkata Palace.

Aset was thinking whether she would pass on Sitre's warning to Kiya or not. She cared about Kiya's safety but also did not want to make her worried, especially since Kiya seemed to enjoy herself so much since she returned to the palace.

The friendly welcome by the Pharaoh and Nefertiti had done her good. They had even invited her for a festive dinner where she had been celebrated like a guest of honour.

Amenhotep had given Kiya a private apartment in the palace compared to which Panehsy's villa appeared poor. The apartment consisted of several rooms including a living area, a sleeping area and a room for washing and bathing. Kiya even had her own kitchen with a cook so she could have her meals in her own room when Amenhotep did not ask her to join him. All the rooms were richly furnished and the walls freshly painted. Aset could read a little and recognized Kiya's name together with the Pharaoh's name on the wall under a depiction of the Pharaoh with a lady. The areas where Kiya's titles were supposed to be written were still blank and would probably only be filled in after the wedding.

"Maybe I was wrong and life in the palace will be good," Kiya spoke. "Everybody is so kind to me."

They were in Kiya's bedroom. Kiya was lying on her comfortable bed while Aset was sitting on a chair next to her. Aset had her own small room next to Kiya's room so she could always be available to her but Kiya did not want to sleep alone and asked Aset to stay with her.

"Amenhotep is so friendly and Nefertiti is also so good to me," Kiya went on.

Hearing Kiya speaking Aset decided to wait with warning her about Nefertiti and to let her enjoy the moment.

"They told me I was going to learn how to read and write and how to behave like a real queen," Kiya spoke again enthusiastically.

"You have to go to school before you can marry the Pharaoh?" Aset asked jokingly.

"No, of course not!" Kiya replied, pretending not to understand Aset was joking and, speaking in a serious tone, she continued: "I will have my own private teacher who will teach me everything I need to know."

"Maybe it will be a young and handsome man," Aset remarked smilingly.

"I hope so. I am sure he would be able to teach me a lot," Kiya replied and both burst out laughing.

At that moment the door to Kiya's room opened, Aset and Kiya looked up and saw the Pharaoh entering the room.

Unlike usually, he was not accompanied by any servants or guards.

Aset quickly jumped up from her chair, bowed and spoke: "I apologize Your Majesty, we did not expect you to honour us with your presence."

Amenhotep ignored her and with a strange expression on his face and his eyes fixated on Kiya who was getting out of her bed he simply replied: "Get out Aset!"

Next he went on speaking in a friendly tone to Kiya: "You don't have to get up for me, Kiya. We are family now."

Aset hurried to the door of the room but before she left she looked back and saw Amenhotep sitting down on the side of Kiya's bed and noticed fear in

Kiya's eyes. For a moment Aset hesitated but then she left the room.

Not knowing what to do Aset went to her own room right next to Kiya's where she would wait for the Pharaoh to leave.

Her room was dark and when Aset was trying to light her oil lamp she heard Kiya's voice coming from the room; first it sounded begging but a short time later it turned into crying. Aset dropped her oil lamp and sat in the dark against the wall with her hands pressed against her ears, trying in vain to block out the sounds coming from Kiya's room.

The next morning Penthu found the Pharaoh in a particularly good mood. He was in his private quarters when Amenhotep had him called to the audience hall. The hall was filled with high officials and Amenhotep and Nefertiti were sitting on their thrones. Clearly the Pharaoh expected important visitors.

Penthu walked up to Amenhotep's throne to greet the Pharaoh but Amenhotep greeted him already before Penthu could say anything: "Good morning Penthu, I am glad you have come."

"I thank you for your invitation, Your Majesty," Penthu replied.

"I have interesting visitors this morning, Penthu, and I thought you might want to attend when I give them an audience," Amenhotep informed Penthu.

"I once again thank you for remembering me, Your Majesty. May I ask who these visitors are?" Penthu spoke, wondering what kind of audience needed his attendance.

"A delegation of the Amun Temple has asked for an audience and I have decided to grant it," the

Pharaoh answered and continued: "I thought you, as a former priest of Amun, might want to attend this audience."

Cold shivers ran down Penthu's spine and he replied: "Your Majesty, I am still a priest of Amun, I have left the temple but not the priesthood."

"Of course you are still a priest, Penthu, how clumsy of me," Amenhotep answered with a smile and then spoke, while pointing at an empty place next to his throne: "Your friends can come any moment, come and stand next to my throne when I meet them."

Penthu felt uneasy, being invited to stand next to the Pharaoh's throne was a great honour but knowing very well how Amenhotep thought about the priests of Amun, Penthu did not know what to think of the Pharaoh's gesture: Was he really honouring him? Was it meant as a way of taunting the delegation from Karnak? Was it maybe a way of taunting him? Or did the Pharaoh maybe want to show everybody, including Penthu himself, that he belonged on the Pharaoh's side?

The Pharaoh told the Royal Announcer that he was ready and he could announce the delegation of the Karnak Temple who had been kept waiting outside the audience hall.

When they entered Penthu immediately recognized Maya, the Second Prophet of Amun, Wenamun, the Third Prophet of Amun and Wennefer, a young but high ranking priest at Karnak Temple.

The priests walked up to the Pharaoh's throne and bowed. Wenamun and Wennefer pretended not to notice Penthu but for just a short time Penthu's eyes met Maya's and during that moment Penthu noticed a burning anger in the priest's glance which immediately disappeared again.

Maya started to speak politely: "Greetings Your Majesty. The High Priest of Amun, Meryptah, sends you his well wishes and prays that the Great Lord Amun will grant you many years on the throne!"

When Maya finished speaking he waited for the Pharaoh to acknowledge his greeting but the Pharaoh did not reply, causing a silence that left Maya and the two other priests feeling extremely uncomfortable.

In an attempt to end the uncomfortable situation, Maya went on speaking: "The High Priest of Amun congratulates Your Majesty on the upcoming wedding and informs Your Majesty that the Temple of Amun is at your service to perform the blessing ceremony in the presence of Amun as the holy tradition requires."

After he had finished speaking Maya held out a papyrus roll to the Pharaoh and added: "This is a personal message from the High Priest to Your Majesty, he wants good relations to exist between the palace and the Temple of Amun."

"Penthu, take that message and hand it to me," Amenhotep spoke and then continued speaking to Maya: "Why does Meryptah, the High Priest of Amun, not come personally to convey his message to his Pharaoh? Why does he insult me by sending mere servants?"

Penthu felt his heart beating in his chest when he walked to Maya to take over Meryptah's message while hearing the Pharaoh accusing the High Priest of insolence.

When Maya handed him the papyrus roll Penthu avoided looking at him finding it too uncomfortable. Penthu quickly walked back to

Amenhotep and handed him the message which the Pharaoh left unopened.

Maya, in the meantime, replied to the Pharaoh: "The High Priest apologizes for not being able to come personally. His fragile health unfortunately prevents him from leaving the temple."

"That is indeed very unfortunate. I hope he will recover soon!" Amenhotep replied but by the lack of emotion with which it was said Penthu knew he did not mean it.

Amenhotep seemed to think a short moment about what to say but then continued speaking: "I do hope that what I am going to say is not going to damage the fragile health of your High Priest any further but I am afraid that I will have to disappoint him by not accepting his offer."

"I deeply regret your decision, Your Majesty," Maya replied and went on in a loud tone so everybody could clearly hear him: "May I remind Your Majesty of the holy traditions and the long existing relationship between the Royal Palace and the Temple of Amun? And my I remind you of your duty to maintain Ma'at?"

After Maya's last words all the murmur in the audience hall suddenly stopped. Accusing the Pharaoh in public of neglecting his duties towards Ma'at, which stood for justice, cosmic order and harmony and had to be maintained by the Pharaoh through correctly performing his religious duties, was unheard of.

"No you may not!" Amenhotep snapped at Maya, standing up from his throne and losing the calm demeanor which he had maintained throughout the meeting.

Standing in front of his throne on the raised platform the Pharaoh pointed down at Maya and yelled: "Who do you think you are to lecture your Pharaoh?"

Everybody in the hall held their breath and Wenamun and Wennefer, both standing next to Maya, turned white.

Equally shocked, Penthu silently prayed to Amun to guard Maya's speech and to restrain the Pharaoh.

The only person who seemed to remain calm was Maya who stood defiantly opposite Amenhotep who was breathing heavily while trying to control himself.

Finally Amenhotep sat down again apparently having regained the calm composure he had before.

However, when he went on speaking his voice betrayed his continuing anger: "As I told you, I have to reject your offer. I don't feel bound by the traditions and relationships of my forefathers. The wedding will be blessed by the Aten in the Gem Pa Aten. Meryra, the High Priest of the Aten, will conduct the ceremony."

While speaking the Pharaoh pointed at a priest who stood close to the throne and was wearing the insignia of the Aten. When Maya looked at him the priest smiled and greeted him with a slight bow.

Maya turned again to the Pharaoh and remarked, genuinely surprised: "Your Majesty, I don't mean to be insolent but the wedding is in two weeks and the Gem Pa Aten is far from finished."

"The temple does not have to be finished for Aten to bless my marriage. The land on which the wedding will take place has been consecrated and belongs to Aten, that is the most important," Amenhotep replied, this time not being offended by Maya's words and then added curtly: "I believe you now have an answer which you can deliver to Meryptah. This audience is now over."

As soon as he had finished speaking Amenhotep got up from his throne and walked away, followed by Nefertiti who had remained silent throughout the whole meeting.

Maya and the two other priests, surprised by the sudden end of the audience, after some hesitation turned and started to walk out of the hall while Penthu hurried after them.

"I see you have risen in the Royal Court, Penthu," Maya spoke when Penthu caught up with them.

"I was only invited to the audience because you were coming," Penthu explained his presence and continued: "You should not have provoked the Pharaoh, Maya. This did not do the position of the Amun Temple any good."

"Are you implying that I damaged the position of the temple?" Maya exclaimed. "For somebody who lives in the presence of the Pharaoh you seem to be very badly informed, Penthu. The temple means nothing to the Pharaoh but nobody seems to dare to confront the Pharaoh with the fact that he is neglecting his sacred duties. Today I decided to do that!"

Penthu wanted to say something in the Pharaoh's defense but Wenamun was faster and spoke: "Maya was right to confront the Pharaoh with his negligence, Penthu. The position of the temple could hardly get any worse. Didn't you notice the Pharaoh did not even care to read Meryptah's message?"

"And don't forget that the Pharaoh had already turned down Meryptah's offer before Maya upset him," Wennefer added to the conversation.

"But you don't know the Pharaoh like I do. He usually listens to me. I can try to influence him positively. Please be careful not to do anything hasty," Penthu pleaded.

"Penthu," Maya spoke, looking him straight in the eyes. "You will have to decide on whose side you want to be. You are either with the Pharaoh or with us, you can't be on both sides."

Maya finished speaking but then, after a short silence, he added slowly: "But maybe you have decided already and you just don't know it yet."

After the last remark Maya turned and, just like the Pharaoh before, walked away without any further words, followed by Wenamun and Wennefer, leaving Penthu alone.

Penthu had never been a very social person and never felt the need of having people around him. That morning, however, he felt truly lonely. He wondered how his life had turned so complicated; he only wanted to be a physician which was what he was good at and what he enjoyed doing but now he felt being torn apart between the two strongest powers in Egypt: the Royal Court and the Amun priesthood.

Hemienu walked over the construction site of the Gem Pa Aten. It was a noisy place with everywhere the sound of hammering and chiseling and workmen yelling at each other.

The noise, however, pleased Hemienu, it meant progress of his temple. Work actually progressed so well that he was feeling confident they would be able to finish the temple in time. They had almost made up for the time they had lost because of the accident and all technical problems had been solved.

The Pharaoh kept a close watch on the progress of the construction and every day sent inspectors to the site who reported back to him. Hemienu did not mind these inspectors because they never interfered with his work and through them he could request from the Pharaoh everything he needed and the Pharaoh always gave him everything he requested whether it was more workmen, material, tools or anything else.

Even though Hemienu still considered the Pharaoh to be very demanding he liked the way he was leading his project. Apart from sending inspectors the Pharaoh also regularly summoned Hemienu to the palace to personally report to him about the progress of the Gem Pa Aten. This also gave Hemienu opportunities for making requests and suggestions about changes in the construction of the temple. The Pharaoh never rejected his suggestions without considering them; instead, he always listened to Hemienu's advice and thought about it carefully before taking a decision.

After he had finished his round over the construction site Hemienu returned to his working place which consisted of only a simple desk laden with papyruses containing plans of the Gem Pa Aten and lists of building materials, tools and provisions for his workmen. Hemienu was responsible for everything on the site.

The only shade Hemienu had while working at his desk came from a simple canopy made out of the leaves of palm trees.

Returning under his shady canopy Hemienu found a man waiting for him whom he immediately recognized to be Hatiay, the Aten priest who had visited the temple during the construction accident.

He was not surprised to see Hatiay since he regularly visited the temple. Over time Hemienu had got to like Hatiay who was a reasonable person as long as they were not discussing religious matters.

That morning, however, Hemienu thought Hatiay looked particularly serious which made him afraid something could be wrong.

"Good morning, my lord," Hemienu greeted the priest and asked: "Is something troubling you?"

"I see work is progressing well. You are doing a very good job, Hemienu!" Hatiay replied not answering Hemienu's question.

"Yes, my workmen have been working very hard every day from sunrise to sunset," Hemienu spoke, feeling proud of the accomplishment of both his workers and himself and added: "We are almost on schedule again and I expect to be able to finish the temple within the time the Pharaoh has set for us!"

Hatiay looked a bit uncomfortable but did not say anything so Hemienu went on: "I don't think you came here to compliment us on our progress. What is it that you want to tell me, my lord?"

"You have probably heard about the upcoming wedding of His Majesty?" Hatiay asked.

"Of course, everybody must have heard about that," Hemienu replied wondering what Hatiay wanted.

"His Majesty has decided to get married here in the temple," Hatiay spoke after a moment of hesitation.

"But the temple is not finished and the wedding will be soon!" Hemienu exclaimed. "Even Ptah, the Great Creator, could not finish the temple on time!"

The moment Hemienu mentioned the God Ptah he regretted it, fearing he might have offended the

Aten priest who, just like the Pharaoh, did not seem to have much sympathy for the old Gods.

To Hemienu's great relief Hatiay was not in the mood for an argument and simply replied: "Please, Hemienu, remember that we are on the sacred ground of the Aten."

After these words the Aten priest kept silent for a moment but then went on: "And that sacred ground is also the reason why the Pharaoh wants his wedding ceremony to take place here. This land belongs to Aten and is the most sacred piece of ground of the Two Lands."

"And what is that going to mean for us?" Hemienu asked, gesturing at his workers who were still continuing their work.

"You will have to stop your work temporarily," Hatiay replied and added: "His Majesty also wants you to remove all the scaffolds and to make the site as presentable as possible. The temple must breathe a holy atmosphere and should not look like a construction site."

"But it is a construction site!" Hemienu exclaimed, starting to get angry, and then complained: "Breaking all the scaffolds down while having to build them up again later and not being able to do any construction until after the wedding will set us far back on schedule! We will never be able to finish the Gem Pa Aten on time!"

"I understand your complaints, Hemienu," Hatiay spoke in an effort to calm the architect down but then went on in a strict tone: "But I am afraid you have no option but to do what you are told. We all have to listen to our Pharaoh."

While speaking Hatiay produced a papyrus roll out of his robe, broke the seal and opened it.

Without waiting for Hemienu to say something he continued to speak: "His Majesty knows that part of the structure of the Holy of Holies is finished so he wants the ceremony to take place there."

Hatiay handed the opened papyrus roll to Hemienu, pointed at its contents and spoke: "His Majesty wants your artists to paint these scenes of the Aten giving life to him and his new wife together with these prayers to the Aten on the walls of the Holy of Holies and the Sun Court."

Hemienu looked at the drawings and texts on the papyrus roll and after some moments resigned himself to the situation and answered reluctantly: "Of course I will do as His Majesty wishes."

Hatiay smiled and replied: "Of course you will, I did not expect anything different. I will now return to the palace to inform His Majesty the temple will be ready on time for his wedding."

While Hatiay walked away Hemienu sighed, got out from underneath his canopy into the burning sun and shouted at his workers: "Everybody stop your work immediately!"

The Pharaoh's reply to Meryptah's offer came as another blow to the priests of Karnak even though it was expected.

After Maya, Wenamun and Wennefer had returned from the palace they went immediately to Meryptah's office to report about the audience with Amenhotep. The meeting with Meryptah was meant to remain confidential but somehow its contents started to circulate amongst the priests in the temple later that day.

After Maya had given his report to the High Priest, Meryptah looked like a defeated man and spoke softly: "I have done everything to maintain good relations with the Royal Palace. Today I have extended a hand of friendship to the Pharaoh but he did not accept it. Maybe you were right after all Maya. Maybe I was wrong to believe that everything was going to be fine as long as we do not upset the Pharaoh and pretend nothing is happening."

Upon Maya's question if Meryptah was ready to follow a harder line against the palace the High Priest just answered: "I don't know Maya, I really don't know. I will go to the Holy of Holies and pray to Amun. I hope He will tell me what to do."

The old priest was weak and Maya had to support him on his way to the holiest part of the temple where the statue of Amun was being kept. There, Meryptah wanted to be left alone and gave orders not to be disturbed by anybody.

Ipi had also heard about the priests who had returned from the palace and was trying to find Wenamun. He was just as concerned about the position of the temple as everybody else but he was also hoping to hear some news about Penthu, his former mentor.

When Ipi finally found Wenamun in his private room he found an exhausted looking man.

"Forgive me if I come at an inconvenient moment, my lord," Ipi apologized.

"Don't worry about that, Ipi," Wenamun reassured him and asked: "What can I do for you?"

"I heard you were in the palace this morning and I wanted to know if you heard something about Penthu," Ipi asked.

"I met Penthu this morning," Wenamun replied and then stopped for a moment, thinking about what to say, before continuing: "Penthu is doing well in the Royal Palace. You don't have to worry about him."

"Did he say something?" Ipi kept inquiring.

"Not much, Ipi, but you should go now. I am tired and have a lot to think about," Wenamun replied, starting to sound a little irritated.

Confused about Wenamun's unusual behaviour Ipi wandered back to his room when he saw a group of priests standing in the shade of a large pillared hall. Amongst the assembled priests Ipi recognized Maya and Nebamun so he walked over to see what was happening.

"Should you not wait for Meryptah to return from the Holy of Holies?" Ipi heard a priest ask to which Maya replied: "We have waited long enough and, besides that, there is nothing wrong with having a meeting with the High Priest of the Southern Temple."

"Is Maya going to the Southern Temple?" Ipi asked Nebamun.

"Yes, our sister temple's relationship with the Pharaoh is as bad as ours. Just like us, until now, the priests there have ignored the situation but Maya thinks we will have a better chance against the Pharaoh when we stand together," Nebamun replied.

"He is right about that but that is a decision for Meryptah, not for Maya or Amunherkhepeshef, who is the High Priest of the Southern Temple but still subordinate to the High Priest of Amun," Ipi spoke.

"Maya has decided to meet Amunherkhepeshef without asking permission of Meryptah. If Meryptah still refuses to take a harder line against the Pharaoh he hopes he will have a strong ally in

Amunherkhepeshef to help him to convince Meryptah," Nebamun explained.

When Maya went to the Southern Temple he was joined by a small group of priests who agreed with his idea or just followed out of curiosity.

Trailed by Ipi and Nebamun, the small party crossed the avenue which ran through the centre of Thebes and connected the two temples of Amun.

Arriving at the Southern Temple Maya asked to meet Amunherkhepeshef, the temple's High Priest, who was immediately ready to meet him.

"Welcome to the Southern Temple, Maya. How nice of you to visit us," the High Priest spoke, clearly happy with the unexpected visitor.

"Thank you, Amunherkhepeshef," Maya replied but then continued: "Unfortunately, however, this is not just a normal visit. I came here to discuss our relations with the Royal Palace with you."

"I understand, maybe we should discuss this somewhere where we have more privacy," Amunherkhepeshef spoke, gesturing at the other priests who respectfully kept a distance but still tried to overhear what the two high ranking priests were talking about.

"No!" Maya replied resolutely and explained while also gesturing at the priests: "They are also priests of Amun and this concerns them as well. We can speak here!"

While listening to the conversation of Maya and Amunherkhepeshef, Ipi looked around him.

They were standing on a large open court that connected to a colonnade which led in the direction of the Holy of Holies. A big part of this temple, Ipi knew, had been built by the Pharaoh's father, the great builder Amenhotep the Third.

The Southern Temple was only about three kilometers from Karnak and Ipi had visited it already a few times but it still impressed him every time he returned, even though this temple was not built on such a large scale as Karnak Temple.

"I agree with you that we cannot ignore this situation any longer and I am willing to help you to try to convince Meryptah to take a firmer stand against the Pharaoh," Ipi heard Amunherkhepeshef say. "But before I do that we should agree on what steps we are willing to take. We must always consider the safety of our temples. I don't want to provoke a violent reaction from the Pharaoh."

"Of course, I agree with you on that but if we don't do anything the Pharaoh will think we are weak and who knows what will happen to us then?" Maya replied and added: "We must show him somehow that we are a force he cannot keep ignoring. We must make it clear to him that Amun deserves the respect and worship that the previous Pharaohs gave Him."

Priests of the Southern Temple started to join the priests who had followed Maya and they started their own discussions amongst each other; some priests wanting to stay passive and others to be more aggressive towards the Pharaoh.

Here and there the discussions started to get heated which made Nebamun remark to Ipi: "This situation is splitting our priests into two different factions. If nothing will change soon we will be doing more damage to the temple ourselves than the Pharaoh could ever do."

After a while the discussions had got so heated that only a few people noticed the messenger from Karnak who ran into the court and went straight to Maya.

"Forgive me, my lord," the messenger spoke in an urgent voice to the Second Prophet of Amun, interrupting his conversation with Amunherkhepeshef. "The High Priest Meryptah is not well and you are urgently needed at Karnak! There is already a chariot waiting for you in front of the temple to take you back."

Maya did not waste any time and immediately ran out of the temple, followed by Amunherkhepeshef.

On his way out Maya noticed Ipi and spoke: "Ipi, come back to Karnak with me. Intef might need you!"

Aset was feeling bored. Queen Teye had insisted on Kiya's lesson on Royal etiquette to take place in her private chambers so she would be able to observe it personally but she did not allow any other servants except her own to enter and her chamberlain Kheruef maintained this rule strictly.

So after delivering a very nervous Kiya to Teye's chambers Aset had nothing to do.

Feeling hungry she decided to go to the palace bakery where the bakers usually gave her a piece of freshly baked bread or cake.

Leaving Teye's chambers and passing the Pharaoh's private chambers which were next to his mother's she met Merykare, the Royal Scribe.

"Hello Aset, nice to have you back in the palace again," the scribe spoke friendly.

Aset was surprised and did not know how to answer. She had secretly liked Merykare for a long time but never dared to say anything because, like most scribes, he seemed arrogant, not like the kind of person who would get involved with a simple servant. Aset could actually not remember him ever talking to her before.

"Ah, uhm, yes I am happy to see you again too, I mean to be back in the palace again," Aset stuttered and blushed.

"I am happy to hear that," Merykare answered smilingly and added: "I hope you won't be leaving us again Aset."

Without waiting for any further words from Aset, Merykare continued to the Pharaoh's chambers, leaving behind a happily confused Aset.

When, some time later, Aset entered the bakery she was welcomed by Harkhuf, the chief baker at the Royal Palace: "Ah, Aset, what a surprise to see you again. My staff and I have missed your and Kiya's visits every morning."

"I am also happy to meet everybody here again," Aset replied, looking at all the bakers who were busy with their work in the hot and uncomfortable environment between the many burning ovens preparing bread and pastries for the Royal Family and everybody else that lived or worked in the palace.

"But I am afraid Kiya will not come to visit here anymore," Aset went on speaking.

"We have heard about that," Harkhuf replied. "Soon you will have a Royal Wife as your best friend."

"Maybe," Aset answered. "Or maybe I will lose a friend and just have a new mistress to serve."

"Don't be so negative Aset, you should know Kiya better than that. She will always be your friend," Harkhuf reprimanded her while taking some pieces of bread out of one of the large ovens. He took one of the freshly baked pieces of bread, sweetened it with honey and offered it to Aset while speaking: "Just remember that whatever happens, you will always have us!"

At that moment Sitre entered the bakery to fetch bread and cakes for Nefertiti. Aset noticed she was very tired.

"Are you all right?" she asked, feeling concerned about the young new servant who probably had the most difficult mistress of all the servants in the palace.

"I am fine," Sitre replied and continued in a lowered voice so nobody except Aset could hear her: "It is just that the Great Royal Wife is very unhappy about the wedding between Amenhotep and Kiya and that makes her act difficult. And now the Pharaoh has also decided to have the wedding ceremony in the new Aten Temple which means that the first ceremony in the Pharaoh's new temple will be his wedding with Kiya. My mistress is jealous and sees Kiya as a threat, so please Aset, take good care of Kiya!"

Harkhuf also offered a piece of sweetened bread to Sitre but she was too much in a hurry, took what the Queen had ordered and disappeared again after quickly reminding Aset: "Remember, take good care of Kiya!"

"That poor child," Harkhuf remarked in a compassionate voice to nobody in particular. "She is running all day for the Great Royal Wife with hardly any moment of rest."

Then he turned to Aset and went on: "You see, Aset, you are very lucky to work for Kiya!"

Penthu felt like a broken man. He had been thinking about the situation he was in and his position at the court. The audience with the priests of Karnak that morning and his private confrontation with them afterwards had shaken him.

He decided not to remain passive anymore and to confront the Pharaoh about what was happening and what he wanted from him. He had asked for a private meeting with Amenhotep and to his surprise he received it immediately.

Standing in front of the doors of the Pharaoh's private office and remembering the Pharaoh's anger when being criticized by Maya that morning Penthu started to wonder whether his idea was very wise but it was too late to turn back.

The doors of Amenhotep's office opened and Sahure, the Pharaoh's personal assistant, invited Penthu to enter after which he himself left the office and closed the doors behind him. Penthu was alone with the Pharaoh.

Amenhotep sat kneeling on a cushion in front of a shrine dedicated to Aten with his hands raised in reverence towards a depiction of the Sun Disc. Contrary to the shrines of the traditional Gods, Aten's shrines did not have a statue.

"I heard you asked to see me alone, Penthu. What can I do for you?" Amenhotep suddenly asked in a friendly but tired tone, without getting up or looking at his personal physician.

Penthu was worried he might have come at a bad moment, however he had no choice but to continue and reasoned that risking the wrath of the Pharaoh was probably not as bad as continuing in his current situation.

"Your Majesty," Penthu started speaking, "I have been your loyal servant for some time now and I hope to be able to remain in your service for many years to come. But I don't understand what is happening or why I am here."

The Pharaoh got up and reverently took a couple of steps backwards before turning his back to the Aten shrine and walking to his desk where he sat down on his beautifully gilded chair.

"You are here because you are an excellent physician," Amenhotep finally replied, pretending not to understand what Penthu was talking about.

"Your Majesty, I don't mean to be insolent but I am being invited at meetings concerning the Gem Pa Aten and this morning I joined the audience with the priests of Amun. Being a priest of Amun myself this places me in a difficult position, the priests at Karnak seem to hate me now, while attending meetings and audiences has nothing to do with my duty as your personal physician," Penthu complained.

"I asked you to attend those meetings and this morning's audience because I value your opinion and because I want everybody to know that you work for me and that I appreciate you. If this causes your colleagues at Karnak to hate you then maybe you should look for the problem with them, not with yourself or me. We are simply fulfilling our duties; you your duty towards me and I my duty towards the Aten and the Two Lands," the Pharaoh reassured Penthu and after a moment, when Penthu wanted to speak again he went on: "Penthu, you are capable of much more than just being a simple physician. I have great plans for the future and I want you to play an important part in those plans."

"Will these plans involve the Temple of Amun?" Penthu asked.

"I have no plans for the Temple of Amun, or any other temple or any god, except for the Aten," Amenhotep replied bluntly.

"Why do you hate the Lord Amun so much?" Penthu asked, for a moment forgetting his place, before quickly adding: "Apologies, Your Majesty, I did not mean to be insolent."

Amenhotep got up from his chair again and started pacing his office without saying any words, his face betraying he was feeling uneasy. Penthu got nervous but the tension in the room was finally broken when Amenhotep spoke again: "There is no reason to apologize Penthu. It is a reasonable question which, unfortunately, is hard to answer. But, being a priest, you will probably understand what I am going to say."

Amenhotep returned to his chair, poured wine in his cup from the jar he always kept on his desk and took a sip.

For a moment the Pharaoh seemed lost in his thoughts but then, unexpectedly, he surprised Penthu with a question: "Penthu, what is the source of all life on this world? The one thing that we cannot live without?"

"I don't know, I guess that would be the sun?" Penthu replied.

"You are right!" Amenhotep exclaimed, delighted with Penthu's answer and went on: "But if the sun is the source of all life then why don't we give it the worship it deserves?"

"But, Your Majesty, we worship the sun. Everywhere in the Two Lands there are temples dedicated to Ra, the Sun God," Penthu answered, not understanding what the Pharaoh meant.

"No Penthu," Amenhotep corrected him: "Ra is only an aspect of the sun, that is why He is depicted as a falcon-headed God. Aten is the source of everything and that is why the Aten is depicted as a Sun Disc with rays ending in hands giving the ankh, the symbol of life. The Sun Disc is the source of all life!"

Penthu thought about the Pharaoh's words for a moment and then asked: "I understand what you mean, Your Majesty, but that does not have to be a reason to be against the Lord Amun."

"Amun has taken the position that belongs to the Aten. Amun is worshipped as the King of the Gods! His name means 'the Hidden One' and they could not have found a better name; I never see Him and I never hear Him. Contrary to the Aten, Who can be seen in the sky clearly and Whose warm rays can be felt on your skin, Amun is indeed hidden, yet a large part of our country and its treasures is offered to Him while it should be offered to the life-giving Aten," Amenhotep spoke angrily.

"Your Majesty," Penthu protested, "the Lord Amun is everywhere, He is the life force, He is like the wind, you don't see Him but He is there!"

"You don't understand it, Penthu," Amenhotep spoke as if he were lecturing a schoolboy and continued explaining: "For centuries the people of the Two Lands have been worshipping dozens of Gods, aspects of the sun or animals, but we never worshipped the source from which everything originated. That is something I want to change. Under my rule the Aten will receive its rightful place. I will bring the Two Lands back to its source!"

From the tone the Pharaoh had been speaking in, Penthu could hear that he was absolutely convinced he was doing the right thing.

"But Your Majesty," Penthu exclaimed, "our Gods are part of our long tradition. Are you intending to change a tradition of a thousand years old? Are you intending to replace all the Gods by a single, new God?"

"Sometimes it is better to abandon certain traditions, Penthu," the Pharaoh sighed and took another sip of his wine before continuing his lecture: "Don't forget that the earliest rulers of the Two Lands used to take some of their servants with them in their tombs when they died. You probably don't mind us having abandoned that tradition, don't you Penthu? And as a priest you should know that the Aten is not a new God. It is little known, unfortunately, but certainly not new. My father used to worship it already and my forefathers as well but they still always gave preference to Amun and other Gods."

For a moment nobody spoke and Penthu was thinking about everything he had just heard from the Pharaoh. He had to admit to himself that Amenhotep had set an amazing task for himself and he understood his reasoning behind it even though he did not fully agree with his ideas.

Then after, some moments of silence, the Pharaoh looked sharply at Penthu and asked slowly: "Penthu, do you understand everything I have just told you?"

"Yes, Your Majesty," Penthu replied meekly.

The Pharaoh kept staring at Penthu and went on: "As I have told you already, I have great plans for you Penthu. You can have a great career under my rule if you decide to support me. If you don't want to be part of my plans you are free to return to your temple, however, when you accept my offer I will demand your unquestioning loyalty!"

Amenhotep stood up behind his desk again, pointed at the door and spoke: "I want an answer from you before you walk out of that door!"

Pressured by the Pharaoh but also genuinely impressed and curious about the career promised to him, Penthu replied: "I accept your offer, Your Majesty, and give you my unquestioning loyalty."

Ipi was sitting next to Meryptah's bed, keeping watch on the frail High Priest who slowly started to wake up.

Meryptah had been found lying unconscious in front of the statue of Amun by Wenamun who, when the High Priest after a long time still had not returned from the Holy of Holies, had decided to disregard the instructions not to disturb the priest and had gone to see if everything was in order.

After the first quick examination Intef had said Meryptah's weak body could not handle the pressure the High Priest was under anymore and his heart started to give up.

"The High Priest has to stay in bed and should not be bothered with any business that could cause him stress," Intef had instructed and also ordered that there should be a physician with him in his room at all time to watch him until he started to regain his strength.

It was evening and Meryptah's room was lit by oil lamps. Ipi looked around in the simply furnished room; it had only a bed, a desk, a chest that probably contained Meryptah's private belongings and a couple of chairs. On the beautifully decorated walls there were shelves which contained many papyrus rolls and in a corner of the room stood Meryptah's private shrine for Amun which he kept meticulously clean.

It was the first time Ipi entered Meryptah's private room and it was a bit disappointing, he had expected the High Priest of the wealthy and powerful cult of Amun to live in more luxurious surroundings.

After a while Maya entered the room to see if the High Priest had already started to recover.

"How is the High Priest doing, Ipi?" Maya inquired.

"He starts to move again, my lord, and sometimes he opens his eyes but he hasn't spoken yet," Ipi answered.

"I have seen you working, Ipi. You are becoming a fine physician. I am very impressed with you," Maya complimented Ipi.

"I hope the Pharaoh will not steel you away from us in the future like he did with Penthu," he added jokingly but Ipi noticed there was a serious undertone in his voice.

For a while Maya looked at Meryptah who lay motionless again and appeared to sleep. Then he went to Meryptah's shrine, lit incense and kneeled to pray to Amun for the High Priest's health.

"I will come back again later to see if there is any improvement," Maya told Ipi after he finished praying and started to walk to the door. He was about to leave the room when suddenly Meryptah opened his eyes, started to moan and tried to speak.

"Don't speak, my lord," Ipi warned Meryptah. "You must rest."

Maya stopped and hurried back to Meryptah who by then was even trying to get up right in his bed, something Ipi did not allow.

"I must speak with you, Maya," Meryptah spoke barely audible.

Ipi looked at Maya and shook his head.
Maya understood the signal and spoke: "We can speak tomorrow, Meryptah. You should rest first."

"No!" Meryptah replied, more forcefully this time. "This cannot wait! We must speak now!"

For a moment Maya hesitated but then he took a chair and sat down next to Meryptah's bed.

"We can speak but not too long. You must not exert yourself," he told the High Priest.

Meryptah looked very tired and seemed to gather all his strength before speaking: "Maya, I will soon join Osiris in the Netherworld."

"No, don't speak about that!" Maya interrupted him but before he could say more Meryptah cut him off: "Let me speak, Maya, this has to be said! After I have joined Osiris you will be the new High Priest. I know we have had our differences recently but I also know that you take all your decisions with the interests of temple and the Lord Amun in mind. I know that I can go peacefully with the thought I leave the temple in capable hands."

Meryptah had been speaking slowly and with difficulty but Ipi had heard every word and to his amazement saw tears rolling down Maya's face. Ipi knew that, in spite of their differences over how to handle the Pharaoh, Meryptah had been the mentor of the younger Maya and that they had always respected each other.

"You have thought me well, Meryptah. I will follow your example when I lead the temple," Maya spoke in a voice choked by suppressed grief.

Meryptah raised his bony hand, put it on Maya's shoulder, pulled him nearer so their faces almost touched and spoke forcefully: "But I implore you Maya, act thoughtfully when it concerns the Pharaoh. Always keep the future of the temple in mind and don't take any rash decisions! Before you take a decision always think carefully about its possible consequences!"

It was early morning when Ipi was relieved of his watch over Meryptah and he could finally get some rest himself.

On his way to his room, when walking through one of the temple's enormous halls Ipi heard chanting coming from the direction of the Holy of Holies. He knew it to be the morning ceremony that was normally led by Meryptah but, as long as he was incapable to do so, would be conducted by Maya.

After ritually bathing in the temple's sacred lake Maya would go into the Holy of Holies and at dawn unlock the doors of the shrine that contained the statue of the Amun just in time for the God's statue to receive the first rays of sunlight.

Maya would then tell the God he came on behalf of the Pharaoh, who officially was the High Priest of every Egyptian God, and then clean the shrine and the statue with water from the temple's sacred lake, change the statue's clothes and offer it food.

During the evening a similar ritual would again be conducted when the statue's shrine was being closed.

Ipi had never entered the Holy of Holies, a right that was reserved for only a few priests, but he did not mind not being allowed to come near the holy statue of Amun. Ipi understood that the statue was not the God itself but merely served as a vessel that the God could enter to receive His offerings, just like the ka of a deceased person could enter his mummy to receive offerings. And just like the mummy at a funeral, the holy statue in the temple also underwent the 'opening of the mouth ceremony' before it was placed in the temple to receive the God.

As far as Ipi knew he was as close to Amun at shrines that were accessible to him and others as the High Priest was in the Holy of Holies and there were even some priests who said Amun was everywhere and that worshippers actually did not need a statue at all to get close to Him.

Ipi loved the music of the sistra and the singing of the priests and priestesses that accompanied the rituals so when he was close enough he sat down against a wall to listen.

He had only sat there a short time when he heard two people walk through the hall, whispering to each other. They stopped close to Ipi and continued their conversation.

The first rays of the sun had only just appeared over the horizon, illuminating the tips of the temple's obelisks and shining through the central aisle of the temple to touch the statue of Amun inside His sanctuary. However, inside the pillared hall where Ipi was sitting it was still dark with the only light coming from torches that were placed on set distances of each other and were kept burning throughout the night. In the dark hall the two priests did not notice Ipi who was sitting beyond the reach of the torchlight.

"This is an opportunity that will never come again. You should take it with both hands!" the voice of an older man whispered.

"I don't know. It goes against the divine rules of the temple," another, younger voice whispered back.

Instinctively Ipi withdrew into a dark corner that was within hearing range and continued to listen.

"It will save the temple!" the older voice spoke again, louder than he had wanted, and immediately went on in a lower voice: "Maya will continue the leadership of the temple in the same way as Meryptah did, he might be talking about action against the Pharaoh but he will do nothing. There is already considerable dissatisfaction amongst the priests and we can use that to our advantage. If you support me to become the next High Priest there will be great rewards for you and you will do our Lord Amun a great service!"

For a moment nobody spoke, the younger man was apparently thinking about the older man's proposition.

Ipi tried to see who the two priests were but, just like him, they remained in the darkness giving Ipi the impression they purposely stayed out of the light of the burning torches.

When he did not get a reply from the younger man the old man went on speaking: "I know you feel you deserve a better position in the temple and I agree with you. I also know that your family has held high positions here and that this puts a lot of pressure on you. I promise you that when I am High Priest you will have a career which will outshine all your family members that preceded you, Amenemope!"

"Amenemope the temple scribe!" Ipi thought to himself. "But who is he talking to?"

"How will you prevent Maya from becoming High Priest when Meryptah dies?" Amenemope asked.

"I can discredit him and you can help me by starting to carefully set the priests up against him and to help me gain their support. Use the dissatisfaction amongst the priests to incite them, tell them that nothing will change with Maya's leadership or that things will get worse," the old man replied and asked again: "Will you help me?"

"Are you sure it is for the good of the temple?" Amenemope asked.

"He is going to give in to the old man," Ipi knew when he heard the tone of Amenemope's voice.

"I love the temple. I have served it all my life, the Lord Amun may strike me down right now if I have ever done anything to hurt His temple!" the old man replied, getting annoyed by the hesitating Amenemope.

At that moment a group of priests came into the hall, talking loudly. The two men quickly ceased their conversation and continued further down the hall but just before they left Ipi heard Amenemope say: "I will help you. But I will do it for the Lord Amun and for the temple!"

More rays of sunlight were starting to shine into the hall and when the two priests walked through a ray of light Ipi recognized the old man: it was Wahankh, the priest who earlier had criticized Meryptah in front of the other priests.

"Hasn't that man got a shred of decency left in his body?" Maya raged. "He probably can't wait for Meryptah to die so he can try to become High Priest himself!"

Ipi had told Wenamun about the conversation between Wahankh and Amenemope he had overheard that morning and he immediately took Ipi to Maya's office to repeat his story.

Maya sat down in a chair, sighed and spoke in a tired voice: "I don't know why Meryptah retained that power hungry priest in the temple in the first place and especially in the position of Overseer of the Distribution of Offerings. We haven't been able to prove it but everybody suspects him of stealing from the offerings to the temple which he is supposed to take care of."

"Meryptah will have had his reasons for keeping him. You should know by now that he usually tries to solve problems by diplomacy and showing goodwill," Wenamun answered, trying to calm the emotional Maya down and then in a more serious tone continued: "But how are we going to deal with this situation?"

"That is easy!" Maya replied. "We will expel both these treacherous priests from Karnak!"

"We should not act too hasty, Maya," Wenamun cautioned and explained: "If we expel them now the other priests in the temple will suspect you of purging the temple of possible opponents in preparation for the succession of Meryptah after his death. That will make you appear like the aggressor."

"You are right, Wenamun," Maya admitted and then spoke: "I will have both Wahankh and Amenemope watched and as soon as I have proof against them I will deal with them!"

Not knowing whether he was supposed to stay or not Ipi remained in Maya's office during the conversation between the two high ranking priests who seemed to have forgotten about him.

Looking around he was surprised to notice that Maya's office was much richer furnished than the High Priest's room where he had stayed during the previous night. Here there was more furniture and all furniture was decorated with gold and precious stones. But, Ipi thought, considering that Maya was, after Meryptah, the highest ranking person of the most powerful priesthood in the country it was still modest.

Ipi knew Maya had lived in luxury all his life. He was a member of a wealthy, noble Theban family and he had decided relatively late to dedicate his life to Amun. Even while he served in the temple Maya still possessed a villa in Thebes where his wife and son lived with whom he rarely had any contact and who had become estranged from him.

Finally Maya noticed Ipi and told him: "Thank you, Ipi. You can go now."

Ipi was about to leave the room when Maya added with a smile: "You keep impressing me, Ipi. You are not only a good physician but also an excellent informer!"

It was two days before the wedding of Amenhotep and Kiya. High dignitaries from every corner of the country streamed into Thebes and all brought their servants and guards with them.

All the guestrooms in the palace were full as well as every tavern in the town.

The harbour of the city was also crowded with the boats of rich business men or government officials such as provincial governors, mayors of important cities and the boats of Aperel, the Vizier of Lower Egypt, who had made the long journey from Memphis to Thebes with such a large escort of guards and servants that his party had arrived with three boats.

The most impressive arrival in Thebes, however, was without a doubt, Thutmose, the Viceroy of Kush. He came with a small fleet bringing an army of soldiers and servants as well as boats laden with gifts from exotic countries far south of Egypt for the Pharaoh and his new wife. Some of these gifts were precious materials or jewellery and the Viceroy had even brought strange animals which were unknown to most Egyptians.

The Viceroy stayed as the Pharaoh's personal guest in the Royal Palace together with his personal servants and a few guards. The rest of his soldiers were accommodated in tents outside of Thebes.

Aset had been busy; when Kiya was taking her lessons in Royal etiquette or reading and writing she had to help taking care of the many guests in the palace. She had no more time to visit her friends in the bakery or trying to 'accidentally' meet Merykare again in the hope of getting into a conversation with him as she had, unsuccessfully, tried to do before the palace was overrun by wedding guests.

When the wedding was only two days away Aset accompanied Ranefer and a group of other members of the Royal Court to the Gem Pa Aten to watch the final preparations.

The group also included the person who would be leading the men carrying the Royal Family's litters and the fan bearers of the Pharaoh's family.

As a measure of practice they walked the exact route the wedding procession would take two days later. Hekanakht, the Head of the Royal Guard who had taken Aset and Kiya to Panehsy's villa, also joined them to observe the security measures that had been arranged. He took his responsibility very seriously. He had often visited the Gem Pa Aten and many times walked the route of the wedding procession to see where possible dangers to the Pharaoh and his family could come from.

When Aset arrived at the Aten Temple she was very impressed by the work that had been done.

She knew the temple was not yet finished and had found it a strange decision of the Pharaoh to hold the wedding ceremony there. But now that she saw the site for herself she was, in spite of the fact that it was unfinished, struck by its beauty and by the holy atmosphere that the temple breathed.

In preparation of the wedding the complex had been completely cleaned and almost everything that reminded of the construction work that, until recently, had been going on had disappeared.

Aset walked between the new white walls with images of the Aten and the Pharaoh depicted here and there and, even though her knowledge of hieroglyphs was limited, she was able to make out Kiya's name on some places. For a moment Aset could not help feeling some jealousy towards her best friend. Temple walls were meant to stand forever so having her name written on a temple wall was not only a great honour but would also guarantee that Kiya's name would be remembered. Even after her death priests would read Kiya's name which would help her ka to survive.

"What do you think of the temple?" a voice suddenly asked.

Aset looked at the man who had spoken to her and recognized him immediately as Hemienu, the architect and the Pharaoh's chief of construction. She had often seen him in the palace but had never spoken to him.

"It is so beautiful," Aset replied.

Hemienu looked tired but was clearly proud of the result of his hard work.

"We have been very busy to meet the Pharaoh's demands. The past week I even stayed in the temple during the night. I had so much work to do I did not have time to go home and meet my family,"

Hemienu spoke and went on with a smile: "My wife will probably be very upset with me when I come home again."

"I hope she will appreciate your work as much as I do," Aset smiled back and continued further down a roofless, pillared aisle into the temple.

In a small room that, like most of the temple, was also roofless Aset saw Meryra, the High Priest of the Aten, who was engaged in a discussion with another priest.

"Maybe something about the wedding ceremony," Aset thought to herself.

When she came closer Meryra noticed her and shouted: "Don't go any further! This is the Holy of Holies! Turn back immediately!"

Aset quickly turned around and while walking back she looked up at the tall pillars that flanked the aisle until another voice made her look down again.

"There you are, Aset!" Ranefer spoke. "I have been looking everywhere for you. Come with me, they are waiting for us."

Ranefer took her to a small group of priests and members of the Royal Court that was waiting on the large open court at the temple's entrance.

The court was surrounded by enormous, partly undecorated, pillars that made Aset feel tiny.

"This court is probably meant for public services to the Aten," Aset thought.

Aset's group was soon joined by Hekanakht whom Aset had earlier seen wandering around the Gem Pa Aten by himself.

The priest who earlier had been talking with Meryra came to the waiting group and started speaking: "I will now take you through the route the procession will take through the temple on His Majesty's wedding day."

"The High Priest of the Aten will welcome His Majesty and his bride here on the Sun Court at the entrance of the temple," the priest started explaining and continued, pointing towards the aisle flanked by two rows of still undecorated pillars: "Then he will lead the procession this way down the aisle towards the sanctuary of the Aten. Only the Royal Family's personal servants and a few selected guards will accompany the procession this way. Everybody else will remain here on the Sun Court until the ceremony is finished."

The group started to move and followed the Aten priest down the aisle.

"How far will the Pharaoh's guards be allowed to escort him, lord Hatiay?" Hekanakht asked the priest.

"Until the end of this aisle," the priest answered and explained: "That is where the Holy of Holies starts. There, nobody except the Pharaoh, his bride and the High Priest will enter. But don't worry, Hekanakht, the Pharaoh and his wife will be safe in the Holy of Holies, even without your guards."

Halfway down the aisle Hatiay stopped at an altar and spoke: "Here the Pharaoh and his new wife will perform an offering to the Aten before continuing towards the Holy of Holies."

The group went further into the temple and at the end of the aisle Hatiay stopped again and said: "This is where everybody will stop. As I explained earlier already only the Pharaoh, his bride and the High Priest will continue into the Holy of Holies to conduct the actual blessing ceremony of the marriage. When the ceremony is finished we will follow the same route back and again stop halfway down the aisle for the Pharaoh to perform an offering to please the Aten."

Aset started to feel uncomfortable in the roofless temple. The higher the sun rose the hotter it got and there were not many places to find shade.

"Was the temple roofless because it was not yet finished or was this part of the design?" Aset wondered. "And was she really the only person who was bothered by the hot sun?"

To Aset's annoyance Ranefer and Hekanakht continued asking Hatiay about the ceremony and Hatiay patiently answered all their questions.

Finally, after what seemed as an endless conversation with the Aten priest, Ranefer announced it was time to return to Malkata Palace where the Pharaoh would be waiting for his report about the visit to the Gem Pa Aten.

The sun was already setting when the group walked back over Thebes's dusty roads to the harbour where a boat was waiting to bring them back to the palace.

Aset trailed behind the group when she suddenly heard a voice behind her calling her name. Looking around Aset saw a tall man who put his hand on her shoulder. Aset's immediate reaction was to scream and run but the man put his hand over her mouth and quickly pulled her in a small, quiet side street without anybody noticing.

"Don't be scared, Aset. Don't you remember me? It is me, Montu," the man spoke.

Relieved to see it was the former palace guard whom Kiya was in love with and whom she had intended to marry Aset stopped struggling and spoke angrily: "What are you doing here? Could you not greet me like any normal person would do?"

"I am sorry," Montu explained, "but if Hekanakht sees me he might prevent me from meeting you and I really need to speak with you, Aset."

"What do you want to say?" Aset asked while looking at the group that disappeared into the direction of the harbour. "You'd better speak quickly because I have a boat to catch."

"I am a guard at the palace of the Viceroy of Kush now and came with him to Thebes for Kiya's wedding. Aset, I must see Kiya before she gets married! Please help me to meet her!" Montu spoke in a desperate voice.

"That is impossible!" Aset replied and went on explaining: "I am her personal servant now and even I hardly get to see her. During the day she is taking lessons which are often under the personal supervision of Queen Teye."

"Then I will see her during the night!" Montu insisted.

"Montu, you know how strict the security of the palace is. You will never get in and Kiya will not get out," Aset spoke but when she saw tears in Montu's eyes she added in a more compassionate tone: "I am sorry, Montu, but I think it is also better for Kiya when you two don't meet. This time is already difficult enough for her without you returning in her life."

"Then please tell her I came to Thebes and tried to see her. I want her to know that I still love her," Montu begged.

"I will tell her this. But now I have to go," Aset told Montu and immediately ran away to meet up again with Ranefer and the rest of the group.

While she was running Aset decided not to tell Kiya about her meeting with Montu.

CHAPTER 9
A DEATH IN THE TEMPLE
AND
A ROYAL WEDDING

Wahankh and Amenemope had been busy spreading rumours in Karnak Temple. They were spreading fear and uncertainty amongst the priests about what would happen if Maya would become the next High Priest and continue the same kind of leadership as Meryptah.

Without having been asked to do so Ipi had been watching them whenever he had the opportunity and saw they were successful in spreading discontent amongst the priests in the temple. He informed Wenamun and Maya about it but to his surprise they were not too concerned.

"I know exactly what is going on," Maya spoke and explained: "I have the treacherous Wahankh and Amenemope being watched by reliable priests who report directly to me. Tonight Wahankh will most likely again be inciting the priests against me and then I will confront him and expel him from the temple, together with Amenemope!"

That night, however, Maya's plans were upset by something that every priest in Karnak had expected to happen, yet, when it happened, it still took everybody by surprise; Meryptah, the High Priest of Amun who had ruled the Amun priesthood for many years through one of its most influential periods, died.

Immediately after his death Meryptah's body was taken to the House of Death were a seventy-days mummification process would start to prepare him for his funeral.

Everybody at Karnak was genuinely upset. Even priests who did not agree with his style of leadership were sad to see the man who had led them for such a long time pass away.

The temple went into mourning, priests and priestesses tore their clothes as a sign of grief and a special ceremony was hastily prepared to pray that Meryptah's ka would safely make the hazardous journey to the Kingdom of Osiris.

Amunherkhepeshef, the High Priest of the Southern Temple, was quickly informed about Meryptah's death and, followed by many other priests, immediately came to Karnak to mourn.

Word about Meryptah's passing away also travelled through Thebes and soon people from the city started flocking to the temple to pay their respects to the High Priest who after the Pharaoh had been the most powerful person in the country.

Within two hours of Meryptah's death the forecourt of Karnak was filled with mourning Thebans.

Just like everybody else Ipi also felt upset; not only because of the death of Meryptah but also because of the uncertainty about what would happen next. Would Maya be a good successor to Meryptah? Or would Wahankh maybe manage to become the new High Priest? Or, even worse, would a period of infighting amongst the temple priests follow?

Added to this uncertainty was the Pharaoh's unfriendly policy towards Amun and his priesthood.

At that moment Ipi thought it was impossible to say what the future would bring for him and the temple.

Seeing the temple court filled with grieving people, however, Ipi found some consolation.

"Maybe the Pharaoh does not love Amun," he thought to himself, "but the people of the Two Lands still love Him and His temple."

Penthu sat alone in his room having a late dinner. He was wondering what future plans the Pharaoh had for him. Since the Pharaoh was a healthy man being his personal physician was not as demanding as his position in Karnak had been so he looked forward to extra responsibilities.

A knock on the door woke Penthu up from his thoughts.

Upon opening the door he saw a palace messenger who spoke: "Lord Penthu, I bring you tragic news from the Temple of Amun. This evening Meryptah, the High Priest of Amun, has joined Osiris in the Netherworld."

"What happened? How did he die?" Penthu asked, feeling upset.

"I don't know anything more than I just told you, my lord," the messenger answered and added: "His Majesty has just received this news and asked me to inform you immediately."

The messenger left again leaving Penthu alone in his room. He sat down again but was unable to finish his dinner.

Many thoughts started to race through Penthu's head. He knew Meryptah had been having problems with his health, Maya had told that during the audience with the Pharaoh. Would he have been able to save him if he had returned to Karnak to treat him?

Then Penthu's thoughts started to go back to the day the Pharaoh ordered him to leave the Temple of Amun to come and serve him in the Palace. He remembered the conversation he had had with Meryptah that day and the promise he had made to him. He had promised to represent the temple at the Royal Court and to try to influence the Pharaoh so he would have a more positive attitude towards the Temple of Amun.

Had Meryptah felt disappointed, betrayed or deserted by him? What had his thoughts about him been when he died? Penthu started to feel guilty and angry at himself. He buried his face in his hands and started to cry.

Kiya had been very nervous over the past days. She had been under a lot of pressure because of the wedding but also because of the responsibilities that would come with her new life after the wedding day.

Aset tried to cheer her up as much as possible and did not mention anything about Sitre's warning about Nefertiti or her meeting with Montu. The last thing Kiya needed was extra worries.

The first private wedding ceremonies already started the evening before the wedding day in the temple that was attached to Malkata Palace. These ceremonies were conducted by Meryra, the High Priest of the Aten, and only attended by the Royal Family, a few special guests and high ranking officials.

After the ceremonies the Pharaoh invited everybody to attend a private banquet with him and his bride.

It was already late in the evening when Kiya finally could return to her apartment to rest.

"For almost two weeks I have been learning from morning to evening about how to behave at the Royal Court but this evening during the banquet I felt completely out of place between the viziers of Upper and Lower Egypt, the Viceroy of Kush and all these other high officials," Kiya complained to Aset.

"You did very well, Kiya. You will make a wonderful Royal Wife! You just have to get used to your new position," Aset replied in an attempt to reassure Kiya.

"I am afraid I will not live up to the Pharaoh's high expectations," Kiya went on, not feeling reassured by Aset's words. "Everybody was looking at me this evening to judge whether I am suitable for the Pharaoh or not. Will they know already that I am actually a servant? How many nobles will approve of a servant as a Royal Wife?"

Kiya, still wearing her dress and jewellery from the banquet, had been pacing the room while speaking agitatedly. Aset took her by the arm and pulled her to a chair to sit down. When Kiya was sitting Aset went behind her to unfasten her wesekh collar and started to remove the other jewellery, hoping it would help her feel more comfortable.

While doing this Aset spoke: "All the Pharaoh's guests loved you today, Kiya, and most important: the Pharaoh loves you! Nobody can reject you when the Pharaoh accepts you."

Kiya did not say anything but still looked worried. Aset took another chair, came to sit next to Kiya, put her arm around her shoulders and continued with a smile: "Between all the boring Royalty and nobility your cheerful and warm personality will win everybody's heart. Everybody has always liked you, Kiya, and that will not change just because you are married to the Pharaoh."

This time Kiya forced a smile and answered: "This cheerful personality is exactly that part of me that they are teaching me to suppress during my lessons at Queen Teye's chambers."

The next morning the difference between the two neighbouring temples of Amun and Aten could not have been bigger.

The unfinished Aten Temple was festively decorated with colourful banners and everywhere there were garlands of flowers representing Upper and Lower Egypt and fertility. The priests and visitors to the temple all had put on their finest robes for their attendance of the Royal wedding.

In contrast to the Gem Pa Aten the atmosphere in the Temple of Amun was one of sadness. The coloured banners that normally hung in front of the temple had been removed and priests had torn their clothes and threw dust on their heads as a sign of mourning for the death of their High Priest.

Whether it was out of respect for Meryptah or because they had understood it was not the right time: the evening of the High Priest's death Wahankh and Amenemope had kept quiet.

The next morning, however, they had decided it was time to act again.

"If Maya will succeed Meryptah as the next High Priest there will be nothing left of our beautiful temple in the future! There will be nobody left to worship our Lord Amun unless we have a strong leader who can stand up to the heretic Pharaoh!"

Amenemope spoke passionately from a raised platform in the temple hall that was normally used by high ranking priests to address the other priests.

Ipi had been listening and thought Amenemope was personally convinced about what he was saying.

"Are you going to be this strong leader, Amenemope?" somebody from the group of assembled priests shouted, causing some laughter amongst the group which immediately stopped when another priest shouted: "Shame on you, Amenemope! You are using the death of Meryptah for you own ambition!"

Amenemope was stung by the last remark and retorted angrily: "This has nothing to do with my own ambition! I respected Meryptah just like everybody else but now he is gone and we have to find the right person to guide us through this difficult and dangerous time! And no, I am not the right person for that task. I think that person should be Wahankh!"

For a moment there was a lot of murmur amongst the crowd; some persons seeming to agree with Amenemope's suggestion while many others disagreed.

"Wahankh is untrustworthy! He steals from the temple offerings!" a voice shouted again from the crowd.

"Can you prove that?" Wahankh's voice suddenly intervened while he appeared next to Amenemope.

There came no reaction to Wahankh's question, instead, everybody went silent and waited for what he would have to say.

"I am the right person to lead the Karnak Temple through this dangerous time. Maya is too young and inexperienced for that!" Wahankh spoke in his old cracking voice.

"With Wahankh as the next High Priest we will be having the same problems about the succession again within two years!" a voice sounded from within the group of priests causing laughter again.

Wahankh heard the derisive remark and shouted in a voice that trembled with anger: "Is this a joke to you? We are talking about the future of our temple! I have devoted my life to Amun and I won't stand by watching while this unholy Pharaoh destroys His temple! This is not a matter to make fun about!"

For a moment everybody was quiet, overwhelmed by Wahankh's aggressive but also passionate retort while Wahankh himself stood looking at the assembled priests with angry flashing eyes.

Ipi had been listening and, in spite of his dislike for Wahankh, he was impressed by the conviction with which he was speaking. Maybe Wahankh was not just an ambitious man but, contrary to what Ipi had been thinking all the time, was actually acting out of love for his temple.

"How do you know the Pharaoh wants to destroy the temple, Wahankh?" Wenamun, who had entered the hall unnoticed by anybody, suddenly asked.

Wahankh looked surprised for a moment about Wenamun's unexpected appearance but he quickly recovered and answered: "Wake up, Wenamun! Don't you see what is happening? Step by step the Pharaoh is going to make our life more difficult and I dare to prophecy here that unless we act, our temple will not survive this Pharaoh's reign!"

Ipi listened to Wahankh's words, they made him think of something that had been bothering him for a long time and it sent a chill through his spine.

"Maybe you are right, Wahankh, but does this make you the right person to lead the temple?" Maya also joined into the discussion. He walked through the group of assembled priests straight to the platform where Wahankh and Amenemope were standing.

In an angrier tone Maya went on speaking: "Does this give you the excuse to upset the temple's laws of succession and to show disrespect to our late High Priest by agitating against his lawful successor only one day after he joined Osiris?"

For a moment Wahankh seemed concerned about Maya's appearance but then he recognized the opportunity to confront him publicly and replied: "That is the reason why I am better qualified to lead the temple during this period!"

Speaking passionately while gesturing in the direction of the Gem Pa Aten he went on explaining: "The Pharaoh is going to have a wedding ceremony right next to our temple. Our High Priest has died but we haven't received one word of sympathy from him and his big wedding celebration will continue as if nothing has happened. I want us to have a strong leadership for our temple as soon as possible so we will be able to face whatever challenge might come, and this challenge will come, I promise you that! You, Maya, seem to prefer to follow traditions and hold ceremonies for the next seventy days, until the funeral and pretend that we are not in a crisis. Unfortunately we are in a crisis and there is no time for ceremonies and traditions. We must prepare ourselves now for a long and hard battle for survival!"

Wahankh's speech had impressed everybody, even Maya was quiet for a moment and seemed to think about what he had just heard.

Then Maya climbed onto the platform where Wahankh and Amenemope were standing, ordered Amenemope to leave and started addressing the gathered priests: "I fully acknowledge that our temple is in a crisis, just as Wahankh has said! And just like him, I agree that we must not waste any time and start preparing ourselves for whatever may come. But this does not mean that we can't show our beloved High Priest, who has led our temple for such a long time, the proper respect he deserves. We will not be worthy to call ourselves priests of Amun if we forget our duties towards our dead at the first sign of danger."

Maya looked at the group of priests in front of him to see if his words had any effect, Wahankh tried to use the moment of silence to start speaking again but Maya cut him off immediately: "There is no reason for any discussion about the succession of Meryptah. It is tradition that the Second Prophet of Amun succeeds as High Priest unless the previous High Priest has clearly designated another person to succeed him. Meryptah has designated me, the Second Prophet, and since Meryptah represented the Lord Amun that means that Amun designated me!"

Maya was silent again for a moment but then asked in a challenging tone: "Is there anybody who disagrees with this?"

When nobody spoke a word the old Wahankh, fearing he was losing ground, started shouting with a red and angry face: "Maya is not as experienced as I am and he did not grow up in the temple like I did! He joined the temple very late in life and has only reached his elevated position because he comes from a noble family. He does not deserve to be the next High Priest!"

Ipi watched the two shaven headed priests arguing, both had torn their fine white robes as a sign of mourning, just like every other priest in Karnak, and Maya even had removed the insignia of his high rank, even though Wahankh still wore his usual jewellery. It was an unusual sight and it reminded Ipi of two children. He was, however, very worried about what Wahankh had said and Maya had confirmed: the temple was in crisis, its survival might be threatened by their own Pharaoh.

Maya suddenly seemed to compose himself and in a quiet and assured manner spoke directly to Wahankh, ignoring the crowd who were trying to overhear what was being said.

Ipi was unable to follow the conversation between the two priests but he saw Maya had a confident bearing when he spoke to Wahankh whose face had turned white and had lost all the signs of arrogance and pride that it usually had. Within minutes the proud Wahankh had been reduced to a defeated man who, without any further words, left the platform from which just moments ago he had spoken so passionately. The battle for the succession of Meryptah was over.

The Pharaoh had declared that the Royal wedding should be celebrated in the whole country. Messengers were sent to every town and city in the Two Lands to proclaim the new Royal Wife's name and titles. Messages were even sent to foreign kings to inform them about the Pharaoh's new wife.

Kiya's wedding day had started early when Titi, the Royal Beautician whom she had already met at Panehsy's villa, came to her room to help her prepare for the important day.

Aset wanted to help Kiya with washing and getting dressed but Titi spoke: "No, Aset, today that is my duty. But stay here so you can watch and learn."

Kiya had been too nervous to sleep the previous night and was clearly feeling very tired, forcing Titi to remark: "My lady, this is the most beautiful day of your life and you are looking as if you could fall asleep any moment!"

"Believe me Titi, I am much too nervous to sleep," Kiya replied in a tired voice.

"You should bathe in cold water and then have a good breakfast that will make you feel better, my lady," Titi advised Kiya.

"Oh no, I could not eat anything. My stomach feels upset," Kiya answered again while raising her hands defensively as if Titi personally tried to feed her.

Titi looked at Kiya and then spoke optimistically: "After I have finished taking care of you, you will feel much better, my lady!"

Titi had not said a word too much; after bathing and a massage with fragrant oil Kiya felt much better. Titi continued to comb her hair, apply cosmetics on Kiya's face, then painted her finger- and toenails with henna and helped her get dressed in her wedding robes made of the finest linen available in the country.

Finally Titi helped Kiya putting on jewellery that had been produced especially for this occasion by the Pharaoh's craftsmen. It was the second time

Aset saw her friend being transformed into a real Royal lady.

After she had finished her work with Kiya, Titi left, leaving Aset and Kiya alone.

"How do I look?" Kiya asked nervously.

"You look beautiful, Kiya. Like a real Royal Wife," Aset replied.

"I am worried I am not yet ready to become a member of the Royal Family," Kiya went on in a trembling voice.

Aset wanted to say something to reassure her when they heard a knock on the door.

Aset opened the door to see Ranefer, who asked: "Is Her Highness ready to attend breakfast with His Majesty?"

Aset was surprised to hear Kiya being referred to so formally but quickly replied just as formally: "Yes, my lady is ready."

When Kiya appeared Ranefer spoke politely: "May I compliment you on how beautiful you look, my lady?"

"Thank you, Ranefer," Kiya replied hesitatingly, still feeling uncomfortable in her new position.

They were walking through the corridors of Malkata Palace when Aset noticed Kiya started shivering with nervousness. She squeezed Kiya's hand and whispered reassuringly: "Don't be scared. Everything will be fine!"

Ranefer, who walked in front of them to lead their way, overheard Aset's whisper, turned around and spoke to Kiya with a comforting smile: "I promised His Majesty to keep this a secret so I actually should not be saying this but His Majesty has a special surprise for you at breakfast which I am sure will make you very happy, Kiya. So cheer up and try to smile when you enter the breakfast room."

Curious about the special surprise Aset and Kiya continued on their way.

When they arrived at the breakfast room Ranefer opened the door and announced in an official tone: "Her Royal Highness Kiya!"

Then he smiled at Kiya and nodded her to enter the room. Aset followed Kiya into the large room that had big windows on two sides which caught the early sunrays and created a breeze that kept the room cool.

Except for the usual depictions of the Aten and the Royal Family the room was decorated with colourful scenes of animals and flowers.

Inside Aset saw the whole Royal Family, dressed in their finest clothes, already sitting on comfortable cushions on the floor around a large breakfast spread; they had clearly been waiting for Kiya to arrive.

Aset was surprised not to see any high officials attending the breakfast as would have been the custom on this special day. Not even the Viceroy of Kush or the Viziers of Upper and Lower Egypt.

There were, however, two middle aged people, a man and a woman, whom Aset had never seen before.

"Father! Mother!" Kiya exclaimed in surprise, for a moment forgetting the court protocol she had been studying every day for the previous two weeks. She ran up to her parents who had got up immediately to embrace their daughter whom they hadn't seen for years.

Even when Kiya was still working for prince Thutmose in Memphis she almost never had an opportunity to meet her parents.

"We have missed you so much!" Kiya's mother spoke in a voice choked by emotion and then continued, looking at her daughter: "You are so beautiful! You look like a real princess!"

"How did you come here?" Kiya asked with tears of happiness in her eyes.

"His Majesty arranged everything. He sent a boat to Memphis to take us to Thebes to attend your wedding. We arrived here yesterday," her father answered, controlling his emotions better than his wife and daughter.

Pharaoh Amenhotep had also got up but did not intervene in the family reunion.

After a few moments he finally spoke while not being able to suppress a smile about his bride's happiness: "I could not get married without the attendance of my new parents-in-law and Kiya should have her parents close to her on her wedding day."

Still not considering any protocol Kiya went to her groom and hugged him while exclaiming: "Thank you! Thank you so much!"

Like Amenhotep, Aset also could not help smiling while seeing her friend so happy, all her nervousness had suddenly disappeared. She noticed that even the Pharaoh's mother, the stern Queen Teye enjoyed watching the scene. The only person who did not seem happy was Nefertiti, the Great Royal Wife. She watched her husband being embraced by his new wife with a depressed expression on her face. Even the smiles of her youngest daughter, Meketaten, who was sitting on her lap, and Meritaten, the oldest daughter, sitting next to her, could not bring a sign of happiness on her face.

After Wahankh had left the meeting hall Maya called upon all the priests to forget their differences and unite behind him to face any challenge that might come.

There were no protests anymore and Maya left the gathered priests, convinced that his succession of Meryptah would not be challenged anymore by ambitious or dissatisfied priests.

Ipi also left the hall, hoping to be able to meet Wenamun and Maya. Something had been bothering him after he had heard Wahankh speaking and he wanted to talk with them about that.

Ipi was also curious about what made Wahankh back down so suddenly from his claim on Maya's position and about what was going to happen to him and Amenemope.

He went to Maya's room which also served as his office and found many priests in front of it who had come to congratulate Maya on becoming the new leader of the Temple of Amun. For a moment it looked as if the events of that morning had made everybody forget their High Priest had only just died.

After a short while Wenamun and his wife Tahat came to visit Maya and upon seeing Ipi, Wenamun told him: "Everything is going to be fine now, Ipi, and that is also thanks to you. You have done Amun and His temple a great service. Come with me to see Maya, he probably wants to see you too."

They entered Maya's room and found him sitting behind his desk, looking very content.

"It seems like the situation is now under control again, Wenamun," Maya spoke, sounding relieved.

"Maybe he hadn't been as confident as he earlier had pretended to be," Ipi thought to himself.

"What are you going to do with Wahankh and Amenemope?" Tahat asked while she sat down in one of Maya's comfortable chairs.

Due to her strong character and her position as First Chantress of Amun she had a lot of influence in the temple which would probably only increase now Wenamun was going to succeed Maya as the new Second Prophet of Amun.

"I will expel both of them from Karnak. I will send Amenemope north, to a temple in the delta and Wahankh to a temple in an oasis in the desert," Maya replied to Tahat's question.

"May I speak, my lord?" Ipi, who had been listening to what Maya had been saying, carefully inquired, fearing his intervening would be regarded as disrespectful.

"Of course, Ipi," Maya spoke, not being upset by his interruption. "What do you want to say?"

"My lord," Ipi started speaking, "when I overheard the conversation between Wahankh and Amenemope I heard Amenemope say clearly that he was acting in the interest of the temple and not out of personal ambition. I am sure he meant what he said."

"Are you trying to say that punishing Amenemope by expelling him from Karnak is too severe, Ipi?" Maya asked and before Ipi could reply he went on, this time sounding annoyed: "I think I am actually being very lenient to both Amenemope and Wahankh. I could have forbidden them to serve in any other temple. And even if Amenemope was trying to serve the temple I still can't forgive him for his lack of respect for the memory of Meryptah this morning!"

"You could use this opportunity to make a positive gesture, Maya," Wenamun now joined in the conversation and explained: "By banishing Wahankh you can show that you will be a strong leader but by allowing Amenemope to remain in Karnak you will show that you can be merciful as well."

"Maybe you are right, Wenamun. I agree to let Amenemope stay," Maya replied reluctantly but then added threateningly: "But he had better not cause any further problems or he will find himself serving the temple by quarrying stones in one of the mines in the desert for our construction projects!"

"With Wahankh gone I am sure Amenemope will keep quiet," Wenamun reassured Maya and after a slight hesitation asked: "Forgive me my curiosity, Maya, but what exactly did you tell Wahankh this morning that made him give up his claim on your position?"

Maya listened to Wenamun's question and started to smile before speaking: "As you know he is suspected of stealing from the offerings to the temple which he was supposed to take care of. I had often asked Meryptah to relieve him from that position because of these suspicions but with Wahankh's long service and without proof Meryptah did not want to move him to another position. After Meryptah had got ill I contacted the treasurer from the palace to give me exact information about the donations of the Royal Palace to Karnak of the last years. I wanted to compare this information with the lists Wahankh made about what the temple received from the palace. I was sure there would be discrepancies between the lists from the palace and the lists from Wahankh."

"And were there any discrepancies?" Tahat asked curiously.

Maya did not answer her question but instead continued his story: "This morning I told Wahankh about my contact with the palace treasurer and I gave him the opportunity to leave with honour or being exposed publicly as a thief."

Ipi listened to Maya's words and was shocked to hear that a priest could steal from the temple. He knew priests could be ambitious but thieves?

"I did not know we received any information about temple offerings from the Royal Palace," Wenamun remarked.

"Actually, we did not," Maya replied and explained: "Sutau, the overseer of the treasury, was forbidden by the Pharaoh to help us."

"But how did you know this morning..." Wenamun asked, not understanding what had happened.

"I did not know anything but as I said already: I was sure there would be discrepancies! So I took a gamble that I was right about that when I confronted Wahankh. If he had been innocent I would have looked like a fool!" Maya told and started to laugh when he remembered how he outsmarted Wahankh. But then he suddenly turned serious and got up from behind his desk.

"We have already wasted too much time on this business!" he spoke and went on: "We have been neglecting our duties to the ka of Meryptah! I will go now to the Holy of Holies to pray and tonight I want a ceremony to help Meryptah to reach the Kingdom of Osiris safely. Help me to organize this ceremony, Wenamun."

Without waiting for a reply from Wenamun, Maya left the room and went to the holiest part of the temple to pray for Meryptah.

"You heard what Maya said, Ipi. It is time to go back to work," Wenamun spoke. "You should go to Intef, he is probably wondering why you are not at your work."

"But I need to speak with you, my lord. It could be very important," Ipi begged.

"Then tell me fast because I have many things to do," Wenamun replied, sounding annoyed about the delay.

"Do you remember what Wahankh said about the Pharaoh wanting to destroy the temple?" Ipi asked.

"Yes, of course, I was there!" Wenamun replied agitatedly.

Ipi was quiet for a moment, shocked about the tone with which Wenamun had spoken but then quickly continued speaking: "For a long time I have been having nightmares about the Pharaoh's soldiers coming to our temple to close it. These dreams are the same every time! The soldiers come here and..."

"Those are just dreams, Ipi. It is no reason for any concern," Wenamun cut him off before he could tell more.

"Dreams might be messages or warnings from the Gods, my lord. The priests in the House of Life have taught me that," Ipi replied, his voice trembling with indignation about not being taken seriously by the man whom he almost regarded as a second father, and went on speaking while his eyes started to fill with tears: "When the soldiers come something very terrible is going to happen!"

"You are right that dreams may contain messages from the Gods and sometimes even predict the future. If your dream is a prediction about what is going to happen then we cannot change it and just have to accept it," Wenamun spoke, sounding a bit calmer than before and then, while walking to the door, he added: "If that was all then I have to go now. I have to pray for Meryptah and then organize a ceremony."

Just like Maya before, Wenamun left the room without waiting for any reply.

Tahat, who had been following the conversation, got up from her chair and came over to Ipi.

She was a middle aged woman who had retained much of the beauty of her youth. Her marriage to Wenamun had never produced any children, a fact that hurt the couple very much and maybe was the reason why Wenamun always took care of Ipi.

Tahat put her arm around Ipi's shoulders and spoke in a comforting voice: "Don't worry about Wenamun, Ipi. He has been under a lot of pressure lately because of everything that has happened but he was right when he said that we have to accept whatever happens. We will defend our temple if necessary and if the Gods want us to survive we will, but if They decide differently then we have to resign ourselves to Their will."

"But something terrible is going to happen. Is there nothing we can do to stop this?" Ipi asked, feeling desperate.

"What is going to happen, Ipi?" Tahat inquired, finally starting to get curious.

"People will die," Ipi answered.

"Do you see who will die?" Tahat continued asking, this time sounding genuinely worried.

"Yes," Ipi replied barely audible.

"Do you often have this dream and is it every time exactly the same?" Tahat asked again.

"Yes," Ipi replied, relieved that Tahat seemed to take him seriously.

Tahat sighed and seemed to think about what to do next. Finally she spoke: "People should not know the fate the Gods have in store for them. Don't talk with anybody about your dreams, Ipi. Later we can speak to Wenamun about it."

Ipi was about to leave the room when Tahat, in an attempt to reassure him, spoke: "Ipi, don't worry too much about it. Most dreams are just dreams and don't have any special significance."

The wedding procession had crossed the Nile River and went through Thebes into the direction of the Gem Pa Aten. The Pharaoh and Kiya were sitting in an open litter, it was one of the few times the Pharaoh was clearly visible for the Egyptian people.

Hekanakht had organized strict security measures; the whole route of the procession was lined by soldiers to prevent anybody from getting too close to the Pharaoh and his family. The Royal Guards joined the procession, flanking Amenhotep and Kiya's litter and those of the other Royals and high officials who followed behind the Pharaoh and his bride.

Aset and other servants followed the procession on foot. As usual it had already got hot early. The Royal Family had fan bearers accompanying them to keep them cool while they travelled the dusty Theban streets under the morning sun but the servants had nobody keeping them cool making Aset not looking forward to the wedding ceremony in the hot and roofless Gem Pa Aten.

The streets were lined with the people of Thebes who wanted to see their Pharaoh and his bride. Normally the people behaved formally and respectfully when the Pharaoh passed but on this special day everybody seemed caught by the festive atmosphere and as soon as the Pharaoh and his bride came into view the people broke out in a cheer with some of them shouting well wishes to the couple.

Aset saw that the soldiers charged with keeping the people under control sometimes had difficulties preventing them from coming onto the street.

Just before they reached the Aten Temple the procession passed the Temple of Amun.

Aset noticed the coloured banners that normally hung at the temple's entrance were missing. She had heard the High Priest of Amun had joined Osiris the previous day and wondered why the Pharaoh allowed the festivities to continue as if nothing had happened and why he still let the joyous wedding procession pass the mourning Amun Temple.

After finally arriving at the Aten Temple on the large open Sun Court, which was basking in the rays of the sun, Amenhotep and Kiya were welcomed by Meryra, the High Priest of the Aten, and a group of Aten priests which included Hatiay.

"Welcome to the Gem Pa Aten, Your Majesty and Your Highness!" Meryra's voice echoed over the large temple court and went on: "Before we ask the Aten for the blessing of your marriage please allow me to say how honoured we are that Your Majesty has chosen our, still unfinished, temple for this holy ceremony."

"The honour is ours, lord Meryra," Amenhotep answered. "We are deeply honoured to have our wedding blessed here in the House of the Aten."

Aset watched the Pharaoh and the High Priest talking while Kiya stood next to her groom and kept silent. Amenhotep was wearing the double-crown of Egypt, a combination of the white crown of Upper

Egypt and the red crown of Lower Egypt, which signified the Pharaoh's power over both lands, while Kiya wore only a simple headscarf against the sun. Later during the ceremony, Aset knew, Kiya would also receive a crown which would signify her new position.

After a few moments the Pharaoh gave a signal that he was ready for the ceremony to start and Ranefer started to order everybody who was allowed to follow Amenhotep and Kiya further into the temple to prepare themselves to continue.

Aset took her position close to Kiya and the group slowly started to move. Since they had left the palace Kiya had not had any opportunity to talk to Aset but Aset could see that her friend was fine. The surprise of her parents joining her wedding did Kiya good.

The wedding party walked down the aisle flanked by white pillars that gleamed in the sunlight, some decorated with images of the Aten and the names of Amenhotep and Kiya while others were still bare, without any kind of decoration. The decorations must have been hurriedly added since Aset's visit to the temple two days earlier when all the pillars were still bare. Aset looked at the decorations and remembered Hemienu's words about how busy he and his workers had been preparing the temple for the wedding.

The group was preceded down the aisle by Meryra and other priests and priestesses who were chanting prayers to the Aten and rattled with sistra.

Halfway down the aisle the priests stopped at an altar setup before a large image of the Aten. The altar was filled with bread, meat, fruit, wine, perfumes and flowers and contained two incense burners.

Meryra asked Amenhotep and Kiya to come forward, handed both of them an incense burner and asked them to hold it up towards the image of the Aten.

While Amenhotep and Kiya raised their incense burners Meryra touched every piece of offering on the altar with a ceremonial rod to dedicate it to the Aten and started to recite a prayer out loud:

"Aten, father and mother of all that is alive, source of everything that exists, here we, Your humble servants make an offering to You of gifts that have been made possible only through Your life-giving rays. With this offering we ask for the blessing of the marriage of Your son and first servant, the Lord of the Two Lands, His Majesty Amenhotep to Her Highness Kiya. We ask this marriage to be fruitful with healthy offspring that can continue His Majesty's task of bringing the Two Lands into Your service."

After Meryra had finished his prayer he invited Amenhotep and Kiya to follow him further down the aisle, towards the Holy of Holies. Amenhotep, however, was whispering a prayer to the Aten himself and everybody respectfully waited for him to finish.

After a while Amenhotep was ready and the group went further into the temple.

At the Holy of Holies Hatiay, the Aten priest, spoke politely: "Only the High Priest, His Majesty and Her Highness will enter the Holy of Holies. Everybody else is asked to wait here for them to return."

When Meryra led the bride and groom into the most sacred part of the Gem Pa Aten the priests who stayed behind with the Royal Family and their servants and guards started chanting in praise of the Aten.

It took a long time for the Pharaoh and Kiya to return. Aset wondered what was happening inside the Holy of Holies but because of the chanting priests she was unable to hear anything of the ceremony that was being conducted inside the holiest part of the temple.

While waiting everybody was expected to respectfully remain standing and pray to the Aten but the burning sun started to take its toll on the Pharaoh's aging mother, Queen Teye, she was unable to remain standing any longer and one priest quickly had to fetch a chair for her to sit down while another brought her something to drink.

After a long wait the Pharaoh, Kiya and Meryra finally returned from the Holy of Holies of the Aten Temple.

Kiya's headscarf had disappeared and on her head with her beautiful long black hair a golden crown had been placed, it had inlays of precious stones and at the front, just above Kiya's forehead a golden uraeus, the rearing Egyptian cobra, reared its head to protect the wearer of the crown.

Amenhotep was holding Kiya's hand while Meryra announced to the people who had been waiting patiently for them: "I am proud to present to you The Great Lady Kiya, whose titles shall be: The Favourite and The Greatly Beloved Wife of the Lord of the Two Lands, Child of the Aten Who Lives Now and Forever!"

After Meryra's announcement everybody clapped and cheered, even Queen Teye, who had started to recover again, got carried away in the moment and clapped her hands.

Aset noticed that again Nefertiti was the only person who did not seem happy.

Kiya's parents had also followed their daughter and son-in-law to the entrance of the Holy of Holies and were bursting with pride to see their daughter wearing a Royal Crown. Kiya was only a common girl but had become the wife of the Pharaoh.

Meryra started to lead the way back to the Sun Court, half way down the aisle they stopped again to make another offering to the Aten before continuing on their way.

Arriving at the Sun Court all the gathered people started to cheer at the sight of Amenhotep and his new wife.

The Pharaoh, Kiya and the other members of the Royal Family and their guests were offered wine and other refreshments before they would return to Malkata Palace where a large banquet was being prepared.

Aset went to Kiya to offer her specially prepared cake and wine and she hoped to be able to speak with her for a moment but because Amenhotep kept Kiya close to himself, Aset, to her regret, did not have the opportunity to say anything to her newly wedded friend.

Unexpectedly to everybody, even to Meryra, the High Priest of the Aten, Pharaoh Amenhotep decided to return alone to the Holy of Holies saying he wanted to pray to the Aten in private. This gave Aset an opportunity to talk to Kiya.

"How are you feeling?" Aset asked.

"I am so happy!" Kiya answered excitedly, clearly overwhelmed by everything that had happened that morning.

Aset wanted to ask more but was pushed out of the way by a group of high officials and noble men and women who wanted to congratulate the Pharaoh's bride. Aset noticed that Panehsy, the man who had abused her in his villa, was amongst them.

After the Pharaoh returned from his private prayer it was time to return to the palace.

Amenhotep and Kiya climbed into their litter and the other members of the Royal Family followed their example.

They followed the same route as they had taken on the way to the Gem Pa Aten and the streets were still lined with soldiers to guarantee the security of the Pharaoh and his family.

Aset followed closely behind the litter of Kiya and the Pharaoh. While they walked through one of the main streets of Thebes Aset suddenly heard a lot of commotion to her left.

"Kiya!" she heard a voice shouting and at almost the same time a tall man burst through the line of soldiers in the direction Amenhotep and Kiya's litter while shouting: "Kiya, I still love you! I will always love you!"

To Aset's shock she saw it was Montu, the former palace guard. His last words would probably not have been understood by anybody because by the time he uttered them he had been pushed to the ground by four or five soldiers.

Walking behind the litter Aset could not see Kiya's reaction but she could imagine the horror on her face at seeing her former fiancé appearing so unexpectedly on her wedding to declare his love and then to be violently apprehended by the Pharaoh's soldiers.

Aset wondered what would happen next to Montu and she knew Kiya would be thinking the same.

Montu's action could be interpreted as an attempted assault on the wife of the Pharaoh and punishments on such an act were severe, most likely death, unless maybe Kiya could convince the Pharaoh to intervene on his behalf.

After Montu's unexpected action the procession started to move faster and the Royal Guards were more alert in case there would be any further threats to the Royal Family. The festive atmosphere of the procession had completely disappeared.

After his conversation with Tahat, Ipi went back to work at Intef's practice. It was busy but he had trouble concentrating on his work, many things had happened recently and he felt disappointed that Wenamun did not take his dreams seriously even though it were the priests who had taught him during his lessons in the House of Life that dreams contained messages and warnings from the Gods.

While he was feeding a patient who lay on a simple reed mat on the floor and was too weak to eat by himself, Ipi heard a voice quietly calling his name. Looking in the direction it came from he saw a cheerful looking Nebamun standing at the entrance of the hall where he was working holding a papyrus roll.

Ipi asked him to wait and after he had finished with his patient he went to Nebamun asking what could make him so happy during this time of mourning.

"Two things make me happy!" Nebamun replied and explained: "The first is that during the Pharaoh's wedding several of his high ranking guests quickly visited Karnak to pay their respects to Meryptah. Even the viziers of Upper and Lower

Egypt came. That means that amongst the high officials there is still support for us."

"That is very good news," Ipi spoke, feeling genuinely relieved, and then went on asking: "And what is the second thing that makes you happy?"

"A letter from my family!" Nebamun replied holding up the papyrus roll.

"That is nice, what do they say?" Ipi asked.

"They inquire about you, even my sister Sithathor asks about you," Nebamun replied with a smile. "They also say that they pray for the Lord Amun to bless you with happiness and good health and they hope to see you again."

Ipi smiled and spoke: "I like your family very much and also hope to meet them again sometime."

"That is great," Nebamun answered, "because they write you are welcome to visit them in Mendes any time."

"That is very friendly but I am very busy here and it takes a long time to travel to the delta," Ipi replied.

"They are not asking you to come now!" Nebamun spoke, pretending to be annoyed by Ipi's reply, and continued: "But you can at least think about it before you turn the invitation down. Just remember that whenever you have the opportunity you can go and visit my family."

"Fine, I will think about it," Ipi replied. He liked Nebamun's family and really wanted to go to Mendes to meet them again but he just could not imagine himself travelling all the way to the delta which was far away from Thebes, the only place he had known in all his life.

"How is Montu doing now?" Amenhotep asked. The Pharaoh controlled himself but was clearly upset about the disturbance during the wedding procession.

"He is fine, Your Majesty. He resisted when the guards took him so they had to use force to subdue him but he will recover from the wounds he received," Hekanakht informed the Pharaoh and, while producing a dagger, continued: "We found his army dagger on him but fortunately he did not use it when he tried to fight off the soldiers."

Kiya who, together with Aset, was present at the meeting of Amenhotep with his Head of the Royal Guard and the Viceroy of Kush about the incident on the way back to the palace, paled when she heard Hekanakht speak.

Nefertiti and her father Aye also attended the meeting in the Pharaoh's private office and the Great Royal Wife remarked: "That man is lucky to be still alive after what he did."

"What do you think I should do with Montu, Thutmose? He is after all one of your guards," Amenhotep asked the Viceroy of Kush.

Even though the Pharaoh did not seem to blame him for what his soldier had done Thutmose clearly felt uneasy and tried to give Amenhotep the answer he would like to hear.

"It is unacceptable what he did and only the most severe punishment will suffice!" Thutmose replied, while overdoing his effort to sound indignant about what had happened.

"Do you mean he should be executed?" Amenhotep asked.

"Could there be any other punishment for the crime this man has committed? He could have hurt your bride or maybe even Your Majesty," Thutmose spoke, hoping the Pharaoh would be impressed by the stern manner he advised to deal with Montu.

"No," Kiya suddenly intervened in a pleading voice while grabbing the Pharaoh's hand. "Please don't kill him! I beg you!"

Aset watched Amenhotep and saw he was in doubt about what to do.

While the Pharaoh was thinking Aye took Nefertiti by the arm and took her to a corner of the room where they whispered for a moment.

"If I don't punish Montu the people will think I am weak," the Pharaoh finally spoke. "I am sorry, Kiya, but I have to set an example to prevent this from happening again."

"Dear husband," the calm voice of Nefertiti suddenly sounded in the room. "Why don't you show mercy? After all Montu is just in love and did not mean to hurt anybody. Give him a symbolic punishment and let him go."

"The Great Royal Wife is right!" Aye now spoke. "Tell the people you let Montu live because it is your wedding day. The people will see this as proof that you are a merciful Pharaoh."

"I cannot go against the will of both my wives and my closest advisor," Amenhotep spoke, raising both his hands in front of him in a mock sign of surrender, and after a moment of thought went on speaking to Thutmose: "Give Montu a beating of twenty strokes with a stick on his back and keep him imprisoned until you return to Kush. After that he is never to enter the Two Lands again. If he ever returns he will be executed immediately!"

"It will be done as you say, Your Majesty. This is a very wise and merciful decision," Thutmose replied in a humble voice.

"Thank you so much, Your Majesty!" Kiya exclaimed, feeling so relieved Montu would stay alive that she, for a moment, forgot she was now the Pharaoh's wife and did not have to address him in such a formal manner anymore.

Then she turned to Nefertiti and embraced her, speaking: "Thank you so much. I will never forget this."

"That is what sisters are for, Kiya," Nefertiti answered with a smile.

There were already many guests waiting in the banquet hall when Amenhotep and Kiya finally arrived.

The Pharaoh had invited almost all the high officials and many members of the nobility to attend the Royal banquet and the parties he had organized for the coming days.

Upon entering the banquet hall all guests received a garland of fragrant flowers around their neck and a wax-cone on their head. When the banquet would progress the wax of the cone would melt and drip down, mingling its scent with the fragrant smell of the flowers and adding to the atmosphere of the party.

The banquet started as soon as the Pharaoh and Kiya sat down at a large table where the other members of the Royal Family and guests of honour, which included Kiya's parents, were already waiting.

Servants entered the hall carrying trays laden with dishes ranging from beef, fish and duck to pastries and various kinds of bread. The palace kitchen had also prepared fruits and vegetables and the Pharaoh had arranged for a wide variety of wines and beers to be poured for his guests.

The guests were entertained by musicians, singers and dancers. Accompanied by the musicians on their drums, harps and lutes the singers sang folk songs and encouraged the guests to join them in their songs while male and female dancers danced between the guests, clapping their hands in time with the music.

During the party many of the guests came forward to the table of Amenhotep and his bride to wish them happiness and good fortune and to offer them wedding presents.

Aset stayed around Kiya but since Kiya was busy acknowledging the many well-wishers she did not have to do much except for taking over the presents Kiya received.

When the banquet finally neared its end Aset looked through the hall and saw many men and women being clearly drunk, some of them had even fallen asleep in spite of the loud music and the noise of the partygoers.

Aset looked at Kiya who was really enjoying the party and was engaged in a conversation with her parents while Amenhotep was speaking with his mother and Meryra who, as a guest of honour, was invited to sit with the Royal Family.

"You are looking very lonely, Aset," a voice suddenly spoke.

Aset turned to see who it was and saw Merykare, the Pharaoh's scribe. He was also one of the wedding guests but contrary to many others he did not seem drunk.

"I have to be here in case Kiya needs me," Aset replied trying not to stutter or blush like she did the last time they spoke.

"I am sure she won't mind if you join me for a glass of wine for a moment," the scribe replied.

"I don't know," Aset spoke, feeling really tempted. "I have to..."

"It is after all the wedding party of your best friend," Merykare insisted.

Aset still doubted but then Merykare spoke: "I have an idea. I will bring two cups of wine here. We can drink here while you can watch Kiya."

Without even waiting for an answer Merykare left to fetch two cups of wine leaving Aset behind with her heart beating heavily in her chest. She had always looked forward to a moment like this but now she was afraid she would not know what to say.

Merykare quickly returned with two cups of red wine, one of which he offered to Aset.

"I brought you the best wine I could find," the scribe told.

"Oh, thank you," Aset replied, desperately thinking about what more she could say.

"Did you enjoy the party?" Merykare asked.

"Yes, I liked it very much," Aset answered, even though she didn't really enjoy it because she was not allowed to actually take part in it.

"Kiya is very lucky to marry the Pharaoh," Merykare continued speaking.

"Yes, she is very lucky," Aset answered after taking a sip from her wine; it was another lie because she doubted whether Kiya should be considered lucky.

"Have you ever thought about marriage, Aset?" the scribe asked again.

Aset had to hold her cup with both hands to keep her from dropping it and replied in shock: "What do you mean with such a question?"

"I am sorry. I didn't mean to be intrusive," Merykare retorted defensively. "I just meant...."

For a moment Merykare stood there quietly looking at Aset before he emptied his cup in one gulp and spoke: "Forget about it. Thank you for drinking a cup of wine with me, Aset."

Merykare quickly left, leaving Aset behind wondering about what he had been trying to say.

A few moments later the Pharaoh and Kiya got up from their chairs and were ready to leave. They thanked their guests for their attendance and started to walk out of the banquet hall.

Kiya would spend the rest of the evening and the night in the Pharaoh's chambers where Aset was not allowed to enter.

Aset escorted Kiya to the entrance of the Pharaoh's chambers and when she entered it Aset grabbed her hand and squeezed it encouragingly. Kiya looked at her with a thankful look in her eyes and squeezed Aset's hand back.

Tired after an eventful day Aset went back to Kiya's apartment. She poured herself a cup of wine, sat down in one of Kiya's comfortable chairs and stared out of the window at the bright stars in the evening sky.

Aset started to think about the events of the past day; she remembered the incident with the poor Montu and the surprising intervention of Nefertiti to save him.

Aset also thought about how Kiya was being addressed in the Aten Temple as The Great Lady Kiya and the titles she had received: The Favourite and The Greatly Beloved Wife of the Lord of the Two Lands, Child of the Aten Who Lives Now and Forever. These were impressive titles but Aset wondered why Kiya was not referred to as Royal

Wife as would have been normal. Was it because Kiya was not of Royal or noble blood?

Finally Aset's thoughts went to her strange meeting with Merykare. What did he want? Was he trying to get closer to her and, if that was the case, had she pushed him away?

The next morning when Aset woke up she did not feel well. She wasn't used to drinking wine and the two cups she had drunk the previous night had already been too much for her.

She could not eat anything so she immediately went to assist preparing the breakfast for the Royal Family and then went to the entrance of the Pharaoh's chambers to wait for Kiya to appear.

She did not have to wait long before Amenhotep and Kiya came out to have breakfast.

"Good morning Your Majesty, good morning My Lady," Aset greeted politely while she made a bow.

Amenhotep and Kiya were in the middle of a conversation. Kiya acknowledged Aset's greeting with a nod and a smile while Amenhotep ignored it completely.

"I will show you my wedding present for you after breakfast, Kiya. I am sure you will love it," Aset heard the Pharaoh say.

Aset was not the only person who suffered from the effects of the previous night. Kiya's parents looked very tired at breakfast while Queen Teye and Aye did not even attend and had ordered their breakfast to be delivered to their private quarters.

Kiya and Amenhotep seemed to be the only people who felt well. Aset noticed Kiya was genuinely happy.

"Please tell me now what my present is. I can't wait any longer," she begged jokingly.

"No Kiya, I told you to wait until we have finished our breakfast," Amenhotep replied and then added with a smile: "And I feel very hungry this morning so I am planning on having a long breakfast."

After they had finally finished their breakfast the Pharaoh ordered everybody to follow him. He took Kiya by the arm and walked out of the palace in the direction of the palace dock.

Arriving there they saw a new bark with the sailors on board and ready to sail.

"This is my present to you, Kiya. I have named her Daughter of the Aten, just like you are," Amenhotep spoke, gesturing at the boat.

"It is beautiful!" Kiya exclaimed and immediately ran on board over the gangway.

Amenhotep followed her more slowly and invited Kiya's parents to join him on board.

They inspected Kiya's new boat which had a large cabin with a sleeping compartment, a living area and even a small kitchen that made it suitable for long journeys. It had a single mast with a sail and seven oars on both sides to propel it when there was no wind, steering was done by means of two large rudder oars on the stern.

After a while everybody disembarked again and Amenhotep took Kiya by her hand, looked at the Daughter of the Aten and spoke casually: "Next week we will use your boat for a trip to Memphis."

"What?" Kiya asked excitedly. "Are we going to Memphis?"

"Of Course!" Amenhotep replied and explained: "We will have to bring your parents home to the new villa which I have ordered to be constructed for them. And the people in Memphis and the cities along the way have to see their Pharaoh's new wife."

"Have you built a villa for my parents?" Kiya asked again, the surprises of that morning almost getting too much for her.

"The parents of a Pharaoh's wife have to live in a decent environment," Amenhotep spoke with a big smile. Aset saw he was clearly enjoying seeing Kiya so happy.

While Amenhotep was speaking a court official appeared, he waited for the Pharaoh to finish then bowed and spoke: "Your Majesty, a messenger has arrived with a message from King Tushratta of Mitanni."

The smile on Amenhotep's face immediately disappeared and his expression became somber.

"Take your parents with your new boat for a cruise on the Nile, Kiya. Unfortunately I have important business to attend to. Come to see me in my office after you return so I can inform you further about our journey next week," Amenhotep told his wife and after having given a friendly nod to her parents he returned to the palace.

Penthu had not enjoyed the wedding party the previous day. The Pharaoh had invited him personally which forced him to attend but to celebrate so shortly after the death of Meryptah did not seem right to him.

Early that morning he had been asked to come to the chambers of Queen Teye who was not feeling well. Penthu concluded that the excitement of the previous day combined with excessive wine drinking during the party had been too much for her. He gave her an herb potion against the headache and advised the Queen to rest for the coming day. Knowing Teye, however, Penthu knew she would probably not follow his advice.

After visiting Teye he decided to go to the Karnak Temple to pray for the ka of Meryptah. Not sure about how the priests in the temple were thinking about him Penthu was nervous to go there but he felt he owed it to his High Priest.

He took a boat from the palace that was going to Thebes that morning and arriving there he walked through the city's busy streets to the temple.

Penthu entered Karnak through its enormous pylon and immediately noticed the temple was busier than normal but he had already expected that. Worshippers of Amun had come from the whole region, probably even from the whole country, to the temple to mourn the High Priest.

After crossing the forecourt Penthu entered the second court of the Karnak Temple.

On the second court he met a few of his former colleagues from the temple's practice amongst the priests but they ignored him or just greeted him coldly.

A shiver went through Penthu when behind his back he heard an angry voice saying: "You are too late! Our High Priest has departed already!"

Feeling hurt Penthu looked behind him but did not know who of the many priests in the court had made the remark.

Penthu could not pay his respects to the body of Meryptah because it was being prepared for the afterlife in the House of Death, so he went to the shrine that was dedicated specially to the memory of the High Priest.

Here all the priests of Amun came to pray for the man who had been in charge of the temple during one of its most glorious periods and here the ceremonies ordered by Maya were held.

After burning incense in front of a statue representing Meryptah and offering fruit, bread and wine which he knew the High Priest to like, Penthu knelt on the floor and asked Amun to help Meryptah arrive safely in the Kingdom of Osiris and to protect his ka for all eternity.

Penthu also prayed directly to the ka of the High Priest to ask for his understanding of his difficult position and to ask forgiveness if any of his actions had hurt him or the temple.

When he was finally ready Penthu wanted to leave but found Maya and Wenamun waiting for him.

"It is too bad you could not have come earlier Penthu," Maya spoke with a calm voice but his eyes had an angry glare. "Meryptah could have benefited more from a visit of the best physician in the Two Lands while he was still alive."

"Don't you think I haven't thought about that myself?" Penthu replied angrily and continued: "I was never aware that Meryptah's condition was that serious and I also had my responsibilities in the palace. But if you had wanted me to come to Karnak to treat Meryptah you could have asked His Majesty to send me. I am sure he would have agreed."

"We have actually considered that but Meryptah himself rejected that idea. He was so disappointed in the Pharaoh that he did not want the priests of Amun to go to him and beg for help. The Pharaoh would have reveled in such an experience," Maya scoffed and went on aggressively: "The Pharaoh must have known that Meryptah's condition was critical but he did not send you here to help. Only now he is dead he allows you to come."

"What are you trying to imply about His Majesty? He has respect for the dead so he let me come here and if His Majesty would have thought I could have saved Meryptah's life he would have sent me to the temple earlier," Penthu spoke in defense of Amenhotep and before Maya or Wenamun could say anything he attacked Maya: "You don't know His Majesty as I do. You are always negative about him and now you actually blame him for Meryptah's death. If you won't change your stance towards him, now you are going to be High Priest of Amun, the consequences for the temple and the Two Lands can be very serious. It is now time for you to start acting responsibly as your new position demands from you. His Majesty is aware of his responsibility for his country and his people and he takes this responsibility very seriously even though maybe not in a way that you like!"

Penthu paused a moment to catch his breath before pointing his finger at Maya and speaking: "You, Maya, could learn a lot from His Majesty. You are the most powerful person in the Two Lands after him. Think further than the interests of the temple, use your influence for the benefit of the whole country!"

For a moment Maya and Wenamun were too overwhelmed to say anything but then Maya became red with anger and just when he wanted to speak Wenamun put his hand on his shoulder to stop him and spoke in a calm voice in which a suppressed anger was clearly audible: "Penthu, you might be a good physician but have you no idea of the function of our temple? Don't you know of the importance of our position for the country and the people? Look at all the people that come to mourn our High Priest, many of them have travelled for days just to come here to pray for him. This temple is the link between the King of the Gods and the world. All the Pharaohs in the past have respected our position and been loyal to Amun and the Gods have rewarded them for this loyalty with a prosperous country. If the Pharaoh takes his responsibility seriously then he will maintain the balance created by his predecessors that has made the Two Lands into the great country it is now."

When Wenamun stopped speaking Maya remarked: "If your Pharaoh respects the dead, as you said, then why don't we hear from him personally? We have received nothing from him, not even a simple message!"

Maya had been speaking with an obvious contempt but Penthu was not sure whether Maya's contempt was meant for him or the Pharaoh.

"I don't know why," Penthu replied. "His Majesty is very busy, especially now because of his wedding, or maybe he is still angry because of your disrespectful behaviour towards him during your audience, I really don't know. But why do you ask me this? His Majesty does not explain his actions to me."

"I ask you this because you seem to approve of almost everything the Pharaoh does, even if it damages the temple where you grew up! The temple that has given you everything you ever needed," Maya spoke and then added in a voice that suddenly sounded very tired: "Please leave, Penthu, just go back to the palace. You don't belong here anymore."

Not wishing to speak any further with Penthu, Maya left the room.

Wenamun had been left alone with Penthu and before he followed Maya he spoke calmly: "You are right that we don't know the Pharaoh as you do but when you spend all your time in the palace you don't see the consequences of the Pharaoh's reign. Times are getting hard, not just for us but for most of the temples in the country and it looks like it is only going to get harder in the future."

Shortly afterwards Penthu was on his way back to the palace. He reflected on his meeting with Maya and Wenamun and hoped they would come to understand the Pharaoh's motives for his actions.

He was surprised to find out that he did not feel sad about his argument with the two priests. The argument and the cool reception he had received at Karnak had taught him that Maya had been right about at least one thing: He did not belong at Karnak anymore. He was still a servant of Amun, and he would remain that for the rest of his life, but he no longer considered himself to be attached to the temple. He could now devote himself completely to his service to the Pharaoh and to any task he would receive from him in the future.

Aset and Kiya thoroughly enjoyed the cruise with Kiya's parents on the Nile with the Daughter of the Aten. They sailed far down the river and had lunch on the boat.

After they arrived back at Malkata Palace they immediately went to the Pharaoh's office as Amenhotep had asked Kiya to do.

They were surprised to find a guard in front of the Pharaoh's door who did not want to let them in, explaining that the Pharaoh was in a meeting with his mother, Queen Teye. Kiya insisted that Amenhotep wanted to see her and even reminded the guard that he was talking to the Pharaoh's wife. The guard finally relented and allowed them to enter Amenhotep's private office.

Inside Aset and Kiya were again surprised to walk into what appeared to be a serious argument between the Pharaoh and his mother.

"I thought you were going to support me in whatever I do!" Amenhotep, who was sitting behind his desk, complained.

"And I still do," Teye replied, sitting opposite her son and having apparently recovered from the wedding party of the previous day. "But I can't stand by without warning you when you are about to make a mistake that could have very serious consequences."

"Why do you think I am making a mistake, mother?" Amenhotep asked in a sulky voice.

"Just look at these letters!" Teye exclaimed angrily, standing up and pointing at clay tablets containing correspondence which lay between them on the Pharaoh's desk.

She took a heavy breath to calm down and then continued as if she were a teacher lecturing a difficult student: "King Suppiluliuma of the increasingly powerful Kingdom of Hatti complains that you don't give him the gifts he asked for and that you have insulted him by writing your own name above his on your correspondence with him. And you also offend our ally Tushratta of Mitanni by refusing to send him the gold which he needs to maintain his army. Let me remind you that Mitanni is the barrier between us and Hatti. Hatti starts to behave more aggressively towards Mitanni and us. We must do our best to maintain good relations with Hatti and in the meantime help Mitanni maintaining their army to keep Hatti under control."

Teye stopped speaking for a moment and Amenhotep also remained quiet. Neither of them seemed to notice Aset and Kiya who were standing at the door, not knowing what to do or say.

Queen Teye sat down again in her chair and finally went on speaking, this time in a milder tone: "With the work for the Aten that you intend to carry out war with Hatti is the last thing you need, my son. So try to buy their friendship and help Mitanni to keep them under control. Let Mitanni do the fighting for us when necessary so you can devote your time to the Aten."

After another short silence Amenhotep spoke reluctantly: "You are probably right, mother. I will follow your advice."

Then the Pharaoh started to smile and remarked: "You are so wise. Where would I be without you to guide me?"

"I have learned from your father. He was a master at foreign diplomacy. That is how he managed to maintain a prosperous country without having to go on military campaigns all the time," Teye replied in admiration of her late husband.

"I don't mean to intrude but you have requested me to come here," Kiya finally found the courage to intervene in the conversation.

The Pharaoh and his mother both looked up in surprise with Teye having an annoyed expression on her face because of the disturbance. "You wanted to inform me about the journey to Memphis," Kiya clarified her presence nervously.

CHAPTER 10
A JOURNEY DOWN THE NILE

A week later a fleet of fifteen boats left Thebes for Memphis. Apart from Kiya's boat there was also Amenhotep's private bark called the Shining Aten as well as boats for accompanying officials, servants, guards and boats which transported provisions for the Pharaoh and his escort. Meryra, the High Priest of the Aten, also escorted the Pharaoh in his private boat.

Five boats of the fleet belonged to Aperel, the Vizier of Lower Egypt. He joined the Pharaoh on his journey back to Memphis to return to his residence after his stay in Thebes for the Royal wedding and the week of parties and ceremonies that had followed.

Queen Teye and Nefertiti, the Great Royal Wife, remained in Thebes and would take care of the daily business in the palace.

Nobody of the Royal Family accompanied the Pharaoh and Kiya on their trip north which made the journey more comfortable for Kiya. This trip, the Pharaoh had said, was to introduce Kiya to the people of Egypt.

Even though his personal bark was sailing with the fleet Amenhotep travelled with Kiya and her parents on the Daughter of the Aten.

On their way north the crew did not need to unfold the sails of the boats or to row but instead they could just let themselves drift down the river on the current making the journey relatively easy for everybody.

Kiya and her parents were sitting on deck, on comfortable chairs in the shade of a canopy while Amenhotep was inside the cabin dictating letters to Merykare. "Affairs of state never stop," he explained the reason of his absence.

Aset stayed close to Kiya, feeling afraid to make herself too comfortable because of the Pharaoh's presence on the boat.

Since the wedding she had hardly had an opportunity to have an informal conversation with Kiya and even though she was always near her, Aset missed her friend.

The further they sailed from Thebes the fewer signs of population there were on the banks of the Nile. The last of the villas of wealthy Thebans had disappeared from view a while ago and after that they only saw the simple thatched or mud brick houses of poor farmers who tended to small plots of land.

Every time the fleet passed such farms the people on the fields would stop their work and bow respectfully for the boats of their Pharaoh. The farmer's children were often too enthusiastic to bow and waved and cheered to the Royal Fleet and Kiya, who greatly enjoyed the cruise down the Nile, waved back just as enthusiastically.

"I remember the trip from Memphis to Thebes with Crown Prince Thutmose," Kiya told her parents. "It is only a few years ago but it seems so long and so much has changed since then."

Waving to some children who were playing on the bank of the river she went on: "At that time I was still a servant and I did not have the opportunity to enjoy the trip like I do now."

Then suddenly Kiya thought about her friend and spoke: "Aset, come sit with us. This should be a fun trip for you too."

Fortunately for Aset, the Pharaoh remained inside the cabin of the boat for a long time being occupied with his work and giving her the chance to relax.

That evening the fleet arrived in a city called Gebtu and since it was too dangerous to sail in the dark they would spend the night there.

The mayor of Gebtu, who had been informed of the arrival of the Royal visitors, was already waiting for them at the harbour, together with the city's officials, noblemen and most of the population.

"Your Majesty, my name is Djedkare and I am the mayor of Gebtu. It is my great honour to welcome you and your beautiful new wife to the city of Min, the great God of fertility," the mayor of Gebtu spoke in a loud pompous tone, as soon as Amenhotep and Kiya disembarked.

Aset, who followed them, smiled when she heard the mayor, an old, obese man wearing an ill-fitting robe and a wig, speak. He was clearly indulging in the importance of his duty to welcome the Pharaoh in front of all the inhabitants of his city.

"We are pleased to have such a warm welcome in your beautiful city," Amenhotep replied.

After inquiring about the journey and introducing the city's high officials to the Pharaoh, Djedkare spoke: "Your Majesty, allow me to invite you and your new wife to visit the Temple of Min, the chief God of Gebtu and God of fertility. A visit to His temple will surely guarantee your marriage to produce a lot of offspring."

Aset noticed Kiya looking down uncomfortably after listening to the mayor's words.

"That won't be necessary," Amenhotep replied to Djedkare, who was visibly surprised and upset by the unexpected rejection of his invitation.

It was common practice for official guests of an Egyptian town to visit the local temple and worship the chief God during their visit.

"I will leave it up to Aten to decide if our marriage will be fruitful or not," the Pharaoh clarified his decision to the mayor.

Aset saw Djedkare was completely taken by surprise by the Pharaoh's unusual decision and that he did not know what to do with the Pharaoh.

It was a hot evening and the mayor dabbed sweat from his forehead with a napkin before he spoke in a voice which had lost all its previous confidence: "Your Majesty, may I invite you and your wife to my villa for a banquet?"

"We accept your invitation, Djedkare," the Pharaoh replied to the mayor's great relief.

Later that evening the Pharaoh, Kiya and her parents, Meryra and Aperel with his wife were attending a large banquet at Djedkare's villa.

They were joined by Gebtu's high officials and nobility who were also invited by the mayor.

Djedkare's villa was a large walled complex on the riverside with lush gardens and a pond.

Aset, who had followed Kiya to the banquet, watched the depictions on the walls of the mayor's home; apart from religious scenes, most of which involved the city's chief God Min, Who appeared to be Djedkare's favourite God, many scenes depicted parties and banquets.

"The mayor of Gebtu clearly liked the finer things in life," Aset thought to herself.

The banquet was not as grand as the banquets in the palace but with three musicians and two dancers and a large amount of good food and wine Djedkare did not disappoint his guests.

Having the Pharaoh as a guest in his villa and seeing everybody having a good time at his banquet Djedkare regained his self-confidence and pompous manner of before.

"Drink some more of my wine, Your Majesty. It comes from my private estate and, if I may say so, it is the best wine in the Two Lands," the mayor spoke while he personally refilled the Pharaoh's cup as well as his own.

Amenhotep politely sipped from his wine but Aset saw he was not comfortable. She hoped that Djedkare, who was starting to get drunk, would be able to control himself when being around the Pharaoh.

Earlier, when she had had a quick meal herself in the kitchen with one of Djedkare's servants, Aset had asked about the mayor to which the young man had replied: "He is a good man when he is sober, however, he often drinks too much and then he sometimes loses his self-control."

Contrary to her husband, Djedkare's wife was very thin. She was wearing too much jewellery and cosmetics which made Aset think her husband had ordered her to do so in a failed attempt to emphasize their high status, because she could not imagine a woman dressing up like that voluntarily.

Seeing Djedkare getting drunk she constantly tried to stop her husband from drinking more wine but he brushed off her warnings and complaints.

Finally that which the mayor's wife, Aset and many other attendants to the banquet had feared happened.

"Why don't you want to visit the Temple of Min? You have just got married so he is more useful to you than Aten," Djedkare spoke to Amenhotep with a hardly understandable voice because of the amount of alcohol he had drunk.

Then, to nobody in particular, he went on: "Min is an old and well-known God but I have hardly ever heard of Aten!"

Before he could say more three of the city's officials who were sitting close to Djedkare jumped up and dragged the mayor, who resisted kicking and screaming, out of the room. At the same time another official, together with Djedkare's wife, apologized to the Pharaoh and begged him to forgive the drunken mayor.

Immediately after the incident with Djedkare, the Pharaoh decided to leave.

Aset could not make out what Amenhotep really thought about what had happened - he acted as if he had been insulted - but she also noticed a glimpse of a smile on his face the moment the drunken Djedkare was removed by his own subordinates.

The next morning, just after Amenhotep had finished his offering to the Aten and was ready to leave Gebtu to continue the journey to Memphis, a tired looking Djedkare escorted by his officials appeared in the harbour.

The officials stayed at a respectful distance of the moored fleet but Djedkare continued forward until he was as close to the Pharaoh's boat as he was allowed to get by the Royal Guards.

The Pharaoh and everybody else were curious about what the mayor wanted and came on deck to watch.

When Djedkare noticed the Pharaoh he threw himself in the dust and started crying and wailing: "Your Majesty, please forgive me! I have insulted you and disgraced myself and my city! You have honoured me by visiting my house and I offended you and the Aten!"

Aset stood next to Kiya watching the mayor wailing while he threw dust on his head.

Pharaoh Amenhotep stood on Kiya's other side and spoke: "Last night I decided his behaviour was unacceptable and Djedkare should be relieved of his position but, Kiya, you are my wife and should learn to make difficult decisions. I let you decide whether he should be forgiven or not."

Kiya thought for a moment and then replied: "He disrespected you and the Aten but it was because he was drunk, not out of disloyalty. He can stay in his position but in return he will have to build a small temple to the Aten in Gebtu to make up for his wrongdoing."

Both Aset and the Pharaoh looked at Kiya in astonishment because of her decision. Then Amenhotep smiled and kissed his wife on the cheek, something Aset had never seen a Pharaoh do before, and spoke proudly: "That is an even better solution than I had. It will be done as you said."

The following days they passed through many towns and cities and spent the nights in Iunet and Abedju, the burial ground of Egypt's earliest Pharaohs and city of the God Osiris, the King of the Netherworld.

Abedju's mayor welcomed the Pharaoh and Kiya on their arrival and even managed to persuade Amenhotep to visit the Temple of Osiris, the holy place where every year the reenactment of the death and resurrection of the popular God was carried out during the Mysteries of Osiris, an event that attracted pilgrims from all over the country.

Their next stop was Khent-Min, the city from which Nefertiti's family originated.

Contrary to the other towns, where Amenhotep and Kiya spent the night on their bark, in Khent-Min they stayed at the villa of the Great Royal wife's family which had been specially prepared for their visit.

The following morning they left the Pharaoh's family-in-law later than planned and to make up for their lost time the ship's crew had to row in order to reach Khmun, the city of Thoth, the ibis-headed God, before dark.

"I am looking forward to arriving in Khmun," Merykare told Aset excitedly and explained: "Thoth is the patron of the writers. As soon as we arrive I will visit His temple to worship Him."

That afternoon a strong wind started to blow from the north and slowed down the speed of the fleet.

At the end of the afternoon some of the sailors started to talk about not being able to reach Khmun before the evening and when at dusk there was no settlement in sight the Pharaoh agreed to spend the night on the river bank.

They stopped and set up a camp on the east bank of the Nile on a large desert plain that was surrounded by rock formations.

Merykare was very disappointed and during a simple dinner, cooked on fires on the riverbank, complained to Aset: "Worshiping Thoth in His temple in Khmun was what I was looking forward to during this trip. Now, I will miss that opportunity. Tomorrow we will pass through

Khmun but won't stop long enough for me to visit the temple."

The Pharaoh and Kiya withdrew early to their sleeping quarters on Kiya's boat leaving Aset with time for herself.

In the bright light of the moon and the stars Aset could oversee the whole plain until the mountain range in the distance which was clearly silhouetted against the night sky. She could even see the guards that Hekanakht had sent out as a precaution against any possible danger that could come from the desert.

Aset was sitting between a group of soldiers and servants who were spending their free evening in the desert with drinking wine around a fire and looked at Merykare who was also sitting between them with a sulky face.

Aset drank two cups of wine to encourage herself and then walked over to Merykare and asked him to join her for a stroll. The scribe's face immediately brightened and he answered: "Yes, of course!"

They strolled onto the desert plain while they heard some of the soldiers and palace servants who stayed behind laughing and yelling remarks to them.

Aset and Merykare, however, did not care, it was the first time they had the opportunity to be alone and even though they did not say it to each other they knew both of them had been longing for it.

Strengthened by the two cups of wine Aset took Merykare by his hand and pulled him nearer to her. Merykare replied by putting his arm around her waist.

"Maybe we are lucky to have stranded here in the desert tonight," Aset remarked.

"I am happy to be here with you, Aset," Merykare replied. "But I really wish we could have made it to Khmun."

Getting irritated Aset sighed and spoke: "Forget about not being able to visit the Temple of Thoth, Merykare. Think about what you can do instead of what you can't do."

Merykare suddenly let go of Aset and replied angrily: "How can you say that? I am a scribe and a devout worshipper of Thoth. If you expect me to forget about visiting His temple, the temple that I have wanted to visit for as long as I remember, so easily then you are not the right woman for me!"

Immediately after he finished speaking Merykare turned around and walked back to the camp and left a crying Aset behind.

That night Aset did not sleep well. She had been thinking over and over about what went wrong between her and Merykare.

The next morning, as usual, she got up early to help Kiya wash and get dressed.

Like every day, Pharaoh Amenhotep was already up so that he, together with Meryra the High Priest, could greet the Aten as soon as He rose over the horizon.

Kiya decided to join her husband on the desert plain that morning and so did her parents, Aperel the vizier with his wife and many of the servants and soldiers.

More and more people at the Royal Court started to worship the Pharaoh's favourite God.

Aset did not understand much of the religion of the Aten and remained at a discreet distance while the others worshiped the rising sun.

As soon as the sun appeared over the horizon everybody fell on their knees and started praying, everybody except Amenhotep and Meryra who fell on their knees but instead of praying just stared in amazement at the sun.

Aset wondered what happened and moved closer. "Do you see that?" she heard the Pharaoh say.

"Yes, I see it," the High Priest replied in amazement without turning his gaze away from the sun.

"This is the place!" Amenhotep spoke again excitedly. "This is the place where Aten wants me to build His city!"

Aset looked at the sun and suddenly understood why the Pharaoh and the High Priest of the Aten were so excited. The sun was rising into the red and purple coloured sky out of a valley between two mountains and as such created a perfect image of the hieroglyph symbolizing the word 'horizon'.

That morning the Pharaoh changed all plans and instead of continuing further north he decided to stay longer on the desert plain.

"I want a stele erected here to commemorate this important day!" Aset heard Amenhotep say to Ranefer in a voice that was still filled with excitement. A few moments later the Pharaoh went on speaking: "I also want a boat to return to Thebes within an hour to fetch my architect Hemienu. I want him here as soon as possible!"

"But Hemienu works on the Gem Pa Aten," Ranefer protested.

"The work there will be able to continue without him for one or two weeks. He has experienced overseers who can keep the construction going," Amenhotep explained in a tone that did not accept any contradiction. "I need Hemienu here to inform him about my new project. A project that I have been dreaming of for a long time and this morning Aten finally gave me the sign to start working on it."

Amenhotep was sitting under the canopy on the deck of his private bark and stared at the empty plain where he planned to build Aten's city and to the valley on the horizon from where the Aten had risen that morning.

Kiya was sitting near her husband but did not dare to disturb him.

"I am going to need a lot of funds to complete this project," the Pharaoh quietly spoke to nobody in particular. "I should not have agreed to send so many treasures to the kings of Hatti and Mitanni."

Suddenly Amenhotep woke up out of his thoughts and called for his scribe, Merykare.

"I want to dictate a letter to my mother," he told Kiya and added: "Tushratta of Mitanni and Suppiluliuma of Hatti will have to do with half of what I had agreed to send them. I have a better use now for these treasures."

"I don't want to know who dies, Ipi, but tell me everything else that happens in your dream," Wenamun ordered Ipi.

As Tahat had told Ipi earlier Wenamun would speak with him about his recurring dreams.

Ipi was sitting in Wenamun's room and spoke in an emotional voice: "I see soldiers coming to the temple, I don't know why they come but they tell everybody to leave, civilians and priests. They beat everybody who doesn't obey their orders. Some priests want to stop them from continuing further into the temple and the soldiers remove them violently and some of the priests get killed."

After he finished describing his dream Ipi asked Wenamun: "Do you believe this dream is a prediction of the future? Will this happen for real? It makes me very scared."

"That is difficult to say," Wenamun replied and then asked: "Do you still regularly have this dream?"

"Not since I last told you about it," Ipi answered. "That is a good sign," Wenamun spoke. "If it is a prophetic dream it will most likely continue until this event you described actually happens. If the dream does return you should inform me about it."

When Ipi remained silent Wenamun, in an effort to reassure him, went on: "Ipi, I know you are very worried about the situation our temple is in at the moment and you are right to be worried. But the chance that something violent will happen or that the existence of our temple will be threatened is very small."

Wenamun paused a moment and then continued: "You have probably heard that Maya and I have been making use of the Pharaoh's absence by having meetings with Ramose, the vizier of Upper Egypt and mayor of Thebes. He serves the Pharaoh and even the Aten but has also remained a devout worshipper of Amun. He told me he is very sympathetic to our temple and promised to do what he can to support us at the Royal Court. Ramose is a very influential person so he will be an important ally!"

After telling Ipi the news about Karnak's important new ally Wenamun suddenly changed the topic of the conversation and spoke: "Ipi, I remember you told me about your nephew who died and for whose ka you promised to care."

"That is my nephew Djehuty. He died while I was working at Karnak," Ipi replied, not understanding why Wenamun so unexpectedly mentioned his nephew.

"You haven't visited his grave anymore since you returned from your visit to your family. I think you should return to your family for a couple of days to visit Djehuty's grave and take care of his ka," the priest explained.

Ipi understood what Wenamun meant and was happy he would have some days away from the temple to visit his family again and he would indeed also have the opportunity to fulfill his promise to Djehuty.

Penthu had also been travelling down the Nile with the Pharaoh but since both Amenhotep and Kiya were healthy there was not much to do for him except for the short examinations of the Pharaoh's and Kiya's health which he performed every morning.

Penthu did not have to treat the Pharaoh's servants and soldiers because there were other physicians to take care of them. He only had to take care of the Pharaoh and his new wife.

Since they had left Thebes Penthu had hardly spoken with Amenhotep, the only times they spoke was during the short daily examinations. The Pharaoh was always preoccupied and also sailed most of the time on Kiya's boat while Penthu travelled on the Pharaoh's private bark.

The first morning they spent on the desert plain Penthu wanted to see the Pharaoh for their daily meeting but to his great surprise he was told that the Pharaoh had no time for him and would be busy all day.

During that day the Pharaoh's guards erected tents for the Pharaoh and his escort to make their stay in the desert more bearable.

Penthu was also shown a tent but like everybody else, except the Pharaoh and Meryra, he had to share it with others.

Aperel and his wife preferred to keep living on their boat and had no tent erected. "Maybe they are not planning on staying long," Penthu thought to himself.

The following morning he was able to see Amenhotep again in his private tent which had been set up for him by the riverside but when Penthu started to make the usual inquiries about his health the Pharaoh replied: "I know exactly what you are going to ask me, Penthu, it is the same every time. So to save your precious time, before you ask me anything, I will tell you that I am healthy and have never felt better."

"It pleases me to hear that, Your Majesty," Penthu replied hesitatingly, believing the Pharaoh's words meant he came at an inconvenient moment and added: "If Your Majesty's health is excellent then you don't need me and I shall go again."

"No Penthu, I want you to stay for a moment," Amenhotep spoke and continued: "You must have heard rumours amongst the men about the reason why we are here. Can you tell me what you have heard?"

"I have heard that Your Majesty wants to build a city on this location," Penthu replied.

"That is correct. And what do you think about this plan?" Amenhotep went on.

Penthu felt uncomfortable, thought for a moment, and then replied: "Any idea that comes from a Pharaoh must be good."

The Pharaoh smiled and spoke: "A very diplomatic answer, Penthu. Maybe I will consider you for the post of ambassador to a foreign country in the future."

Seeing Penthu turning pale at the thought of being sent abroad Amenhotep started to laugh but then suddenly turned serious again.

"Penthu," the Pharaoh continued speaking: "I have told you already many times that I have great plans for the future. This is one of those plans."

While he spoke the last words Amenhotep gestured in the direction of the empty plain.

Then he went on: "For a long time I have been thinking about building a city dedicated to the Aten and yesterday morning Aten has showed me this is the place for His city. Here on virgin land, land which has never been dedicated to any God or has never belonged to any person, I will build a city that belongs only to the Aten! No longer will Aten be a minor God or will He be in the shadow of Amun. Here, in this city, Aten will be the only God and all the temples will be dedicated to Him!"

"Will the priests of the other religions accept this?" Penthu wondered.

"They will have no choice!" Amenhotep replied. "I am Pharaoh and I will do what is best for the Two Lands with or without their approval. The Aten has ordered me to build Him a city far away from all the other cities with their multitude of temples dedicated to I don't even know how many Gods, so I have to obey that order to please Him. And when Aten is pleased He will reward our country with prosperity."

After a brief silence Amenhotep spoke again and both his voice and face betrayed his enthusiasm about his latest project: "I had everything already planned for this city, the only thing that was missing until yesterday was a location. Now that the Aten has shown me the location, the construction of the city can start soon. In the palace in Thebes I have papyruses on which I have drawn maps of the entire city. They will be brought here so I can show them to Hemienu, my architect, but I myself don't even need them; I know every line on those maps, every house and every street has been designed by me personally! When I look at the empty plain outside I don't see sand and mountains but an entire city. A city like no other in the Two Lands!"

Aset was standing outside the Pharaoh's tent and waited for Kiya to return from her private meeting with her husband.

She wondered how long they would stay on that deserted plain. She had already heard some of the soldiers and servants complaining about their presence in such uncomfortable surroundings. They wondered about the reason for their prolonged stay and wanted to return to civilization.

Apparently the Pharaoh was going to build a city there but Aset could not understand his motivation. It was a remote area, far from everything, and it was a dry and barren place. And what would happen when the construction of the city was finished? Was the Royal Family going to move to this place and would she have to follow them? Was she expected to live there in the future?

While Aset was waiting and thinking about the Pharaoh's unusual plans Merykare came walking up to her.

He looked a bit uncomfortable and spoke: "Aset, I want to apologize for my behaviour the other night. I did not mean to get angry at you, I was just very disappointed about us not reaching Khmun."

"But you said I was not the right woman for you," Aset replied, feeling hurt again when remembering the scribe's words.

"I know and that was wrong of me," Merykare spoke. "I hope you will forgive me and I want to invite you to take another walk with me tonight."

When Aset seemed to doubt about accepting his invitation Merykare added: "I promise you I will be in a better mood this time."

Aset started to laugh, feeling relieved that their relationship seemed to normalize again and replied: "I accept your invitation. I am looking forward to seeing you tonight."

Merykare smiled and spoke: "I am so happy you accept. Tonight I will make up for my bad behaviour."

Soon after Merykare had left Kiya appeared from the Pharaoh's tent.

"We will be leaving tomorrow morning, Aset," she told.

"Has the Pharaoh decided to leave? I thought he planned to stay here a long time," Aset replied surprised.

"We are leaving, Aset," Kiya clarified. "Amenhotep, together with most of the soldiers and servants, will stay here. We will go with Aperel and his escort to Memphis to bring my parents back."

"Will Merykare also come with us to Memphis?" Aset asked.

"No, Amenhotep needs him here. Why do you ask this?" Kiya replied.

"For no reason, never mind," Aset spoke, feeling depressed. Just when the contact between her and Merykare was improving and she started to see the bright side of their stay at this deserted area she had to go and leave her scribe behind.

That evening Aset was waiting for Merykare to come. She sat by the riverside and watched a group of soldiers who were sitting around a fire.

The mood amongst to soldiers was bad, they were drinking and complaining about the prospect of a long stay in the desert and the more they drank the louder they became.

When Hekanakht, during an inspection of the guards, passed the small group he reprimanded them sharply.

"Never complain about anything the Pharaoh demands from you!" he spoke strictly and before continuing his inspection he remarked: "Consider it an honour that you may serve him here!"

The soldiers stopped complaining but Aset knew it would only be temporary. She was afraid that if they would have to stay there much longer without anything more to do than guarding the Pharaoh's camp on an empty desert plain some soldiers might even rebel.

Aset waited for a long time but Merykare did not come.

The soldiers by the fire had kept drinking and eventually went to sleep in one of the tents that had been erected or fell asleep by the fire.

Disappointed Aset finally went to Kiya's boat where she and Kiya still spent their nights together with Kiya's parents who had their own private room on the boat.

Kiya would not spend the night before her departure with her husband who had said he would be busy working all night.

Aset felt humiliated and decided she did not want to have anything to do with Merykare anymore.

Kiya had given Aset permission to go out that evening and when she returned Aset was relieved to see that Kiya was already asleep. Aset was feeling very depressed and the last thing she wanted was having Kiya asking her what she did that evening.

Even though Kiya was her best friend she did not want to have to tell her about her humiliating experience.

Quietly Aset lay down on her sleeping mat on the floor next to Kiya's bed when Kiya opened her eyes and spoke: "You returned very late. Where did you go?"

"Nowhere," Aset replied, lying on her mat with her back turned to Kiya to prevent her from seeing that she had been crying. "I just spent some time around the fire with a few guards."

"Is there something wrong, Aset?" Kiya asked, sounding worried.

"No, I am fine," Aset replied to which Kiya immediately answered in a strict tone: "Aset, I know you long enough to know that you are not fine. Tell me what happened and turn around so I can see your face!"

Aset obeyed and turned to Kiya.
"Have you been crying?" Kiya asked after seeing Aset's face.

Aset decided to tell Kiya everything. She told about her meeting with Merykare at the wedding, of their fight on the evening they arrived on the desert plain and about how Merykare had come to her that day to invite her to meet him that evening but then never came. She even told Kiya that she had decided never to speak to Merykare again.

Kiya started to smile and spoke: "Merykare was really planning to meet you, Aset, but Amenhotep is keeping him busy. He told me he would spend most of the night dictating letters to government officials in Memphis that Aperel will take with him tomorrow morning. I actually visited Amenhotep's tent a short time this evening and saw that Merykare looked very unhappy."

"So Merykare did not make me spend the whole evening waiting for him on purpose?" Aset asked, feeling relieved.

"No, of course not! He wanted to spend the evening with you," Kiya replied.

Kiya got up from her bed and poured a cup of wine.

"This will help you to get over your spoiled evening," she said while handing the cup to Aset, which was a very unusual act for a Pharaoh's wife, and then went on speaking: "I see how Merykare looks at you and I have seen you two drinking together at my wedding. I know Merykare likes you, Aset. You should go and see him tomorrow morning before we leave."

CHAPTER 11
A NEW PROJECT FOR HEMIENU
AND
A VISIT TO THE OLD CAPITAL

Hemienu arrived at the Pharaoh's camp together with a small fleet bringing provisions. When he disembarked he looked around, feeling surprised by the barren features of the area.

"Why would the Pharaoh want to build anything at such a deserted place?" he wondered.

Hemienu had been surprised when the Pharaoh ordered him to abandon the Gem pa Aten immediately and leave Thebes on a boat that had already been waiting. He had had only a short moment to inform his family that the Pharaoh demanded his presence at an unknown place somewhere between Thebes and Memphis and that he did not know when he would return. Hemienu's wife and children had not been happy that he was leaving since they already rarely saw him because of his work at the Aten Temple. But because he had to be on the boat departing northwards on the same day he received the Pharaoh's order he did not have time to argue with his wife. He had quickly packed a few belongings he wanted to take on his trip, hugged and kissed his wife and children and rushed to the harbour where the boat would be waiting for him.

On board of the boat he had already heard some rumours about the Pharaoh planning to build a city in the desert. Hemienu had wondered whether those rumours were true, if so, it would be a logistical nightmare.

Almost immediately after his arrival Hemienu was summoned by the Pharaoh.

"How is the construction of the Gem Pa Aten progressing?" Amenhotep inquired in a businesslike manner.

"It is progressing very well, Your Majesty, but we need extra time to make up for the time lost because of the wedding ceremony," Hemienu replied.

"Do you have reliable and qualified overseers on the construction site who are able to finish the construction of the temple without your guidance?" the Pharaoh continued asking.

"Yes, Your Majesty, my workers and overseers are very skilled," Hemienu answered, already fearing what the Pharaoh was going to ask of him.

"Hemienu," the Pharaoh suddenly started speaking in an enthusiastic tone, "I have a task for you that is the dream of every architect!"

"That is a great honour, Your Majesty," the Pharaoh's architect replied, his voice betraying his own lack of enthusiasm.

"Do you know what I am going to ask of you?" Amenhotep inquired before he explained his new project.

"I believe Your Majesty wants me to build a city for him on this desert plain," Hemienu replied again.

"And what do you think of this assignment, Hemienu?" Amenhotep continued his questions but then, before Hemienu could speak, added: "You don't seem very excited, while building a completely new city should be a challenge for an architect."

"It is indeed a challenge, Your Majesty," Hemienu replied. "But I foresee many difficulties."

"What kind of difficulties?" the Pharaoh asked irritated, not appreciating any criticism of his plan.

"The biggest problem is the isolation, Your Majesty. We are far away from everything. To build a city here we will have to move thousands of workers to this place and support them with living quarters and food. We will also have to transport the building material. Everything we need has to be transported over a huge distance," Hemienu explained and after some hesitation he went on: "And, if I may add, Your Majesty, when the city is finished it will still be very remote. Who would want to leave their own home town, the place where their ancestors are buried to live here?"

The Pharaoh remained silent, his face showing that he was trying to suppress his anger.

Then suddenly he smiled and spoke: "I appreciate your honesty, Hemienu. I will need honest people like you if I want to successfully complete the task the Aten has given to me."

Next he placed a couple of papyrus rolls on his desk, opened them and spoke in a voice that did not accept any further criticism: "The city will be built! Here are maps of the city as I designed it. I will give you everything you need to complete your task and whatever happens after the city is finished does not concern you!"

Hemienu decided not to contradict the Pharaoh any further and looked at the maps on the desk in front of him. It was a city as he had never seen before. It was going to be the first city on such a scale that had been completely designed from the beginning.

Looking at the maps containing drawings of impressive palaces and large temples he started to feel some enthusiasm for his new assignment. The Pharaoh had been right: it was a challenge.

Aset and Kiya had arrived in Memphis where they would stay for a month before returning to Thebes.

To Aset's great relief she had been able to see Merykare before they left the Pharaoh's camp site in the desert. Merykare came to apologize again and confirmed what Kiya had told Aset the previous night.

Their journey further north had been uneventful. When they started to near Memphis Aset noticed the strip of fertile land along the Nile started to become wider; a sign they were nearing the lush and green Nile Delta.

She was relieved when they arrived safely in the former Egyptian capital because life on the boat had started to become very monotonous.

Even though Thebes was now both the religious and administrative capital of the Two Lands, Memphis was still an important administrative and economical center.

Aperel, the Vizier of Lower Egypt, invited Kiya to take residence in his palace during her stay in Memphis but Kiya preferred to stay with her parents in the villa that Amenhotep had built for them.

Kiya's family had never been rich, they had always lived in a modest house in the centre of Memphis.

When returning to her native city Kiya was happily surprised to see that her parents' villa was located on the outskirts of the city with views over green fields and the river.

"The Pharaoh gave us this villa just before we departed to Thebes," Kiya's father told when they arrived at the villa's gate. He was obviously proud of his new possession. They had been taken there by chariots provided by Aperel and had been escorted by twenty Royal Guards who would stay with Kiya at her parents' villa and would follow her everywhere during her stay in Memphis until she would return to Thebes.

As soon as they arrived the gate of the villa was opened by a guard and they were welcomed by servants who also had been given to Kiya's parents by Amenhotep.

They entered through the gate and found themselves in a large enclosure with a garden with fragrant flowers, fruit trees and a fish pond. It was similar to other villa's Aset had seen but on a bigger scale. Amenhotep had done his best to please Kiya's parents and seeing how proud they were he had succeeded.

They entered the main building where refreshments had already been prepared on a table. The servants had clearly been warned that they were coming.

Feeling tired from the long journey Kiya sat down in a comfortable chair leaving Aset standing uncomfortably.

"Sit down, Aset," Kiya spoke. "As long as we are at my parents' house you are not my servant but a guest."

"Come to have a look upstairs, Kiya," Kiya's mother spoke excitedly. "The view from there is magnificent."

With a tired look on her face Kiya got up from her chair and beckoned Aset to follow her.

On the rooftop a canopy had been constructed with a table and chairs underneath it.

Aset had to agree with Kiya's mother about the view. From the rooftop they had a stunning view onto the surrounding countryside, the Nile River and Memphis.

Kiya's parents were still showing all the luxurious rooms on the second floor when they heard loud and hurried footsteps coming up the stairs. A young officer of the Royal Guard arrived with another soldier and inspected every room.

"What are you doing here? You cannot come here without permission!" Kiya's father spoke angrily.

"I apologize, my lord," the officer replied politely, addressing Kiya's father with 'lord' even though Kiya's parents were not members of Egypt's nobility nor did they occupy any important positions, and went on just as politely but in a voice that did not accept any contradiction: "My name is Horemheb, I am commander of His Majesty's Royal Guards in Memphis. His Majesty has ordered me to guard Her Highness Kiya. To guarantee her safety I need to know the precise layout of this building, I need to know every possible means of entry and I will also need to know where she will be sleeping."

"But you can't..." Kiya's father started to protest but Kiya quickly intervened: "Let him do his work, father. He is only doing what Amenhotep has ordered him to do."

"Thank you, Your Highness," Horemheb spoke, made a small bow and then continued: "As long as Your Highness will be staying here my soldiers and I will need to have unrestricted access to the house to guarantee your safety. We will, however, do our best to make our presence as little intrusive as possible."

Kiya's parents grudgingly accepted the inconvenience of having soldiers in their house and from then on did their best to ignore them.

Even though Kiya was staying at her parents' villa she was expected to attend a banquet in her honour at the palace of Aperel. That evening a messenger of the vizier arrived at the villa to inform Kiya and her parents that in the evening of the following day they would be picked up by chariots of the palace to be taken to the banquet.

Ipi returned to Thebes after having visited his family. He had enjoyed seeing his family again and to have been away from Karnak with all its problems and tensions.

He could, however, never completely let go of his worries about the temple and, even though he could not do much to help the Temple of Amun during that difficult period, he felt he had to be there instead of in the countryside.

Tuya, the wife of his brother Ankhaf, was about to give birth to her baby and Ipi had been taking care of her during his stay at his parents' house. He expected Tuya to give birth to a healthy baby soon.

The day before he returned to Thebes he had conducted another ceremony at Djehuty's grave to sustain his nephew's ka, as he had promised. He had been pleased to notice that his family also regularly brought offerings to his nephew's grave.

When he was on the ferry crossing the river back to Thebes Ipi saw five boats laden with workmen and construction materials sailing down the river.

He had heard rumours about the Pharaoh having a big construction project somewhere in the desert, far north of Thebes. Ipi found it strange but seeing these boats on their way north he wondered whether those rumours could be true.

Arriving at Karnak Ipi noticed a litter with guards and fan bearers waiting outside of the temple gates. He immediately recognized it as the litter of Ramose, the vizier.

Ramose had always had good connections with the Temple of Amun and Ipi was glad to see that during the Pharaoh's absence these connections seemed to get even better.

When Ipi was about to enter the temple Ramose and Maya came outside.

"Don't worry about Queen Teye being informed about our meetings, my lord," Ramose spoke to Maya. "That was expected to happen. Knowing her, she will inform His Majesty, who will probably summon me as soon as he receives her message to explain to him the nature of our meetings."

"Won't that bring you into trouble?" Maya asked the vizier.

"I am an old man, Maya," Ramose replied. "I have been serving at the Royal Court almost all my life. I had already served at the court of Thutmose the Fourth and I became vizier under Amenhotep the Third. I have been dealing with the politics of the Royal Court long enough to know how to handle this."

"But our current Pharaoh is unlike any of our previous Pharaohs, Ramose," Maya continued cautioning the vizier.

"I know His Majesty from the moment he was born and know his typical behaviour. However, I respect him and he respects me, when I give him advice he always listens and considers the advice carefully," Ramose explained and added full of confidence: "There are two persons to whom the Pharaoh still listens, his mother and me. If I will be summoned by Amenhotep that will most likely be positive for the Temple of Amun. I will be able to convince him of the importance of retaining the prominent position of the temple and that he should change his attitude towards the Lord Amun."

While speaking the vizier had stepped into his litter and after he had finished he gave an order to his bearers who immediately picked up the litter and started to walk in the direction of his palace. The fan bearers also started to move and escorted the litter on both sides to keep the vizier cool.

Maya stayed behind with a relieved look on his face. Ramose's optimism had infected him.

When Wenamun came to him to ask about his meeting with the vizier, Maya spoke: "Ramose is convinced he can positively influence the Pharaoh."

"I hope Amun will give Ramose strength when he meets the Pharaoh. He will need it!" Wenamun replied.

Wenamun and Maya went back into the temple followed by Ipi. Ipi was relieved to finally hear some positive news. If Ramose was right and could really convince the Pharaoh to change his policy towards Amun and His temple then the future of the temple, and with it the whole country, seemed much brighter.

Penthu was worried about the effects a long stay in the desert would have on the Pharaoh's health. He had tried to convince him to return to Thebes but Amenhotep would not listen. He was too busy with the preparations for the construction of his city and with honouring the Aten on what Amenhotep regarded as the Aten's sacred land.

Every morning the Pharaoh and the priest Meryra worshipped the rising sun and made offerings on an altar that had been constructed during their stay on the desert plain.

When he was not worshipping, the Pharaoh was usually looking at maps of his new city, having meetings with Meryra or his architect or dictating letters.

"You cannot believe how much I have to arrange to start the construction of my city," Amenhotep told Penthu and before he could answer the Pharaoh went on to give examples in a tone that sounded as if he was complaining: "I have to find enough workmen, I have to arrange the transportation of men and equipment, I also have to order to start the work in the stone quarries and I even have to arrange living quarters for the workers here on the construction site! And all this is only a fraction of everything that has to happen before construction of the city can even begin! Aten has given me a very difficult task."

"Your Majesty, if you want to successfully complete the task the Aten has given to you then you should take better care of your health. Staying in this barren environment for too long will have a negative influence on you. We have already been here for more than two weeks," Penthu spoke in another attempt to convince the Pharaoh to return to Thebes.

Amenhotep did not seem to care about Penthu's worries and replied in an uninterested tone: "The Aten will protect my health. Don't worry about me, Penthu."

While Amenhotep was speaking Ranefer entered the tent holding a sealed papyrus roll and handed it with a bow to the Pharaoh.

"Your Majesty, Her Highness Queen Teye sends you a message," Ranefer spoke before leaving again.

Amenhotep broke the seal and read the letter written by his mother. Penthu, who was not yet excused, watched the Pharaoh while he was reading.

Teye and Nefertiti wrote almost daily to Amenhotep about the affairs of state and they seemed to manage well without having the Pharaoh in the palace. Amenhotep wrote them back regularly, sometimes giving them directions about what to do but more often he was informing them about his plans for his city.

Seeing the Pharaoh sitting in his chair behind his desk in a tent that was almost as comfortable as his chambers in Malkata Palace, while he had his wife and mother taking care of the daily business of running the Two Lands, Penthu knew Amenhotep was not going to leave the barren desert plain soon.

While reading his mother's message Amenhotep's face turned red as if he was getting angry.

"Is there something wrong, Your Majesty?" Penthu inquired worriedly.

"There is no problem, Penthu, it is more a disappointment," the Pharaoh sighed and told: "Apparently my Vizier of Upper Egypt has been meeting many times with the High Priest of Amun since I have left Thebes. I always knew Ramose was a worshipper of Amun but after I became Pharaoh he started to worship the Aten as well and he did not visit Karnak so often anymore. I thought that he probably was an opportunist who just followed the God that was the most powerful but maybe I was wrong. He could be conniving with the priests of Amun against the Aten and me. If that would be true I would be very disappointed since I have known Ramose all my life and have always trusted him."

Amenhotep seemed genuinely upset by the thought that Ramose could have betrayed him so Penthu spoke, trying to sound as reassuring as he could: "It is probably nothing, there are many reasons why Ramose could visit the Temple of Amun."

"Maybe," Amenhotep answered, "but I want to be sure. Tell Merykare, my scribe, to come here immediately. I am going to dictate a message to Ramose. I will order him to come here to meet me as soon as possible."

A moment later Penthu stood outside while the Pharaoh was dictating his message to Ramose. It was extremely hot and apart from the tents that had been set up close to the riverside there was no place that offered any shade.

The first workmen that had arrived on the plain had started with building a small village consisting of basic buildings that were going to serve as living quarters, store rooms and kitchens for the workers.

The Pharaoh had been right when he said that a lot needed to be done before the actual work of constructing the city could start.

When Penthu was on his way back to his tent he heard the voices of many men shouting. Looking in the direction where it came from he saw a group of Royal Guards doing exercises and combat training in the distance.

He remembered that after a couple of days in the desert some guards had started to complain about having nothing to do and that as a result of these complaints Hekanakht had prepared a training schedule to keep his soldiers busy.

On the riverside Penthu noticed two boats arriving, one filled with more workmen and construction materials and another loaded with food supplies to sustain the community which had started to form on the desert plain.

Penthu went over to Hemienu who was watching the disembarkation of his new workmen.

"There seems to be no shortage of workers," Penthu remarked to the architect. "I have seen many boats arriving the past days."

Hemienu looked worried and replied: "I have received many workers but not enough. Just as with the Gem Pa Aten His Majesty is also in a rush with this project. I need many more workers and, more important, skilled overseers."

"I am sure His Majesty will give you everything you need," Penthu tried to reassure the architect.

"If he has all the resources I need he will give them to me, I am sure about that. But I don't know if he has enough workers to build a complete city within a few years," Hemienu replied.

He watched how some of the workmen started to unload boxes containing tools while other men started to unload the food supplies from the other boat. The supplies consisted of fresh fruits, bread, dried salted meat and even live ducks which would serve as a rare supplement of fresh meat to the few birds or other desert animals the workers and soldiers were able to catch in their free time.

Finally there followed a load of large jugs containing wine and beer that was received with cheers by some of the workers who came to watch the unloading of the two vessels.

"I will be on one of these boats when they return to Thebes," Hemienu told Penthu. "I will have to go to the Gem Pa Aten to hand over the control of the construction. At the same time I will try to find capable workers and overseers who can support me here."

Aset was sitting next to Kiya in the banquet hall of Aperel's palace. Kiya had told the vizier that she would come to his banquet and that Aset would attend as her guest instead of her servant. Aperel conceded to Kiya's unusual request and for the first time in her life Aset attended a state banquet as a guest.

They were sitting in a large pillared hall that was filled with officials and the nobility of Lower Egypt. There were large open windows in the hall that allowed fresh air to enter which brought with it the scents of the flowers in the palace gardens.

Aset looked through one of the windows and saw the moon rising over the palm trees into an evening sky filled with stars. She was enjoying the music and the food and the special treatment she received as Kiya's personal guest. Nobody, accept for Aperel, seemed to know that she was in fact a servant and if they knew they did not appear to care.

Kiya, who was sitting next to Aset, was often in conversation with Aperel who sat with his wife on Kiya's other side together with Kiya's parents.

On Aset's other side sat an older man wearing the robes of a high ranking priest together with an older lady who, Aset thought, was probably his wife.

Kiya's conversation with Aperel was often interrupted by guests who wanted to greet the Pharaoh's new wife and offered her gifts. Kiya kept smiling during these interruptions and every time managed to friendly thank the people for their kind words and their presents which she passed on to a servant that Aperel had appointed to her.

"Her Highness, Kiya, seems very promising as a Royal Wife," the priest next to Aset spoke and before Aset could say anything he went on: "She is doing very well even without having the Pharaoh to support her."

"Yes," Aset concurred when she watched Kiya speaking with the vizier and acknowledging all the high dignitaries who came up to her. "I think the Pharaoh has made a very good choice when he married her."

"May I introduce myself?" the priest spoke again. "My name is Hetepka. I am the High Priest of Ptah."

For a moment Aset felt intimidated by the high position of the man next to her. Ptah was the patron God of Memphis but, because He was also the God Who had created the world, He was worshipped throughout the whole country. Being a creator God also made Ptah the patron God of the Egyptian workmen.

The High Priest of Ptah seemed very friendly so the intimidation that Aset felt quickly disappeared.

"My name is Aset, I am a close friend of Kiya," Aset introduced herself to Hetepka, not wanting to lie but also not daring to add the fact that she was not only Kiya's friend but also her servant.

"Have you accompanied Kiya on her trip from Thebes to Memphis?" Hetepka inquired.

"Yes, she invited me to join her on this journey," Aset replied.

"Are you a native of Thebes, the great city of Amun?" the High Priest asked again.

"I was born in Thebes and have lived there my whole life," Aset told, enjoying receiving attention of a person with such a high position.

"It must have been a shock for you, as a Theban and worshipper of Amun, that the High Priest of Amun died," Hetepka spoke and after a moment of silence continued: "I knew Meryptah very well and I have mourned for him when I heard he joined Osiris in His Kingdom. I will soon travel to Thebes to attend his funeral."

Aset, who respected but rarely worshipped Amun and preferred the Goddess Hathor, felt uncomfortable and did not know how to answer Hetepka. Finally she spoke: "Everybody in Thebes has grieved over the passing away of the High Priest."

Hetepka seemed to notice Aset's discomfort and changed the conversation: "I have heard Kiya comes from Memphis. Is that true?"

"Kiya grew up in Memphis and her family is still living here," Aset told, wondering if the High Priest just showed a general interest in where Kiya came from or whether there was a more specific reason for his question.

Hetepka ate a piece of roasted beef, washed it away with wine before bending towards Aset until their faces almost touched and speaking in a confidential tone: "Aset, with your friend coming from Memphis, do you know her thoughts about our city's patron God Ptah?"

Aset thought for a moment, looked at Kiya, who was in an, at that moment undisturbed, animated conversation with Aperel and his wife, then turned back to the priest and answered: "I know she highly respects Ptah and sometimes even prays to Him but I think she is expected to follow the Pharaoh in his Aten worship."

This reply did not seem to satisfy the High Priest of Ptah. He watched the musicians and dancers for a moment, who were very successful in livening up the party, but Aset could see Hetepka was somewhere else with his thoughts.

Aset took some more food from the plates that had been put in front of her by servants and had her cup filled up again with wine from the nearby delta.

Next to Aset, Hetepka whispered for a moment with his wife, then turned back to her and spoke: "May I invite you and Kiya to visit the Temple of Ptah while you are staying in Memphis? It would be a great honour if the Pharaoh's new wife would visit our temple."

When Aset hesitated with her answer the priest added: "It would also be expected that Kiya would visit the temple of the God of the city where she is a guest."

"Of course," Aset quickly replied to Hetepka but then went on: "I am sure she will visit the Temple of Ptah during our stay here but I cannot decide when. It is Kiya's decision."

"What is my decision?" Kiya's cheerful voice broke into the conversation.

"I was just inviting you and your friend Aset to visit the Temple of Ptah while you are staying in Memphis," Hetepka informed Kiya and asked: "Do you accept my invitation?"

Two days later Aset was standing in front of the enormous Temple of Ptah. It was bigger than she had expected and it reminded her of the temple complex of Amun in Thebes.

Kiya had accepted Hetepka's invitation and when Aperel heard of it he insisted on joining her. So when they arrived at the temple Aset and Kiya were accompanied by the vizier, Kiya's parents and Horemheb and his guards.

At the temple's entrance they found Hetepka waiting for them. He made a bow to Kiya and politely greeted Aperel.

"Welcome to the Temple of Ptah!" he spoke to everybody and then went on speaking to Kiya: "May I have the honour to escort you around the temple?"

Kiya agreed and walked with the High Priest into the temple while the rest followed them.

"This temple is named Hi Ka Ptah 'Temple of the Ka of Ptah' and was originally founded by our earliest Pharaohs," Hetepka started lecturing his visitors. "Since its construction it has been expanded by all our Pharaohs because they understood the importance of Ptah, the Creator God. They understood that without Him there would be no world!"

They walked over open courtyards and through impressive pillared halls and everywhere Aset saw depictions of Ptah, sometimes He was depicted as a pottery maker Who was creating the world but most depictions showed Him standing, wearing a blue head gear and a tight robe while holding a scepter.

The High Priest continued explaining about the temple and its history and function and proudly told how he used to work under the Pharaoh's brother, Crown Prince Thutmose, the previous High Priest of Ptah who had died so unexpectedly.

When they reached a gate that led into a corridor which ended at a pair of closed doors the priest suddenly went silent.

"Here the Holy of Holies starts," Hetepka finally spoke in a voice in which his reverence for Ptah was clearly audible. "This area is only accessible for the highest ranking priests of Ptah and for His Majesty but as a rare exception I want to invite Her Highness Kiya to enter the Holy of Holies with me."

Surprised and honoured Kiya agreed and followed Hetepka into the most sacred part of the temple where the statue of Ptah was being kept, leaving the vizier, her parents, her guards and Aset behind.

"This is a great honour for Kiya," Aperel told Kiya's parents. "I have never seen any Royal Wife being invited to visit the Holy of Holies."

It took almost an hour before Kiya and the High Priest returned from the temple's most sacred area.

Aset had wondered what took them so long and Horemheb had been pacing up and down, clearly feeling uncomfortable not being able to watch the person he had been ordered to protect.

As soon as Kiya appeared from the Holy of Holies Aset knew something had happened which had angered Kiya. Kiya looked upset while Hetepka also seemed distressed and was not as informative anymore during the rest of the visit to the Temple of Ptah as he had been before.

They continued their tour around the temple with the High Priest only making a few remarks every now and then.

Finally Hetepka said they had seen every part of the temple and offered everybody refreshments to drink before they would leave.

Aperel was about to accept the offer but Kiya quickly turned it down before he could say anything. She was clearly in a hurry to leave the temple.

A moment later chariots of the Temple of Ptah brought Aset, Kiya and her parents back to their villa while Horemheb and his soldiers followed in their own army chariots.

On the way back Kiya was quiet and as soon as they arrived at the villa Aset dragged her friend to their private room and asked: "What happened in the Holy of Holies, Kiya?"

Kiya remained silent for a moment as if she did not know what to answer but finally she started speaking: "Hetepka asked me why Amenhotep did not fulfill his obligations towards the Temple of Ptah. When I said I did not know the reason for this and that it probably had to do with Amenhotep's Aten worship he told me that it was my duty to change my husband's mind. He said that the Pharaoh was betraying Ma'at and that if I would not convince him to support the Temple of Ptah, as he was supposed to do, I would be betraying Ma'at as well!"

While Kiya was speaking she got more and more upset until she finally broke down in tears and spoke: "I have nothing to do with Amenhotep's religious ideas! I have only just married him! How can he blame me for betraying Ma'at? I have no control over the Pharaoh!"

"What did you answer to Hetepka?" Aset asked curiously.

"After Hetepka would not listen to me when I told him I had very little influence over the Pharaoh, I told him that the High Priest of Ptah is not such an important position to Amenhotep anymore and that

I probably have enough influence over Amenhotep to be able to have him replaced," Kiya answered while she managed to produce a smile.

Hemienu had returned to Thebes. The first thing he did after arriving was inspecting the Gem Pa Aten and appoint a new head of the construction site to replace him.

But after that, as the Pharaoh's chief of construction, he would still be obliged to follow the temple's progress and give advice to his successor as much as he could from his new construction site in the desert.

At the Aten Temple Hemienu met Thutmose, the sculptor, and Rensi, the relief artist. He informed them of the Pharaoh's new project and told them they would later have to move to the new city to help with the construction. There would be a lot of work for them to be done.

"But how about the temple? Should that not be finished first?" Rensi asked.

"It will take a while before we can even start with the construction of the city," Hemienu replied. "By the time you and Thutmose will be needed to work on His Majesty's city, work on the Gem Pa Aten will have progressed far and your artists will have obtained enough experience to finish the last part of the temple without you."

Rensi and Thutmose agreed Hemienu was right and accepted that they would move to the construction site of the Pharaoh's new city in the future.

Hemienu was also considering which of his overseers working on the Gem pa Aten he would take with him to help leading the Pharaoh's new project but he decided that would have to wait. First he had to see his family and inform them about the new task the Pharaoh had given to him.

While walking home Hemienu wondered what had happened to Nebtawi. After he had been fired by the Pharaoh he had disappeared from Thebes and nobody knew where he was, not even his family.

"He must have felt too ashamed and humiliated to stay in his native city where everybody knew him," Hemienu reasoned. "But for the Pharaoh's new project I would gladly use his knowledge and experience."

As soon as Hemienu thought about using Nebtawi's help he rejected that idea: "Even if I could find him, the Pharaoh would not allow him on any of his construction sites."

When he arrived home Hemienu's son and daughter, Hemaka and Achtai, came running up to him. Hemienu kneeled down to hug his twin children, whom he had missed so much during his trip to see the Pharaoh.

Hearing the children yelling with happiness Hemienu's wife Ahotep came rushing to see what was happening.

"Hemienu!" she also exclaimed with happiness.
"I am so happy you have returned!" she continued while she threw her arms around her husband, who was still hugging his children.

Hemienu let go of his children and got up to kiss his wife.

"I hope His Majesty will not take you away from us anymore," Ahotep spoke while she embraced him again.

Hearing his wife's words Hemienu thought it was better not to say anything about the Pharaoh's new project yet.

With Hemienu coming from a well-to-do family and being promoted to the Pharaoh's chief of construction his family was not short of anything.

However, contrary to most rich Egyptian families who lived in opulent luxury, they preferred to live a simple life. They had a modest house with a garden on the edge of Thebes and only one servant girl who helped Ahotep with the housework.

But that day, to celebrate her husband's return, Ahotep decided to prepare a special dinner. She bought the best fish and meat she could find at the market and the most expensive wine. Together with her servant, a girl named Kiki who came from a poor family of farmers from the countryside south of Thebes, she had been busy for hours preparing the festive meal.

That evening they had dinner in the garden surrounded by trees and flowers by the light of oil lamps.

"Is there something wrong, my dear?" Ahotep asked Hemienu worriedly during their dinner.

"No, everything is fine," Hemienu replied in a tone which clearly betrayed to his wife that something was bothering him. Hemienu was feeling uncomfortable, he was waiting for the right moment to tell his wife about his new task which would take him far from Thebes for a very long period but he did not want to spoil the joy his family was experiencing about his return.

"What did the Pharaoh want from you?" Ahotep went on asking.

"He inquired about the progress of the Gem Pa Aten," Hemienu answered, thinking he wasn't lying to his wife because the Pharaoh actually asked about the Aten Temple.

The rest of the dinner passed mostly in silence with the only real conversation coming from the children.

Later in the evening Ahotep asked Kiki to take Hemaka and Achtai into the house to sleep, leaving her alone with her husband.

Ahotep refilled Hemienu's cup with wine and then her own cup.

She took a sip of the wine and spoke in a sad voice: "You have to build the Pharaoh's new city in the desert, don't you?"

Hemienu looked surprised and replied: "Do you know about this project?"

"Of course I do. Everybody knows about it!" Ahotep replied and after a short silence she went on: "The Pharaoh intending to build a city in the middle of nowhere is the latest story going around in the city. Do you know how many people have asked me lately if you have anything to do with the construction of this city? I had no idea what to answer them because I never received any message from you. I, the wife of the Pharaoh's chief of construction, had to hear all the news from others. The sellers gossiping at the market know more about your new project than I do!"

While speaking the last sentences there was an obvious irritation audible in Ahotep's voice.

Hemienu felt guilty about neglecting his family and asked: "Has somebody told you already that I was going to lead the construction of the city?"

"No," his wife replied in a calmer voice. "But it would only be logical that you were going to be in charge of such an important project."

Hemienu sighed, took a grape from a bowl that was standing in front of him and put it in his mouth, thinking about what he would say to his wife.

"You are right that I am going to be in charge of the construction of the Pharaoh's city," he finally spoke but then added: "But that does not have to mean that we will be separated for a long time."

"What do you mean?" Ahotep replied hopefully. "Are you saying that you can regularly visit Thebes during the construction?"

"No," Hemienu spoke. "I mean that you and the children can come with me to the new city."

Ahotep looked dismayed at Hemienu.

"Do you want to let the children grow up on some remote construction site in the desert?" she asked, not being able to believe her husband could seriously mean what he had suggested.

"We are going to build a village for the workers. We will be able to live in a decent house," Hemienu defended his idea.

"But it is not a good environment for our children to live in. Would you like Achtai to grow up in the middle of the desert between thousands of men? And what can they do there? There are no opportunities for them to study anything. Here in Thebes there are temple schools they can attend, in the desert there is nothing!" Ahotep exclaimed, getting upset by her husband's suggestion.

Stung by his wife's words Hemienu replied: "My workers are all decent men. They would never hurt Achtai, so that is one worry you can forget. I agree that at this moment the building site is not an ideal place for a family but that will change soon and I can always arrange for tutors to come there to teach Hemaka and Achtai!"

He stopped speaking for a moment and then continued in a softer voice: "This is the only way I can find for us to be together, Ahotep, and as the chief architect I can make the construction site into what I want. I can make it into an ideal place for you and the children."

When he finished speaking Ahotep did not say anything, so Hemienu went on in a begging tone: "Ahotep, I will have to go there whether I like it or not. The Pharaoh has given me this assignment and would not accept a refusal from me. Please come with me!"

"But the tombs of our family are here. I want to stay close to my parents' tomb to be sure they are well taken care of," Ahotep, who, like most Egyptians, took the cult of the dead very seriously explained, while her eyes started to fill with tears.

"Your living relatives can take care of their tomb and you can return to Thebes on special occasions such as the Beautiful Feast of the Valley," Hemienu persisted, hoping his suggestion would be an acceptable solution for his wife.

Ahotep remained silent for some time, thinking about her husband's idea and finally spoke: "I don't know what to do. I just don't like the idea of me and the children living in the desert, faraway from Thebes and our family's tombs."

Ahotep stopped speaking for a moment and started to cry when she went on: "I am sorry but I think I want to stay here with the children."

Not wanting to continue the discussion Ahotep got up and quickly went inside.

Hemienu stayed behind alone, feeling depressed. He heard his wife crying inside the house but thought it was better to leave her alone for the moment. Instead, he emptied his cup and refilled it again with the wine Ahotep had bought for him.

CHAPTER 12
UNREST ON THE CONSTRUCTION SITE
AND
A VISIT TO MENMADE MIRACLES

Penthu was asleep in his private tent which had recently been appointed to him. He woke up from noise outside and when he opened his eyes he saw a bright light entering his tent.

The first thing that crossed his mind was that it was morning already but almost immediately he noticed this light was different from daylight and started to smell something unusual.

Having just woken up from a deep sleep Penthu felt drowsy and did not immediately understand what was happening until he heard somebody shout: "Fire!"

Penthu quickly got up and ran outside.

In the darkness of the night he saw a big pile of wood, which had just been delivered from the delta the previous day, burning.

Some workers already started to try to put out the flames with buckets of water from the river but Penthu saw it was already too late and the wood that had been intended for use on the construction site was lost.

Getting nearer to the fire Penthu noticed Hekanakht, who was already at the scene and questioned a member of the Royal Guard.

"It was not an accident," Penthu heard the guard say.

"We saw somebody running away when we discovered the fire. I stayed here to raise the alarm while two other guards chased the man in that direction," the guard told his commander, pointing northwards along the riverbank.

Hekanakht immediately ran into the direction the guard had pointed at and was followed by other soldiers. Penthu followed them more slowly wondering whether they would find the arsonist.

A few minutes later he caught up again with Hekanakht, who was kneeling next to a body that lay on the ground. In the light of the torches that some of the soldiers carried with them, Penthu immediately recognized the man as one of the Royal Guards.

Without waiting for anybody to say something Penthu started to examine the guard.

"He is just unconscious. Probably hit on the head with a heavy object," Penthu spoke.

"Is it serious?" one of the soldiers asked.

"I don't think so but bring him to my tent where I can examine him better," Penthu replied.

Hekanakht had just ordered two soldiers to help Penthu bring the unconscious guard back to the camp and was himself about to continue his search for the mysterious arsonist and attacker with the remaining soldiers when suddenly everybody was startled by a horrible scream.

"Penthu, follow me! I might need you again!" Hekanakht ordered Penthu and started running in the direction where the screaming still continued.

"Whatever is happening, that person must be in real agony," Penthu thought, while he ran after Hekanakht and the other soldiers.

As abruptly as it had started the screaming stopped again.

Penthu and the soldiers kept moving along the river into the direction where it had come from when they found two pale looking soldiers standing by a person who was sitting on the ground shaking heavily and who appeared to have been beaten up.

"What has happened here?" Hekanakht demanded and then recognized the man on the ground as one of his Royal Guards and asked: "Ineni, what happened to you?"

"He was deserting. We followed him here," one of the two soldiers guarding him explained when Ineni, refusing to look at his commander, stared at the ground and kept silent.

"What? Is that true?" Hekanakht exploded in a mixture of anger and disbelief.

For a moment it appeared as if the Head of the Royal Guard would hit the sitting man but he quickly controlled himself again.

"What was the screaming about?" Hekanakht asked the two soldiers. "It sounded like you were torturing Ineni!"

"That was not Ineni," the same soldier spoke again. "We did have to use violence to subdue Ineni but he was not the one you heard screaming."

The soldier paused a moment before he went on: "Ineni was not the only deserter. There were two of them."

When he heard about the second deserter Hekanakht looked like he was going to explode again but that time he controlled himself and remained silent, waiting for the soldier to go on with his report: "We followed the two deserters who were trying to hide there in the reed on the river bank when a crocodile caught his accomplice and dragged him into the river."

While the soldier was pointing at the place of the attack and explaining what had happened to the other deserter, Penthu saw a shiver going through

Ineni, who was still sitting on the ground and looked miserable in the light of the soldiers' torches.

For a moment he caught Penthu's gaze but then averted his eyes and continued staring at the ground again.

Hekanakht did not seem too upset about the fate of the second deserter and after the soldier had finished his report mumbled quietly: "Sobek, the crocodile God, punishes quickly."

Next Hekanakht turned his attention again towards Ineni.

"Look at me!" he shouted when the deserter kept avoiding looking at him.

"I cannot believe that I live to see a person calling himself a member of the Royal Guard acting so shamefully!" Hekanakht raged.

Suddenly Ineni turned his gaze at his superior and spoke with contempt: "I have served the Pharaoh's father for years and I would have given my life for him. But this Pharaoh does not serve his country or the Gods like his father did. I refuse to spend my time on this depressing empty plain for a Pharaoh who will bring nothing but disaster over the Two Lands by angering the Gods!"

Hekanakht was surprised by Ineni's sudden angry reaction but then hissed back: "I should throw you in the river so the crocodiles will have another meal."

Then Hekanakht unexpectedly smiled and spoke: "You should at least know that your plan of starting a fire as a diversion for your desertion worked against you. Without the fire you might have actually succeeded!"

The expression on Ineni's face turned from defiance to surprise.

"That fire was not started by us," he spoke. "We just ran out of the camp and on the way we were forced to hit a guard unconscious but we did not start any fire."

The next morning Ineni was standing with his hands bound behind his back between two soldiers on a large open space between the tents and buildings that were still under construction.

All the members of the Royal Guard and all the workers had been ordered to attend Ineni's punishment which would serve as an example to everybody.

Hekanakht was still in the Pharaoh's tent to discuss the punishment of the deserter with Amenhotep and the High priest of the Aten.

It was early in the morning but it was already getting hot.

Penthu looked at Ineni who awaited his fate calmly. He appeared even worse than during the night, he had clearly been mistreated after his capture.

Ineni obviously deserved whatever punishment the Pharaoh decided to give to him but Penthu could not help admiring his calm attitude under such difficult circumstances.

Penthu had not slept anymore after the events of the past night and felt tired. He had been taking care of the guard who had been attacked by the two deserters and who had regained consciousness and would soon be able to take up his duties again.

After that Penthu had been joining discussions with workers, soldiers and officials about who could have been responsible for the mysterious fire but nobody seemed to have any idea.

It took a long time before Hekanakht and Meryra appeared from Amenhotep's tent.

Penthu held his breath for a moment, if the Pharaoh did not come personally that most likely meant that something was about to happen that he did not want to witness.

The Head of the Royal Guard walked up to Ineni while Meryra stayed back to observe from a distance what was going to happen.

When he stood close to Ineni, Hekanakht for a moment looked at him with a scornful gaze but then turned to the attending soldiers and workers and shouted: "His Majesty has asked me to advise him on the fate of this man, whose name I don't want to mention, and I advised him the only correct punishment for desertion from the Royal Guard: Death!"

Hekanakht paused for a moment to see the effect his words had on the attending people. The soldiers did not move or speak but amongst the workers, Penthu heard murmuring.

Penthu felt himself turn cold in spite of the morning's heat. He was a physician who had devoted his life to saving people and as such he felt revulsion towards killing, even if the person actually deserved it.

Ineni himself did not show any emotion and just stared at the ground as if he had not heard Hekanakht's words.

After looking around at the assembled people Hekanakht started speaking again: "However, His Majesty, in his wisdom, has decided to be merciful and to spare this criminal's life!"

This time there was even more chatter amongst the people, even the soldiers seemed surprised about the unexpected mercy for the deserter.

Ineni, however, still did not react and kept looking at the ground. It seemed as if he did not care anymore about his own fate.

"As an alternative punishment," Hekanakht spoke again, "His Majesty sentences this man to a beating of fifty strokes with a stick for making insulting remarks about His Majesty after his capture. For desertion and attacking a comrade His Majesty sentences this man to hard labour in the stone quarries in the south of the country until death or until His Majesty decides to pardon him."

After he had passed the sentence Hekanakht turned to Ineni and spoke: "The sentence for insulting His Majesty will be carried out immediately!"

The moment Hekanakht finished speaking one of the soldiers guarding Ineni pushed the prisoner on his knees while the other took his dagger and started to cut the rope that bound Ineni's hands behind his back.

A moment later a heavy stick started descending on Ineni's back, each time breaking more skin and drawing more blood.

Ineni tried to remain calm but eventually it was impossible keep his pain hidden and he started to cry out. He sat kneeling in front of Hekanakht who counted out loud the beatings given by one of the soldiers. Three times Ineni fell over and had to be helped up again to continue the carrying out of the sentence.

All the onlookers were quiet, even those who thought Ineni deserved his punishment did not seem to enjoy the sight of a man being beaten so violently.

Penthu could see that even Hekanakht, who had been so upset about two of his men trying to desert, did not feel any satisfaction during that moment.

After the last stroke Ineni fell down again but that time nobody helped him up anymore.

Hekanakht looked at his assembled soldiers and spoke: "Let this be a lesson for anybody else who thinks about deserting!"

As soon as he finished speaking he walked away from Ineni and the assembled workers and soldiers as if he wanted to forget the unpleasant experience as soon as possible.

Penthu quickly walked over to Ineni who was still unattended to but Meryra stopped him and spoke: "Leave him, Penthu. You are the Pharaoh's physician and should not lower yourself to treating criminals. One of the physicians of the workmen can take care of him."

An officer of the Royal Guard heard the High Priest speak and immediately ordered two soldiers to drag the heavily bleeding Ineni away so he could be taken care of.

Aset and Kiya had left Memphis early in the morning on Kiya's private bark the Daughter of the Aten.

They followed Aperel's boat through the green fields northwards followed by another boat containing the guards who were responsible for Kiya's safety.

Aperel, the vizier, did his best to make Kiya's stay in Memphis as pleasant as possible and had invited her on a trip down the Nile.

Aset watched the farmers on their fields and witnessed glimpses of life in the small villages they passed. Coming from Thebes and having lived and worked most of her life in the Royal Palace, life on the Egyptian countryside seemed very hard to her.

"Look over there!" one of the boat's crewmen suddenly exclaimed excitedly while he pointed towards the horizon.

Everybody looked in the direction he pointed at on the west bank of the Nile and there Aset saw three unnatural shapes towering over the horizon.

Her heart started to beat faster with excitement. She immediately recognized them as the structures built by legendary Pharaohs a long time ago.

Aset remembered that when she was a child and served at the court of Amenhotep the Third an old priest working in the palace used to tell her stories about Egypt's glorious past and one time he told her about the great Pharaohs who had created mountains that reached to the heaven in which they were laid to rest after they joined Osiris in His Kingdom.

"These mountains must have been built by giants," Aset heard one of the crewmen speak in awe when they came nearer to the enormous structures.

The mountains' white limestone covering reflected the rays of sun and almost blinded everybody who directly looked at them.

Getting closer Aset saw an enormous head wearing the nemes headdress of a Pharaoh and part of a lion's body sticking out above the trees that grew on the bank of the river.

Aset felt intimidated by the statue that seemed to guard the mysterious gleaming mountains behind it in which some of Egypt's greatest Pharaohs were entombed.

She had often seen statues of this kind, a human head on a lion's body, in Thebes and other Egyptian cities where she went when following the Pharaoh on his visits but none of these statues were on such a scale as what she saw at that moment.

The boats kept nearing the enormous face that stared towards the river with the gleaming men-made mountains behind it and Aset noticed similar but smaller constructions around the bigger artificial mountains and also that temples had been built in their direct vicinity.

Aperel's boat started to sail towards a harbour that seemed connected to these temples and the impressive structures behind them.

Kiya's boat and that of her guards followed Aperel's boat and shortly afterwards they were disembarking onto the dock.

Almost immediately they were welcomed by a group of about ten priests who seemed to have been waiting for them. Aset immediately recognized them as mortuary priests.

"Welcome to the necropolis of the greatest family that ruled the Two Lands," one of the priests spoke.

Aperel greeted the mortuary priests with a polite bow and said: "May I introduce the Pharaoh's new wife Her Highness Kiya, The Favourite and The Greatly Beloved Wife of the Lord of the Two Lands, Child of the Aten Who Lives Now and Forever."

"We are honoured to welcome Your Highness at the mortuary complex of our great lords," the priest spoke to Kiya while referring to the Pharaohs whose funerary cults they served.

While the priests were welcoming Kiya and the vizier Aset looked around at the sacred area where they had just arrived. From the harbour on the green riverside she saw a causeway leading to a temple next to the gigantic statue of the human-headed lion on the edge of a desert plateau. From there another causeway continued onto the plateau to another temple next to one of the gleaming white mountains which dominated the entire necropolis.

"The Pharaoh who built this complex must have been extremely powerful," Aset thought to herself.

"May I invite Your Highness to visit the Royal Necropolis?" one of the priests asked Kiya.

Kiya agreed and a moment later they were walking up the causeway towards the first temple that was built next to the intimidating statue that guarded the way to the enormous Royal Tomb further up the desert plateau.

Kiya and Aperel were walking together with the priests in front followed by Aset, Horemheb and his guards and Aperel's servants and personal guards.

The priests were explaining the history of the area to Kiya but Aset was too far behind and too impressed by what she saw to listen to what they were saying.

Reaching the first temple Aset heard one of the priests speak: "This is the valley temple of the funeral complex of His Royal Majesty, the Great Pharaoh Khafre, who reigned over the Two Lands more than a thousand years ago!"

The temple appeared very old, had a gloomy feel about it and, contrary to the temples in Thebes and other temples she had visited, there were no inscriptions on the walls.

In the temple Aset was impressed by a pair of black statues of the Pharaoh seated on a throne with Horus, the God in the form of a hawk, perched on the back of the throne, protectively spreading His wings behind the Pharaoh.

Kiya and the vizier burnt incense in honour of the Pharaoh who had ruled the Two Lands during a period which was sometimes referred to by the

Egyptians as the golden age while Aset stayed behind at a respectful distance.

"Before we continue to His Majesty's mortuary temple we will visit the temple of Horus of the Horizon," one of the priests told.

The temple at the feet of the human-headed lion was situated right next to the valley temple of Khafre's funeral complex.

Standing at the feet of the largest statue Aset had ever seen she felt awed and when Kiya and Aperel were invited again to burn incense to worship the power reflected in this enormous statue, Aset, in an unusual action, asked permission to join them and burn incense as well.

After initially being surprised by Aset's question the High Priest of the temple's cult smiled and replied: "Of course, everybody is allowed to worship Horus of the Horizon."

After they had finished the priest explained how the human-headed lion represented the strength of the powerful lion combined with, and tamed by, human intelligence; a combination which symbolized Royal power.

Turning to Kiya, the High Priest went on speaking: "Your Highness, now I would like to show you how much influence Horus of the Horizon has on Royal power."

They walked between the paws of the lion's enormous body and looking up Aset saw the human head wearing the Pharaoh's nemes headdress with the uraeus and the beard of a Pharaoh towering high above her.

"Your Highness, please have a look at this stele which has been erected here by your husband's grandfather, the famous Pharaoh Thutmose the Fourth," the priest spoke, pointing at a large stele.

When the priest made a connection between the statue and Amenhotep's family, Kiya became very interested and, while looking closely at the stele and trying to read it, she asked: "Why did my husband's grandfather erect this stele here?"

Satisfied that he had received the interest of his important visitor the priest of Horus of the Horizon began to tell: "His Majesty Thutmose the Fourth came visiting here after a hunting trip in the desert when he was still a prince, who was not in line to the throne. At that time the body of Horus of the Horizon was covered with sand blown there over the course of centuries by the strong desert winds that occur sometimes on this plateau."

The High Priest was talking excitedly while gesticulating with his arms. He clearly enjoyed telling about his God and His temple.

The priest's enthusasm was contagious and everybody was caught by his story and listened with complete attention while he continued telling:
"Exhausted from his hunting trip His Majesty Thutmose the Fourth, at that time still just prince Thutmose, decided to rest in the shadow of the head of Horus of the Horizon, which was the only part of the God's body that was not covered by the desert sand. The young prince fell asleep and in his dream Horus of the Horizon came to him and complained about His body being covered by the sand. He then promised that if Thutmose would clear away all the sand He, Horus of the Horizon, would make him the next Pharaoh."

The Priest stopped speaking for a moment and smiled before continuing: "And you all know what happened next. Thutmose did as Horus of the Horizon requested and he became the next Pharaoh. To commemorate this important moment in the history of the Two Lands and to honour Horus of the Horizon, Thutmose had this stele erected after he had become Pharaoh," the priest finished his story while pointing again at the stele between the lion's paws.

The priest had been right when he said that the event he had been telling about was an important moment in the history of the Two Lands.

Aset not only knew Pharaoh Thutmose the Fourth as the father of the previous Pharaoh Amenhotep the Third but, maybe even more important, he was also the Pharaoh who made peace with Egypt's old enemies the Mitanni. He even sealed the peace treaty by marrying one of the daughters of the King of Mitanni, an act which Pharaoh Amenhotep repeated when he married Tadukhipa. Without Thutmose's wise diplomacy the present situation in the Two Lands could have been very different now that Hatti, the neighbouring Kingdom of Mitanni, was becoming more powerful. Amenhotep the Third had used the legacy of his father wisely and used Egypt's new allies to keep Hatti under control.

They left the temple of Horus of the Horizon and continued under the burning sun over the causeway towards the mortuary temple of Pharaoh Khafre that was constructed at the base of his massive tomb.

While the High Priest of Khafre's funerary cult kept telling details about the funeral complex and details about the Pharaoh's life Aset looked at another tomb similar to Khafre's.

"Impressive isn't it?" one of the other priests spoke to her. "That is Pharaoh Khufu's tomb. It is almost similar to Khafre's but even higher."

Then, before Aset could say anything, he introduced himself: "My name is Nedjem, I am a priest of the cult of Khufu."

Aset introduced herself and Nedjem went on speaking: "These three great tombs have all been built by one family. Khufu was Khafre's father and that smaller but still impressive tomb there is built by Menkaure, who was the son of Khafre. They must have been taught about building these tombs by Khufu's father, the great Pharaoh Snefru. During his reign he had built three constructions such as these further to the south from here. Even though they are on a smaller scale, his constructions are very impressive but Snefru was only satisfied with- and finally laid to rest in the third and last tomb he had built."

Nedjem stopped speaking, stared at the three enormous Royal tombs and then added: "Without Snefru gaining such a vast amount of experience in construction these wonders could not have been made."

Aset kept listening to Nedjem who continued telling about his favourite Pharaohs Snefru and Khufu until they reached Khafre's mortuary temple.

It was getting very hot so Aset was relieved to finally receive some shade after the long open causeway.

The temple and the Pharaoh's tomb were built on higher ground from which Aset could oversee the whole surrounding area. Rows of tombs seemed to continue endlessly, tombs of Royals but also private tombs.

"There might even be more burials here than in the famous Theban necropolis," Aset thought.

Inside the temple there was a court and a pillared hall with more statues of Khafre and the same undecorated walls Aset had seen in the valley temple.

This was as far as they could go into the complex of Khafre the priests said. Entering the massive tomb itself was not possible and only Kiya was invited to go further and enter the Holy of Holies of the temple to privately worship the Pharaoh in the shadow of the wonder he had created more than a thousand years ago.

Pharaoh Amenhotep was not feeling well, he was suffering from fever and could hardly eat.

Penthu tried to treat him as well as he could under the primitive circumstances they were living under on the desert plain but he worried the Pharaoh's health would only deteriorate further unless they would return to civilization.

"Your Majesty, I beg you to take my advice and return to Thebes as soon as possible," Penthu tried to convince the Pharaoh.

"I appreciate your advice, Penthu. I know you are trying to help me but I cannot leave yet. I must first be assured that the construction here will get underway as soon as possible. Only then I will allow myself to leave," the Pharaoh spoke, rejecting Penthu's plea.

Penthu and Amenhotep were interrupted when Ranefer entered the Pharaoh's tent and announced that Ramose, the Vizier of Upper Egypt, had arrived as the Pharaoh had requested.

"Show him in!" Amenhotep spoke. "I want to speak him immediately."

A moment later Ramose was sitting in a comfortable chair opposite the Pharaoh's desk.

"He looks exhausted. The long journey down the Nile must have been hard for him," Penthu thought when he saw the old vizier.

Amenhotep showed the vizier maps of his city and asked his opinion about it.

"It is very impressive, Your Majesty, and you will have my full support to complete the enormous task the Aten has given to you," Ramose assured him.

"I had been hoping for that answer," Amenhotep replied but then went on: "However, I receive reports that during my absence you frequently have been having meetings with Maya, the High Priest of Amun."

"Your Majesty," Ramose spoke, trying to put a surprised tone in his voice, "I did not know it was forbidden for the Vizier of Upper Egypt to meet the High Priest of Amun!"

"Ramose, I am too tired to play games," Amenhotep spoke in a weak voice and then asked: "Just tell me what is happening. What are these meetings about?"

"We were discussing the situation of the Temple of Amun," Ramose told the Pharaoh, sounding as if he wasn't speaking about a subject that was very sensitive to Amenhotep.

This answer made an expression of surprise appear on the Pharaoh's face but he quickly recovered and replied as if he genuinely cared about Amun's temple: "And, how is the situation of the Temple of Amun? Is everything well?"

"For the moment everything is well. But the priests are worried about their future. They are scared that Your Majesty's rule is going to damage their temple," Ramose informed the Pharaoh and stopped speaking a moment. Then he looked directly at Amenhotep and added slowly: "Or maybe even worse."

Amenhotep listened to his vizier and in spite of his fever managed a smile, as if he was satisfied to hear that he had an effect on the priests of Amun.

When he received no reply from the Pharaoh, Ramose leaned over to him and spoke softly: "Your Majesty, I have served your family for most of my life and I have been your servant since the moment you were born. Please permit me to speak to you as your friend instead of your vizier and advisor."

"You have my permission, Ramose. What do you want to say?" Amenhotep sighed and took a sip of water from a cup on his desk.

All the way from Thebes Ramose had been thinking about what he would tell the Pharaoh at that moment but while sitting in front of him he did not know where to start.

Finally, after a long pause, just when Amenhotep began to lose his patience, Ramose started to speak: "I know that the priests of Amun have a lot of power, maybe even too much power. But their temples are also an important factor in the society of the Two Lands, both religiously and economically."

Ramose stopped speaking a moment to see if his words had any effect on the Pharaoh but Amenhotep just kept staring with a blank expression on his face past the old vizier at an unspecified point behind him.

Again getting no reaction from the Pharaoh, Ramose continued speaking: "It is important that the Temple of Amun survives. I am not asking you to make donations or to take part in the temple cults, the Temple of Amun is rich enough to take care of itself and I know you need all your resources and time for doing Aten's work, but I implore you to acknowledge its right to exist."

"Have I ever told you that I want to close the Temple of Amun?" Amenhotep interrupted his vizier.

"No," Ramose replied and went on hesitatingly: "But your dislike for Amun and His priests is well known."

"Amun and His priests are very powerful and have the position that the Aten should have. The Aten should actually be the only God in the Two Lands!" the Pharaoh spoke in an unexpectedly loud voice.

"I know and I agree," Ramose replied quickly. "You can concentrate yourself completely on the Aten. I ask you to just tolerate the existence of the Temple of Amun. If you leave the Amun priests to fend for themselves they will become weaker and many people will turn away from them and towards the Aten, the new and powerful God of Egypt. You can accomplish all of this without the use of any force that could cause destabilization of the country, a situation that you do not need while building your new city for the Aten!"

Penthu was listening to Ramose's reasoning and to his surprise he saw that the Pharaoh seemed to seriously consider what the vizier was telling him.

Apparently it was true that Ramose was one of the very few people to whom Amenhotep would listen. Any other person who tried to talk the Pharaoh ideas out of his head would have surely been unsuccessful.

Even though Penthu's relationship with the priests of the Temple of Karnak had deteriorated he did not wish them any harm and he still regarded himself as a servant of Amun and as such he hoped Ramose would be able to convince Amenhotep to spare the Amun Temple any hardship.

"Maybe you are right, Ramose. Maybe I wanted to act to rashly. Thank you for giving me such good advice," Amenhotep spoke, even though his voice betrayed he did not like Ramose's idea.

"Will you leave the Temple of Amun in peace?" Ramose asked, looking for a confirmation that he had successfully changed the Pharaoh's mind and saved Amun and His priests.

"I guess that is the wisest thing to do," Amenhotep replied quietly.

Ramose looked relieved and spoke: "Thank you, Your Majesty. You have indeed made a good decision in the interest of the Two Lands."

As if he had enough of the conversation Amenhotep suddenly changed the topic and asked: "How long will you be staying here, Ramose?"

"Not long, Your Majesty," the vizier replied. "I will be leaving tomorrow. With the absence of Your Majesty, I have a lot of work to do in Thebes."

The Pharaoh, who genuinely liked the old vizier whom he had known all his life, looked disappointed when he heard that Ramose would be leaving again the following day and spoke: "In that case I ask you to join me for dinner tonight. Due to my ill health I cannot eat much but I am sure my cooks will be able to prepare something special to celebrate the visit of my vizier."

When he had finished speaking Amenhotep looked at Penthu and said: "I want to take a rest now, Penthu, so I won't be needing you. Take Ramose outside, show him around on the plain and inform him about my plans for the city of the Aten."

A moment later Penthu and Ramose walked over the plain where the Pharaoh's city was going to rise.

Workmen had started to level the plain and soon they would be able to start laying the foundations for the first buildings.

Others were still expanding the workmen's village which would house the many workers who kept pouring onto the plain.

It was hot and there was no place to shelter from the burning rays of the sun. Penthu hoped Ramose would not be too interested in the work on the plain so they could quickly return to the shelter of a tent.

Fortunately Ramose also found the sun unbearable and soon they were walking to Penthu's tent to find shade.

"Thank you for helping the Temple of Amun, my lord," Penthu spoke gratefully to Ramose.

"It was my duty towards the Lord Amun and the Two Lands to speak to His Majesty about his policy towards the Amun Temple," Ramose replied and, knowing that Penthu used to serve at Karnak, added: "The Temple of Amun will survive, I am sure about that."

Penthu looked at Ramose while he was speaking and noticed he still looked very weak and tired.

"My lord, are you not feeling well?" he inquired. "If you are feeling weak I can prepare a potion to help you regain your strength."

"I am fine, Penthu," the vizier replied and explained: "It is just that at my age such a long journey down the Nile can be very tiring."

"In that case maybe you should stay here longer to rest instead of returning to Thebes tomorrow," Penthu advised.

"Unfortunately that is impossible, as I already told His Majesty," Ramose answered. "I have too many tasks waiting for me in Thebes."

Ipi and Nebamun had attended the evening ceremony in the temple and after it had finished decided to go into Thebes.

Ipi's day had been busy, there had been many patients who visited Intef's practice in the temple and Ipi had also received more responsibilities at his work. Lately Intef had started to allow Ipi to take care of patients without the supervision of more experienced physicians.

Next to his work Ipi also still regularly visited the House of Life where he learned skills such as reading and writing and studied about the State God Amun.

Ipi and Nebamun walked down the crowded streets of the Egyptian capital. During the evening the city was illuminated by countless torches and oil lamps and music and singing could be heard from the many taverns.

Ipi loved the chaotic atmosphere of Thebes during the evening to which he still hadn't completely got used after growing up in the quiet and peaceful countryside.

"If you like this then you will also love Mendes, where my family lives," Nebamun spoke and added: "You really should go there sometime, Ipi."

On the streets numerous hawkers were trying to sell their products to passers-by and the local markets also continued their business during the evening.

Many Thebans left their hot homes to find fresh air and coolness outside after the long hot day. Men and women of all ages were outside, on their way to visiting the markets or taverns or to nowhere in particular, just enjoying a beautiful evening and between them children ran around laughing and shouting at each other.

When they neared the river Ipi and Nebamun started to see crewmen of the river boats who had docked in the city for the evening going into the city looking for entertainment.

After reaching the riverside they saw a fleet of boats arriving in the city's harbour.

"They are very late. They must have been sailing in the dark," Nebamun remarked.

When the boats came nearer they saw that they were fully loaded with construction material.

"They must be on their way to the Pharaoh's new city in the desert," Ipi remarked.

"Yes, our great Pharaoh is in a hurry. He wants to finish his city as soon as possible," a voice replied behind Ipi and Nebamun, before Nebamun could say anything.

Startled Ipi and Nebamun turned to see Amenemope. Ipi sighed disappointedly, since Amenemope had supported the banished Wahankh in his attempt to become High Priest, he felt an even stronger dislike towards him than before, even though he knew the young priest had acted out of conviction instead of ambition or greed.

"Well, if the Pharaoh wants to direct all his attention to building a city faraway from here he should do that. It is not hurting us," Nebamun, who did not seem bothered by the priest's unexpected appearance, spoke and added: "I hope he will move there after his city is finished."

Amenemope smiled and replied in a lecturing tone: "In that case I think your wish will probably come true. But are you so naïve to think it won't hurt us when the Pharaoh moves to his new city?"

Before Nebamun could answer Amenemope's question the priest already gave the answer himself: "That new city will then become the new administrative and religious capital of the Two Lands and Thebes will turn into an insignificant desert town and together with Thebes our temple will lose its importance."

Ipi had been listening to what Amenemope had said and replied: "Ramose, the Vizier, will protect us. He won't let anything happen to the temple."

"Maybe," Amenemope spoke. "But Ramose is an old man and the Pharaoh is a young man. How long will Ramose be around to protect Karnak?"

CHAPTER 13
ANOTHER SETBACK FOR KARNAK
AND
ATEN'S CITY RECEIVES A NAME

The next morning Ramose left early so he would be able to travel as far as possible during the day.

He had spent the previous evening in the company of the Pharaoh, who was still not feeling well but had seemed to enjoy the visit of the old vizier. He even came, together with Meryra and Penthu, to say farewell to Ramose before he boarded his boat.

"How are you feeling today, my lord?" Penthu asked when they had a moment alone. He was still worried about the vizier's health.

"To be honest, not so good," Ramose replied with a weak smile. "I might have caught the Pharaoh's illness."

Penthu noticed Ramose was sweating in spite of the cool morning weather. He checked his temperature and noticed the vizier had a light fever.

"My lord," Penthu spoke earnestly, "I advise you seriously not to travel today."

"I appreciate your concern but I have a lot of business in Thebes that cannot wait. But there is no need to worry, my personal physician accompanies me and he will take care of me during the journey," Ramose replied, trying to give the impression he was confident about being able to make the long journey.

Before he went to say farewell to Amenhotep and Meryra, Ramose padded Penthu on the shoulder and spoke: "I will be fine, Penthu! I might be old but I am strong!"

A short time later the vizier's boat departed. While they watched it sailing up the river the Pharaoh spoke: "I feel very weak, Penthu. Bring me something that will help me to regain my strength. I will be waiting in my tent."

Penthu went to prepare a medicine for Amenhotep and not much later arrived at the Pharaoh's tent to administer it.

Upon entering the tent Penthu was surprised to hear Amenhotep and Meryra, the High Priest of the Aten, arguing.

"How could you agree to Ramose's request?" Meryra asked indignantly.

"Because it is the best thing to do," Amenhotep replied in a tired voice.

"But the Aten should be worshipped exclusively. He does not accept other Gods next to Him," Meryra continued to which the Pharaoh replied: "I know that and the Aten is going to be the only God. After I have made the Aten the state God, the people will turn to Him without me having to forbid the worshipping of other Gods. It will be better for the stability of the country this way, Meryra."

"I understand, but Ramose not only worships the Aten but is also still loyal to Amun. I don't understand why you gave in to him at the expense of the Aten without even asking my advice," Meryra complained, his voice betraying that he felt insulted.

Apparently there were even limits to how far the High Priest of the Aten could go with the Pharaoh. Amenhotep turned red and suddenly yelled at Meryra: "I can give in to anybody I want without asking your advice, Meryra, because I am the Pharaoh and you are only a priest! And besides the Pharaoh, I am also the only representative of the

Aten on earth! I am the son of the Aten, so it is not your place to tell me whether my decisions are good or bad for the Aten! If I take a bad decision Aten will give me a sign. I don't need you for that!"

Penthu was shocked, he had never heard Amenhotep speaking in such a way to one of his most trusted and loyal servants.

Meryra also felt upset about the unusual outburst of the Pharaoh against him and as soon as Amenhotep stopped speaking he ran past Penthu out of the tent. While he passed him, Penthu thought he saw tears in the High Priest's eyes.

After Meryra's sudden departure the Pharaoh turned to Penthu.

"Come here, Penthu. Did you bring a medicine for me?" Amenhotep asked, the annoyance about Meryra's insolence still audible in his voice and, while rubbing his hands over his face, he went on: "I have a terrible headache and Meryra's visit only made it worse."

A few days after Ramose's departure Hemienu returned to the construction site of the City of the Aten.

The whole journey down the Nile he had felt depressed. He hadn't been able to convince his wife to follow him with the children to the desert plain. He had tried several times to change her mind but most attempts only turned into a fight.

Finally he had given up and resigned himself to the fact that he would rarely see his family in the coming years.

On the way to the construction site Hemienu had stopped to visit several stone quarries to inspect the progress of the work and he was satisfied to see that there were already many blocks of stone ready to be shipped.

After the success of the working method they were using at the Gem Pa Aten Hemienu decided to implement the same method for the construction of the Pharaoh's new city. That meant that all the stones would already be cut in the quarries into a standard size which could be quickly and easily handled by the workers at the building site.

As soon as he arrived Hemienu asked for a meeting with the Pharaoh, which was immediately granted.

When he entered the Pharaoh's large and luxurious tent Amenhotep was visibly pleased with his return and spoke: "Welcome back, Hemienu. Has your trip been successful?"

"Yes, Your Majesty. I have brought capable overseers with me who will be able to help me leading the construction. I have also recruited more workers," Hemienu answered.

"With the number of workmen you have now, how long will it take to build my city?" the Pharaoh inquired.

"Seven to ten years, Your Majesty," Hemienu replied.

"That is too long! I want the city to be habitable in five years," Amenhotep demanded.

"But Your Majesty," Hemienu protested, "That is almost impossible! We don't have enough workers! To finish the city in such a short time we will need much more workers, not only here but also in the stone quarries and on the river for the transportation of the construction materials."

Hemienu had been talking excitedly and paused a moment to catch his breath before adding: "And all these workers will need tools and have to be fed and taken care of when they are ill or wounded, they will need housing and..."

"I know all that!" Amenhotep snapped, cutting his architect off and when Hemienu was quiet repeated more quietly: "I know about all the extra responsibilities that come with more workers but we can take care of that."

"But I don't know where to find extra workers, Your Majesty. We have already recruited workers from all over the country," Hemienu spoke, continuing to see too many obstacles to be able to finish the city within the time period the Pharaoh demanded.

"I have thought about that," Amenhotep replied and went on: "I have decided to recruit farmers. Each village will have to send a part of their farming population to work on my project."

"But that will have a disastrous effect on the harvest which we will need to feed the workers," Hemienu spoke horrified.

"That will be solved by increasing the taxes, Hemienu. We will take a bigger share of the harvest. I spend a large part of my wealth on this city so I can also demand a contribution of the people for the construction," Amenhotep spoke, starting to get annoyed by his architect's unwillingness to simply try to meet the target set by him.

"But how about the people. Will they be able to..." Hemienu started to speak again, trying to convince the Pharaoh that his idea had many disadvantages but again he was cut off.

"The people will be fine!" Amenhotep almost shouted now. "As I have already said: I am sacrificing a lot for the Aten so the people can do so too!"

Amenhotep paused a moment and then spoke in a voice drained of any emotion: "Let the workmen work hard. The sooner they finish the city the sooner all the farmers can return to their fields."

Then suddenly the Pharaoh calmed down again and said in a very serious tone: "Hemienu, before you start construction on the city I want you to create boundary steles that will indicate the boundaries of Aten's land. These steles will be cut in the cliffs around the city on both sides of the river."

The Pharaoh handed Hemienu a papyrus roll and spoke: "These are the texts I want to be written on the steles."

Hemienu opened the roll and quickly ready the first text:

"My father the Aten has shown me this land. Here, I will build Akhetaten for my father the Aten on the land which He has created, which is protectively surrounded by rock formations and which has never belonged to any other God."

'Akhetaten', the Horizon of the Aten; it was the first time Hemienu read the name of the city that was going to control his life in the coming years.

Ipi was working at Intef's practice at Karnak. Intef had left for the afternoon and Mereruka was in charge until he would return.

The last days it had been very busy, many people were getting sick and Ipi wondered whether the Gods were unhappy and punishing the people.

He tried to forget these thoughts and started to prepare medicines for the patients, who were lying on reed mats on the floor; most of them would be staying there during the night.

While he was working Ipi heard the sound running feet coming nearer. When he looked who it was he saw Nebamun hurrying into the practice, his face looking very upset.

"What happened?" Ipi asked.

"A messenger just arrived at the temple and said Ramose has died on his way back to Thebes after visiting the Pharaoh," Nebamun replied, speaking excitedly and after a short pause to catch his breath added: "His boat will be arriving in Thebes soon."

Ipi felt as if the ground had disappeared beneath his feet.

"What happened?" he asked again.

"I don't know," Nebamun replied. "But maybe we will know more when his boat arrives later today."

Early that evening Ramose's boat arrived in Thebes.

Word of the vizier's death had already started to spread around the city and his boat was met by a mourning population. Ramose had been a popular person in Thebes because he was not only the Vizier of Upper Egypt but also the mayor of Thebes.

Together with many priests of Amun, including Maya, Wenamun and his wife Tahat and Amunherkhepeshef of the Southern Temple, Ipi and Nebamun were waiting to meet the boat carrying the deceased vizier.

Amongst the priests many rumours started to circulate some of which even suggested that Ramose was murdered by the Pharaoh. Maya had quickly tried to end these rumours by saying that there was no proof for such a theory and pointed out that the Pharaoh had always been close to the vizier and that it was unlikely he would have killed him.

"Whatever happened," Ipi spoke tearfully, "we have lost our only supporter at the Royal Court. First we have lost Penthu and now Ramose. There is nobody left anymore in the palace who will defend the temple against the Pharaoh."

"Don't worry so much, Ipi," Wenamun replied reassuringly. "Maybe everything will turn out to be fine. Maybe Ramose has been successful during his meeting with the Pharaoh before he died."

Ipi was not reassured by Wenamun's comforting words. His nightmares had returned again which he regarded as a bad omen. He decided, however, not to tell anybody about it anymore, since he felt his dreams were not taken seriously.

Ramose's boat docked at the harbour and priests of the House of Death immediately went on board to take the simple coffin in which the vizier had been temporarily laid to rest after his unexpected death and take him away to start the mummification process.

When the priests of the House of Death left with Ramose's body they were followed by the vizier's grieving family and many mourning Thebans.

Since Ramose was already old Ipi knew he would probably have been well prepared for his journey to the Kingdom of Osiris and he would without doubt have an impressive tomb in the Theban necropolis waiting to receive him.

"What happened to Ramose?" Maya asked Ramose's personal physician when he disembarked to follow the priests who carried his master to the House of Death.

The physician politely bowed for the High Priest and replied: "My lord, my master was already weak from the journey down the Nile when we arrived at the site of His Majesty's new city in the desert but he insisted on leaving again early the next morning. During his stay with His Majesty my master was attacked by a fever but he still insisted on returning to Thebes. On the boat I could not do much for him and after the fever got worse both I and the ship's crew advised my master that we should stop for a rest and treatment at a city along the way but he ordered to continue sailing to Thebes. When he finally agreed to stop at Abedju it was too late. He died just before we reached the city. We stopped in Abedju to have my master laid in a coffin with natron to preserve his body for the rest of the journey home to Thebes to receive proper mummification. That was all I could do for him."

The last words had been spoken by Ramose's physician in a voice choked with emotion and as soon as he had finished he quickly followed his master's body to the House of Death.

"He must feel he has failed his master whom he was supposed to take care of," Ipi thought, feeling compassion for the physician.

There was a cold look in the Pharaoh's eyes. His condition had improved significantly due to Penthu's treatment but the news of Ramose's death has shaken him.

Penthu had tried to keep Amenhotep calm but the Pharaoh started pacing up and down while he kept saying: "This must be a sign! This changes everything!"

Suddenly he stopped pacing and ordered Ranefer, who was waiting to be available for when the Pharaoh might need him: "Tell Meryra to come here immediately!"

"Have you heard the news about Ramose, Meryra?" Amenhotep asked a few moments later when the High Priest of the Aten had arrived.

"Yes, Your Majesty, it is very tragic," Meryra replied.

"How do you interpret this tragic event?" Amenhotep asked.

Meryra kept silent for a moment, as if he was thinking about how he should answer, and then finally spoke: "Your Majesty, it means that Aten does not agree with the fact that Ramose has changed your mind about your religious policies. The Aten does not accept other Gods next to Him."

"That's exactly what I thought," Amenhotep replied to Meryra's visible relief.

"Your Majesty, may I speak?" Penthu nervously interrupted the conversation.

"What do you want to say, Penthu?" Amenhotep reluctantly gave permission.

"Your Majesty, as a physician I believe Ramose died of a combination of exhaustion, fever and old age. These are natural causes and are not divine interventions," Penthu explained.

He wanted to add that he believed Ramose had probably caught the fever which had caused his death from the Pharaoh, who was himself ill during the time he had met with the old and weak vizier but Penthu did not have the courage to give this information to the Pharaoh.

Meryra stared angrily at the physician and, before the Pharaoh could reply, spoke condescendingly: "You are a good physician, Penthu, but you don't understand how the Aten works. The Aten has given His Majesty a holy task and Ramose has tried to divert him from this task. Because of this interference Ramose unfortunately had to pay a price!"

"I know how the Gods work, Meryra," Penthu replied, feeling insulted by the way the Aten priest addressed him. "Don't forget that apart from being a physician I am also still a priest of Amun!"

Meryra wanted to reply but Amenhotep stopped him before he could say anything. He seemed to be deeply in thoughts when he spoke: "I interpret whatever has happened to Ramose as a sign, I don't believe this is a coincidence. But what if you are right, Penthu? We have to be careful with making decisions."

"What is this going to mean for the temples of the other Gods, Your Majesty?" Penthu asked, feeling a glimmer of hope.

"They will have to accept Aten as the supreme God, that is for sure, and I might have to close the other temples if the Aten asks this from me," Amenhotep replied but then went on: "The first priority, however, is to finish Akhetaten as soon as possible. Aten needs a city that is exclusively dedicated to Him!"

"Are you not going to do away with the other temples immediately?" Meryra asked, sounding disappointed.

"Not yet, unless the Aten gives me a clear sign that He wants me to do so," Amenhotep replied and added: "As I said: the first priority is to finish Akhetaten."

Penthu and Meryra both tried to speak but the Pharaoh held up his hand as a sign to silence them.

The expression on the Pharaoh's face softened and for a moment Penthu thought he saw tears in his eyes.

After a long silence Amenhotep finally spoke: "Maybe Ramose was wrong when he asked me to spare the temple of Amun. But he was a good vizier, whom I have known my entire life and who was like family to me. I don't want any further discussion at this moment. I want everybody to leave so I can mourn Ramose in private."

Aset and Kiya had been travelling up the Nile for about a week when they reached the plain surrounded by rock cliffs where Amenhotep's city was going to rise.

Their last days in Memphis had been quiet, only on the day before they were going to leave the city Aperel had insisted on a farewell banquet.

During the banquet Aset saw Hetepka, the High Priest of Ptah, again but she managed to stay out of his way.

When they had been about to leave Memphis Horemheb told Kiya he had received orders to escort her to the Pharaoh's construction site. Since there was no Royalty staying in Memphis at that moment the Pharaoh had apparently decided it was not necessary to maintain the presence of the Royal Guards there.

On the way to the south Kiya's boat had overtaken many transport boats which were heavily loaded with men and materials.

"I wonder how far Amenhotep's city will have progressed," Aset remarked, watching a boat crowded with workers.

"They haven't even started building yet," Kiya replied and when Aset looked at her in wonder about how she knew this Kiya explained: "I have received a letter from Amenhotep in which he explained that at the moment they are still preparing the surface of the ground and are building houses for the workers. But I am also looking forward to see the changes that will have been made since we left."

Aset had double feelings about returning to Amenhotep's construction site and to Thebes. She looked forward to meeting Merykare again but the moment she would arrive she would also be demoted again to Kiya's servant while in Memphis and on Kiya's boat she was accepted as Kiya's friend and guest.

When they turned around a bend in the Nile they saw the river was filled with boats. They had reached the Pharaoh's building site where transportation vessels came and went, bringing supplies to support the community which had formed on the plain in the desert.

The experienced helmsman expertly navigated the Daughter of the Aten through the busy river stretch and a short while later they safely docked next to Amenhotep's bark.

Looking from the river onto the plain Aset saw Kiya was right; construction of the Pharaoh's city had not yet started but a village of simple buildings had formed which obviously served the workers. The Pharaoh and his officials were still living in luxurious tents.

Word had already spread that the Pharaoh's wife was returning from her trip to Memphis so when her boat arrived Amenhotep was waiting together with Meryra, Hekanakht, Hemienu and other dignitaries who stayed with the Pharaoh at his construction site to welcome Kiya.

When Kiya disembarked Amenhotep took both her hands and spoke: "I have missed you, Kiya. There are hundreds of people with me on this plain but I felt lonely without you."

"I am pleased to join my husband's side again," Kiya replied.

Having returned to her husband Kiya also needed to adept to the court protocol again after the freedom of Memphis. But Aset noticed her friend was genuinely happy to see Amenhotep again.

Amenhotep and Kiya walked past the line of dignitaries, giving them the opportunity to welcome her.

"My heart is delighted to see Your Highness again," Meryra greeted Kiya when she passed him. Contrary to the Pharaoh he spoke very formal.

A short time later the Pharaoh and Kiya had withdrawn to the privacy of their tent and Aset was free to look for Merykare.

She did not have to search long, Merykare had already seen Aset and Kiya arriving and had been waiting for Aset to be released from her duty.

The moment they met Aset wanted to say how she had missed Merykare but Merykare just threw his arms around her and kissed her passionately. It was the first time in Aset's life that she was kissed in such a way.

Hemienu had returned to his work after welcoming Kiya. Since he was going to spend the coming years working on Akhetaten he had a private house being built but because it was not yet ready the Pharaoh had given him a tent where he could work in privacy.

He was sitting bent over a simple table filled with maps of the future city and lists of numbers of workers and materials that he had received or was going to receive.

He had heard disturbing stories about arson during his absence and later on tools had also mysteriously disappeared from storerooms. Starting to worry about security the Pharaoh had ordered the Royal Guards stationed in Memphis to follow his wife Kiya to the construction site to strengthen the security there.

Hemienu was relieved to have extra guards. The fire puzzled him, he could understand that poor workers would steal valuable tools but he could not understand why anybody would deliberately set fire to construction material.

After a moment Hemienu shrugged off these thoughts, he could not change anything to what had happened and with the extra security he hoped such things would not occur again. Besides that, he had already more than enough problems to deal with.

He looked on the map of Akhetaten with its temples and palaces constructed along a road which would run parallel to the Nile. There was even going to be a covered bridge across this road that would connect two palaces.

"This city is going to be unique in the Two Lands," Hemienu thought to himself. "But how am I going to build it within five years without enough skilled workers? The Pharaoh can send me farmers but will they make much difference? Will this not negatively influence the food-supplies of the country and maybe even the Pharaoh's project?"

While pondering over these questions he, almost automatically whispered a short prayer to Ptah, the Creator God who was popular amongst the Egyptian workers.

Being an active man who liked to be around his workmen on the construction sites Hemienu eventually could not stand sitting and worrying and staring at maps and documents alone in his tent anymore. He got up from behind his desk and decided to see how the work on the steles which the Pharaoh had ordered to be created on the boundaries of Akhetaten was progressing.

A few days after Kiya had returned to Akhetaten Amenhotep had decided it was time to return to Thebes. He had been away from the capital for too long already and Ramose's death made his return even more urgent; now he had to appoint a new vizier to replace him.

Before he left Amenhotep met with Hemienu, who was going to be in charge of the construction site of the new city after his departure and he appointed Horemheb, the commander of the Royal Guard of Memphis, as the new head of security since Hekanakht with his soldiers was going to escort the Pharaoh back to Thebes.

At Hemienu's request more regular soldiers had already been sent to Akhetaten to help maintaining security after Hekanakht's Guards' departure.

After having given everybody who remained behind the necessary instructions the Pharaoh left, taking a large escort with him.

Amenhotep sailed on his private bark the Shining Aten while Aset and Kiya followed on Kiya's boat.

From the moment they left Kiya felt tired and moody. Aset did not know what was wrong and unsuccessfully tried to cheer her up, she even told her about her recent meetings with Merykare which under normal circumstances would have interested and amused Kiya.

"Are you worried about returning to Thebes?" Aset asked while they were eating lunch on the boat.

"No, why should I worry about that?" Kiya replied annoyed.

"I don't know, I just want to know what is bothering you," Aset spoke, getting worried about her friend.

"Nothing is bothering..." Kiya started to say but then suddenly had to throw up.

All the boat's crew came to see what happened to the Pharaoh's wife but Aset quickly told them to leave them alone.

"You are getting sick, Kiya," Aset spoke and in a voice that did would not accept any contradiction she added: "You have to let Penthu examine you!"

The crew of Kiya's boat signaled to the crew of Amenhotep's boat on which Penthu was travelling.

Soon afterwards both boats moored on the riverside and Penthu boarded Kiya's boat to examine the Pharaoh's wife.

Everybody was waiting nervously and Aset was very worried; she had heard stories about Ramose, the Vizier of Upper Egypt, dying only a short while ago, while making the same journey they were making.

She looked at Amenhotep, who was pacing up and down on the riverside close to the gangway of the

Daughter of the Aten, his face showing he was just as worried as Aset.

Finally, after what felt as a long time, Penthu appeared from the cabin of the boat.

Aset looked at his face but could not make up whether the news was going to be good or bad.

Penthu walked straight to the Pharaoh, made a small bow and spoke formally: "Your Majesty, allow me to be the first to congratulate you. Her Highness Kiya is pregnant!"

There was a festive atmosphere when the fleet of Amenhotep arrived back in Thebes.

The Thebans lined the side of the river to welcome their Pharaoh and his wife, who had been away for so long.

The news of Kiya's pregnancy had not yet reached the people but if they would have known about it it would have surely heightened the atmosphere because after Nefertiti having given birth to two daughters everybody was waiting for a son, the Crown Prince, to be born.

Ipi was standing amongst the people at the Theban harbour and watched the boats sailing past them.

When he first heard the Pharaoh was returning to Thebes he had regarded it as bad news. He had felt more comfortable knowing the Pharaoh was far away, building his new city. But now that he was standing on the riverside between the cheering and waving people he got carried away by their excitement and when some of the people on the Pharaoh's boats started to wave, to his own surprise he waved back.

As soon as the Pharaoh's fleet had passed Ipi returned to reality. He remembered Amenemope's words from the evening they had met at the harbour. Ipi had not paid much attention to them at that time but now that Ramose had so unexpectedly died the situation had changed completely. He realized that maybe he should listen more to what Amenemope had to say.

Ipi looked around at the large crowd lining the riverside in the harbour and wondered if the people knew they had been cheering for the Pharaoh who was possibly going to take the privileged position of their city away.

The Royal Fleet reached the docks of Malkata Palace where everybody was already waiting to welcome the Pharaoh back home after his long absence.

Since the discovery of Kiya's pregnancy Kiya and Aset had been travelling on the Pharaoh's boat because Amenhotep wanted to guarantee that his wife would stay safe and, as he hoped, would give him an heir to the throne.

Along the way the Pharaoh had ordered to stop at Gebtu where he had been pleased to see the mayor had kept his promise and was building a temple dedicated to the Aten.

Queen Teye and Nefertiti, the Great Royal Wife, were the first to welcome the Pharaoh when he disembarked.

"Welcome home, my son. You have been away longer than a mother can bear," Teye spoke while she hugged the son to whom she had always been very close.

"Your Great Royal Wife also welcomes you home and lets you know that all the affairs of the Two Lands have been well taken care of during your absence," Nefertiti spoke in a tone that was both businesslike and affectionate.

Amenhotep greeted his wife and his mother and Aset could see by the way he greeted both that he had really missed them.

Finally Teye and Nefertiti also started to give attention to Kiya.

"Welcome home, Kiya," Queen Teye spoke.

"Did you have a pleasant journey, Kiya? You look pale. Are you all right?" Nefertiti inquired, sounding genuinely concerned.

Amenhotep, who overheard Nefertiti's words, replied before Kiya could say something: "Kiya is fine."

Next he put one arm around his mother's shoulders and the other around Nefertiti's and spoke in a voice that gave away his happiness: "Kiya is with child!"

Aset watched when the Pharaoh was giving his mother and wife the good news; Queen Teye was happy and immediately congratulated Kiya but Nefertiti's face, which had been smiling just a moment before, turned dark and worried.

Aset seemed to have been the only person who noticed it and she immediately remembered Sitre's warning from the day they had arrived back in the palace after staying at Panehsy's villa: Kiya giving birth to a son before she did would be one of the worst things that could happen to Nefertiti.

Seventy days after his death the mummification process of Meryptah, the High Priest of Amun, had been completed and he was ready to be interred in the tomb which he had started preparing many years before his death.

Meryptah's funeral procession had started early in the morning from the Karnak Temple and would lead across the river to the Theban necropolis.

Having served well as the High Priest of Amun for a long period, Meryptah had become well known and popular amongst the Egyptians and his funeral attracted people from all over the country, including priests and priestesses of other Egyptian Gods. The Pharaoh, however, had not sent anybody to represent him.

The temple of Amun had arranged boats to help all the participants of the funeral procession to cross the river.

Ipi, also taking part in the procession, had just arrived on the west bank of the Nile and would walk in the front of the procession together with the other priests of the Karnak Temple. Standing on the west bank Ipi looked around himself, he saw Thebes on the other side of the Nile and the Theban Mountains rising high above him on his side of the river.

Looking at the mountains Ipi remembered how he used to climb them, he remembered the day he had witnessed the funeral procession of Crown Prince Thutmose arriving at exactly the same place where he was standing. That was the day his parents had told him he was going to be sent to the Temple of Karnak, it was maybe only two years ago but it seemed much longer, so much had changed for him since then.

The funeral was presided over by Maya, who would act as the Sem Priest and would perform the Opening of the Mouth ceremony.

When everybody had arrived on the west bank a priest bearing a standard of the jackal God Wepwawet, the Opener of the Ways, started to lead the procession to Meryptah's tomb followed by Maya and the richly decorated coffin containing Meryptah's mummy on a sledge drawn by two bulls.

Behind the coffin the priests and priestesses of Amun followed, next came professional mourners and finally the rest of the people, which included friends and family of the High Priest, devout followers of Amun and state officials.

Arriving at the tomb in one of the many valleys of the Theban Mountains Maya conducted the highly important Opening of the Mouth ceremony to enable the ka of Meryptah to return to his body, breathe again and to receive offerings.

After the ceremony the coffin of the High Priest was taken into the tomb that had been dug into the mountain. To his surprise Wenamun invited Ipi to join the few selected priests who would follow the coffin into the tomb.

Ipi felt nervous, he had never before entered a tomb, all the funerals he had ever attended had been of poor farmers who could not afford anything more than a pit in the ground on the edge of the desert.

Upon entering the tomb Ipi saw an enormous portrait of Meryptah holding a large scepter on the wall facing into his tomb. The portrait must be picturing Meryptah entering the Netherworld, Ipi reasoned.

He read the hieroglyphs below the portrait: "The first servant of the Lord Amun, Osiris Meryptah."

Ipi knew that adding the name of Osiris, the Lord of the Underworld, to a person's name meant that this person had joined Osiris in His Kingdom.

Ipi followed the priests who were constantly chanting prayers for the protection of the ka of their High Priest while they followed behind the coffin that was slowly carried further into the tomb through a long passage that led deep into the mountain.

The only sources of light they had inside the tomb were the torches the priests had brought with them and in their flickering light Ipi tried to interpret some of the scenes he saw depicted on the walls of the passage.

In the first half of the passage he saw Osiris Meryptah in front of strange looking creatures which Ipi knew to be the guardians of the gates to the underworld. There were several gates and at each gate Meryptah would have to recognize the demonic guardian and call him by his name to be able to pass through. Fortunately for Osiris Meryptah, to help him through his perilous journey, the names of the guardians had been written on the walls of his tomb.

Further down the long passage Ipi recognized scenes where Osiris Meryptah was welcomed by Gods and Goddesses which meant he had reached the Kingdom of Osiris successfully.

Deep inside the mountain, at the end of the passage, the priests reached the first chamber. In the chamber Ipi noticed it was already filled with everything the former High Priest might need in the afterlife. He saw simple and daily products such as bread, beer, and wine but also more luxurious items such as expensive ointments, a chariot, gilded furniture and golden statues of various Gods.

The chamber gave access to three more chambers in which Ipi also saw the glimmer of gold and precious stones in the light of the torches.

The priests did not pay any attention to the chambers on their left and right sides but continued into the chamber right in front of them. They only stopped a short moment when Maya, who was leading the group, seemed to hesitate a moment in front of a wall with a large depiction of Osiris Meryptah playing senet, the popular Egyptian board game which the High Priest loved to play during his life, with a lady.

Ipi read the hieroglyphs written under the beautifully painted scene and was surprised to read that it depicted Meryptah playing senet in the afterlife with his wife Nefertari. Ipi had never known Meryptah had been married. According to the hieroglyphs under the painted scene Nefertari had joined Osiris already and Ipi thought she must have died a long time ago because he had never heard anything about her having ever existed.

Maya stared a short moment at the depiction of Meryptah together with his wife but then continued into the next chamber, a large four-pillared chamber where an empty sarcophagus was waiting to receive the High Priest's coffin.

Priests bearing torches took up positions at the chamber's four corners, illuminating the complete room and revealing more riches and the large red quartzite sarcophagus.

The sarcophagus was decorated with the four winged Goddesses Isis, Nephthys, Selket and Neith; each Goddess standing on a corner and protectively spreading Her wings.

Looking up Ipi saw the ceiling of the chamber depicted the Goddess Nut arching over the entire length of the ceiling. Her body was decorated with the stars and constellations of the night sky. Nut was the Goddess of the sky Who also symbolized rebirth because every evening She ate the sun and give birth to it again the next morning.

The priests who carried the coffin containing Osiris Meryptah's mummy carefully placed the coffin into the sarcophagus while they, together with all the other attending priests, were chanting hymns to Osiris asking Him to accept their former High Priest into His Kingdom.

While the priests were chanting Maya had been reciting a prayer wishing Osiris Meryptah a prosperous afterlife. Finally they slid the lid on the sarcophagus leaving Meryptah in the darkness of the Underworld.

After the sarcophagus had been closed Ipi noticed the scene of the Hall of Judgment on the wall. It showed Meryptah in front of Osiris while his heart was being weighed against the feather of Ma'at.

Ammit, the creature that ate the heart of people not worthy to enter the Kingdom of Osiris, was shown waiting to devour Osiris Meryptah's heart but Ipi knew she would be disappointed; a person like Meryptah would without doubt be found worthy to enter the realm of Osiris.

Four more priests, Wenamun, Intef, Amunherkhepeshef and Wennefer, the young high-ranking priest who earlier had joined Maya and Wenamun at the audience with the Pharaoh, entered the chamber; each of them solemnly carrying a jar with a lid shaped like the head of an Egyptian God.

These were canopic jars, the jars that contained the High Priest's vital organs which had been removed during mummification.

The priests placed the jars in a container which stood close to the sarcophagus while the whole time they had kept chanting prayers.

Finally, after the last prayers had been recited the priests started to leave the burial chamber and move up the long passage again towards the daylight that beckoned them back to the land of the living.

As soon as they arrived outside officials of the necropolis locked the doors of the tomb and sealed them to prevent the doors from being opened without the necropolis guards noticing it.

After the tomb's doors had been locked Ipi suddenly started to feel the loss of the High Priest more than ever. Before Meryptah had been buried Ipi felt as if he was still present but now that he was lying deep in his closed tomb, ready to meet Osiris, it finally got through to him that Meryptah was really gone.

Ipi was walking back to the Nile River together with all the other attendants of the funeral. It was hot and Ipi felt uncomfortable, he hoped the boats would already be waiting to bring them back to Thebes on the east bank.

When they came near the Nile bank Ipi noticed a large group of men, who looked like workers or farmers gathering together and a number of boats waiting close to them on the river. Getting nearer to the group Ipi could hear some of the men shouting angrily.

"What is happening there?" Ipi heard one of the priests behind him remark. Ipi was wondering exactly the same.

The boats that were going to take the participants of the funeral procession back to Thebes were lying next to the boats that were apparently waiting for the group of men that was standing on the bank of the Nile.

When he passed the group Ipi saw the angry men were being kept under control by soldiers. They were all standing in lines and had to give their names to scribes, who wrote them down on rolls of papyrus.

"What about my fields? Who is going to harvest them?" Ipi heard somebody shout desperately.

"Who is going to take care of my family?" another person yelled in the same desperate tone.

Ipi continued further towards the river, not understanding what was happening, when he heard somebody call his name. Looking around he noticed Huni, his brother and father of his deceased nephew Djehuty, amongst the group.

Huni walked towards Ipi but when he wanted to leave his line he was stopped by a soldier armed with a stick.

Ipi then walked to Huni and asked what was happening.

"The Pharaoh has ordered us to leave our fields and work on his construction site. Every village in the country has to give a certain number of farmers to serve on the Pharaoh's project," Huni explained and went on: "Many people here have nobody to replace them or to support their wives and children. Aha had offered to go in my place to let me stay with Tahat but the Royal official who came to our house wanted me to come because I was younger and stronger."

"And Ankhaf?" Ipi asked. "Does he not have to go?"

"No," Huni replied. "Tuya has just given birth to a daughter so they let him stay home."

"Is the baby healthy?" Ipi asked, feeling happiness for a moment.

"She is very beautiful and healthy. Her name is Henutsen," Huni replied with a warm smile.

"You have talked long enough! Get back in line, it is almost your turn!" the soldier with the stick ordered Huni and after noticing Ipi's robes of the Amun priesthood he bowed reverently and spoke politely: "I apologize for disturbing your conversation but this man has been ordered to serve His Majesty."

Before he went back in line to give his name to the scribes and continue to the boats that were waiting to bring the farmers to their new working place Huni spoke hurriedly: "Ipi, try to visit our family sometimes when I am gone! Tell Tahat that I love her and that I will come back to her as soon as possible and please keep making offerings to Djehuty's ka!"

"You there! What is your name?" a scribe shouted at Huni.

The soldier pushed Huni towards the scribe where Huni gave his name after which he was directed to a boat that had already started to fill with the Pharaoh's new workmen.

By the time Ipi had boarded his boat to return to Thebes his brother had boarded an uncomfortable transport boat crowded with men who were angry and nervous about being forced to leave their families and fields to work at a place faraway of which they had never heard.

CHAPTER 14
A MURDER ON THE CONSTRUCTION SITE
AND
A TRAGEDY IN THE PALACE

It had been more than two months since the funeral of Meryptah.

Ramose, the Vizier of Upper Egypt and mayor of Thebes, had just been buried in his magnificent tomb in the Theban Mountains with a large state funeral ceremony attended personally by the Pharaoh.

After the funeral Amenhotep had appointed Nakhtpaaten as Ramose's successor as Vizier of Upper Egypt. His choice had surprised many since it was expected that one of the prominent court officials such as Aye would become the next vizier.

Nakhtpaaten was, however, of Royal blood and carried the title of prince and, more importantly to Amenhotep, he loyally supported him in his Aten worship. As a sign of his devotion to the Aten he had even taken a new name that praised the life-giving Sun Disc.

The appointment of Nakhtpaaten had caused consternation amongst the priests of Amun. Where Ramose, besides being a follower of the Aten was also a worshipper of Amun who showed sympathy for the situation of His temple, the new Vizier of Upper Egypt, just like the Pharaoh, only worshipped the Aten. The priests of Amun did not have to expect any support from Nakhtpaaten.

"Your Majesty looks very worried this morning," Penthu spoke to the Pharaoh.

Penthu came to the Pharaoh's private office for his usual morning's meeting but the Pharaoh seemed elsewhere with his thoughts; instead of answering Penthu's inquiries about his health Amenhotep sat behind his desk and kept staring at a message in front of him.

"Is it bad news, Your Majesty?" Penthu finally asked.

Amenhotep did not immediately reply but after a while spoke slowly: "This message from Tushratta, the King of Mitanni, arrived yesterday."

The Pharaoh held out the clay tablet on which the message was written to Penthu and said: "Read it yourself."

Penthu was shocked, it was highly unusual for a Pharaoh to show private correspondence from another king to his subjects.

Hesitatingly he took the tablet, feeling privileged by the trust Amenhotep apparently had in him.

The message was written in cuneiform, the diplomatic language of the region which Penthu had studied at the House of Life at Karnak when he was a young priest.

Trying hard to remember what he had learned a long time ago but after that had never used anymore Penthu started to read:

"To my brother Amenhotep, Lord of the Two Lands from Tushratta, King of Mitanni.
How is my brother and how is his mother, the Great Lady Teye? How are your Great Royal Wife, your new wife Kiya and my daughter Tadukhipa?

I pray daily to the Gods of my country that all of you may enjoy excellent health.
My brother has not sent me everything I have requested from him. Does my brother not care about me? Recently King Suppiluliuma of the Kingdom of Hatti has plundered my lands and even taken land from me. King Suppiluliuma is also threatening vassal kingdoms of my brother.
I ask my brother one more time to send me gold so I can maintain my army and protect both my brother's lands and my own."

When he finished reading Penthu put the clay tablet carefully on the Pharaoh's desk.

"I haven't got many resources to spare, Penthu, but I have to do something to please Tushratta. What do you advise me to do?" Amenhotep asked, looking up at his physician who was standing in front of his desk.

"Forgive me, Your Majesty, but I am not an expert on diplomacy or military strategy. I am not the right person to advise Your Majesty on this affair," Penthu replied.

The Pharaoh kept staring at Penthu and spoke in a very serious voice: "Since you are not an expert you might have a fresh approach, different from my advisors, to this matter. What do you advise me to do, Penthu?"

Penthu thought for a moment and then suggested: "You could raise the taxes, Your Majesty."

Amenhotep smiled and spoke: "That was my idea but some of my advisors said that could cause unrest amongst the people and that is something I do not need at the moment. I have to keep the people calm so I can complete the task the Aten has given to me."

"Maybe Your Majesty can send King Tushratta grain instead of gold or other treasures," Penthu suggested as a new idea and explained: "Tushratta's army needs to be fed and you will prove to him that you value him as an ally."

"That is a good idea, Penthu," Amenhotep spoke without any enthusiasm but then went on: "But where would I get enough grain? I have sent many farmers to Akhetaten to help with the construction of the city. I am not even sure if all our fields will be completely harvested during the coming years."

"I am sure they will be harvested, Your Majesty," Penthu replied reassuringly. "Farmers are hard workers and help each other when necessary. They will harvest their fields!"

"And what if they won't?" Amenhotep remarked, still not being convinced.

"Trust me, Your Majesty, they will!" Penthu spoke and then added: "And if there are farmers who won't harvest their fields Your Majesty can have them ordered to be harvested by other farmers and keep that harvest to be sent to Mitanni."

Penthu paused for a moment and then went on, speaking slowly: "Since this is a matter of national interest force should even be applied when necessary to finish the harvest."

"Maybe you are right," the Pharaoh spoke, this time sounding more enthusiastic. "I will send Tushratta a part of our harvest."

Kiya returned from Nefertiti's apartments to her own quarters.

Her pregnancy made her often feel tired but Amenhotep surrounded her with the best possible care. Penthu regularly checked her health and her relation with Nefertiti was very good so Kiya felt very satisfied with her life.

Nefertiti regularly invited her to spend time and have meals with her and to play with her daughters Meritaten and Meketaten because, as she explained: "Soon you will be a mother and you will have to know how to take care of your child."

Since Amenhotep's return to Thebes he had spent a lot of time with Nefertiti, whom he had clearly missed during his time away and since a few weeks Nefertiti was also pregnant again, making his chance on having a Crown Prince soon even bigger.

"Nefertiti is very supportive during my pregnancy," Kiya told Aset when they were alone and then added in a whisper: "When I was still a servant I never knew she is actually a very kind person."

"Maybe she is very kind, Kiya, but I think you should be careful. You should understand that you pose a threat to her," Aset replied with a warning tone in her voice.

Feeling tired Kiya lay down on her bed while speaking admonishingly to Aset: "I cannot accept you talking like that about the Great Royal Wife, Aset! Nefertiti and I are sisters and she would never do anything to hurt me!"

Aset did not say anything in reply to Kiya since she obviously liked Nefertiti and could not be convinced by her about any possible danger coming from the Great Royal Wife.

"And maybe Sitre could have been wrong?" Aset thought. "Maybe Nefertiti really is trying to help Kiya during the difficult months of her pregnancy and helping her preparing herself for her motherhood?"

Laying on her bed Kiya looked at her big belly with a tender expression on her face and while stroking it with both her hands spoke: "If I will produce the future Pharaoh of the Two Lands Nefertiti will be happy for me. Sisters are never jealous of each other."

"You are probably right," Aset replied and left the room to let Kiya have her afternoon rest.

Aset went to her small private room and before getting some rest herself burnt incense at her little Hathor shrine and said a short prayer asking her favourite Goddess to protect her friend, just in case Sitre had been right.

As his brother Huni had asked him to do moments before being sent away to work for the Pharaoh Ipi had gone to visit his family.

They had not heard anything from Huni since he had been taken away by the Pharaoh's officials and Tahat was scared her husband would never return.

"Don't worry," Ipi had tried to reassure her. "He only has to help on the Pharaoh's construction site. When his city is finished Huni will return home."

Apart from reassuring his family about Huni's situation Ipi held another ceremony for Djehuty's ka.

After having seen Meryptah's elaborate tomb Ipi wondered whether Djehuty's simple grave was sufficient for him to survive in the afterlife even though Wenamun had already assured him that with the proper prayers and offerings Djehuty's ka would survive.

While being home Ipi had met his niece Henutsen, the daughter of his brother Ankhaf and his wife Tuya, for the first time. Meeting her had been the only thing that made him feel happy during the visit to his family.

Ipi was relieved to return to Karnak Temple. Arriving there Ipi noticed a middle aged woman and a boy about his age who were just leaving.

He recognized them immediately as Maya's wife Hetepheres and her son Amenemhet, who sometimes came to visit their husband and father at Karnak.

Ipi had seen them for the first time at the inauguration of Maya as the new High Priest, almost two months earlier. Out of respect for the previous High Priest Meryptah, Maya had not wanted the inauguration ceremony to take place during the mourning period before the funeral.

It had been a solemn ceremony without any festivities but it drew a lot of attention from the Egyptian people, who kept showing devotion to Amun, the King of the Gods, even though their Pharaoh had deserted Him and most other Gods.

Since he had become High Priest, Maya had been trying hard to improve his relation with his wife and son from whom he had been estranged for many years.

Maya had joined the Amun Priesthood relatively late but after he had joined he had devoted himself completely to the temple and God and had had no more time for his family. After a while his wife had not accepted being neglected anymore and had cut all contact with him.

Maya's attempts to renew his relationship with his family had led to rumours amongst some of the priests of Karnak, who claimed that Maya had started to prepare for a new life after the temples of Amun would be closed. Ipi did not believe these rumours but he did wonder what had made Maya decide to meet his family again after so many years without any contact.

"Did you have a nice time with your family, Ipi?" Maya, who had followed his wife and son to the temple gate, asked Ipi when he entered Karnak.

"I was happy to meet my niece, my lord," Ipi replied. "But my family is very worried about my brother Huni, who is working for the Pharaoh now. They are very unhappy that they don't receive any news from him. I did not enjoy this visit as much as the earlier visits."

"Are you not worried about your brother, Ipi?" Maya asked.

"I think he will be fine, he is a strong man and when the Pharaoh's city is finished he will return home again," Ipi replied.

"Maybe you are right but you should take good care of your family, Ipi. Family is very important!" Maya lectured Ipi and continued: "For a long time I neglected my family and I almost lost them forever. It was only recently that I found out the mistake I made when I banished my wife and son out of my life."

"What made you change your mind, my lord?" Ipi asked, thinking only after he had voiced his question that Maya could feel offended by the inquiry.

Luckily Maya was not insulted by Ipi's directness and replied very seriously: "Do you remember the scene in the tomb of Meryptah where he is playing senet with his wife?"

"Yes, I remember it. It was a very beautiful depiction," Ipi replied.

"Yes it was very beautiful," Maya agreed and went on: "When I saw that painting I thought about my own afterlife. Would my wife want to meet me in the afterlife? She did not want to see me in this life anymore and I suddenly realized that that meant I was also going to spend the next life alone and that I had committed an injustice towards my wife and child."

Maya stopped speaking, was silent for a moment and then added: "So I decided to try to renew my contact with them before it would be too late."

A moment later the High Priest returned to his private quarters and Ipi continued on to his own small room while he was thinking about what Maya had told him.

"Hello, Ipi," Nebamun greeted him when he entered their room. "How is your family? Did you have a good time with them?"

"Yes, I was very happy to see them again," Ipi replied.

It was early in the morning and the sun had only just started to rise.

Hemienu still was asleep in his newly built house when he was woken up by a loud knocking on his door. Half asleep Hemienu opened the door to see it was one of Horemheb's Royal Guards.

"What is so important that you have to wake me up?" Hemienu asked annoyed.

"I apologize, my lord, but I have to ask you to follow me immediately. One of your workers has been murdered," the soldier replied.

Moments later Hemienu was standing next to the dead body of the workman. He was lying close to the river on an open space far from the workmen's village. The dead worker lay face down on the ground and had a gaping wound on the back of his head where he had clearly been beaten with a heavy object.

"He must have been murdered during the night," Horemheb, who was already on the scene before Hemienu had arrived, spoke and went on: "But he was not murdered here."

"How do you know that?" Hemienu asked.

"If he was murdered here there should have been more blood on the ground but there is hardly any. This man must have been dead for a while before he was dropped here," Horemheb explained.

"Why would anybody drop the body here?" Hemienu asked again, kneeling to look at the face of the victim.

"I think that the murderer intended to throw the body in the river to be eaten by the crocodiles to conceal his crime. While moving the body he was probably disturbed by one of the patrolling guards so he dropped his victim and ran away," Horemheb spoke.

"I suppose you are correct," Hemienu replied while trying to lift the dead man's head without getting his hands stained with blood.

"Allow me, my lord," one of the attending soldiers spoke and turned the body on his back.

Hemienu recognized the man immediately. "This man comes from Thebes," he said. "His name is Sabni and he used to work as a stonemason with me on the Gem Pa Aten from the day we started its construction. He was a highly skilled worker so I brought him here."

"Do you have any idea why anybody would want to kill him?" Horemheb inquired.

"I would not know why," Hemienu answered. "As far as I know he was a calm and peaceful man."

"The workers can drink a lot in the evening after their working day is over and when drunk some of them sometimes can get violent," the soldier who that morning had woken up Hemienu remarked.

"Some of my workers might argue or even fight sometimes but they are not murderers!" Hemienu snapped back at him.

"But we have to consider the possibility that one of the workers did this, Hemienu. It is either a worker or a soldier and I cannot imagine one of my soldiers doing this," Horemheb spoke calmly.

"Well, maybe it was a worker," Hemienu admitted and after a moment of silence went on: "There are of course workmen from all over the country on the site and don't forget all those farmers who have been put to work here. Many of them are very unhappy and angry about being taken away from their farms and families."

While they were speaking curious workmen started to gather at the scene of Sabni's murder. An overseer finally went over to them and told the workers it was time to start working but Hemienu told them to wait; with thousands of workers being employed at Akhetaten he knew the chance would be small but he wanted to try it.

"Does anybody here know Sabni, the stonemason from Thebes?" he shouted so all the gathered people would be able to hear him.

All the workers shook their heads but from the back of the crowd Hemienu heard a voice: "Yes, I know him!"

A tall thin man, wearing only a simple loin cloth like most of the workmen came forward and repeated: "I knew Sabni, we worked together and lived in the same house."

"When did you last see him?" Horemheb asked. "Yesterday evening," the worker replied. "He liked to be on his own and usually went out to take a walk outside the village after his working day. I saw him leave last evening but never saw him return."

Sabni's colleague could not give any further clues about why or by whom Sabni had been murdered and to Hemienu's dismay Horemheb said he had not enough time or people to search for the murderer.

The only thing Horemheb could do was advise the workers not to wander alone outside of the workmen's village at night.

Sabni was buried that same morning in a simple grave in the ground outside of Akhetaten's boundaries. There was no mummification for the workmen who died at Akhetaten; their way to the afterlife consisted of serving their Pharaoh and hoping they would be rewarded for their service by gaining entrance into the Netherworld.

Hemienu attended the simple funeral ceremony which was led by a priest who was part of a group of Aten priests who were on the construction site to mark the correct alignments in reference to the sun along which the Aten Temples and palaces of Akhetaten had to be built.

After the funeral Hemienu went to visit the construction site to see the progress that was being made. He was pleased to see that the first walls of the main palace and the biggest Aten Temple of Akhetaten had started to rise.

It was getting hot and Hemienu was just about to get something to eat in the cool environment of his home when a guard came running up to him.

"My lord," the guard spoke hastily, "one of the boundary steles that have been cut into the rock formations around the city has been severely damaged during the night!"

The damaged stele was a long walk from the construction site so Hemienu was driven there by the guard in a chariot. Horemheb who was warned around the same time as Hemienu followed in his own chariot.

The stele had been cut high in the rock face but as soon as he arrived Hemienu climbed up easily using steps that had been cut out of the rock by his workers when they created the boundary stele.

Assessing the damage to the large stele Hemienu was shocked by its extend; large parts of the text had been chiseled away.

"It must have been done last night," Horemheb, who had followed Hemienu up the rock face, spoke. "My guards passed here yesterday and reported that everything was in order."

"Who would do such a thing?" Hemienu wondered, being too surprised to be angry.

"The Pharaoh's policy towards the traditional Gods makes him quite a few enemies amongst the people and especially amongst the various priesthoods. Maybe it is a very devout follower of Amun or any of the other Gods, or maybe even one of the disgruntled farmers you have mentioned earlier this morning," Horemheb suggested.

"Whoever did this must be a skilled worker," Hemienu reasoned and explained: "He chiseled large parts of text away working only with the light of the moon and without using any scaffolding."

"Do you think it is one of your workers?" Horemheb asked.

"I would not know who else it could be," Hemienu sighed, accepting the painful fact, while looking towards the workmen's village in the distance.

"Could the person who did this also be the murderer of Sabni?" Hemienu suddenly asked and continued: "Could Sabni maybe have been attracted by the noise that the chiseling must have made and surprised the perpetrator during his work?"

"That is possible," Horemheb replied and, pointing in the direction of the river, went on: "There, close to the river, we found Sabni's body. If Sabni was killed near here and the murderer would take the shortest way to the river to dispose of the body then he would pass that area."

Horemheb thought for a moment and then spoke again: "I am almost convinced that you are right and both crimes have been committed by the same person!"

Aset was happy with Kiya's pregnancy but it also meant that she had to take more care of her friend than before.

Since they had arrived back in Thebes from their journey to Memphis and the desert plain where the Pharaoh's city was going to be built Aset hardly had had any opportunity to meet Merykare. The only moments they could meet for a short time were when Kiya sent Aset out on an errand or when Kiya was sleeping during the afternoon and Aset could quietly go out hoping Kiya would not wake up before her return.

A few times Kiya did wake up early but when Aset explained where she had gone Kiya smiled and inquired for more details about her meeting with Merykare.

Since their return in the palace Aset slept most of the nights in her small private room. While earlier Kiya had liked Aset to share the same room with her she preferred to sleep alone after she had become pregnant.

Aset was sleeping when, in the middle of the night, she was suddenly woken up by screams coming from Kiya's room which was located right next to hers. Aset immediately got up and hurried to Kiya to see what was happening.

In the light of the oil lamp that was burning in Kiya's room Aset saw her friend sitting upright in her bed crying and staring down with an expression of both pain and horror on her face.

To her own horror Aset saw that the bottom of Kiya's white dress and her bed had turned red.

"Please, Aset, call Penthu! Something is wrong with my baby!" Kiya begged, holding her stomach and writhing in pain.

Aset was about to run out of Kiya's chambers to find the physician when Penthu already came running into the room together with Ranefer, the Head of the Royal Servants.

As soon as Penthu entered the room and saw Kiya's bloodstained dress his face darkened.

"Bring me a bowl of water and a towel so I can wash Her Highness," he ordered Aset.

Aset did as she was told and then left Penthu and Kiya alone.

While she waited outside of Kiya's room with Ranefer, the Pharaoh and Nefertiti entered Kiya's chambers.

"What is happening?" Amenhotep asked agitatedly.

"I don't know, Your Majesty," Aset replied. "But Her Highness is bleeding heavily and Penthu is now examining her."

"Has she lost her child?" Nefertiti asked and before Aset or Ranefer could say anything she added: "If so that would be most tragic."

Aset did not say anything but contrary to Amenhotep who was genuinely worried about Kiya and her unborn baby, Nefertiti, in spite of her words, did not seem to care very much.

Amenhotep could not wait for Penthu to return from Kiya's room and went inside to personally see what was happening and was followed by his Great Royal Wife.

Aset and Ranefer stayed behind and Aset quietly prayed to the hippopotamus Goddess Tawaret, the protector of pregnant women, to protect Kiya and her baby.

"What will happen when Kiya will lose her baby? Will the Pharaoh blame her?" Aset, worried about the fate of her friend, finally asked Ranefer.

"I don't know. I think he will accept it as the will of the Aten," Ranefer answered after thinking about the question for a moment.

Not much later Amenhotep stormed out of Kiya's room with a furious expression on his face followed again by Nefertiti on whose face Aset thought to see a sign of relief.

A moment after the Pharaoh and his wife had left Penthu appeared with a sad look on his face and

Aset could hear her friend crying in the room behind him.

"Unfortunately the Gods think it is not yet time for Her Highness to give birth to a baby," Penthu spoke.

"What went wrong?" Ranefer asked the physician, not accepting the will of the Gods as an explanation for Kiya's loss.

"I have no idea. When I examined Her Highness in the afternoon everything seemed fine," Penthu replied.

Aset fetched some more water and went into Kiya's room to wash her, help her into a clean dress and meanwhile tried to comfort her.

All the time Kiya kept crying about the loss of her baby but seemed even more upset about what the Pharaoh would think.

"I have failed the Pharaoh!" Kiya cried. "I have disappointed my husband!"

After a while Kiya calmed down and her crying changed into a quiet sobbing.

Aset looked at Kiya who was lying in her bed again when she heard a sound at the door. Looking who it was she saw Amenhotep. The angry expression that had been on his face earlier had been replaced by an expression of sadness.

While he walked to Kiya's bed the Pharaoh beckoned Aset to leave the room. Just before she left Aset looked back at Kiya and saw the Pharaoh sitting next to her on the bed while kissing her on her forehead.

Hemienu was walking during the night through his workers' village which had formed on the desert plain.

He had not been able to sleep that night, his thoughts kept wandering to his family in Thebes which he had not seen for a long time and to the events of the past day on his construction site.

After a while he had given up trying to catch any sleep and decided to take a walk through the small village, hoping that it would help to clear his mind.

Most of the buildings, each of which housed a large number of workers, were dark and quiet but Hemienu saw light coming out of a few houses and with it the sound of voices.

Passing these buildings Hemienu heard that most of the people who were still awake were drinking or gambling. He wondered whether these people did not need any sleep but he left them alone; as long as they performed well during their working day he did not care what they did during the night.

Passing one building that was still lit Hemienu heard a different kind of voices. The people inside were arguing excitedly but they sounded as if they were completely sober.

"What stops us from just walking away from here and return to our families and fields?" he heard a voice speaking loudly.

Hemienu knew the buildings around him were occupied by the farmers sent to him by the Pharaoh. Instead of continuing his stroll Hemienu decided to wait a moment and listen how the argument would develop.

"What do you think about the soldiers and the desert surrounding us?" another voice replied to the first speaker.

"They cannot keep us here. We have the right to work on our fields. If the Pharaoh wants us to work as construction workers he should help us support our families and pay us like any other worker," the first speaker spoke again and his remark was followed by agreeing murmurs amongst some of the listeners.

"But we are all subjects of the Pharaoh," a new voice spoke.

"Yes, we are his subjects but does that mean he can just remove us from our houses?" the first voice replied and another voice shouted: "He moves us around like we are cattle and we don't get anything in return!"

Hemienu had heard enough, he opened the door and stepped into the house that was lit by oil lamps.

He looked around in the simple building and saw a group of about thirty men sitting and standing in a scarcely furnished room that only contained a table with a few cups and a couple of sleeping mats.

The assembled group recognized the unexpected visitor immediately and everybody fell silent.

Hemienu looked at the people and spoke: "I believe you were having a discussion? Please continue and allow me to join in."

For a moment nobody said anything but it did not take long before a tall young man started to speak in an aggressive tone: "We don't want to be here. The Pharaoh might need us but our families need us more."

By his voice Hemienu recognized the man as the first speaker he had heard while he was outside.

"I understand your situation," Hemienu answered and went on: "Just like you, I also have a family in Thebes and just like you, I would rather be with them than being here. However, we are all servants of the Pharaoh and have to do as he wishes."

"And what would the Pharaoh do if we would walk out of here?" another farmer asked defiantly.

"The soldiers here will prevent you from doing that," Hemienu replied and added threateningly: "With violence when necessary!"

After his last threatening remark, before anybody could say anything, Hemienu continued in a more accommodating tone: "Listen, as the Pharaoh's chief of construction I am not only here to construct his city but also to take care of his workers. If there is anything I can do to improve your working and living conditions just tell me and I will try to help you."

"Can you also improve the living situation of our families who have to survive without the help of their sons, brothers and fathers?" the first speaker, who seemed to act as the leader of the group, spoke again.

"We are all here against our will, that is a situation we cannot change and will just have to accept," Hemienu spoke in a tired voice and went on, trying to sound optimistic: "But for as long as we are here we will have to make the best of our situation. So I ask you again: is there anything I can do for you to improve your situation?"

For a moment nobody spoke but soon some of the men started to come with suggestions: "Can we have better food?" "If we are to stay here for a long time we need a better living environment!" "We want longer breaks during our working day."

Hemienu had listened to the suggestions of the farmers and promised he would consider them seriously.

He expected their dissatisfaction to be over for the moment but he would have to keep watching these workers to prevent it from returning and maybe causing serious problems in the future.

The farmer who appeared to act as the leader of the group had not given any suggestions for improvement and seemed dismayed that his colleagues were accepting the fact that they would stay at Akhetaten for a long time. He did not seem to want to settle for anything less than returning home.

"I will especially have to watch him," Hemienu thought to himself. "We cannot allow him to start agitating again."

The news of Kiya losing her baby had spread quickly through Malkata Palace. Everybody felt sympathy for the poor Kiya and wanted to visit and comfort her. Penthu, however, had forbidden any visits to her with the exception of Amenhotep and other members of the Royal Family and Aset who was taking care of her.

The following day Kiya was still being attacked by violent stomach cramps for which Aset gave her potions prepared by Penthu to relieve her pain and to help her sleep. She was sure that Kiya's loss was not an accident and suspected Nefertiti of being behind it, even though she had no idea how the Great Royal Wife had done it.

The guard in front of the door of Kiya's chambers carefully opened the door and told Aset that there was somebody who wanted to talk to her. Aset told him to let the person in and a moment later Aset and Sitre were talking in Kiya's living room.

"What happened last night? How did Kiya lose her baby?" Sitre asked.

"We don't know what happened exactly," Aset replied.

"I don't know if it means anything," Sitre whispered hesitatingly while looking around as if afraid that someone could hear her, "but Nefertiti acted strangely last night. She spoke about what happened to Kiya as a great tragedy but she also seemed relieved. This morning Nefertiti even remarked to me with satisfaction that she will be the one who will produce the new Crown Prince and not Kiya."

"Why are you telling me this?" Aset inquired surprised but relieved that Sitre seemed to confirm what she had been suspecting.

"I want you to convince Kiya to stay away from Nefertiti. I don't know whether Nefertiti had anything to do with what has happened to Kiya, we cannot do anything against her anyway, but if Nefertiti will give birth to another girl and Kiya will get pregnant again I would fear for her safety."

After Sitre had left Aset suddenly felt depressed; if she would have been able to convince Kiya to be careful of Nefertiti after Sitre's earlier warnings, could Kiya's terrible loss have been prevented?

Penthu stood in front of the window of his room, staring outside.

He had just visited Kiya whose situation had started to improve again even though she had not yet recovered from the shock of what had happened.

Penthu was pleased to see that the Pharaoh regularly came to visit her and supported his wife during this difficult time.

"What could have happened to Kiya's unborn baby?" Penthu wondered, he did not understand it. He had followed the progress of Kiya's pregnancy closely and everything seemed normal; Kiya as well as her baby had always been healthy.

Looking outside Penthu saw the Nile River with vegetation of different kinds of flowers and plants growing on its banks.

Suddenly Penthu went cold all over his body while he remembered a visit of the Great Royal Wife a few weeks earlier.

Nefertiti had come to his private practice and inquired about a little known plant that grew only to the west of the Two Lands on a small piece of shoreline of the Great Green Sea.

This rare plant had many medicinal characteristics that Penthu had explained to the Queen and he had even helped her to obtain a few specimens.

At that time Penthu had not thought it to be strange for the Pharaoh's wife to inquire about the medicinal workings of this plant, even though he had wondered how Nefertiti knew about it since it was little known. But thinking back to that moment Penthu remembered one specific characteristic of that plant: it was a very powerful abortifacient!

He knew Kiya had regularly been visiting Nefertiti and had had meals with her; could the Great Royal Wife have used this plant to kill the Pharaoh's unborn child?

Penthu shivered at the thought of this possibility and whether he had to act upon this knowledge. But as soon as he started wondering about what he could do he rejected the idea of taking any kind of action. The Great Royal Wife was one of the most powerful people in the Two Lands and Penthu could do nothing against her. Even if he would inform the Pharaoh, he would not believe him since he had no proof. Penthu decided to remain silent.

YEAR 3 OF THE REIGN OF AMENHOTEP THE FOURTH/ AKHENATEN

CHAPTER 15
A STRIKE
AND
AN UNEXPECTED ENCOUNTER

Hemienu walked over the construction site of Akhetaten. Work was progressing well, the city's main temple and the Royal Palace had started to take shape as well as some of the smaller buildings surrounding the temple and palace.

Hatiay, the Aten priest whom Hemienu had earlier met at the Gem Pa Aten, had arrived already in Akhetaten, bringing with him a few lower ranking priests to make sure the details of the construction of the Aten Temple would be done correctly.

Rensi and Thutmose, the relief artist and sculptor, had also arrived already together with their workmen to start their work on the Pharaoh's city.

In spite of all the progress Hemienu was not satisfied. He had always wanted the best for his workers and did his best to give them everything they needed but he could not prevent life on the desert plain from becoming harder for them.

The harvest of the Two Lands had been reasonably good in spite of the fact that many farmers had been put to work on the Pharaoh's construction site but to Hemienu's dismay rations for the workers had been cut and they deteriorated in quality. Apparently, Hemienu had heard, the Pharaoh had sent a lot of grain to Egypt's northern ally Mitanni, even a part of the grain stored for times of famine had been sent abroad.

Hemienu regularly corresponded with the Pharaoh about the progress of Akhetaten and had often begged to increase his workmen's rations but his requests had always been rejected and once, when Hemienu had told that his workers might lay down their tools in protest if they would not get more to eat, he had been told to use force when necessary to keep the construction of Akhetaten going.

Since he had left the site of his future city Amenhotep had returned only once to personally inspect the progress of his project. The Pharaoh had been satisfied but wanted the work to progress faster.

In order to please the Pharaoh and to speed up the construction by making it more efficient Hemienu and his overseers had opened a stone quarry close to the new city. This would save valuable time on transportation but it forced the workers to carry stones or pull them on sledges over a distance of two and a half kilometers.

Hemienu had always been popular amongst his workmen and had felt comfortable to walk amongst them on construction sites but things had started to change as well as the attitude of the workers towards him. The last few months Hemienu had started to feel more and more uncomfortable meeting his men on the work site.

"When are we going to receive better food?" a worker who was constructing a scaffold shouted at Hemienu when he passed him.

Earlier Hemienu would have stopped to encourage him or say a few kind words but this time he did not know anymore what to say, so he walked further without saying a word.

It was getting hot and Hemienu returned to his house where Horemheb was waiting for him, sitting at his desk and looking at the maps of the city.

"You are looking worried, Hemienu," Horemheb remarked.

"Have you seen my workers?" Hemienu asked in reply. "They are starting to become exhausted and malnourished and many accidents are occurring as a consequence of this. There is a lot of dissatisfaction amongst the men."

"I have noticed that," Horemheb replied. "I have ordered my guards to be alert for workers trying to escape or to commit acts of sabotage."

Hemienu smiled wryly and spoke: "Soon I might need your guards to escort me over the construction site."

For a moment nobody said anything but then Horemheb mentioned: "The good news is that the saboteur seems to have given up his attempts to sabotage the project. For a long time nothing has happened."

Hemienu poured two cups of wine, handed one to Horemheb while taking a sip of the other before sitting down opposite the soldier and saying: "That is the only good news, Horemheb. If nothing changes soon I fear that we will have to follow the

Pharaoh's orders and use force to keep the men working."

While Hemienu was speaking there was a knock on the door and without waiting for permission an overseer entered the house and spoke: "My lord, two men have just collapsed during their work. One has already died."

Life in Karnak went on as usual, the Pharaoh was too busy with his new city to interfere with what was still the most powerful temple of the Two Lands.

How long their influential position could be maintained, however, the priests of Amun did not know. As they had expected the new Vizier of Upper Egypt, Nakhtpaaten, was not as sympathetic to them as his predecessor Ramose had been.

Next to the Karnak Temple the enormous Gem Pa Aten had, in spite of the delays during the construction, opened ahead of the schedule the Pharaoh had set for its construction.

The Pharaoh had been pleased by the temple's swift construction and had said this had proven his idea that 'everything could be done as long as one was determined enough' but had then immediately added that the extraordinary effort of the construction workers could not have succeeded without the help of the Aten.

The Gem Pa Aten had opened with an impressive ceremony but the priests of Amun had not been invited.

Ipi had wanted to enter the temple once to have a look inside, just like the Temple of Karnak the forecourt was accessible to everybody, but Maya had said that priests of Amun should not go there.

"I have sent the High Priest of the Aten a letter to congratulate him on the opening of the Aten Temple and invited him to visit Karnak so our relationship could improve," Ipi had heard Maya say but then he had continued: "The reply I received back from Meryra was that he could not visit Karnak because as an Aten priest he could not visit the temple of another God."

Meryra's reply also came without an invitation for the High Priest of Amun to visit the Gem Pa Aten. Apparently the Aten priests did not care much about relations with other temples.

Ipi tried to visit his family as often as possible since his mother's health had started to fail.

They had not heard anything from Huni since he had left and his wife Tahat was worried he might never return. Ipi also feared that his mother's declining health was caused by her worrying about her son.

A few months earlier Ipi had finally accepted the invitation of Nebamun's family and joined Nebamun on a journey to Mendes in the Nile Delta of Lower Egypt.

On the way they had passed the site where the Pharaoh's new city was being built and where his brother was working. Seeing the construction site of Akhetaten Ipi had felt shocked. It was a hot and dusty environment and the work seemed hard. He had also noticed a large presence of soldiers which he viewed as a bad sign. He had decided, however, not to tell anything of what he had seen to his family.

Nebamun's parents had warmly welcomed Ipi and he had enjoyed meeting them again. Ipi had also been happy to see Nebamun's younger sister

Sithathor again and been surprised about how much she had grown up since their last meeting.

Ipi had enjoyed his stay in the green delta which he had never visited before. Nebamun's parents had two villas, one in the city and another in the countryside and they had invited Ipi to visit both.

He had been surprised by the luxury the family lived in. Ipi had seen luxury in the temple but, even though his life there was definitely not uncomfortable, during his stay with Nebamun's family it had been the first time he could experience such luxury himself.

After staying for about a month in Mendes Ipi returned to Thebes.

"How was your journey to the north, Ipi?" his mother asked him when he came to visit his family.

"It was very beautiful there mother," Ipi replied and started to describe the green delta to her.

An area like the Nile Delta was hard to imagine for Ipi's mother since she had never left the surroundings of Thebes. Her world existed only of the Nile Valley with its narrow strip of green fields along the river.

"Did you see the place where Huni is working?" Nefer, Ipi's mother, asked.

"Yes, it looks like a good place to work," Ipi replied, speaking half the truth.

After their conversation, for a short time, Nefer was relieved and felt better but soon she sunk back again into a depression. Ipi thought that the only thing that could really improve her health was the return of Huni.

After spending four days with his family Ipi returned to Karnak. He took the ferry across the

Nile and from the Theban harbour walked back to the temple.

Just before he reached Karnak Ipi passed the newly finished Gem Pa Aten. He saw the large gate with enormous depictions of the Sun Disc with its rays ending in hands giving the Ankh, the symbol of life, to the Pharaoh on both sides of the entrance.

Ipi was intrigued by this temple and in spite of Maya's order not to enter it he decided to have a quick look.

He entered through the open gate and walked into a massive forecourt. It was around midday and most people were having lunch and seeking shelter against the sun causing the temple court to be almost deserted.

Standing in the center Ipi looked around the forecourt of the Gem Pa Aten and saw rows of pillars with depictions of the Aten giving life to the Pharaoh on every side and between these pillars statues of the Pharaoh had been erected.

This court looked different from the court at Karnak but the most unusual, Ipi thought, were the statues: they had a strange elongated face, small eyes and broad hips. Some of the statues even had very pronounced female features. Ipi had never before seen a Pharaoh been depicted in such a way.

He walked past a row of pillars and looked at the depictions on the wall behind them. Apart from the scenes containing the Pharaoh, Ipi, to his surprise, also noticed depictions of daily life taking place under the rays of the Aten and all the scenes had been created in the Pharaoh's new and unusual style.

After his short visit Ipi continued to Karnak where he only told Nebamun of his visit to the Gem Pa Aten.

Kiya's physical health had recovered quickly after the loss of her baby but mentally it took a long time before she was the same person again that Aset had known earlier.

Even though Amenhotep did not blame her and had taken care of her well after she had lost her child Kiya felt extremely guilty towards him.

In the meantime Nefertiti had given birth to her new baby but to her great disappointment it was another daughter. Even Amenhotep, who was hoping for an heir to the throne, was visibly disappointed when he found out he still did not have a Crown Prince.

Nefertiti's new daughter was named Ankhesenpaaten and, like her older sisters, she was a healthy child.

Nefertiti had stopped contacting Kiya after she had lost her baby and Aset had managed to convince Kiya to stay away from the Great Royal Wife even though she had not told her that she suspected Nefertiti of killing her unborn baby, something which Kiya would never have believed.

As the Pharaoh's wife Kiya had attended the opening of the Gem Pa Aten, the first great temple in the Two Lands dedicated to the Aten.

Aset had escorted her on that day and had been impressed by the enormous temple and the large depictions of the Aten and the Royal Family. She had even recognized the name of Kiya under a depiction of a Royal Lady who, in the company of the Pharaoh, received the symbol of life from the Aten.

The ceremony of the opening of the Gem Pa Aten had been as impressive as the temple itself. Aten priests made countless offerings on endless rows of offering tables while the Pharaoh and the High Priest Meryra were reciting hymns to the Aten.

Impressive as the temple and the ceremony were, it made Aset feel uncomfortable. It seemed too different compared to the traditional temples and ceremonies that she was used to.

A few days after the opening of the Gem Pa Aten Merykare, to Aset's great surprise, asked her to marry him. After recovering from the initial shock she gladly accepted his offer.

As her servant Aset had asked Kiya for permission to marry Merykare which she immediately gave while Amenhotep had also given his permission to his scribe to get married.

Since they were not Royalty their wedding had been very simple. They promised to be loyal to each other and a scribe made a record of their promise, making their marriage official.

Having officially been married they made offerings of incense to their ancestors asking for their blessing of the marriage.

There had been no wedding party and since Aset's parents and Merykare's father had already died they held the offering ceremony at the family altar at the house of Merykare's mother in Thebes.

Except for his mother the only attendant of the ceremony was Merykare's brother, who worked as a scribe in the Pharaoh's army. Kiya had also wanted to attend but Amenhotep forbade it, even though he liked his scribe he thought it was not suitable for a Pharaoh or his wife to attend a wedding of mere servants.

After their marriage not much had changed for either Aset or her husband. Merykare had received a larger room in the palace where he and Aset could live but Aset still had to spend most of her days and nights at Kiya's chambers.

It was early in the morning and Hemienu had just got up. After having washed himself and eaten a simple breakfast he left his house to go to the construction site.

Leaving his house the first thing he heard was the laughter of a child. Hemienu looked in the direction where it came from and saw Thutmose, the sculptor, playing with a little boy in front of his house.

Seeing Thutmose playing with his son, Hemienu felt upset at his friend, even though he knew it was unreasonable.

Hemienu had not been able to return to Thebes after the visit during which he had begged and argued with his wife to join him at his working site.

Contrary to his wife Thutmose's wife had followed her husband with her son to Akhetaten and Rensi had brought his family as well.

Hemienu regularly corresponded with his wife and every time he asked her to come to Akhetaten but she kept refusing, saying that it was not suitable for the children and that she wanted to stay close to her family's tombs.

Hemienu walked onto the construction site and a short time later found himself between the unfinished walls of what was going to be the Aten Temple, joined only by a few guards, overseers and priests.

"What is happening? Where are the workers?" Hatiay, the Aten priest, asked with a look of wonder on his face.

"They should be coming any moment," Hemienu replied reassuringly, already fearing that he was wrong.

He went to the unfinished palace but found it also deserted except for the presence of Horemheb with a few more guards and overseers.

"I think we have a problem!" Horemheb simply spoke when he noticed Hemienu.

"We will not return to work unless our food and our living and working conditions improve!" a worker, who appeared to be speaking for all the workmen, said when Hemienu and Horemheb arrived at the workmen's village to find out why nobody came to work.

"Can we not discuss your complaints while the other men return to work?" Hemienu asked.

"We have already discussed them with you but things have only got worse since then!" another worker snapped at him.

Hemienu immediately recognized him as the farmer who had acted as the leader of the group of farmers with whom he had spoken during that night, already so long ago.

"He is right," the first worker spoke again and went on: "We are not going to discuss anything! You have our demands and we won't work until you meet them!"

As soon as he stopped speaking the worker turned and disappeared into one of the workmen's buildings as to prove his point that he was not going to discuss anything.

Hemienu thought for a moment about what to do and quickly conferred with Horemheb.

After a short conversation with the soldier he shouted, so everybody could hear him: "You have until midday to return to work! Everybody who does not start working at midday will be sent to work by force!"

"They won't come to work," Horemheb spoke to Hemienu after they returned to Hemienu's house.

"Why do you think so?" the architect asked in a tired voice.

"They are too determined," Horemheb replied and continued: "This had to happen sometime, Hemienu. Don't tell me you did not see this coming. The workers are malnourished! Nobody can keep working on an empty stomach for a long time!"

Hemienu did not answer but knew the officer of the Royal Guard was right. It had been more than a month since the first workers had collapsed during their work due to malnourishment and many more had followed since then.

"I cannot sit here waiting and doing nothing," Hemienu finally spoke. "I go to the village to see what the workers are doing."

"I will send some guards with you for your safety," Horemheb replied.

"No, that will give the wrong impression," Hemienu answered, declining Horemheb's offer, and then added: "I want my workers to see me as one of them, not as a slave driver who only dares to come with soldiers to protect him."

Hemienu walked through the narrow streets of the workmen's village. Most workers were inside and the few who were outside quickly entered their buildings as soon as they saw him coming.

Hemienu felt hurt that the relationship with his workers, that had always been very good, could have turned so bad.

Passing the workmen's buildings Hemienu could hear parts of lively discussions that were going on inside.

"At least some of the workers seem to want to return to work," Hemienu thought to himself.

Inside one building he heard somebody speak particularly fierce.

"Don't give up now! There are many of us! Even if the soldiers decide to use violence against us we will still have a large majority! We should prepare to fight back when necessary!" Hemienu heard the man speak in a loud, aggressive voice.

"That sounds serious," Hemienu thought and decided to return to Horemheb to inform him about what he had heard, so that he could prepare for possible resistance. But then suddenly Hemienu stopped; the voice of the speaker had sounded familiar to him.

He immediately turned around and entered the building where he had heard the man speak.

"Nebtawi!" Hemienu exclaimed when he recognized his former superior.

He looked older, had lost weight, was badly shaven and wore only a simple worker's loincloth but it was clearly the former chief of construction.

"It was about time that you would recognize me," Nebtawi spoke with a triumphant smile and then added tauntingly: "I have been here almost from the beginning of the construction!"

"What are you doing here?" Hemienu asked in surprise.

"Can the master not visit the construction project of his student?" Nebtawi spoke, still smiling; emphasizing that Hemienu was actually his subordinate.

"Why don't you want the workmen to continue their work? Don't you want the Pharaoh to finish his city?" Hemienu went on asking.

Nebtawi's smile suddenly disappeared from his face and was replaced by an expression of burning hatred.

"I could not care less whether the Pharaoh finishes his city or not but I definitely don't want you to be the person who finishes it!" Nebtawi spoke angrily. "This project should have been mine, not yours! It was not my fault that that wall at the Gem Pa Aten collapsed!"

Suddenly something started to become clear to Hemienu.

"Are you the person who has been sabotaging the construction of Akhetaten?" he asked.

"Yes," Nebtawi admitted without hesitation, started to smile again, and explained: "There are workers from all over the country here and I could easily hide amongst them. I was determined to sabotage your work in any way I could as a revenge for you stealing my position. The last months, however, I started to realize that you were damaging the construction of Akhetaten yourself more than I could ever do by your treatment of your workmen and I capitalized on that by setting them against you."

"Did the workers never recognize you as the former chief of construction?" Hemienu asked, wondering how Nebtawi could have remained hidden for so long.

"As I have said: there are workers here from all over the country. I spend most of my time amongst workers from places faraway from Thebes, where there was little chance of anybody knowing me. Until I revealed myself as the former chief of construction yesterday evening when I managed to convince the leaders of the workmen to call for a strike, I have been recognized only once," Nebtawi explained.

"And how did you manage to keep the person who recognized you from informing me?" Hemienu asked, already suspecting what the answer would be.

"I had to kill him," Nebtawi replied bluntly. "After you had damaged one of the boundary steles?" Hemienu asked.

"Yes," Nebtawi spoke again, in a tone as if he were talking about some daily occurrence. "It was during the night and I had just damaged one of the steles that were cut into the rock face. Walking back to the village I coincidentally stumbled across a workman who was walking on the plain. He started talking to me and, because it was a clear night and the moon was almost full, after a while he recognized me. Apparently he came from Thebes and had been working with us on the Gem Pa Aten. I was forced to kill him to keep you from knowing I was here so I smashed his skull with a rock. I tried to throw his body in the river for the crocodiles to eat and to conceal what had happened but before I reached the river a few guards came near me so I dropped the body and disappeared. Fortunately the guards had not noticed me but they soon found the body."

"You are correct that the workman came from Thebes and had been working with us," Hemienu spoke, being both surprised and upset by the lack of any trace of feeling or regret in Nebtawi's voice, and added: "His name was Sabni and he worked under you at the Gem Pa Aten as a stonemason."

"Could be, I did not remember him," Nebtawi shrugged and went on: "After I had killed the stonemason I left the construction site for a while to wait for things to calm down. Only after a few months, when I was sure everybody would have forgotten about the dead worker, I returned."

"Do you know what the Pharaoh will do to you after he hears that you have sabotaged his project, killed one of his workers and set up other workers against their architect and overseers?" Hemienu asked.

Nebtawi's expression did not change and he did not show any sign of fear when he replied: "He will have me killed in some horrible way, I am sure about that. But I feel as if I died already that moment when the Pharaoh fired me as chief of construction. I have never returned to my family since that night! Imagine me having to tell my wife and children that the Pharaoh had called me incompetent! I could not bear the shame! I have been back to Thebes a few times and watched my family to see if they are well but I could never bring myself to meet them, as much as I wanted to."

Nebtawi stopped speaking for a moment and Hemienu for the first time noticed a sign of sadness in his eyes while he had been speaking about his family.

After a short pause Nebtawi's gaze hardened, however, and he continued speaking: "If the Pharaoh wants to kill me I am ready. At least I will have one consolation when I die."

"What is that consolation?" Hemienu asked automatically.

"That you will have died before me!" Nebtawi replied while he produced a dagger from underneath his loincloth, jumped on Hemienu and stabbed him.

The workers who had been standing in silence, listening to the conversation between their former and current architect did not know what to do; some of them wanted to help the screaming and wounded Hemienu, who was desperately trying to fight off Nebtawi, while others appeared to have become so upset with him that they were reluctant to do anything to help.

Just as a few workers finally decided to intervene the door flung open and four soldiers burst inside with drawn swords. They quickly subdued Nebtawi and took him and Hemienu, who was bleeding from a wound in his shoulder, with them.

"You are lucky I ignored your wish and had you followed by four of my guards," Horemheb spoke to the wounded Hemienu after he had been taken back to his house.

"I guess I am lucky," replied Hemienu, whose shoulder wound turned out not to be dangerous, and he added with a forced smile: "I would have been even luckier if your soldiers had come earlier."

"I am glad you had the opportunity to join us, Penthu," Aye, the Pharaoh's most trusted advisor and his father-in-law spoke to the Royal Physician when he entered Aye's chambers at Malkata palace during the morning.

Aye had his own villa in Thebes where his wife Tey often lived and another in Khent-Min where his family descended from. Aye, however, preferred to stay in the palace as much as possible and always tried to stay close to the Pharaoh.

Courtiers and officials did not appreciate this behaviour and accused him of trying to gain influence over the Pharaoh.

Apart from Nefertiti, Aye and his wife Tey had another daughter named Mutbenret, who was married to a Theban noble man and with another wife Aye also had a son, Nakhtmin, who was making a career in the army.

Penthu had always kept the secret about what he suspected Aye's daughter, the Great Royal Wife, had done to Kiya to himself and every time he met her he had treated her as respectfully as he always had done.

The Pharaoh respected Penthu a lot and asked his advice about matters of state so often that he had started to attend meetings where under normal circumstances a Royal Physician would not be invited.

"Your invitation came unexpected but it is an honour," Penthu replied to Aye and then politely bowed for Nakhtpaaten, the Vizier of Upper Egypt, who was sitting in a chair next to Aye.

"The Pharaoh values your advice, so why shouldn't we," Nakhtpaaten spoke to Penthu, explaining the reason for his invitation to the private meeting.

"I am at your service," Penthu answered, while he sat down in a comfortable chair, gestured to by Aye.

"Are you aware of the fact that the Two Lands are at the dawn of a new era?" the Pharaoh's advisor spoke slowly, as if to emphasize the importance of what he said.

"I am aware that His Majesty is going to make many changes in the country," Penthu replied.

"I think that 'many changes' is not the right description of His Majesty's plans," Nakhtpaaten remarked with a small laugh.

"The first of His Majesty's 'changes'," Aye began speaking, emphasizing the last word, "is moving the capital from Thebes to Akhetaten as you already know, Penthu."

"Yes, I know about that but it will take one or two years more before Akhetaten is ready to properly function as the capital and Royal Residence," Penthu replied.

"That is correct but by that time we must be ready so we will have to start preparing now," Aye explained and then asked: "What is the most important part of a city? What does every city needs to function, Penthu?"

Penthu thought for a moment and finally replied: "A source of fresh drinking water? Accessibility and farming fields?"

"These are indeed vital for a city, Penthu, but there is something that is maybe even more important," Aye spoke and before Penthu could ask what he meant he went on: "Every city needs people, inhabitants!"

"Of course a city needs inhabitants. They will move to Akhetaten when His Majesty moves his court," Penthu replied, not understanding what Aye was talking about.

"That is exactly what I am saying," Nakhtpaaten intervened. "The people will follow their Pharaoh to Akhetaten like a flock of sheep follows its shepherd!"

"Do you really believe that?" Aye asked, looking at the Vizier with a condescending look on his face.

The room fell silent for a moment until Aye continued to speak: "Of course the courtiers and the nobles, who depend on His Majesty will follow. But do both of you really think that the common people will leave their homes, farms, family tombs, loved ones and the town or city where they have lived for their whole lives to follow His Majesty to a new city in the middle of nowhere?"

"It is not just a city in the middle of nowhere!" Nakhtpaaten argued. "It is the city of the Aten, a piece of sacred land untouched by other Gods. People should be honoured for the privilege of living there!"

"You are right, I completely agree with you," Aye spoke, trying to calm down the Vizier, but then went on in his businesslike manner: "But do the people know that? Do they understand that they are privileged?"

"If the people don't want to come to Akhetaten then we should ask the Pharaoh for advice about what to do," Nakhtpaaten spoke.

"That is exactly why I asked both of you to come here," Aye replied. "His Majesty has many matters to care about. He has to take care of his people, he is busy with building temples for the Aten and the Hittites are causing more and more problems. These are only a few examples of what His Majesty has to deal with. He should not have to think about how to convince the people of the Two Lands to come and live in his city. Why don't we take this responsibility from His Majesty's shoulders so he can concentrate on the more important business of ruling the country?"

Penthu had been listening to Aye and was wondering about what he wanted. Was Aye really only trying to help the Pharaoh? Aye was the father of Nefertiti and this made Penthu feel some distrust towards him.

He watched Aye, sitting in his gilded chair opposite him, speaking and when he finished remarked: "If we want to help His Majesty, how would you suggest we should do that?"

Aye looked at Penthu and replied: "We must begin with offering positive incentives for people to move to Akhetaten and if that doesn't work then maybe we should use..."

Aye stopped speaking a moment as if he was trying to find the right words, then leaned forwards so that his face came closer to Penthu's and the vizier's and finally said slowly and clearly: "Maybe we should use more forceful methods to convince the people to move."

Penthu felt uncomfortable by Aye's words and spoke: "Let's forget about those forceful methods for a moment. What kind of incentives do you suggest to attract the people to Akhetaten?"

Aye leaned back in his chair again and replied in a casual tone: "I have a few ideas of course but I hoped you would be able to help me by giving some useful suggestions."

"We have to tell the people that Akhetaten is the holy city of the Aten. That will make them want to come to the new city," Nakhtpaaten spoke, apparently not convinced by Aye's earlier words.

"First we have to decide who we want to live in Akhetaten," Penthu spoke. "We must have people of each trade needed for the city to function."

"I agree, but how do we get those people?" Aye replied.

"We must only accept qualified people who are good at their trade and are willing to embrace the Aten as their God," Nakhtpaaten stated and added: "We can ask mayors of different cities across the Two Lands to appoint people of each layer of the population who they think are suitable to live in the Aten's city."

"That is a good idea but what if these people refuse?" Aye countered.

"We can attract them with the promise of a new house. The newly built houses in Akhetaten will most likely be better than the houses most people are living in now," Penthu suggested.

"The layout of Akhetaten is completely planned from the start, it will offer an ideal living environment," Nakhtpaaten added.

"And what if, after hearing all the benefits of living in Akhetaten, the people still refuse to move?" Aye asked again, giving Penthu the impression that he wanted somebody else to come with a suggestion that he was already thinking about.

"Then our army will have to help them to move," Nakhtpaaten replied with a face so serious that both Aye and Penthu had no doubt that he meant what he said.

Thutmose and Rensi, whose workers had joined the others and had laid down their tools in protest, had come to visit Hemienu as soon as they heard about the attack on the chief of construction.

They had been shocked to find out the attacker was their former superior, Nebtawi.

Hemienu was pleased with their company but when it was almost midday, the moment when his ultimatum to the workmen would end, he sent them away so he could confer alone with the officer of the guards.

"What do we do if nobody decides to return to work?" Horemheb asked Hemienu, whose wound had been treated and bandaged by a physician but was still hurting, causing his face to twitch with pain frequently.

"I guess we will have to follow the Pharaoh's orders and have your soldiers make the workmen go to work," Hemienu replied with resignation.

Horemheb smiled as if he was pleased with the prospect of his soldiers having some action, even if it was against unarmed workers. "My soldiers are ready!" he spoke.

"But what shall we do with Nebtawi?" Hemienu asked.

"Do you have to ask that after everything he has done?" Horemheb asked in return.

"No, I don't have to ask that," Hemienu spoke downcast and after a moment of silence added: "But it is something I am not looking forward to having to take responsibility for. I had never expected something like this to be part of my work when I became an architect."

"This does not have to be your responsibility, Hemienu," Horemheb spoke. "Let me take care of that dirty business."

Suddenly Horemheb's face brightened and he exclaimed: "This gives me an idea! An idea that could prevent my soldiers from having to use violence against your workers."

It was after midday. Hemienu's ultimatum had already passed when a group of workers, which included the workers who had taken a leading position in the rebellion against Hemienu, assembled on the bank of the Nile River outside the boundaries of Akhetaten.

The rest of the workmen had been forced to stay inside their houses until their colleagues would return.

Hemienu had already been waiting on the riverbank together with Horemheb and a few of his guards when the workers arrived.

The officer of the Royal Guard had offered him the opportunity to remain in his house but, since he was in charge of everything that happened on the construction site, Hemienu thought he had to attend what was going to happen, even though he thought the prospect was terrible.

The workmen were talking amongst each other, wondering why they had been brought there. Some of them showed signs of fear; were they going to be punished for their disobedience?

Shortly afterwards two soldiers appeared with Nebtawi between them, his hands bound behind his back. They were followed by a young officer of the Royal Guard.

The soldiers positioned themselves with Nebtawi in front of the workers and pushed the former chief of construction on his knees.

Horemheb wanted to take a step towards the workmen to address them but Hemienu put his hand on his shoulder and spoke: "As the person in charge this is my responsibility."

He took position next to Nebtawi and started to address the assembled workmen, who looked with pale faces at the kneeling figure: "I know most of you don't want to be here and are not happy about the current working conditions. But, just like me, you unfortunately don't have any choice. The Pharaoh has ordered us to work for him and it is our duty to obey."

Hemienu had been speaking in an accommodating tone but then continued more threateningly: "Some of you might want to disobey the Pharaoh and escape or, like this man here, even want to sabotage his project, murder a fellow worker and attempt to murder me!"

Having said these last words Hemienu felt a sharp pain going through his shoulder where Nebtawi had stabbed him. His face twitched but he kept on speaking: "For those who harbour such ideas remember that that kind of behaviour will be met with the most severe punishment. As you are about to witness, even a former chief of construction will not escape his punishment."

Hemienu swallowed heavily a few times and tears started to roll down his cheeks; he could not carry on speaking anymore. He turned to Nebtawi, who still sat on his knees and stared towards the ground.

"I am sorry but you have left me no choice," Hemienu whispered.

Nebtawi looked up at his former subordinate and spat in front of his feet before staring at the ground again without saying any words.

Hemienu walked back to Horemheb and gave him a nod upon which Horemheb now came forward and spoke to the young officer, who was standing behind the kneeling Nebtawi: "Are you ready?"

"I am ready," the officer replied.

"Then do your duty," Horemheb ordered his subordinate.

The officer grabbed a battle axe in one hand and with the other he took Nebtawi by his hair. Slowly he raised the axe and a moment later let it violently descend on Nebtawi's head, splitting his skull open.

The sight of the execution reminded Hemienu of the scenes of the Pharaoh smiting his enemies which were often depicted on temple walls.

The sound of the axe descending on Nebtawi's head made Hemienu's stomach turn and when he saw his former superior's body fall down in the dust with blood spilling out of his broken skull he had to try hard to prevent himself from throwing up.

Seeing Hemienu was not able to speak Horemheb continued speaking on his behalf: "Let this be a warning to everybody who thinks about disobeying the Pharaoh! Go back to the village, tell your colleagues what you have just witnessed and start your work in one hour!"

Without any protests the horrified workers started to return to the workmen's village.

Horemheb ordered his soldiers to throw Nebtawi's body in the river to be eaten by the crocodiles, destroying the former architect's body and preventing him from having an afterlife.

Having made sure that Nebtawi's body had been disposed of Horemheb walked over to Hemienu, who was sitting down on a rock, holding his wounded shoulder with his pale face twisted by pain.

"Don't worry, Hemienu," the Royal Guard spoke reassuringly. "The workmen will return to work today without any further problems."

Horemheb had been right, an hour later the workers showed up on the construction site with defeated expressions on their faces.

CHAPTER 16
A DISTURBING AUDIENCE FOR THE AMUN PRIESTS
AND
AN ACCIDENT AT THE STONE QUARRY

It was six months after Penthu had attended the meeting with Aye and Nakhtpaaten.

The Pharaoh started to trust him even more and sometimes let Penthu replace him at meetings and audiences.

One morning Amenhotep had called Penthu and told him: "The High Priest of Amun has asked for an audience with me. I have no time to meet him so I have asked Nakhtpaaten to receive him instead. But Penthu, I would like you to attend this audience with the High Priest since my vizier is not as experienced and wise as you are."

The last sentence had been spoken with a smile but Penthu knew the Pharaoh meant it; Nakhtpaaten had been made vizier because of his family relation to the Pharaoh and because of his loyalty to him and the Aten, not because of his capabilities.

In spite of it being an honour to attend the audience together with the vizier on the Pharaoh's behalf Penthu was nervous about dealing with Maya. He also expected the reason for the Pharaoh not to meet the High Priest of Amun himself was not that he had no time but that he did not want to meet him.

Nakhtpaaten, the Vizier of Upper Egypt, sat in the audience hall on a large chair decorated with depictions of the life-giving Aten.

The vizier's chair had been placed at the base of the platform on which the Pharaoh's throne stood which would remain unoccupied during the audience.

At Nakhtpaaten's right stood Penthu, who would support the vizier during his meeting and on his left sat his scribe, who would write down the details of the meeting.

After Nakhtpaaten gave a signal Maya was let into the audience hall accompanied by the Second Prophet of Amun, Wenamun.

Ignoring Penthu, Maya and Wenamun bowed for the vizier and the High Priest started to speak: "Greetings my lord. May the Gods bless you with health and prosperity."

"What can I do for you?" Nakhtpaaten spoke in an accommodating tone.

"I apologize, my lord, but I have requested an audience with His Majesty," Maya remarked politely and then added indignantly: "Since when does the Pharaoh not have any time for the High Priest of Amun?"

Nakhtpaaten smiled and replied in the same accommodating way as earlier: "Unfortunately His Majesty has more urgent matters to take care of and he has sent me and one of his closest advisors, Penthu, to meet you."

While speaking the last words the vizier gestured to his right where Penthu was standing and then continued: "I am sure we will be able to help you as well as His Majesty would."

Maya looked upset but Wenamun's face remained emotionless.

Penthu knew it was uncommon for a Pharaoh not to receive a high priest, especially the High Priest of Amun, personally. To Maya and Wenamun this must be another sign of the declining importance of the God Amun and His priesthood.

"What can I do for you, Maya?" Nakhtpaaten asked again.

Maya sighed and, realizing that getting upset would not help him, spoke: "My lord, we have noticed that the construction of His Majesty's city is progressing swiftly. Since we have never received any word from His Majesty about his future intentions we come here to ask about his plans and what they will mean for our temple."

Nakhtpaaten remained silent for a moment and also Penthu had no idea what to say.

The Pharaoh had often spoken about the future but it was never clear what he was going to do and when he would do it. Penthu feared he might close all temples not belonging to the Aten but he was not certain the Pharaoh would dare to take such a drastic measure.

"His Majesty will move the court to Akhetaten which will become the new capital of the Two Lands," Nakhtpaaten finally spoke.

"And what will this mean for our temple?" the High Priest of Amun asked nervously and went on: "Will the Pharaoh respect the rightful position of our Lord Amun?"

"Amun will have His rightful position under the Aten," the vizier replied and while Penthu watched Maya and Wenamun turning pale he continued in the same calm tone in which he had been speaking all the time: "The Aten shall be elevated to His rightful position of the supreme God."

Penthu was impressed by the way Nakhtpaaten conducted the audience. He knew him to be as fanatical in his devotion to the Aten as the Pharaoh and just like him he had a strong dislike for Amun and His priesthood. However, to Penthu's surprise, he remained friendly and respectful towards the two Amun priests.

"But Amun has been the King of the Gods for ages, it is a sacred tradition that can't be changed from one day to another!" Wenamun exclaimed dismayed. "It will upset the balance of Ma'at!"

"Times are changing," the vizier replied patiently. "Amun's rule as King of the Gods is coming to an end. Meryra, the High Priest of the Aten, has declared that it is the powerful and wealthy Temple of Amun which is upsetting the balance of Ma'at and that this balance shall be restored under the rule of the Aten."

Still being a worshipper of Amun, these words hurt Penthu but he had to admit to himself that the Temple of Amun had accumulated enormous power and wealth. Maybe Meryra had been right that this had negatively influenced the balance of Ma'at.

"What do you think of this, Penthu? Will you let this happen to the Temple of Amun without any protest?" Maya asked.

Contrary to their previous meetings, this time Maya did not sound angry or insulting, this time the tone of his voice sounded desperate, as if he was begging Penthu to do whatever he could to save the temple.

Penthu did not know how to answer but, remembering his promise to the Pharaoh to stay loyal to him, with pain in his heart he finally spoke: "The vizier has spoken correctly. Amun will receive the position He deserves but Aten will be the new supreme God."

"Then there is no reason for us to take any more of your time, my lord," Maya spoke in a trembling voice to Nakhtpaaten.

The priest was clearly trying to suppress different kinds of emotions that were welling up inside him.

Maya and Wenamun bowed for the vizier, turned and walked out of the audience hall.

Penthu felt sympathy for them but decided not to go after them since he could not give them any kind of reassurance.

There had been no more protests from the workers after the execution of Nebtawi and Hemienu's shoulder had healed well but apart from that there was little Hemienu was satisfied about.

The working conditions had declined even further since then and the rates of accidents and deaths due to exhaustion, disease and malnutrition amongst the workers had risen significantly.

The physicians on the construction site could not cope anymore with the number of wounded and as a result many were left unattended to for a long time.

The wounded who could not recover were sent home but the others were sent back to work as soon as possible.

The workers who had died were buried in a mass grave outside Akhetaten's boundaries. Hemienu had suggested a gravesite within the city's boundaries but Hatiay, the Aten priest, had disagreed, saying: "While appreciating the workers' sacrifice for the Aten, we cannot bury them in the Aten's sacred land. Most of them are not even worshippers of the Sun Disc."

While the work still progressed on schedule it went slower than before due to the exhaustion of the workers. Sometimes Horemheb's guards even had to threaten to use force to make them work faster.

During the nights Hemienu could not sleep anymore and often he wondered why the Gods had punished him by putting him in this situation. His workers hated him and his family was also upset with him for leaving them for such a long time.

Never in his life had he felt so alone. Sometimes Hemienu remembered his words to his wife about the construction site during the last time they met in Thebes, when he was trying to convince her to follow him: "As the chief architect I can make the construction site into what I want." Had he been right when speaking those words? If so it meant he was responsible for all the suffering of his workmen.

Every time these thoughts came up in his mind Hemienu tried to shake them off and reasoned that he was not to blame about anything since he could only work with the means that the Pharaoh had given him. He could not feed his workers when he had no food to give and since the Pharaoh demanded the work to remain on schedule he had to force them to work harder.

Hemienu had, however, one consolation: by now he was glad his family had not followed him to Akhetaten. He did not want his wife and children to see what was happening there.

Hemienu walked over the boulevard which ran from north to south over the entire length of Akhetaten, cutting the city in two.

He passed the main temple of the city that was called Per Aten em Akhetaten, the Mansion of the

Aten in Akhetaten, and contained several open courts lined with pillars and filled with altars.

Rensi's workers had already started chiseling and painting the reliefs on the outside of the temple even though on the inside the construction had not yet been completed.

Together with Hemienu's workers Thutmose's sculptors were also working inside the temple, finishing the statues of the Pharaoh that were going to be erected inside the Per Aten.

While Hemienu walked further down the boulevard he was followed by two of Horemheb's guards.

Horemheb had insisted on him being escorted everywhere he went since the attack by Nebtawi.

Hemienu reached the Pharaoh's main palace that was going to be known as the Great Palace.

Amenhotep had ordered another palace to be constructed in the northern part of the city but Hemienu was not going to start its construction until the Great Palace was finished.

Standing on the main street Hemienu looked up and saw a covered bridge which was still under construction. This bridge connected the Pharaoh's working palace with his residential palace. It was a unique structure in Egypt and Hemienu felt proud on having constructed it.

Further down Akhetaten's main road many other smaller buildings were being erected, which were going to be offices, workshops and villas, with some of them already nearly finished. The houses for the common people were being built further from the city centre.

Hemienu turned into a narrow side road, walked further between the unfinished houses and came at the edge of the construction site.

In the distance he saw sledges laden with blocks that were being drawn towards the town by exhausted and malnourished workers.

They were coming from the stone quarry close to the construction site and since the transportation of the blocks only required strength and not much expertise it was mainly done by the farmers that had been sent to Hemienu by the Pharaoh.

He watched the workers pull the heavy sledge through the desert sand and then decided to visit the stone quarry where the blocks came from.

It was a walk of about two and a half kilometers that the workers had to make several times a day with their heavy load.

After arriving at the large quarry Hemienu watched the stone blocks being cut out of the rock deep inside the mountain by workers with bronze chisels and heavy wooden mallets. The blocks were then taken over by other workers, who chiseled them into the right shape and size so they could be used easily in the construction of Akhetaten. Finally other workers had the heavy task of carrying the blocks of stone out of the quarry over an uneven footpath. At the end of the path a sledge would be waiting to transport the blocks to Akhetaten.

Working in the quarry was extremely hard and Hemienu knew that a significant part of the workmen who had died had worked there.

The workers noticed the chief of construction watching them but they were too exhausted to care, nobody said anything and all of them continued their task as if he were not there.

The overseer of the quarry came to speak with Hemienu and assured him that the work was progressing well.

After a while Hemienu had seen enough and just as he had decided to return to Akhetaten he witnessed a worker carrying a large stone block on his back collapsing on the footpath leading out of the quarry.

He remained lying face down on the uneven surface of the path with the weight of the heavy block of stone on his back. A few other workers dropped their blocks to help him but the overseer looked worriedly at Hemienu and shouted: "Leave him! Work must continue at all costs!"

"Let them help the poor man," Hemienu reacted immediately, feeling shocked that even the overseer appeared to be afraid of him, and added: "And get a physician to treat him!"

Hemienu went down the path to where the worker was lying. His colleagues had already removed the heavy block from his back and an on-site physician came running towards him.

The physician quickly started examining the worker and almost immediately shook his head. He got up and spoke to Hemienu: "The heavy stone has crushed many bones in this man's body and has probably damaged vital organs. This man will die soon."

Hemienu sighed, feeling frustrated he could not do anything to lessen the hardships of his workmen.

"Somebody bring him some water!" he shouted and kneeled down next to the wounded man.

"Where are you from?" Hemienu asked in a caring voice.

The man, who could not be turned on his back because of his fractured bones, slowly looked up at him and Hemienu felt his body turn cold; the wounded worker was the same man with whom he had argued earlier, the man who had acted as the leader of the group of disgruntled farmers.

His face, however, did not show any anger but only sadness.

"I come from Thebes," the man replied to Hemienu's question while he started to cough up blood.

"So do I," Hemienu replied with a forced smile, trying to comfort the man, for whom he had not been able to do anything earlier, as much as possible during his last moments.

"All I wanted was to stay home to take care of my wife and parents," the man went on speaking, his voice becoming harder to understand while he was getting weaker.

Another worker came with a cup of water but after trying to drink the wounded man coughed and spat the water out again.

"I understand you. I am so sorry for all of this," Hemienu replied, taking the dying man's hand and for a moment imagined how he would feel when he knew his own wife and children would be waiting for him to return home without him ever arriving and without them ever knowing what had happened to him.

Hemienu was relieved that the man squeezed his hand, something he understood as a sign that the worker forgave him.

"What is your name?" Hemienu asked while tears started to roll from his eyes.

"Huni," the man replied, speaking very weakly by that time and added in such a soft voice that Hemienu was not sure whether he had understood his words correctly: "At least I will soon be with my son Djehuty again."

After speaking these last words Huni's eyes closed and he did not react anymore to anything Hemienu said.

"I am sorry, he has started his journey to the Kingdom of Osiris," the physician spoke quietly.

Suddenly all the emotions that Hemienu had been trying to suppress for a long time welled up inside of him and, still sitting next to the dead Huni, he started to cry in front of his amazed workers.

Kiya was starting to get worried, she still hadn't got pregnant again after she had lost her first baby.

Penthu had examined her and could find nothing unusual but it did not make her feel less worried.

"What if I cannot get pregnant again?" she frequently asked Aset. "Will Amenhotep still love me if I cannot give him any children or will he send me away?"

"Don't worry, Kiya," Aset usually replied. "I am sure you will get pregnant again and that you will give Amenhotep the Crown Prince he is waiting for."

Aset did her best to sound positive but she was not sure whether it was justified. What if whatever had killed Kiya's baby had also damaged her womb, preventing her from getting pregnant again?

At the same time Aset was also worried about her own chances of raising a child. The Pharaoh kept Merykare permanently occupied and she spent most of her time taking care of Kiya.

"You have probably more chance of getting pregnant than I have since Merykare and I can hardly ever meet," Aset once remarked to her friend, making it sound like a joke but actually meaning it seriously.

"What do you mean?" Kiya replied sharply, understanding what Aset referred to. "Are you complaining that I keep you away from your husband? Are you not happy when you are working for me?"

"I am your friend Kiya. I am helping you and not working for you," Aset retorted and added more calmly: "I am happy to be with you but I wish you and the Pharaoh would also realize that Merykare and I are married and like to spend time together sometimes. Amenhotep keeps my husband almost permanently occupied!"

"That is because Amenhotep has many businesses to take care of," Kiya spoke again, sounding annoyed about Aset's complaint. "You know that he is preparing for the moment he is going to move the capital. These days, even when he spends time with me, he is somewhere else with his thoughts."

While Kiya spoke the last words she had a sad look in her eyes but then she suddenly spoke in an optimistic tone: "Maybe everything will change once we are in Akhetaten!"

Everybody in Karnak knew about the visit of Maya and Wenamun to Malkata Palace and was eagerly awaiting their return, hoping to receive more clarity about the temple's future. Many priests and priestesses who had the opportunity remained near Karnak's dock to meet the two highest ranking priests of the temple as soon as they arrived back.

Amongst these priests were Ipi and Nebamun, who were just as worried as everybody else about the temple but also about their own future.

Maya's wife Hetepheres and son Amenemhet had reconciled completely with Maya and had even moved into the temple to live with their husband and father. Together with the other occupants of the Temple of Amun they also were awaiting the news Maya and Wenamun would bring.

Finally the boat transporting the High Priest and the Second Prophet of Amun appeared in the distance and a few moments later moored at the temple's dock.

Ipi saw the expression on the faces of Maya and Wenamun when they disembarked and remarked to Nebamun, who stood next to him: "It is going to be bad news."

Maya did not say anything to the assembled people and, with a worried expression on his face, even walked past his own wife and son without noticing them and hurried into the direction of the Holy of Holies.

"He is probably going to beg Amun for help," Ipi thought.

Wenamun apparently thought the waiting priests and priestesses deserved some kind of an answer and spoke loudly, so everybody surrounding him could hear his words: "The best news I can give you is that we have not heard that the Pharaoh intends to close the temple!"

He did not want to say anything more and took his wife Tahat by her hand and walked to their apartment.

"You were right, Ipi," Nebamun spoke. "They must have received bad news in the palace."

YEAR 5 OF THE REIGN OF AMENHOTEP THE FOURTH/ AKHENATEN

CHAPTER 17
A NEW BEGINNING

The moment that many Egyptians had either feared or looked forward to had come: Pharaoh Amenhotep had moved his capital from Thebes to Akhetaten.

Apart from his officials and courtiers he was followed by many noblemen who hoped to further their careers by joining the Pharaoh in his new city and by common people who saw new opportunities in Akhetaten.

But except for these people who went voluntarily there had been many others who had been forced to move so the city would have representatives of every layer of the population and every trade that it needed to survive.

Aset stood in front of a window of the Pharaoh's new residential palace, next to the entrance of the covered bridge that connected it to the Pharaoh's working palace.

She looked outside onto the street where the inhabitants of Akhetaten were assembled to listen to the Pharaoh, who was standing with his mother,

Nefertiti, Kiya and his closest advisors on the bridge in front of a window which was called the Window of Appearance to give a proclamation.

In the front of the crowd stood the nobility while the commoners stood more to the back.

Aset looked at the assembled people and amongst them recognized Panehsy. She felt shivers going through her spine when she remembered the last evening at his villa in the Theban countryside.

Aset quickly turned her gaze away from him and looked at the gleaming white buildings with depictions in the brightest colours she had ever seen. Akhetaten appeared surreal to her, she had never seen a city that was completely new and, even though the city was not yet finished, she could not believe this was the same area as the barren desert plain which she had visited the first time on the way to Memphis.

The previous day Amenhotep and the High Priest of the Aten, Meryra, had organized a large ceremony to dedicate the Per Aten, the Great Aten Temple.

The Royal Family, all the state officials and the Aten Priests who were going to serve in the temple had attended the ceremony.

Aset had not been allowed further into the temple than the forecourt but she had been impressed by the rows of offering tables laden with fruits, flowers, meat and bread, that were being offered to the Aten and everywhere she smelt the scent of incense and heard the sound of hymns being sung in honour of the Sun Disc.

On the temple walls Aset had seen large and lively scenes of the Royal Family worshipping the Aten and depictions of flowers and animals whose existence has only been made possible by the life-giving rays of the Aten.

Aset woke up out of her thoughts when the Pharaoh, wearing the double-crown of Egypt and holding the crook and flail as symbols of Royal Power, started speaking: "Today is a memorable day for the Two Lands and its people! Today is a new beginning because we dedicate our new capital Akhetaten and by doing so we dedicate our country to the Aten, the source of all life in the world! From today and forever after the Aten shall not be a minor, unknown God anymore but the supreme God of the Two Lands!"

Aset had listened to what the Pharaoh had said and for a moment her breath halted, it seemed that this statement of the Pharaoh made the replacement of Amun as the King of the Gods by the Aten official.

The Pharaoh continued his speech: "To prove that the Pharaoh recognizes the devotion with which his loyal servants serve him I will reward the one person who, under the guidance of the Aten, has created this city: my architect and chief of construction Hemienu."

Hemienu, who had already been waiting, came forward and kneeled under the Window of Appearance. The Pharaoh told him to get up and dropped a large golden collar, called the Gold of Honour, down from the window which Hemienu caught and, in front of all the people of the city he had built, laid around his neck.

"For your great service to the Aten," the Pharaoh spoke.

"Thank you, Your Majesty, this is a great honour. More than I deserve," Hemienu replied humbly while making a bow.

The Pharaoh turned again to the people of Akhetaten and went on speaking: "This city is dedicated solely to the Aten, Who is both my father and my mother, and to emphasize my complete devotion to the Aten I will from now on rule under a new name: Akhenaten, Beneficial to the Aten!"

The Pharaoh stopped speaking while everywhere the surprised murmur of the people could be heard.

Even amongst his closest officials Aset noticed surprise. Apparently the Pharaoh had not informed them about his decision to change his name.

The only people who did not seem surprised where Queen Teye, the Great Royal Wife Nefertiti, Kiya and Meryra.

"Being away from the temples of the traditional Gods and their priests the Pharaoh becomes more confident and starts to implement his ideas faster," Aset thought to herself and wondered what was going to happen in the years to come.

After the Pharaoh had moved his court to the new capital everybody at the Karnak Temple was waiting what would happen next.

Ipi had become old enough to actively take part in the temple ceremonies even though, like most priests, he was not allowed to enter the Holy of Holies.

Apart from taking part in the worshipping of Amun, Ipi still worked every day as a physician with Intef.

His family had never heard anything anymore from Huni and they started to fear that he would never return from his work for the Pharaoh. Ipi's mother could not live with the uncertainty about the fate of her son and her health continued to decline making Ipi fear she might not live much longer.

It was morning and Ipi had taken part in the procession through the temple that was a part of the morning ceremony during which the shrine of Amun was opened for the God to receive the first rays of sunlight and during which the statue of the God and the shrine would be washed and Amun would receive His first offerings of the day.

He was just about to go to Intef's practice to start his daily work when another priest informed him that Maya was going to make an announcement.

Most of the priests, priestesses and other temple personnel had assembled on the large forecourt of Karnak and even priests of the Southern Temple had followed their High Priest Amunherkhepeshef to the Temple of Karnak to listen to what Maya was going to say.

A short moment later a depressed looking Maya appeared, wearing a torn robe as a sign of mourning, and took position in the middle of the court.

"Today is a sad day for our country and for the Gods Who have made our country and its people prosper for many centuries," Maya started speaking and continued while he raised a hand in which he held a papyrus roll: "I have received a message from the Pharaoh in which he officially declares that our God Amun is no longer the King of the Gods and that He has lost its privileged position."

The High Priest stopped speaking for a moment and looked at the reaction his words had on his priests, priestesses and other listeners.

Except for a murmur amongst the people everybody remained quiet since they had already expected this to happen for a long time and had resigned themselves to the inevitable.

"All the Gods," Maya went on, "are now subordinate to the Aten, Who the Pharaoh has declared to be the new supreme God of the Two Lands. And as a final act, to cut his last tie to our Lord Amun, the Pharaoh has renounced his name Amenhotep, Amun is Satisfied, and has taken a new name: Akhenaten!"

This last announcement was not expected and surprised the assembled people.

As soon as Maya stopped speaking conversations sprung up everywhere amongst the priests and priestesses; everybody wanted to know what this name change could mean.

"This is a very bad sign for us," Ipi heard a Chantress of Amun, who stood behind him, say to a priest next to her.

"The Pharaoh no longer wishes to be associated with Amun in any kind of way. Now I fear it can only get worse," she continued in a scared voice.

While the priest tried to reassure the chantress, Ipi feared she was right. Maybe that was also the reason why his nightmares about the Pharaoh's soldiers storming the temple had returned and occurred even more frequent than ever.

Ipi could not believe that Wenamun and Tahat were right when they had told him a long time ago that when dreams contained a prediction of the future the people had to accept what was going to happen as the will of the Gods. If this attack from the Pharaoh's soldiers was really going to come then Ipi was sure the Gods were giving him this warning to be prepared for it.

Finally, after not having seen his family for a few years and with occasional letters as the only contact, Hemienu returned home to his family.

His stay in Thebes would only be temporary because the Pharaoh had many more plans for him to realize. Akhetaten needed to be expanded with more temples, palaces and other buildings; the first being a palace for the Pharaoh's second wife Kiya which was going to be constructed to the south of the new city.

But even the Pharaoh understood that his chief of construction needed to see his family again and allowed him to return to Thebes for two months.

Arriving at his house he opened the door and saw a young girl, his daughter Achtai, sitting inside the living room writing on a broken piece of pottery.

"Probably practicing her writing skills," Hemienu thought, proudly noticing that she was growing up.

"Who are you? What do you want?" Achtai asked surprised and a bit scared but then recognized him and exclaimed: "Is that you, father? What happened to you?"

Upon hearing her daughter's voice Hemienu's wife Ahotep and son Hemaka came into the room but instead of, as Hemienu had expected, running up to him and hugging him they remained distant.

"Has your work been hard?" Ahotep inquired. "Yes," Hemienu replied and asked: "Why do you ask this?"

Ahotep finally came up to her husband and hugged him, speaking: "You look different. You have aged and look as if you have experienced a terrible time. What has happened to you?"

Without letting his wife go Hemienu felt the tears welling up in his eyes again and simply said: "Yes, it was terrible."

It was a week after Akhenaten had dedicated his capital and elevated the Aten to the status of supreme God.

In recognition of his loyalty the Pharaoh had given Penthu the honourary title Chief Servant of the Aten. This was a very important title and showed how much Akhenaten appreciated his physician.

Penthu, besides being proud of the title, also felt uncomfortable with it, since he still worshipped Amun.

Penthu stood in the Pharaoh's new office, together with Aye, Nakhtpaaten and Aperel who had come from Memphis to Akhetaten to take part in the ceremonies to dedicate the new city.

They stood in front of the Pharaoh's desk behind which Akhenaten sat on a large gilded chair.

Penthu looked out of the window behind the Pharaoh over the city, where he saw the large pylons of the Per Aten towering above all the other buildings, with large depictions of the Pharaoh receiving life from the Aten on both sides of the temple's entrance.

The Pharaoh was reading a letter which he had just received from a messenger. Penthu turned his gaze at Akhenaten's face, trying to see whether the message contained good or bad news.

After staring for a long time at the clay tablet on which the message had been written the Pharaoh finally put it away.

"Is it bad news, Your Majesty?" Aye asked.

"It is a letter from my vassal, Rib-Addi, the King of Byblos. He tells me that the Hittites have invaded our protectorates in the north and plundered and burnt the lands. He asks me to send him soldiers to prevent the situation from getting worse," Akhenaten replied without much emotion.

"That is terrible!" Aye exclaimed with a look of horror on his face. "We must act immediately and send King Rib-Addi the soldiers he requests!"

"We have no time for that now, Aye," Akhenaten spoke, sounding annoyed. "Rib-Addi will be able to handle this situation by himself. We have just moved our capital and are making important reforms in our own country. We cannot afford to start a foreign campaign right now. We should trust in the Aten, then everything will be fine."

Penthu wanted to intervene in the conversation but the Pharaoh raised his hand to silence him and, changing the topic of the conversation, asked: "How have the priesthoods of the old Gods received the news about the Aten being the new supreme God?"

"In Upper Egypt and even at the Temple of Amun in Thebes they have accepted it without any protests. They seem to have resigned themselves to the fact that a new era has started in the Two Lands," Nakhtpaaten spoke proudly.

Just like the Pharaoh, he did not seem to be worried about the Hittite threat.

"It is the same in Lower Egypt," Aperel added his experiences. "The High Priest of Ptah came to my office in Memphis to complain and I told him he had no choice but to accept the new situation. But apart from that all the priesthoods have, like in Upper Egypt, resigned themselves without protests to the new situation."

The Pharaoh leaned back in his chair and smiled, he was clearly satisfied that his reforms were implemented without any resistance.

As quickly as the smile appeared on Akhenaten's face it disappeared again and he continued speaking in a very serious tone: "Soon new measures against the other Gods will follow. Aten is not satisfied with the power that the temples of the old Gods are still possessing!"

"What if the priests will resist when we curb their power any further?" Penthu asked, feeling worried about any possible consequences.

The Pharaoh listened to Penthu's question, then looked at both his viziers and spoke: "When the time comes you should be ready to deal with any kind of resistance that the temples may put up!"

After these last words, in spite of Penthu attempting to protest, Akhenaten closed the meeting and a moment later Penthu, Aye and the two viziers left the Pharaoh's office.

King Rib-Addi's plea for help had not been discussed anymore.

Aset was satisfied with her new life in Akhetaten. She had received a large room in the palace next to Kiya's chambers which she could share with Merykare, who had been given more free time by the Pharaoh lately. For the first time Aset started to feel that she and Merykare were living as husband and wife and she felt happy.

However, Aset still spent most of her time with Kiya.

"You are looking pale, Kiya," Aset spoke to her friend.

"I am not feeling so well today," Kiya replied, speaking in a tired voice.

"I have heard Akhenaten is going to build a palace for you," Aset went on speaking to Kiya, trying to cheer her up. "He must really love you."

"I am so happy," Kiya replied, her face suddenly shining with happiness. "It will include pavilions, gardens and lakes and all of that he builds for me. I hope it will be constructed soon."

Suddenly Kiya's happiness disappeared and she started to feel very sick.

"I will tell someone to call Penthu," Aset spoke and started to run to the door of Kiya's chambers.

"No, Aset. I am fine," Kiya reassured her and when Aset turned back to her Kiya spoke, while her smile reappeared: "I am pregnant again!"

It was night and a group of seven men was sitting around a fire, far in the south of Upper Egypt under a bright sky lit by millions of stars.

The men were hungry, poorly dressed and seemed dissatisfied about their situation. One man, however, formed an exception and smiled while staring into the fire.

"What are you smiling about?" one of the other men remarked.

"Yes, what reason do we have to smile?" one more man added. "You promised us treasures but look at us now! We are surviving by robbing lonely travellers and plundering graves which are so poor that they are hardly worth the effort!"

The man stopped complaining for a moment but then continued, sounding threateningly: "When are we finally going to receive our treasures, Paneb?"

Paneb did not answer but just kept smiling and staring into the fire.

He had never forgotten what he had seen years ago in the tomb of Crown Prince Thutmose. The glimmer of gold, silver and precious stones had made an inerasable impression on him and his determination to return to that tomb had kept him going for all those years.

He had been wandering through almost the whole country, living comfortably off the treasures he had managed to take from Thutmose's tomb and after these had been depleted he had survived by robbing travellers and plundering small tombs. Meanwhile he had been assembling a gang of trustworthy men whom he would take with him when the moment came that it was safe to return to Thebes.

"Don't worry," Paneb spoke, looking at the six men sitting with him around the fire. "The time has finally come for us to return to Thebes."

He looked up for a moment when a bird flew up screaming from the marshes on the bank of the nearby Nile River but then continued speaking: "The Pharaoh has left Thebes and moved the capital to his new city. He will have taken most of his security forces with him, leaving all the tombs filled with riches beyond your imagination for us with hardly any guards to defend them."

Paneb's listeners now started to become excited and when one of them asked when they would depart for Thebes the tomb robber replied: "We will leave tomorrow. We will go to the nearest city and take a boat to the north which will bring us to Thebes in about a week."

Paneb smiled a moment before adding: "Soon we will all be very wealthy men!"

Printed in Great Britain
by Amazon